LETHAL INTENT

Also by Quintin Jardine

Bob Skinner series:
Skinner's Rules
Skinner's Festival
Skinner's Trail
Skinner's Round
Skinner's Ordeal
Skinner's Mission
Skinner's Ghosts
Murmuring the Judges
Gallery Whispers
Thursday Legends
Autographs in the Rain
Head Shot
Fallen Gods
Stay of Execution

Oz Blackstone series:
Blackstone's Pursuits
A Coffin for Two
Wearing Purple
Screen Savers
On Honeymoon with Death
Poisoned Cherries
Unnatural Justice
Alarm Call

QUINTIN JARDINE

LETHAL INTENT

headline

First published in Great Britain in 2005
by HEADLINE BOOK PUBLISHING

1

Cataloguing in Publication Data is available from the British Library

0 7553 0406 3 (hardback)
0 7553 0408 X (trade paperback)

Typeset in Electra by Avon DataSet Ltd,
Bidford on Avon, Warwickshire

Printed and bound in Great Britain by
Mackays of Chatham plc, Chatham, Kent

HEADLINE BOOK PUBLISHING
A division of Hodder Headline
338 Euston Road
London NW1 3BH

wwwheadline.co.uk
www.hodderheadline.com

The book is dedicated to the memory of Dr George Armour Bell, OBE, uncle, advisor, friend; a great man, no more, no less.

The author's thanks go to:

Moira McGinley, for her generosity.

'Sir' Stuart MacKinnon, for his.

Scott Wilson and the Radio Forth team, for enabling it.

President George Walker Bush. If I had invented Camp Delta or Camp X-Ray, Guantanamo Bay, Cuba, and then attempted to pass them off as fiction, I'd have been condemned for breaking the bounds of credibility, and probably for insulting the entire American nation by suggesting such an outrage: but he did it for real, so I'm okay.

One

Along Princes Street and George Street, the festive lights shone. It had been a good year, memorable in fact, even when measured by the high standards of Edinburgh, which had seen many glorious passages in the centuries of its evolution into a historic and cultural European capital. As always, it was ending with the season of goodwill, but none of that spirit had found its way into the main drawing room of Bute House, the official residence of the First Minister of Scotland.

She glared at its occupant across the table. He looked blandly back at her, his moustache twitching slightly. Like his hair it was an unusual shade of red, and it was rumoured that he dyed both. He liked to keep his distance; if they had been eye to eye she would have looked down on him, and he was sensitive about his height.

'You can't do that!' the Justice Minister exclaimed, her voice raised in protest.

He smiled, then glanced around the Georgian room, as if he had barely heard her. 'You're one hundred per cent wrong there,' he chuckled, eventually, 'as you'll find out tomorrow.'

'What about the Lord Advocate?' Aileen de Marco demanded. 'What does he have to say?'

'Milton concurs with my view. He's already instructed the prison service to make the necessary arrangements.'

'The Lord Advocate can't instruct the prison service.'

'He can on my authority.'

She leaned across the oval table, staring at him until he was forced to make eye contact. 'And just what authority is that, Tommy, may I ask? You are the First Minister of the Scottish Executive, but you're a member of the Cabinet, just like me.'

'Not quite like you. I appointed you, remember? And you should remember: it was only a few weeks ago. I don't need to tell you that I can fire you just as easily.'

She let out a short bitter laugh. 'Better . . . and bigger . . . men than you have tried to threaten me, Mr Murtagh, only to find that they were wasting their time. On what grounds would you fire me? Because I object to you riding rough-shod over the Scottish judicial process? You try and argue that one out with me in public and see how far you get. Come off it, First Minister. You're just a wee dog jumping because the big dog's barked.'

Thomas Murtagh stiffened and his eyes grew frosty. 'Maybe you haven't noticed but we're all in the same party, whether it's London or Westminster.'

'That wasn't the dog I was talking about, Tommy: the one you mean jumped just as high as you when his master called. I'll ask you straight out, are you going to show yourself worthy of your post by calling a Cabinet meeting to discuss this, then abiding by its majority view?'

'I've already made my decision,' he replied, curtly. 'I only invited you here out of courtesy, so you didn't learn about it second-hand.'

'Indeed.' She made no attempt to disguise the sarcasm in her tone. 'And here was me thinking that you invited your Justice Minister to meet you so that you could consult her on this unprecedented and quite improper request from Downing Street. I should have known better.'

She picked up her bag from the table. 'Call the Cabinet, Tommy. If you don't I'll have to consider my position.'

'I'm already considering it for you. I don't know if I can have a senior minister who's so openly hostile to me.'

De Marco laughed. 'If that's your criterion for appointment you're going to be lonely in this big room.' She headed for the door.

'Sleep on it, Aileen,' he called after her, with more than a hint of a threat in his tone. 'Maybe you should save me the embarrassment of admitting that I made a mistake when I gave you a seat at the top table, and save yourself the indignity of being told that you weren't up to the job after all. Yes, sleep on it.'

She looked over her shoulder with her hand on the door knob. 'I might not get too much sleep, Tommy,' she retorted. 'I may be too busy making phone calls.' As she swept from the room she saw a frown cross his face.

Two

The snow was as deep as he had ever known it, falling so hard that it obscured the bulbs of towering sodium street-lamps above, diffusing and merging their beams into a single glow in the night sky, over-arching everything like a sinister orange cloud.

'Should we be trying this?' he asked, as she turned left at the roundabout and headed up the hill. He thought it was Drumbrae but, oddly, he found that he was not sure. She said nothing in reply, nor did she glance his way. Instead she peered into the blizzard ahead, her knuckles white as she grasped the wheel, her face seeming to reflect the weird light outside.

The incline was slight at first, and the car took it with only a little difficulty. 'Where are the road gritters?' he heard himself mutter.

'This is Sunday night in Edinburgh,' she hissed. 'There are no gritters.'

'Then should we be doing this?' he repeated.

'Shut up!' Her voice became a strange, insistent croak. 'You have to know.'

She drove on, hunched forward in the driving seat, as the slope became more severe. Still the car made steady forward progress, as she kept it in the highest gear possible. But soon they came to the real hill, rearing up before them at an impossible angle. The snow was fresh, crisp and unmarked, forcing upon him the knowledge that not only were they alone but that no vehicle had come this way in some time.

She pressed on, but gravity began to take its toll. They were maybe halfway up the incline, he reckoned, when the wheels began to spin beneath them and they lost what little forward momentum they had left.

'Go on,' he urged, 'we've got this far.'

'We're too heavy,' she snapped. 'You'll have to get out and walk up. Get back in at the top.'

'You're daft!'

'Just do it!' The words came out as a raw scream. He had thought that he was a stranger to fear, but a wave of panic swept over him and he jumped out of the car.

At first he found it difficult to balance on the pavement: he reckoned that the snow had to be at least eight or nine inches deep. He took a step forward and then another, inching up towards the crest.

Yet the hilltop seemed no nearer.

Each pace grew shorter, each footfall more tentative, each movement threatening his precarious hold on the vertical and threatening to send him tumbling backwards into the growing blizzard. His breathing grew heavier, and he felt his heart beat faster in his chest.

'No bloody use,' he gasped, and risked a look over his shoulder, through the snow, for the car. But there was no car: it had gone. He looked for the tyre-tracks: there were none. Even the light had changed: the orange glow of the lamps had turned dull and bluish grey. He gazed around him: if they had started to climb Drumbrae, he was somewhere else now, somewhere alien, somewhere wholly malignant.

He stared and he knew that what he felt had gone beyond panic, transcended fear and crossed the threshold of pure terror. He turned back to face the hill. It looked like Everest before him, but he sensed that there was no way back, only forward. He thrust upwards into the blizzard, gulping in mouthfuls of air and snow. Each step grew more laboured, until he was practically powerless to move.

Yet even standing still, his chest heaved as he forced the cold air into his lungs. The hill had no summit, he realised: it would go on for ever, or at least until it had drawn from him everything that he had. He slumped to his knees, then fell on to his face, his breathing still impossibly heavy.

'*Can you drown in snow?*' The crazy thought bubble seemed to flash up in Neil McIlhenney's mind as the sure knowledge came to him that he was going to die.

5

Three

Robert Morgan Skinner had never been keen on fishing. In his childhood his father had tried to instil into him his own love of the pastime, but his attempts, whether they were on the upper reaches of the River Clyde, or from a boat on their occasional family sorties to the Western Isles of Scotland, had all ended in failure.

The young Bob had been deterred by two things. Although he never said as much to his teacher, his instincts told him that ramming a hook into the mouth of any living creature and heaving it, struggling, from its natural environment might be morally questionable. More off-putting than that, though, he was bored stiff by the long periods of inactivity that angling asks of its devotees.

Eventually Bill Skinner had given the job up as hopeless and instead had concentrated on his son's golf, with much more satisfactory results. A few lessons from the club professional had set the boy up with a smooth, rhythmic swing, and the hours that he was prepared to spend on the practice ground had instilled in him the patience that had been lacking on the riverbank. His handicap had moved into single figures by the age of fourteen and for the rest of his father's life he had given him shots every time they played.

Bob smiled as he recalled their last round together: he had hit irons off every tee so that they could be close together all the way round, and so that the game would be as competitive as they both liked it. When he had been left with a four-foot putt for the match on the last green he had misread the line, and the ball had horseshoed out.

'You missed that on purpose,' Bill Skinner had said.

'You're bloody joking,' he had replied. 'There was a fiver on that putt; I need all the fivers I can get right now.'

So what, he wondered, would his dad have thought if he could have seen him sitting on the back of a cruiser in the Gulf of Mexico, strapped into a chair with a damn great marlin rod in his hand?

'Concentrate!' his wife urged him. For a second he thought that his father's ghost had spoken.

The creature on the end of the line tugged hard, and he had to use all his strength to prevent the rod being ripped from his hands and its socket set firmly in the deck. 'Let him run,' said their guide. 'This is a strong boy: there's fight left in him yet. Give him some more line.'

Bob did as he said, until the skipper put a hand on his shoulder. 'Okay, enough. He's gone as far as we want. Start to put pressure on him now; start to reel him in.'

The struggle lasted for almost an hour, but gradually, Bob's strength overcame that of the fish. Finally, as he drew it nearer the boat, it broke the surface in a great leap, trying to shake itself free of the line. It seemed to hang in the air for a second, a magnificent blue-white creature, its great dorsal fin and long sword in profile, and then dived back beneath the waves.

'Let it go,' said Skinner. 'Cut the line.'

He glanced to his right, and saw the skipper's grin, white teeth gleaming in his black face. 'You sure?' he drawled. 'This is one big motherfu— fish that you got there.'

'Yeah, and I can't kill him. Cut the line.'

'You're in the chair.' The man produced an enormous clasp knife from his pocket, opened it, reached out to take hold of the bow-taut line, and sliced through it. There was an audible 'twang' as the pressure was released from the rod; Bob felt it quiver in his hands.

'You're a good guy, boss,' said the captain. 'I wish more of my clients would do that, but all most of them want is their picture taken with a monster of the deep so they can boast to their beer buddies back in Boise, Idaho, or Middletown, Wherever.'

Sarah Grace Skinner shook her head. 'I don't get it. What's the point of all this? What's the point of fishing if it isn't to catch fish?'

Her husband pointed out across the waves. 'I caught him, didn't I? I just chose not to kill him, that's all.'

'That makes you feel better, does it?'

'As a matter of fact it does.'

She looked at him wryly, as the skipper took the rod and went to store it with the others. 'When did you become so sensitive?'

'When I was about fifteen, and I gave up boxing.'

Her expression changed to one of pure surprise. 'You never told me you boxed.'

'You never asked. And you hate boxing, so why should I bring it up?'

'What made you quit? Afraid of having your good looks spoiled?'

'There was nobody around who could do that,' he shot back. 'No, it was more the other way round. Junior boxers aren't supposed to be able to do much damage. I could. Most of my fights ended early: the referees were good, and got in quick. So they moved me up a grade, let me fight older kids. In three fights I broke two ribs and a nose . . . all other people's. Finally the guy who ran the club put me in with a senior; I think he meant it to teach me a lesson.'

'And did it?'

'It sure did. The guy caught me a good one in the first round, but not good enough. The red mist came down and I ripped back at him, just one punch: knocked him unconscious. It took them five minutes to bring him round and it was another ten before he could stand up. They kept him in Law Hospital overnight as a precaution. I tell you, Sarah, I've never been as scared in my life, before or since. I knew the lad I hurt: he was a decent bloke, with a nice girlfriend and a good job. He hadn't meant me any harm, yet I could have killed him.'

He glanced down at his hands: they were bunched into fists, still clutching the marlin rod. 'So I took my gloves off,' he said, 'and I never put them back on again to hit another man. I joined a martial-arts club instead.'

'What's the difference?' Sarah challenged. 'That's even deadlier.'

'In theory it might be, but in practice it's not. What I did was largely non-contact, but more than that, it taught me mental discipline and self-control, how to sublimate my aggression. I admit that I don't always manage to do that, but over the piece it's served me well. Our kids will all study judo and karate, if I've any say in it, just as my Alexis did.'

8

'Wait a minute,' she protested. 'It may do our younger son some good, but Seonaid's only two! And as for Mark, he's a thinker, not a fighter.'

'Thinking is a big part of what it's about. Plus, he's the sort of quiet kid who can get picked on . . . and our daughter won't always be two.'

'I see,' Sarah mused, 'so it was mental discipline that allowed you to let that fish go, was it?'

He grinned. 'No. I just couldn't see us eating him on our own.'

She laughed in spite of herself. 'What about the hook?' she asked. 'It was hardly humane to leave that in his mouth, was it?'

'He'll get rid of it now the tension's off,' said the skipper, as he returned, with everything tidied away. He looked at her. 'What say, lady? You wanna try the chair?'

She shook her head. 'I don't think so. I'm tired out just watching that. Take us back to Key West, please. The sun's on the way down, and I'd like to get there before dark.'

The captain nodded, and climbed up to the high cockpit. A few seconds later the cruiser's big twin engines roared into life.

The journey back to the dock took almost an hour; they let it pass without conversation, content to watch the ocean, and then, as it came into view, the island chain that formed the southernmost tip of the state of Florida.

On the quayside, as Bob gave the skipper a fifty-dollar tip, Sarah headed for their rental car. She was behind the wheel when he joined her, and the convertible's roof was packed away. 'Straight back to the hotel?' she asked.

'Might as well. We've done the Dry Tortugas National Park, we've taken the Sunset Cruise, we've swum with dolphins, and we've ridden the Old Town Trolley. I reckon we've seen all the sights.'

'There's one more I'd like to see,' said Sarah, casually.

'What's that?'

'I'd like to see you smile as if you meant it. I'd like you to look happy that you came out here to join me.'

'Didn't I look happy last night?'

She shrugged her shoulders. 'I couldn't tell in the dark. But I doubt if you looked ecstatic.'

'You seemed pleased with yourself.'

'I like fucking,' she retorted. 'But that's all it was, and you know it. I enjoy making love a lot more, and you haven't made love to me in a while.'

He shot her a sudden piercing glance. 'Not like he did, you mean?'

Sarah started the Sebring convertible, slammed the lever into drive and roared out of the car park.

'Sorry!' Bob exclaimed, his voice raised over the engine.

'If I believed you really were…' she broke off, easing down her speed '…I'd ignore your question. But I don't, so I'll answer it. You're right: not like Ron did. There's been no real tenderness between us for longer than I can remember and, Bob, that's something I need. I have to feel that you care for me when we're vertical as well as horizontal, and I haven't, not for a while.'

'So you went looking for that tenderness somewhere else.'

'No!' she protested. 'It found me.'

'And if I really believed that . . .'

Four

Neil McIlhenney sat bolt upright. The room was cool, yet he was perspiring, and breathing hard. He felt his heart thumping, seeming to play a rapid, but thankfully steady tattoo against his ribcage.

Louise stirred beside him, but did not waken. He slipped out of bed and went into their bathroom, feeling his way in the darkness and not switching on the light until the door had closed behind him. He stared at his naked self in the mirror, then rubbed the stubble on his chin, as if he was reassuring himself that he was still in the world, that he could still experience ordinary sensations.

As he looked, he saw that his arms and shoulders were glistening, and that the hair on his chest and belly had spun itself into damp curls, black but heavily grey-flecked. He picked up a towel and dried himself off, then brushed his teeth and rinsed his mouth with cold water. When he felt sufficiently composed, he yanked the cord to turn off the mirror's illumination and opened the door once more.

His wife was sitting up in bed as he stepped back into the room. Her reading light was switched on and she was looking at him anxiously, her arms wrapped round his pillow, pressing it to her breasts. 'What's up, love?' she asked, quietly. 'This is damp. Are you feeling ill?'

He shook his head. 'I'm fine: bad dream, that was all. I shouldn't have had that cheese.'

She grinned, reassured. 'When I was a kid, my poor old dad used to warn me, "Eat cheese for supper and you'll see your granny", meaning you'll have dreams. My granny died when I was five and I missed her like hell, so I used to sneak into the kitchen before I went to bed and pinch a big lump of Cheddar, or whatever else was in the fridge. It

11

didn't work, though: I never did see her.' She paused as he slipped back under the duvet. 'Did you?'

'Did I what?'

'See your granny?'

He reached out and ruffled her hair, then took the pillow from her. 'Both my grannies are still alive,' he reminded her. 'I don't need to use dairy products to conjure up visions of them.'

'What did you see, then?'

A corner of his mouth twisted in a slight grimace. 'I don't think I want to talk about it.'

'Scary?'

'Weird.' He gave a shiver, remembering the coldness.

She dug him gently in the ribs with an elbow. 'Go on, tell me. You'll feel better. I used to go to this shrink who made me tell him all my dreams.'

As he looked at her, a broad, incredulous smile spread across his face. 'Why the hell did you need to go to a shrink?'

Lou McIlhenney gave a small frown. 'For the same reason most people go: my head was messed up. It was after my first marriage went down the toilet. I was depressed, lonely, and drinking a bit. My work suffered in the process. For a while I tried to rebuild my confidence with casual affairs, but I found I couldn't do casual.' She shrugged her shoulders. 'So I did what any self-respecting actress would do in the circs: I got the name of a Harley Street psychiatrist from my doctor, and I went into therapy.'

Neil smiled again. 'It worked, that's for sure.'

She snorted. 'Two years and God knows how many thousand quid later it worked. The gremlins were gone and I started to do my best work.' And then she smiled. 'I still suffered from occasional self-doubt, though. Do you know when I realised for sure that I was cured?'

'Tell me.'

'The day I met you: when I went to dinner at Bob and Sarah's and you were there in the fourth chair, I said to myself, "Louise Bankier, this is your moment. You're going to have him." And I did.'

He laughed at her honesty. 'You were that sure of yourself?'

'He really was a very good shrink.'

'And he made you tell him your dreams?'

She nodded.

'All of them?'

'Every one, in all the detail I could remember.'

'Pervert.'

'That thought did cross my mind, but after a while I could tell him the most intimate things without bothering about it.'

'Did you ever worry about your dreams winding up in the Sunday scandal sheets?'

'No. He taped all our sessions but he only worked from notes. He gave me all the tapes; it was his way of making me sure he'd have nothing to gain and everything to lose by leaking to the press.'

'I can see that,' Neil conceded.

'So tell me your dream. I promise I won't sell it to the *Sunday Mail*.'

'They wouldn't buy it. Just your common or garden nightmare, that was all.' The vision was still vivid in his mind; he recounted it for her, step by step, until the moment when he snapped awake.

'I see,' she murmured, thoughtfully, when he was finished.

'So what's your verdict, Dr Lou?'

'Did you ever have any experiences as a child that related to the dream?'

His forehead wrinkled for a second or two, and then his eyebrows rose. 'Now you mention it, yes,' he conceded. 'When I was a kid, like six or seven, we had a very big snowfall and it lay for a while. My pals and I decided we'd build an igloo in my back garden, as you do. It was a real pro job, just like the Eskimos have, only it wasn't quite as good as we thought. I was inside it on my own when it collapsed. I was buried in snow and ice and I thought I was going to suffocate in it. Maybe I would have too, but my dad saw it happen and he hauled me out.'

'There you are, then,' said Louise triumphantly. 'Classic case: I'm pregnant, and you're worried about something like that ever happening to our child. No doubt about it.'

'Mmm.' Neil scratched his chin. 'A couple of small doubts, maybe. I've already got two kids, and I never had that dream or anything like it when Olive was pregnant with either Lauren or Spencer.'

'No, but . . .'

He held up a hand. 'Something else,' he said. 'And this is the scary bit. The woman in the car, the woman driving: it was Olive. It was my first wife, and she took me up there and left me to my death.'

Five

'Get wid da, get wid da hot funky beat!'

The dee-jay's voice boomed out of the speaker array, over a heavy, insistent bass rhythm. On the packed floor dancers moved, some in time to the music, others in the mistaken belief that they were. The hall was decked out for the season: paper Christmas trees hung from the roof, and long strands of tinsel were wound round the lighting gantry. Several of the clubbers were wearing party hats.

The man turned to his companion and nodded in the general direction of the stage as the single line sounded out again and again.

'D'ye think any of those have any fucking idea what that noise is about?' he asked, flashing a wickedly provocative grin that made his teeth shine unnaturally white in the beams of ultraviolet light that wove random patterns around the club.

The other man shrugged, displaying no interest in the question. 'Who the fuck cares?' he growled. 'Is this mate of yours gonnae show or no'?'

'He said he would, but he's an unreliable bastard.'

'He can rely on a sore fuckin' face if he pisses me aboot.' The man's little eyes screwed up, becoming, for a second, mere pinpricks in his fleshy face as if to emphasise his threat, and his menace. 'So can you an' all. Ah'm fucked waitin' for this guy. Dis ye want tae deal or no'?'

'Sure. Same rate as before?'

'Naw. It'll be seventy-five this time.' The man paused. 'Naw, make that a hunner and fifty: yis'll be buying yer mate's as well.'

The sardonic grin was gone. 'Seventy-five a baggie? What happened tae the fifty quid it wis before?'

'Inflation. Supply and demand. Call it whit ye like, but that's the tab, Davie boy. Now stop with the wide-eyed fuckin' innocence . . .' He paused and pointed to a third man standing a few feet to the right: around thirty, well dressed, well groomed, a stockbroker out for a night on the wild side. '. . . before somethin' bad happens tae ye.'

Davie boy looked down at his feet. 'Okay,' he muttered. 'Let's do it. Same place as before?'

'Aye. Just gies a minute tae get in there first. We dinnae want tae ' go in thegither.'

'Like anybody would care in here. Why dae ye use the ladies' anyway? Why no' the gents'?'

'Too easy for the nasty boys tae hide in the gents'. Nae coppers in the ladies'.'

'Man, they have women polis tae!'

The fleshy face split into what passed for a smile. 'Ah kin spot thae a mile-off. Fuckin' dykes, the whole bunch. See yis in there.' He turned on his heel and pushed his way through the crowd. The lyric, and the beat, thumped on relentlessly.

Davie boy waited for two minutes, checking the time on his watch as it passed. Finally he followed the man's footsteps. The toilets were on the other side of the hall, two doors a few yards apart, one marked 'His'. He walked towards 'Hers', noting that, as usual, the stockbroker was standing guard outside. They exchanged a glance as he pushed the door open; the eyes were cold, dispassionate, maybe a little weary of his tedious job.

He stepped inside. There were half a dozen stalls; the second was in use, the door of the fourth bore an 'out of order' sign and was sealed with tape, and the others were vacant. A line of wash-basins faced them, and on the far wall were three slot machines, two selling condoms and the third tampons. A blonde in a dress that might have been painted on was feeding pound coins into the Durex dispenser.

The dealer waited until she had left, and until a wiry red-head had emerged from the second cubicle and returned to the hall without washing her hands. There had been no sound of flushing. Davie boy guessed that either she had been badly brought up, or had been injecting; he placed a bet with himself on the latter. As always, neither woman had paid any attention to the two alien invaders, or even looked in their direction.

'Okay,' said the dealer, as the door closed on the red-head. 'Get your fuckin' money out.'

Davie boy produced a roll from his pocket. He began to peel off notes, then hesitated. 'Ah dunno, man,' he muttered. 'A hunner and fifty's serious cash tae me. Whit if ma mate disnae turn up at a'?'

The stocky man's face seemed to stiffen. 'What if?' he snarled. 'Tell ye something, son: we're here because you told me Ah was going' tae sell two baggies o' smack.' With his left hand, he took two small clear packs of white powder from the breast pocket of his jacket and waved them in the air. 'You're no leavin' till Ah dae . . .' The eyes became tiny once more. '. . . or yis urnae leavin' at a'. Here's another "what if" for yis.' His right hand slipped into his jacket pocket. Davie boy tensed, anticipating a blade, but instead the dealer produced a Nokia cellphone. 'What if I just press that green button there? Ah'll tell yis what'll happen. Ma man's phone'll ring on the other side of that door. When he sees it's me that's callin' he won't bother tae answer. He'll jist come in here and cut your fuckin' face off.'

As if from nowhere, the sardonic grin was back. 'Well, Jingle,' he murmured. 'Maybe you'd better just press it and we'll see.'

A look of fury crossed the dealer's face; a snarl escaped from his lips as he held the Nokia in the air and pressed the send button.

Davie boy took a step to the side, so that he could keep both the dealer and the door in his line of vision. The man he had called Jingle stared at it, waiting for it to burst open, and for the stockbroker to set about his business.

But it stayed firmly closed. Instead, there was a tearing sound as the door of cubicle four ripped free of its sealing tape. A woman stepped out. She wore a black satin trouser suit and her brunette hair was expensively cut; she was pretty, but her face was set and she looked all business.

'Hey, Mavis,' Davie boy exclaimed. 'Jingle here reckons you're a lesbian. Is that right?'

The woman kicked the dealer, once, twice, on each calf with the pointed toe of her shoe, sending him slumping to his knees, seizing his hands as he fell and holding them in the air for Davie boy to bind his wrists together with plastic handcuffs.

Standing straighter now, and looking altogether different, he wrenched the man back to his feet. 'I am Detective Chief Inspector David Mackenzie,' he said. 'Fettes; Drugs Squad commander. My friends and enemies alike call me Bandit. This is Detective Sergeant Mavis McDougall, who is, for your information, as straight as a die. But she didn't take offence at being called a lesbian. No, she objected to you trying to sell me a class A drug, for which offence, Charles "Jingle" Bell, we are placing you under arrest. Now, tell me if you understand the following.'

He recited the formal caution; when it was complete, Bell said nothing, but spat in his face.

'Thank you,' said Bandit Mackenzie, taking a paper towel from the dispenser and wiping himself. 'That'll come up nicely on the video. Camera's in the tampon machine, by the way: we reckoned that was the one that'd get the least use. So, in addition to possession with intent to supply, you'll also be charged with assaulting a police officer. Come on. Let's get you out of here so the ladies can use their toilets.'

He grasped Bell by the arm and marched him towards the door, which McDougall opened for him. Outside a crowd of clubbers had gathered around the stockbroker; he was face down on the floor, bleeding heavily from the nose, with his hands cuffed behind his back. A long knife lay beside him, and there was a smear of blood on the wall, where, Bandit supposed, his face had hit it, hard. As if to confirm this guess, a muscular man in a leather jacket stood over him, with a foot on his neck. His curly blond hair looked surreal as it was caught in the zooming nightclub lights, and his green eyes gleamed.

'You will not try that again,' said Deputy Chief Constable Andy Martin to the prone stockbroker, then he looked up at Jingle Bell. 'And neither will you, my friend. This may not be my patch any more, but I will not tolerate anyone setting up a dope business anywhere, least of all in a place owned by a friend of mine. But you weren't to know that, were you, any more than you were to know that Spike Thomson doesn't scare easily.'

He smiled, even more wickedly. 'You and your pal did me favour, though.' He chuckled. 'After all these months in uniform, I've really enjoyed this wee bit of action.'

Six

They sat side by side on the terrace of their suite in the Pier House, looking out across the Gulf of Mexico, listening to the varied sounds of the resort as they drifted up to them. The sun had vanished below the horizon, but there was still sufficient light for them to take in the waterfront action.

Sarah stretched out her long, tanned legs, resting her heels on the balcony rail and sitting further back in her chair. She swirled the ice round in the Cuba Libre, which she had brought up from the bar, and glanced sideways at her husband. 'It's broke, isn't it?' she whispered.

'I guess so,' he replied.

'Can we fix it?'

'I don't know; my name might be Bob, but I'm no builder. What do I have to do to make it better?'

'You could start by forgiving me.'

Bob looked into her eyes. 'I did that on day one,' he told her. 'And anyway, it's a bit rich for me to be forgiving you. I haven't had an angelic past. Forgiving is no problem, love. It's forgetting that's the hard part.'

'What can I do to make you forget?'

'Nothing. I don't think I ever will.' He gave a small shrug of his shoulders, then reached down to take a can of Miller Lite from the ice bucket by his side and popped the ring-pull. 'The question is, can we live with it, with what we know about each other?'

'I can,' she answered, 'if I know that in spite of it all you still care about me.'

'I do. That's not in question. Plus, I was a lone parent for most of Alex's childhood; I don't really want our three to have that experience.'

'So you'll stay with me for the kids, is that what you're saying?'

'Not entirely, but that's a pretty solid reason.'

'Maybe it isn't for me, though. I'm lonely, Bob. Consciously or not, you've distanced yourself from me; and it's not just because of Ron. It happened before that . . . in fact Ron and I probably happened because of it. You don't realise it, but I've been really lost. I was going crazy back home, waiting for you to unbend and show me some real affection. Eventually I had to do something drastic: that's why I ran off here and challenged you to follow me.'

He laughed softly, then took a mouthful of beer. 'Fine,' he said. 'Let it all be my fault, then.'

Something in his tone made Sarah's eyes narrow. 'It doesn't cut both ways, does it?' she asked. The question seemed to come from out of nowhere, taking him by surprise. A simple snapped 'No!' would have dismissed it, but it hung in the air for a second; a second too long.

'Bob?' She swung her feet off the railing and turned half round in her chair. 'Have you been with someone else?'

'No,' he replied at last, but she had fastened on to his hesitation.

'No?' Her eyes were narrow.

'No, I have not been with anyone else ... certainly not in the Ron Neidholm sense.'

'In what sense, then?' The sudden coldness of her tone seemed to be intensified by the warmth of the sub-tropical evening.

'You want me to be completely honest? Okay. I met someone recently,' he said carefully. 'I find myself attracted to her, and I think it's mutual, but that's as far as it's gone.'

'Someone at work?'

'Not in the force, but someone I encountered recently, in a professional situation.'

'Not a suspect, surely,' Sarah exclaimed, sarcastically. 'You didn't see a hooker and get the hots, did you?'

'Don't be silly. I meet a lot of people in my work without feeling their collars.'

'It wasn't her collar I was asking about!'

'Very funny,' he muttered, unsmiling. 'As I said, there was an attraction, mutual and inescapable, but no more than that. There might have been, but I didn't . . . we didn't . . . because it wouldn't have been right.'

'But the attraction is still there.' There was no question in her tone. 'I'm here, am I not?'

'You wouldn't take that evasion from a suspect, so don't try it with me.'

'Yes, it's still there.'

Sarah stood and looked down at him; then, very slowly, she stretched out her arm and poured her Bacardi and Coke over his head.

'Thank you for that gesture,' he said, running his fingers through his wet hair. 'If I returned it in proportion to our respective sins, it'd probably mean I'd drown you in the bath.'

She stamped off the terrace and into their bedroom; it was almost dark indoors, and she noticed, for the first time, that the red message indicator on the bedside telephone was flashing on and off. 'If it'll help your self-righteousness, I'll run it for you,' she shouted at him. 'But while I do, you'd better check the phone. We've had a call, and since nobody knows I'm here, it must be for you.'

He leaped, growling, out of his chair, wiping the drink from his face, then from his hand on to the side of his shirt. He grabbed the receiver and pushed the play-back button.

'Bob,' said a female voice. 'I need to speak to you, urgently. Call me please, as soon as you get this. I'll be at the flat; the time doesn't matter.' It was Aileen de Marco, and she sounded as angry as he felt. He crossed to the dressing-table, aware that he was being watched, picked up his wallet, and retrieved from it the card that she had given him, with her home number written on the back. He knew that it would be long past midnight in Edinburgh, but he took her at her word and dialled it.

The Scottish Justice Minister answered on the third ring. 'Yes?' She sounded wide awake.

'It's me. I just got your message. Where's the fire?'

'It would be in Tommy Murtagh's jockeys if I had anything to do with it. I'm going to resign, Bob, first thing in the morning; but I wanted to tell you before I did it. I'm sorry to break in on you, but I just had to talk to you, especially since you're at the heart of it.'

'Hey,' he exclaimed, taken aback, 'hold your horses, Aileen. What's this about? What's Murtagh done?'

'He's appointed himself God. Those five terrorists that you and your people arrested two weeks ago: our esteemed First Minister has decided, himself, without reference to Cabinet colleagues, that they will not be tried in Scotland. Instead they'll be handed over to the Americans, right away.'

'What? All of them?'

'All five.'

'But three of them were minor people.'

'It doesn't matter. The Americans want to interrogate every terrorist they can get their hands on, just in case they know the slightest thing that might be important or could lead them to the top guys in the network that they haven't caught yet.'

'Murtagh hasn't done this off his own bat, though.'

'Of course not! He's had his orders from Downing Street.'

Skinner laughed. 'Even though they're illegal.'

'It's not funny.'

'I know. It's pathetic. I take it you've told wee Tommy how you feel.'

'Loud and clear, but it made no difference.'

'What about the Lord Advocate? They're in Crown custody: it's his shout.'

'What do you think?'

'Enough said. But listen to me now. Who will gain if you quit over this? The Scottish Executive? I don't think so. The five people you're talking about? They won't even know about it. This is international arrogance, and while the fact that Murtagh's gone along with it should cost him his job, there's no reason why it should cost you yours.'

'He's half threatened to fire me for disagreeing with him and demanding a Cabinet discussion. I'm just going to beat him to it, that's all.'

'Call his bluff. He won't dare: you're too popular. He might like you to quit, but he can't sack you.'

Aileen paused for a few seconds. 'But, Bob,' she said, 'if I stay in post, it'll look like I support him.'

'No, it won't, not after I've done a bit of judicious leaking to the press. I can play these boys at their own game, don't worry. Now please listen to me: say nothing to Murtagh tomorrow. Stay in your job. There's nothing you can do that'll alter what's going to happen. None of these people are UK nationals, so they'll go. There may be a small row about it, but it'll soon blow over. Even if it does damage the First Minister in the long run, it won't cost him his head now. What you must not do is allow the wee shit to manoeuvre you out of the Executive. You're his biggest potential threat, and everyone knows that, but only if you're in office, so do us all a favour and bloody stay there.'

'Okay,' she acknowledged, grudgingly. 'I'll think about it.'

'No, just do it.'

'If that's what you really believe is best, I will.'

'I do, honest.'

'Right.' She sighed. 'You know, you don't sound surprised by any of this.'

Skinner chuckled. 'Sorry, Aileen, there's little or nothing you politicians can do to surprise me.'

'You can't be pleased by it, though.'

'No, I'm bloody livid, as the Lord Advocate is about to find out.'

'You're not going to call him, are you?'

'On the instant.'

'Look, be careful. Don't do anything that'll put you in jeopardy.'

'I've been doing that for years, so don't worry about me. Now get some sleep.'

'Okay, I will. I'm off to my bed.' She took a breath. 'How's things, by the way?'

'If I knew I'd tell you. So long.'

'Good night.'

He hung up and turned to find Sarah looking at him. 'That was her, wasn't it?' she said. 'Aileen. And going by the conversation, that would be Aileen de Marco, the Justice Minister, wouldn't it?'

He nodded.

'Then we're done. I could tell by the way you talked to her: you used to speak to me like that.'

He took two steps towards her and tried to put his hands on her shoulders, but she twisted away. 'Look,' he murmured, 'you're reading too much into it. I like her. She believes in the same things I do, and she's a member of a rare species, a politician who can make a difference. We bat for the same team, Aileen and me.'

Sarah snorted. 'Bob Skinner in bed with a politician; that's rich. Of course, she isn't the first, is she? There was that other one a few years ago.'

'Shut up, please,' he found himself begging.

'Yes, sir,' she hissed. 'You want to know the truth, Bob? There's only one of your mistresses that I can't stand, the one that I've never fought because I know I'll always lose, and that's your bloody job. You want to leave me for Aileen de Marco, fine. You want to have an affair with her and stay with me, fine. But God help her in the long run, for sooner or later she'll try to put herself above your job, and that'll be the end of her too.'

'So what do you want me to do?'

'Quit!' she shouted. 'How many times do I have to say it? That's what I'd like you to do to save our marriage. Resign from the force. You've given it all your adult life; now you owe your family some.'

He walked away from her and across to the wardrobe, going through his jacket pockets until he had found the palm-sized computer that she had given him for his most recent birthday. He switched it on and scrolled though the phone numbers stored there until he found the one he sought, then walked back to the phone, picked it up again and began to dial.

This time he had to wait much longer before his call was answered. This time, the voice on the other end sounded sodden with sleep. 'Grassick,' it croaked.

'Milton,' he barked. 'It's Bob Skinner here, and I'm hugely pissed off.'

'Do you know what time it is?' the Lord Advocate groaned.

'I don't give a damn what time it is. I'm a policeman and I'm concerned twenty-four hours a day when I hear of the law being broken. So should you be: you're supposed to be the head of our prosecution system, after all.'

'What do you mean?'

'You know bloody fine what I mean. I'm talking about the five terrorists we arrested last month. They've been charged with various counts of murder and attempted murder; you and I both know they're as guilty as sin. Now I hear you're letting Murtagh pack them off to the US, without any trial for those crimes.'

'Not the US,' Milton Grassick replied, wearily. 'Cuba. And there's no point in trying to interfere now: they were handed over to the Americans at midnight, and flown out of Turnhouse on a military jet.'

'Magic! So they'll be interrogated, without any legal or personal representation, and once that's done, they'll probably be stuck before a secret tribunal, then shot.' Skinner drew breath, as if to keep his anger in check. 'The most appalling thing about this,' he went on, 'is that you're a Scottish law officer. You've got legal and constitutional duties and you've ignored them all. These people weren't just in your custody, they were in your care. They had a right to offer a defence against extradition, and they've been denied it.'

'There are great issues at work here,' Grassick protested.

'None of them greater than natural justice,' Skinner fired back. 'Is this what you went to the Bar to do, Milton? To subvert the law and ignore every human-rights accord ever signed? I know that when I took my oath of office it said bugger all about that. As my wife's just pointed out to me, I've spent my lifetime upholding a justice system that I believe in. Now I'm expected to sit on the sidelines and watch you and Murtagh piss all over it. No chance. I can't do anything about the First Miniature, but I can do something about you.'

'Such as?' The Lord Advocate summoned up a degree of belligerence.

'Such as make a citizen's formal complaint to the Dean of the Faculty of Advocates about your professional conduct. And you know what? Even if it's a token gesture, I think it might just be upheld. It might not mean your resignation, but it will for sure put a big barricade across your cushy road to a judge's robes. Sleep on that, mate.'

He slammed the phone back into its cradle and turned back to

Sarah. 'With guys like him in office, you want me to quit?' he said, quietly. He stripped off his stained shirt and walked back out to the terrace. Settling back in his chair, he picked up his beer, drained it in a single gulp, then took another from the ice bucket and ripped it open.

She followed him out and sat beside him. 'I'm sorry about the scene,' she murmured, looking out at the quayside below.

He tossed a little beer towards her, splashing it on her white cotton top. 'There.' He grinned at her, gently. 'We're quits.'

'But are we really?' she asked.

He took another drink. 'No, I don't suppose we are. I can have a career and be a good father, Sarah. Most people can. Ask Alexis if she felt deprived as a child.'

'Very few people are as driven as you, Bob. You're hard to live with.'

'So hard I drove you into another man's bed?'

'No, that was different. I didn't do that out of pique.'

'Maybe you should have waited for him all those years ago: given the guy a chance to get football out of his system.'

'That would never have happened; Ron couldn't have kept that promise. He was as driven as you are in that respect. Once he'd finished playing it would have been coaching or the media, or whatever, but still the same circus.'

'Yet you asked him to quit too?'

'Not in so many words, but I suppose I did.'

'You know that I won't, not as long as I'm fit to do the job?'

'Yeah.' She sighed. 'I know.'

'So don't force me to a choice.'

'I won't, if it's between me and the job. If it's between me and Aileen de Marco . . . well, that's another matter.'

'Let's just say it isn't.'

'In that case I'm the one who has to make the choice.'

'Whether you love me enough to stay?'

She looked at him. 'Do you love me enough to ask me?'

'I'm not going to do that. You have to want me, warts and all, short-tempered, obsessive bastard that I am.'

'And the kids?'

'The kids will have the education we've planned, whatever way it goes. Let's agree that much right now.'

Sarah nodded; she reached out and squeezed his arm.

'I have to go back,' he told her.

'I know.'

'Tomorrow.'

'Yes.'

'And you?'

'If it's okay with you, I'll take another few days out here. I'm calm now. I was a mess when I ran away from Edinburgh; I was on the edge of making an ass of myself, but now I feel better. If nothing else, our shouting match tonight has finally got a lot of stuff out of my system. Now I can think about the future with a clear mind.'

Bob smiled and ran his fingers through his sticky hair. 'I'm glad about that. You take all the time you need. I'll tell the kids you've got some stuff to sort out over here.'

'Mark might not believe you.'

'I can be persuasive, even with him.'

'I promise you that I'll come back in plenty of time to make sure that they all have a great Christmas. We can talk about everything then. You okay with that?'

'Deal.' He finished his beer and glanced down at the ice-bucket; it was empty. 'Dinner?' he asked.

'Yes. Have a shower, and then we'll go out. Let's eat lobster at Alonzo's … and I promise not to throw any over you.'

Seven

Detective Chief Inspector Neil McIlhenney made a point of being first to arrive each morning in the Special Branch suite. So he was surprised, when he reached the door of the outer office, to see light shining through the glass panel.

He turned the handle and stepped inside, expecting to find DC Alice Cowan behind her desk; instead he saw the dark-suited stocky figure of Assistant Chief Constable Willie Haggerty. 'Morning, sir,' he said. 'How did you get in here? This is supposed to be a secure area.'

'I'm an ACC, for fuck's sake,' the gruff Glaswegian replied. 'I'm supposed to be able to go anywhere in this building.'

'Not into my room, though,' said McIlhenney, walking across to his private office and holding a key in the air. 'I put my own lock in it when I took over from Mario McGuire, and there's only one other guy has one of these.'

'Aye,' Haggerty grunted, as he followed him into the modest room, 'and I can guess who that is. Where is he, by the way?'

'How should I know?'

'Because you're his best mate in this building.'

'He doesn't tell me everything, though.'

'And even if he did, I don't suppose you'd tell me.'

'Not if he didn't specifically ask me to.'

The assistant chief glowered at him. 'Maybe you've been in this job too long, Neil. You SB guys can get too comfortable with secrets.'

'That's the whole point of us SB guys, isn't it?' McIlhenney countered cheerfully. He walked over to a small fridge in the furthest corner of the office and took out a bottle of water. He did not drink tea or coffee, and very little alcohol. 'Want one?' he offered. 'Or a Pepsi?'

Haggerty shuddered and shook his head. 'Did you know about the terrorists?' he asked. 'The ones you lot lifted last month.'

'What about them?'

'They're off to the cages in Cuba.'

'Eventually, you mean?'

'No. Now, I mean. They were handed over to the Sherman Tanks last night and flown straight out. The Chief Constable just told me; the First Minister's private secretary only told him after it had happened, and he's not best pleased about that. The Solicitor General will advise the court this morning that all charges against them have been deserted; he'll say that it's *pro tem*, but it might as well be *simpliciter*, permanently. We'll never see them again.'

'Neither will anyone else,' McIlhenney murmured. 'I knew that a couple of them would go sooner or later, but I heard that everybody had agreed they'd be tried here first.'

'Not everybody, the Americans didn't. The Lord Advocate signed the release papers yesterday.'

'It gets them out of our hair, I suppose, but I know somebody who will not be at all happy about it.'

Haggerty glanced at him. 'Naw, he won't. In fact, he'll go ballistic when he finds out.' He took a breath. 'There's other things he's missing out on as well. What do you know about Greg Jay?'

'Between you and me?'

'Of course.'

'I know that he's unpopular with his men, and that the general view is "Don't take your eyes off him." I've never served under him, but I have seen him in action and I didn't like what I saw. He was good in his time, though, and he got where he is, divisional CID commander, on the basis of results. Why are you asking?'

'Because he's gone.'

'Gone?'

'Taken early retirement. Big Bob didn't say anything to you about it, did he?'

The DCI shook his head. 'Not a word.'

'Is that so? Big McGurk, his assistant, had heard nothing about it either, and I think Bob would have told him if he'd known, even if he didn't say anything to you.'

'What happened?'

Haggerty gave him a shrug and a blank 'don't know' look. 'Nothing. He saw the chief last Monday morning, and told him he wanted to go by the end of the week. He said he didn't want any fuss made: no announcement, retirement piss-up or anything like that. He wanted to leave very quietly.'

'He probably figured that if they'd passed the hat round for him, it'd have come back empty.'

'Maybe that's all it was,' the ACC conceded. 'Still,' he mused, 'it intrigues me when a guy does something like that. It usually means he's dodging the bullet, or he's been made a good offer somewhere else.'

'Do you want me to find out?'

'Naw, leave it. He's no' worth your time.'

'As you wish.' McIlhenney smiled. 'You're full of surprises this morning, sir.'

'Ah, there's lots more than that, though: this'll be news to you as well. We had a return visit from Andy Martin last night.'

Yet again, the big DCI was caught off guard. 'How come?' he asked.

'A bit of inter-force co-operation. You know Andy has a friend who owns a disco, or club, or whatever?'

'Spike Thomson? Sure.'

'Okay, and do you know a guy called Charlie Bell?'

'Jingle? Yes, I know him. He used to be a runner for Tony Manson, then for Dougie Terry; got scared and left town after Dougie got done. Strictly small change.'

'Not quite so small now. Bell and a minder called Richard Cable . . . Do you know him?'

McIlhenney frowned. 'Richard Cable? Is that his real name?'

'It was the name on his driving licence and his credit cards.'

'Not one I've heard, then. Has he got previous?'

'None that anybody can trace so far. Anyway, Jingle, with him backing him up, started moving drugs through Andy's mate's club a couple of weeks back; they told him that unless he kept his eyes and his mouth shut he'd never be able to open them again. The guy . . .'

'Spike?'

'Called Andy straight away and reported it to him. Andy came to the DCC and told him, on the quiet; Bob brought me in on it because he was up to his balls in the papal visit, and asked me to brief Bandit Mackenzie. He's new in town, so we guessed right that Bell wouldn't know him. Bandit staged a couple of buys last week, just to test the ground, then went back last night. Got a result; lifted them both.'

'Did you say Andy was there?'

Haggerty smiled and nodded. 'He asked me if it was okay: I told him to be our guest. While Bandit and Mavis MacDougall were in lifting Bell, Andy took care of Cable. The eejit pulled a knife on him; he actually cut his leather jacket. He got his nose smashed for his trouble as well.'

McIlhenney chuckled. 'He's lucky that's all he got burst. Andy loves that jacket: it's the only uniform he ever liked wearing.'

'He might be a happy boy, then,' Haggerty grunted. 'Maybe he won't be stuck in one at Tayside for too much longer.'

'What do you mean?'

The ACC tapped his nose. 'Just a feeling I've got,' he chuckled. 'I don't see Andy as a long-term Dundonian, that's all.'

'Thank you, sir. Is that all this visit was about: to wind me up about things I don't know?'

'Not quite. The chief had another call this morning, and he asked me to tell you about it. We're having a visit tomorrow afternoon from friends in London, and he wants you in on it. Most important of all, they want Bob to be there; their top man insists on it, in fact.'

'Special Branch?'

'Of course not: they'd have called you direct. No, they're from MI5, the Security Service.'

'No point asking what it's about?'

'None. As per usual they won't tell us till we're all in a room that's been swept for listening devices.'

'Is that why you wanted to know where the DCC is?'

'Mainly, yes.'

'Let me guess: so does Sir James, and he told you to ask me.'

Haggerty looked sheepish.

'Silly games, sir. You weren't testing me, were you? Trying to ease me into telling you things I shouldn't?'

'Nothing was further from my mind,' said the ACC disingenuously.

'No, of course not: you wouldn't do that.' McIlhenney smiled, affably. 'Anyway you and the chief can relax. He should make the meeting. I had a call from him at half six this morning. He's flying back today from . . . where he's been; he gets into Glasgow tomorrow morning. I'm picking him up. He might be like a bear from the jet-lag, but he'll be there.'

Eight

Aileen de Marco liked her office. It looked out and down over the Old Town of Edinburgh, and if she got close to the window and leaned to the left, she could see the castle.

In her days as a Glasgow councillor, she had thought that its Victorian marble-lined City Chambers was the finest public building in the world. She had been as loyal a Glaswegian as there was, and had regarded Edinburgh as a pompous place, which looked down its civic nose at the rest of Scotland. Yet now that she was there, installed as a minister in Scotland's first home-based legislature in almost three hundred years, she had to admit that there was something about St Andrews House, for all its allegedly fascist architecture, that she liked even more.

It stood on the site of the old Calton jail . . . legend had it that its execution chamber was still in existence, used as a store deep in the cellars . . . and it had little of the opulence of its George Square counterpart, which had been built to emphasise Glasgow's proud position as the second city of the Empire. Yet it had its own aura, drawn from the city around it.

It was a cold winter day, and the view was hazy, as if the traffic-crippling fog of a few weeks before was threatening a come-back, but the great dome of the Bank of Scotland headquarters on the Mound, with the silver Christmas star on top, still stood out on the skyline, between the crest of St Giles Cathedral and the tall spire of the Assembly Hall that had given the Scottish Parliament its temporary shelter.

She would never give up this room without regret, she realised.

She had just settled into her chair, and was about to buzz for Lena

McElhone, her private secretary, to bring in the morning's in-tray, when the unlisted phone on her desk rang. She wondered if it was Bob again, calling to make sure she had done nothing reckless, but then she realised that it was the middle of the night in Florida.

She picked up the receiver. 'Yes?'

'Ms de Marco?' a male voice asked. 'Lord Advocate for you, ma'am.'

'Put him through,' she said, icily.

'Aileen, how are you?' Milton Grassick began.

'Still here,' she replied. 'Are you surprised?'

'Relieved, actually. I wanted to talk to you about your meeting in Bute House yesterday, with Tommy. I gather it was hostile.'

'I don't think it was even as friendly as that.'

She could almost hear Grassick wince. 'You threatened resignation?'

'Was the First Minister smiling when he told you that?'

'I have to say that he didn't sound too concerned. I am, though.'

'Nice of you, Milton,' she said, casually. 'But isn't it a bit late for that?'

'You haven't . . .'

She paused for several seconds, letting the silence build. 'No,' she told him, at last.

His sigh of relief seemed to explode down the line. 'Thank goodness for that. Listen, Aileen, if anyone should go over this it's me. I had a call from Bob Skinner in the middle of the night; he made his feelings very clear and even threatened to embarrass me publicly. He's not a very nice man when he's angry, is Mr Skinner, but I rather think his view will be shared by most of the police service. It'll be difficult for me to work with him, and maybe with the chief constables, from now on. So I think I may well . . .'

'Tommy won't let you,' she told him, bluntly. 'Your resignation would be seen as a condemnation of his decision . . . or, rather, of his surrender of his powers to London.'

'He may have difficulty . . .' Suddenly Aileen was distracted by the sound of her door opening. Lena McElhone slipped into the room. 'Hold on, Milton. What is it, Lena?' she asked.

'The First Minister wants you,' her private secretary replied. 'Now, was what he said.'

'Okay.' She returned to the phone. 'Milton, I'll need to go. You-know-who's calling for me. Listen, don't you do anything rash; if you feel your position is untenable, do what Lord Advocates have always done, promote yourself to the Supreme Court bench. I'll support that.'

There was another silence, shorter this time. 'Let me consult a few people about it,' he murmured. 'There is a vacancy, and I could probably persuade the Judicial Appointments Board to approve, but . . .'

'Think about it; now I really must go.' She hung up and followed McElhone from the room.

The First Minister's office was almost identical to her own. The furnishings were a little grander but that was the only difference the eye could detect. Tommy Murtagh looked even smaller behind his desk; she looked at him as she closed the door behind her, but saw nothing in his eyes that gave away what he was thinking.

'Thank you for taking the time to see me,' he began.

She looked for sarcasm in his tone, but could detect none. 'My time is your time,' she said. As she spoke, she heard the door open again, then close.

She turned: a tall, slim, man had followed her into the room. He looked to be in his fifties, with muddy grey eyes. His only distinguishing feature was a high forehead, accentuated by a receding hairline. 'I want you to meet someone, Aileen,' Murtagh continued. 'Sit down, please, both of you.' He pointed to two chairs that faced his desk. They were exceptionally low-slung; she knew that he liked to look down on his visitors. She would have preferred to stand, but she did as he asked, keen to see what was coming.

'Ms de Marco, I'd like to introduce Mr Greg Jay,' the First Minister announced. 'As you know, when the office of Secretary of State for Scotland disappeared, I inherited Sir John Govan as my security adviser. Sir John's done a good job, but to be frank, he's establishment, very much in the court of the Association of Chief Police Officers, and that isn't always our side. I've decided to replace him with someone from the . . . dare I say it? . . . more active side of policing. Mr Jay has just retired, with effect from last Friday, in fact, as detective superintendent in charge of a CID division in Edinburgh; he's been doing this job unofficially for a couple of weeks now, but as of today he's full-time. He comes highly recommended by friends of ours.'

She nodded to Jay as she accepted his handshake. 'Congratulations; I'm pleased to meet you.' She looked back at Murtagh. 'At the same time, I'm a bit surprised that you didn't consult me as Justice Minister before making the appointment. I have relations with the police in my portfolio, after all.'

'This isn't a police post, Aileen. Greg's remit is security, in the broadest sense. Besides, there were reasons for not consulting you.' He paused. 'Before I go into those, let's round off our last conversation. You were a wee bit steamed up last time we spoke. Are you still thinking of resigning?'

She shook her head. 'My friends tell me that would be an overreaction on my part. They've persuaded me that since the decision was yours alone and taken behind my back, nobody's best interests would be served by me quitting.'

Murtagh's oval face broke into a smile; it was framed, oddly, by his red moustache. 'Not even mine?' he murmured.

'If you want rid of me, Tommy, you'll have to fire me.'

'I'll bet you think I wouldn't do that, though. Not given the story that's running in the on-line *Scotsman*, and the *Herald*,' he tapped the computer monitor on his desk as he spoke, 'and on the latest radio and television news bulletins.'

'What story's that?' she asked, genuinely surprised. She had rushed to the office, not taking time to read a newspaper.

'I'm sure you know damn fine: the one about the terrorists. Their removal was supposed to be announced in the Sheriff Court this morning, but there's been a leak. The beans are well and truly spilled. You're even quoted.'

'What do you mean I'm quoted?' she demanded.

'Well, maybe not quoted, but you're mentioned. It's all very slanted against government as usual, but this time against the Prime Minister and me in particular. All the stories I've read say that senior police officers are angry and frustrated by the decision, and they say also that it's understood you were not consulted. You can imagine what the opposition parties are saying about it.' The little man frowned across the desk, with a hint of menace. 'I'd love to know who the source was.'

'I'll bet you would,' said de Marco, evenly.

'It shouldn't be too hard to find out, though. There were so few people in the loop: Milton, you, me, the Prime Minister, Foreign Secretary, three private secretaries and Greg here. That's all.'

'I haven't spoken to any journalists since last night, Tommy.'

'I'm sure you haven't.' Murtagh chuckled. 'You're much too shrewd to do that.' He paused, and she could tell that a grenade was about to be thrown. 'You did speak to other people after our meeting, though. For example, you had a twenty-minute conversation with Mitchell Laidlaw, the chairman of Curle Anthony and Jarvis, the law firm. Just before that you made a short call to a number in Key West, Florida; the Pier House Hotel, I believe. A few hours later, you had an incoming call from the same number.'

The Justice Minister managed, but only just, to control the great gusher of anger that she felt welling up inside her. For the first time she understood why Jay was present at the meeting. 'Am I to under- tand,' she asked, calmly, 'that you've had your new security advisor tap my telephone?'

Murtagh raised both hands in mock protest. 'Heaven forbid!' he exclaimed. 'It would be almost unthinkable for me to do that to a senior colleague. But Greg and I did discuss your outburst at our Bute House meeting last night and we agreed, given the sensitivity of the whole matter, that it would be best if we kept an eye on your personal calls: until everything was done and dusted, so to speak. That's as far as it's gone, I assure you.'

He smiled again: thin-lipped, smug, humourless. 'That's to say it's as far as it's gone up to now. I could, of course, ask Mr Jay to obtain a copy of the guest list in that hotel. I'm sure that with the help of the American authorities . . . who now owe us a favour, you'll appreciate . . . he could even identify the occupant of the room you called.'

'I'm sure he could,' de Marco exclaimed. 'Listen, Tommy, I have my own advisors: not on the public payroll like your man here, but friends, experts in their own fields, who can help me do my job better. If I want to seek their advice, that's my business, not yours.'

Murtagh nodded; for a second his sleek, crinkly hair reflected the light above his head. 'Granted. I appreciate that, and it doesn't worry me; I have my private network too. And,' he conceded, 'I'm not above using them to get things into the media that I can't have directly attributed to me. I know what you and Bob Skinner have been up to: you've put a few personal things on the record. Possibly I'd have done the same thing in your shoes. But you know as I do that this will all be forgotten in a week. I'm sure Mitchell Laidlaw told you that these people were handed over legally.'

She nodded. 'That's not quite how he put it: he said it raised a question about human-rights legislation, but he pointed out that these people were hardly in a position to ask the court to stop the hand-over, and he told me what I knew already, that as soon as they were out of our hands they were beyond rescue since they're under American military jurisdiction in Cuba.'

'Exactly. That was the advice the Attorney General gave the Prime Minister in London.'

'All well and good, but let's go back to something. What do you mean by "you and Bob Skinner"?'

Murtagh looked at Jay. 'Greg,' he murmured, 'would you leave us now, please?' As the door closed on his security advisor, the First Minister turned back to de Marco. 'I know,' he resumed, slowly, 'that until he left the country for Key West around ten days ago, you and he had been meeting regularly. At the Scottish Arts Club, of which you're a member, at the flat you share with your private secretary, in his office at Fettes, and, just before he went to join his wife on holiday, in the Open Arms Hotel, in Dirleton. To top it off, I also know that his marriage is in trouble, thanks to his wife's recent indiscretion in the USA.'

Her temper snapped at last. 'You little . . .' she exploded. 'You've been having me tailed!'

'Not in the sense you mean; my information all came after the event, or events, to put it more accurately.'

'And just what conclusions have you drawn from it?'

'It doesn't matter what conclusions I draw from it. What matters is the conclusions that the tabloid press will draw if they ever find out.'

She pushed herself out of the low chair and looked down on him. 'You little snake!' she snapped. 'Are you trying to threaten me? Because if you are, we'll see how long you last with me on the back benches throwing rocks at your administration.'

'No, we won't, Aileen, because I won't let you go to the back benches. I want you all nice and docile and co-operative, not working to undermine me; I want you on the front bench where I can keep an eye on you. So you go back to your office and toe the line.'

'And why should I do that?'

'This is why,' Murtagh told her, his cold smile back in place. 'You may not care about your own office right now, but do you want to sacrifice Skinner's on the altar of your long-term ambition? He's an outstanding policeman, no doubt, but if he thinks he can play politics with the big boys, he's wrong. I intend to take a lot tighter control over the police service, and I want you as my Justice Minister to be my instrument in that.'

He stood up to face her, still not quite at her eye level. 'You asked me about my conclusions earlier. Here they are: I think you care about Deputy Chief Constable Skinner, and I think he cares about you. So here's what I'm telling you. If you do value each other, you will do what I say, and he will lower his profile and stop interfering in things that don't concern him. Otherwise, regrettably, I will fire you and take my chances, and I will ruin him, without a second thought.'

Nine

What knife?' Richard Cable looked across the table at the two detectives.

'The knife with which you attacked my colleague,' Bandit Mackenzie replied. "The knife with which you cut his jacket. The knife that's going to land you in the dock on a charge of attempted murder.'

'It's your colleague that should be in the dock,' said Cable evenly. His voice had little accent, but what there was was cultured, suggesting a comfortable background and upbringing. 'He was the one who did the attacking. I was standing there minding my own business, waiting for my girlfriend to come out of the toilet. My phone rang, I went to answer it and next thing I knew I was having my face bounced off the wall.' He reached up and touched the heavy white plaster that covered his nose. 'This is the result. As soon as I'm released from here, you can expect a formal complaint to the Chief Constable, and probably a civil action too.'

'Feel free to consult a lawyer,' Mavis MacDougall told him. 'We'll stop this interview right now, if you want to change your mind and have one present. Call him; tell him you're being held at Danderhall police office.'

'I don't feel the need for a lawyer at this stage. If and when I do, I will let you know. Can we go on, please? I don't have time for this.'

Mackenzie chuckled. 'Ah, but you do, Mr Cable. Trust me, you do. You've got years for this. Let's go back to your girlfriend. What's her name?'

'If I tell you that you'll haul her in here for questioning and give her a hard time. You don't need to know her name.'

'Can I make that decision for myself, sir?'

'No,' Cable whispered. His eyes had no more expression than they had shown in the club: there was no anger, no defiance, nothing other than boredom.

'When I went into the toilet with Bell,' the detective continued, 'there were two women there, other than DS MacDougall that is: a blonde buying condoms and a red-head with poor personal hygiene. They left one after the other and walked right past you. So where was ' this mystery woman? Or were you just fantasising about the sergeant here?'

For the first time Cable allowed himself something that resembled a smile. 'That might be a fantasy worth having, but I'd never seen her until I was hauled off the floor by your colleague. Where is he, incidentally? I'd like another talk with him.'

'He's not taking part in this interview. Plus, if you have any sense, you will not want to see him again. He's still very upset about his jacket.'

'That old rag?'

'It's one of his best friends, I believe.'

'Too bad he cut it, then.'

'And when did he do that?'

'When he produced the knife that he planted on me.'

Mackenzie sighed. 'Mr Cable, we have three witnesses who saw you produce the knife and thrust it at my colleague. You know the scenario: we have Bell on videotape telling me what will happen if he calls you, then he does. You said earlier that you answered the call, but the fact is you didn't. It rang, you checked the number showing, and then you headed for the ladies' toilet.'

'Nonsense. I went to answer but I pushed the red button by mistake. Then I was attacked by your colleague, who knocked me down and dropped the knife by my side. Are my prints on it?'

'No, because the handle is covered in a special tape that doesn't take prints.'

'It's not my knife, then. I don't carry knives to clubs. Do I look like that sort of guy? I have told you, and you've had time to check it out, I am a salesman with a BMW dealership in London. I had annual holidays to use up and I decided to come to Edinburgh.'

'You were due back at work today.'

Cable nodded. 'But I'm here, thanks to you.'

'You mean you were going to the showroom straight from the nightclub?' MacDougall exclaimed. 'Sure it's only about four hundred miles; no time at all in a Beamer, I suppose.'

'Where have you been living on your holiday?' Mackenzie asked.

'The Travel Inn, at Haymarket: you found my room key-card among my effects.'

'So you hadn't checked out?'

'No, I kept my booking open for another week.'

'So you weren't going back?'

'I kept my options open. I told you, I have a girlfriend; I met her here, and I fancied spending another week with her.'

'Ah, so if we go to the Travel Inn and wait for her she'll turn up there?'

'I shouldn't think so, not if she saw what happened to me. It probably scared the poor kid off.'

'But she was in the toilets. You were waiting for her.'

'She must have come out when my back was turned; before you went in there.'

The drugs squad commander sighed and ran his fingers through his hair. 'It's lucky for you I've got a sense of humour,' he said. 'Mr Cable, this is what happened. You and your associate Mr Bell were pushing drugs through that club; Bell sold me drugs on two occasions believing me to be a punter. When he tried it again last night the whole transaction was filmed and he was arrested. Your job was to guard the door, preventing people from interrupting the transaction, and if necessary, to provide the muscle. How do you respond to that?'

'I deny it. I do not know this man Bell. Let me ask you something. When have you ever seen us exchange a single word, or show any recognition of each other?'

'Last night, when he called you on his mobile.'

'Have you checked the ownership of the phone he used?'

'No. Why should we?'

'Because if you do, I think you'll find it belongs to me. I have two cell-phones, one for business, the other personal. My private phone was stolen the other night, in the club. I guess Bell must have taken it. I suggest to you that the call you saw him make was a simple bluff. He picked a number at random from my phonebook and called it.'

Bandit Mackenzie laughed. 'You're good, Mr Cable, really good. You could sell me a car any time. I think we've both earned a break, don't you? Interview suspended at,' he checked his watch, 'ten fourteen a.m., to be resumed later today.' He reached over and switched off the tape-recorder on the table, then looked up, over Cable's shoulder, to the uniformed constable who stood impassively with his back to the door of the small, windowless interview room. 'Take the prisoner back to the cells, please, Barton, and bring along Mr Bell. Let's see how funny he is.' He looked back at Cable. 'Just so you know, you'll be appearing in the Sheriff Court tomorrow morning; you'll be formally remanded then.'

The car salesman smiled again, and winked; the gesture was made grotesque by the puffiness around his eye. 'I wouldn't lay any bets on that, Chief Inspector, if I was you,' he said.

Ten

When was he reported missing, sir?' Detective Constable Tarvil Singh's voice was flat and toneless as he asked the question. He looked as if he had just seen something that he could not bring himself to believe; in fact, that was the case.

'Ten o'clock last night,' Detective Inspector Stevie Steele replied. 'He and his mates came up town to the Christmas fun-fair in the gardens, and they were all going for burgers afterwards. He was due home at eight; when he hadn't showed by quarter to nine, George and Jen started calling round the other lads' parents. When they got no joy, George called St Leonards, the divisional HQ for where they live, and then he called me.' He looked at the big DC, who seemed bulkier than ever in his white scene-of-crime tunic. 'When I told the chief super, she phoned round the other divisional commanders; just about every copper on duty in Edinburgh's been looking for the lad ever since.'

'Have you let Ms Rose know that he's been found?'

Steele frowned. 'That's no job for me, Tarvil. The chief superintendent will be gutted by this, like we all are. I'm sure that Detective Superintendent Chambers will tell her, but only after she's brought George Regan here and he's formalised the identification.'

Singh looked past him, over his shoulder. 'I've got news for you, boss,' he murmured. 'Somebody's beaten her to it.'

Steele turned and saw a car that had not been there before, parked beside the ambulance on the roadway near the railway line. He knew it well; as he looked at it, the driver's door opened and Chief Superintendent Margaret Rose, commander of Edinburgh's western police division, stepped out. She wore a heavy coat over her uniform, and her close-cut red hair was tucked neatly inside her cap. She walked across to the two detectives.

'You sure?' she asked the DI, quietly.

He nodded. 'I'm sorry, there's no doubt.' He turned and looked over at a large tent that had been erected on the slope that ran sharply down from the western ramparts of Edinburgh Castle; Tarvil Singh had left them and was moving towards it, as if to stand guard. 'I've known wee George since he was eight or nine.' He smiled, sadly. ' 'Whenever the Regans had a party they'd a hell of a job getting him off to bed.'

'How old is he now?'

'He'd have been fourteen in February, poor wee guy.'

'What happened?'

'The doctor's still in there, but his provisional view, and mine when I saw the body, is that his neck's broken.'

Rose looked up at the towering grey castle. 'Does that mean that he climbed up there and fell?'

'Trying to scale the heights, you mean? It looks like it; a daft boy's trick. He'd have been game for it, that's for sure.' Steele shivered: the December morning was grey and cold, and he found himself wishing that he had brought his own overcoat. 'The body's virtually unmarked. There's some facial bruising, that looks like it was sustained when he hit the ground, but nothing more than that.'

'But it was night-time when it happened, wasn't it?'

'It's Christmastime, Mags. With all the decorations and stuff, this whole area's lit up like a football field.'

'I suppose so. Has George been here yet?'

Steele winced. 'No, not yet; Mary's bringing him . . . and I wish I didn't have to be here when he arrives.'

'Not his wife, though?'

'God forbid.'

'He may not have the authority to do that. If it was my son . . .' She broke off. 'Who found him?' she asked.

'He was spotted by somebody in Saltire Court,' said Steele. He pointed at the elegant office block that dominated the far side of Castle Terrace. 'The body can't be seen from the path at all, or from the roadway, but a sharp-eyed worker on the top floor spotted it, took a closer look through a pair of binoculars, and raised the alarm.'

The sound of another approaching vehicle made them look towards the road. 'Oh dear,' Rose whispered. 'Jen is here after all.' The dead boy's mother sat in the back seat of Detective Superintendent Mary Chambers's car. As the two officers moved towards her, they saw on her face the same expression of disbelief that Singh had worn earlier.

The inspector felt a fluttering in his stomach as Detective Sergeant George Regan stepped out on to the hard, rough road. The two friends met, and shook hands formally. 'Jen will stay in the car,' said the bereaved father. 'She wanted to come to the scene, and we didn't try to dissuade her.'

'I'll sit with her,' said Rose, as Mary Chambers came round to join them, her plain square face ashen white.

'Thank you, ma'am,' Regan replied. He drew himself up to his full height, gathering his dignity around him like a protective cloak. 'Let us suit up, Stevie, and then let me see him.'

Steele waved to a crime-scene technician, who brought over two fresh white tunics. He waited in silence while Regan and Chambers put them on, then led the way up the steep slope.

Eleven

Like most people, Bob Skinner tolerated flying, regarding it as a twenty-first century necessity; he believed firmly that those who said they actually enjoyed being in a heavier-than-air machine thirty-five thousand feet above the ground were either liars or idiots.

The part of the whole process that he disliked most was the pre-boarding wait in the departure lounge. The small airport that served Key West, where Sarah had dropped him fifteen minutes before, was reasonably comfortable, and the monitor screens told him that his aircraft was on the ground and was scheduled to leave on time, but still he fretted.

He tried to read a book, a private-detective yarn called *Alarm Call* that he had brought with him from Scotland, but found that he could not give it the concentration it deserved. The small cafeteria was open: he bought himself coffee, and a bagel with cream cheese, but even as he chewed he found himself reaching unconsciously inside his jacket for the cell-phone which, on a whim, he had left at home, so that he could be truly out of contact to all except Neil McIlhenney, Trish, the children's nanny, and Aileen de Marco.

He had given her his contact number because, he had told himself and her, he had promised to be there for her whenever she needed advice, but in truth, he wondered if his motive had been more personal. Whatever was in his head, and his heart, he felt an urgent need to speak to her, to make sure that she had kept the promise she had made to him the evening before.

He gave in. He drained the coffee but left half of the bagel, then walked over to a payphone against the wall, and used a credit card to activate it. He punched in her number and waited. Lena McElhone answered. 'Justice Minister's office.'

'Lena, it's Bob Skinner here. Can I speak to Aileen, or is she at lunch?'

'She's in her office, Mr Skinner. Hold on.' He waited for a minute, watching the cost of the call tick higher and higher. 'I'm sorry,' said the private secretary, when finally she came back on line, 'Aileen's very busy and can't be disturbed.'

He grunted in frustration. 'Okay. Tell her I'll call her from Miami once I get there.'

'She expects to be busy all day, sir.'

'She's not clearing her desk, is she?'

'Pardon?'

'Obviously not. Just give her a message, please: tell her I'm glad she's done the right thing, and that I'll be back in Scotland tomorrow morning. I'll call her then, and if her lunch-hour's free maybe she can keep it that way.'

'I'll pass that on, sir. Goodbye.'

Skinner pulled down the cradle, released it again, and dialled the secure Special Branch number. 'Neil,' he said, as his friend picked up the call. 'What's happening? How are the papers handling the terrorists?'

'As you expected,' he replied. 'They're kicking the crap out of the PM and Murtagh. The Nats and the Tories are having a field day.'

'It won't help the terrorists, though. They'll be touching down pretty soon not all that far from where I am right now. I don't fancy their chances of ever leaving.'

'Are you bothered?'

'About what happens to them? In truth, no, I'm not. But I assured Aileen de Marco that they'd be tried in Scotland. I was wrong, and she's been dropped in it. That's what annoys me.'

'You'll both get over it.'

'You sound harassed, Chief Inspector. What's been happening?'

'Plenty, but I can't talk about much of it over the phone. I can tell you one thing, though. Bandit Mackenzie and Andy Martin were playing cowboys last night.'

'Andy was involved?' Then, 'Tayside must be as boring as I told him it would be. Did they get a result?'

'Big time. Bandit's been like a dog with two cocks all morning. He should enjoy it while he can, poor lad: he's about to be given a high-level vasectomy.' The DCC heard McIlhenney pause, as if someone had come into his office. 'Boss, I have to go. See you tomorrow morning.'

Twelve

The tent was still in place, although the body of George Regan junior, aged thirteen, had been removed to the mortuary in the High Street. The King's Stables Road entrance to Princes Street Gardens had been reopened, and a mobile investigation headquarters caravan, white and imposing, now stood where the cars and ambulances had been parked earlier.

George Regan senior and his wife had gone, with the same composure and grace of bearing they had brought with them, to the unspoken relief of their colleagues. The sergeant had understood how difficult their task would be. The violent death of a stranger child always had a profound effect on those who had to investigate it; when the victim was known to them, inevitably it was even worse. George had realised also that he could not be a member of the team, and had made no such embarrassing request.

'You never know what's in a person till you see them in a crisis,' Detective Superintendent Chambers said quietly, facing Stevie Steele across the small table in the mobile HQ. They had been joined there by Detective Chief Superintendent Dan Pringle, the ageing head of CID, and by Alan Royston, the force media-relations manager. There was a fifth person in the command van: Sir James Proud, the Chief Constable, had come to the scene; he sat next to Pringle, silent and solemn.

'Or in yourself, till you experience one,' the DI added. 'Beneath all his normal banter and stuff, George is a bloke and a half.'

'So let's find out how his son died,' the head of CID pronounced. 'But let's not get ahead of ourselves. We'll reach no conclusions until we have the post-mortem findings. That said, on the basis of what

51

we've seen, provisionally it looks as if it was a straightforward mishap. Young boy out for adventure decides to climb the castle rock, slips and falls, breaks his neck.'

'There were no other injuries on the body,' Steele pointed out. 'Nothing to indicate that he'd fallen.'

'You could fall off a pavement and break your neck,' Pringle countered. 'You might not even have to fall. I heard of a case once where a man was waiting to cross a road and a bus drove past too close to the kerb. Its wing mirror hit the guy, killed him stone dead.'

'It was after dark,' said Mary Chambers, 'and wee George was on an eight o'clock curfew. The other kids were all home on time. Yet he sneaked off on his own and tried to climb a cliff.'

'That would be fairly typical George behaviour,' Steele told her. 'He was a lovely lad, but you'd have thought that mischief had been invented for him. And who says that he was on his own? Maybe they were all there. Maybe it was a dare that went wrong. Maybe the other kids panicked and legged it.'

'That's a possibility,' she conceded.

The Chief Constable leaned forward. 'I don't like to intervene in these situations,' he began, 'but we must interview these boys; quietly and discreetly, but we must do it. We need to eliminate . . . or confirm . . . the possibility that they were all part of this prank and have all been scared into silence. If they haven't, then to complete the picture we need to find out if anyone else saw George junior, after they all went their separate ways.'

'Very good sir,' said Chambers. 'DI Steele, DC Singh and I will get on to that straight away.'

DCS Pringle grunted. 'Mary, big Tarvil on his own will scare the shite out of those kids just by looking at them. With George gone you'll be short-handed, so I've persuaded Maggie Rose to lend us her young *protégé*, PC Haddock, for a while. He's inexperienced, but he's a smart kid, and he's maybe more user-friendly than DC Singh.'

'Okay,' the superintendent conceded, 'but we'll need to get on with it. George Regan gave us the boys' names, and told us where to find them. Two of them are at Heriot's, and the other four are at Castlebrae, where George junior was. We'll try to interview them at school, but first we'll have to contact the parents, tell them what's happened and give them a chance to be present when we speak to their sons, or get their permission to do it with a teacher present. These are minors, so we'll have to ask the schools if they can lay on counselling for them afterwards.'

She looked at Steele. 'You take young Haddock and handle the pair at Heriot's. I'll do the Castlebrae lot with Tarvil.'

'What about the media?' asked Alan Royston. 'We'll have to make an announcement soon. I'd like you to take a press briefing. How about midday?'

Chambers nodded. 'I'll do it, but not until two o'clock; give us a chance to speak to the boys first. Once we've done that I'll have a better idea of what I'm going to say.'

Thirteen

Bandit Mackenzie smiled. 'A good night's work, would you say, Mavis?'

'And half the day as well,' the sergeant replied, drily. 'You might as well lock them up for the night and let us get home for some rest ourselves.'

'You've got no stamina, MacDougall,' he taunted. 'I can go on for ever after I get a good result; there's no buzz like it.'

'If you really believe that, you're a sad bastard . . . sir. I've been on duty for over thirteen hours, several of which I spent sealed in a toilet, sharing the moments as females relieved themselves. Now I would like a pizza, a shower, and a change of clothes, preferably before my boyfriend gets home this evening, or he'll smell me before he sees me.'

'Your boyfriend's a plumber; he'll never notice. Come on, I fancy another go at Bell.'

'He's not going to make a statement, however long you go at him. Guys like that don't. We showed him the video and all he did was shrug his shoulders and say you planted the drugs on him outside. All he's offered to plead to is stealing Cable's cell-phone. He's taking the piss, Bandit. He knows what's going to happen, but he's determined to make it as difficult for us as possible.'

'Let's try Cable again, then.'

She laughed. 'We'll definitely get nothing out of him. He's a really cocky one. I wonder what his background is.'

Mackenzie grunted. 'He's an international man of mystery, as far as I can see. He's got no traceable background, other than as a vendor of German motors. Still, I fancy another go at him. It would be good if he coughed: then we wouldn't have to stick Andy Martin in the witness box.'

'The only way he'll cough is if he catches the flu.'

'He's been in the cells long enough for that. Let's have him.' He pushed himself from his chair, in the office they had been loaned by the Danderhall station commander. He had almost reached the door when the phone rang. MacDougall took the call, frowned, then replaced the receiver. 'We've got a visitor. He's coming up to see us.'

'Who?'

'Bob Skinner's hatchet man.'

'Eh?'

Mackenzie still wore his bewildered expression when the door opened, and a large man stepped into the room. He recognised him at once, but even as they shook hands he struggled to put a name to the face. 'DCI Neil McIlhenney, Special Branch,' said the newcomer, by way of an introduction. 'Our paths did cross a couple of weeks ago, if only briefly.'

'Ah, of course. You're the guy that's married to the actress. What can we do for you? Do you want our autographs for the wife?'

McIlhenney looked at him, stone-faced. 'Save the flash act for the punters, friend. You've got two prisoners in the cells downstairs, Bell and Cable.'

Mackenzie's smile vanished. 'Yes. So?'

'So you're letting them go.'

'I'm what?' the drugs squad commander cried out, spontaneously. It was the first time that Mavis MacDougall had ever heard him raise his voice.

'They're being released, without charge. You will shred all transcripts of interviews and give me all your tapes. Destroy any paperwork you may have relating to this operation. The record of their booking in here has already been erased.'

'On whose authority?'

'Mine. I'm Santa Claus, come to them early.'

Bandit regained his composure. 'You're a DCI, pal. Last time I looked, so was I. You'll need to give me more than that.'

McIlhenney gazed at him. 'No, I won't. You'll do as I ask. But before they leave this building, I will be speaking to your prisoners; alone.'

'And what about Spike Thomson? They'll go straight back to his place and chib him.'

'No, they will not. They will not go near Spike Thomson again, or his place.'

'And who's going to tell them that?'

'I am. Now, give me the tapes, please.'

Mackenzie glowered at him, but took four cassettes from his pocket and handed them over.

'Thanks,' said McIlhenney. 'For what it's worth, I'd be brassed off too, if I was in your shoes. I'm sorry, but this is the way it's got to go.'

'Okay,' Bandit acknowledged. 'I understand. I know that Bell's got form, but Cable, is he an undercover cop, then?'

'Please don't ask, and please don't mention his name again, not here, at home, at Fettes, not anywhere. I know it's frustrating, but . . .'

'Understood,' Mackenzie conceded, grudgingly. 'Even if I do act flash on occasion, and even if I'm new in Edinburgh, I'm a professional.'

'Fine,' said McIlhenney, as he turned to leave. 'Just one more thing. Come and see me in my office tomorrow afternoon, please. Five minutes to three, no later, and don't talk about that either.'

Fourteen

Although she had been a police officer for over twenty years, Mary Chambers had never faced a press conference. She had been given communications training in Glasgow, where she had begun her career, and Alan Royston had briefed her well, but still she felt uncharacteristically nervous as she read her prepared statement to the media, gathered in a conference room at the divisional headquarters in Torphichen Place.

It was brief, naming the victim and describing the circumstances of his disappearance and the discovery of his body. When she revealed that the dead boy was the son of Detective Sergeant George Regan, a collective murmur rippled across the room. Most of the journalists present knew Regan; all of them recognised a page one headline when they heard it.

She completed her text, laid the single sheet of paper on the table and looked out over her audience inviting questions.

'How are you treating this death, Superintendent Chambers?' asked a grizzled veteran in the front row.

'John Hunter, freelance,' Royston whispered in her ear.

'On the face of it, Mr Hunter,' she replied, 'it's a tragic accident. I'm never keen to anticipate pathologists' findings, but I'm not expecting anything from the autopsy to change that view. However, we are keen to speak to anyone who may have seen George, in Lothian Road, or King's Stables Road.'

'When was the last known sighting of the boy?'

'He and his friends parted company in Princes Street, at the foot of Lothian Road. George lived on a different bus route from the rest of them. We've spoken to all of the boys, and they all describe him as heading for the bus stop in front of St Leonard's Church, just after seven fifteen. The spot where his body was found isn't far from there. The medical examiner put the provisional time of death at eight p.m.'

A woman raised her hand. 'Iris Staples, *Evening News*,' she said. 'Was George a bit of a daredevil?'

'George was a normal active boy,' Detective Inspector Steele answered, from the side of the room, 'with a keen sense of adventure. I knew him, but I'm not going to stick any labels on him.'

'Would it have been in character for him to go off to try a spot of rock-climbing?'

'That's a question that would be better put to his parents, when they feel up to seeing you.'

'So, Superintendent,' said John Hunter, 'to come back to my first question, we can safely say that there's no evidence of foul play, and leave it at that? Nothing's going to change overnight?'

'No, it isn't,' Mary Chambers replied, 'nor the night after that. We'll await Professor Hutchinson's report, and any witness statements we receive, but I expect we'll be able to make a report to the Procurator Fiscal pretty soon.'

Fifteen

Rolling his suitcase behind him and with his flight bag slung over his left shoulder, Bob Skinner stepped through the international arrivals gateway and out on to the concourse of Glasgow Airport. It was eight a.m., his eyes were gritty . . . he never slept on aircraft . . . and he felt in dire need of a shower and a shave. He also felt cold: he had left in late-autumn conditions, but he was returning to a full-blown Scottish winter.

He shivered as he looked around for Neil McIlhenney, not bothering to hide his impatience as he failed to spot him. Suddenly he felt a tug on his sleeve. He turned ... to see Aileen de Marco looking up at him. 'Taxi?' she said.

For the first time in a full day he smiled. 'Hi,' he sighed. 'I'd like that, but I'm being picked up.'

'You are indeed: by me.'

'How come?' he asked, bewildered. 'Did you quit after all and go into the car-hire business?'

'Nearly, but I stopped myself. Being chauffeured is one of the perks of my job. I couldn't give that up. As for my being here, I wanted to see you, so I called your pal Neil and persuaded him to let me take his place.'

'I thought you didn't drive.'

'Your information was out of date: I didn't have a car for a while, but I've driven since I was eighteen. I bought myself new wheels six months ago: a sharp deal from Arnold Clark.'

'I'll bet Neil was pleased to hear that.' He leaned forward slightly, and kissed her cheek. 'But I'm glad you did it: I wanted to see you too. I tried to call you yesterday, but Lena said you were tied up all day.'

'I sure was.' She took his arm. 'Come on, let's get out of here.'

She led him out of the terminal building and across the road to the short-stay car park. Her car was a Fiat Stilo hatchback; he put his bags into the boot and climbed in, pleased to discover that the interior was still warm from the trip to the airport.

'Have you come from Edinburgh?' he asked her, as she turned on to the M8.

'No, I stayed at my flat in Glasgow overnight. I thought we'd go there now, actually, to let you freshen up, and to have some breakfast.'

He rubbed his chin. 'Good idea. I feel like I've been travelling for ever; it's three flights from where I was to here.'

'There's a *Scotsman* in the back,' she said. 'There's something in it you should see.'

'Sounds ominous,' he murmured, reaching behind him to retrieve the newspaper.

The report of George Regan junior's death was at the foot of the front page. 'Jesus,' he whispered. 'The poor kid. I met him, too, at the station Christmas party a couple of years ago.' He scanned the report. 'How must George and his wife be feeling?'

'Like any other parents who've lost a kid, I imagine. They'll be going through all sorts of agonies and recriminations: if only they hadn't let him go, and all that.'

'Try caging thunder,' Bob mused. 'My younger son would try to climb Mount Everest if I took my eye off him for a second.'

'Make sure you don't, then. By the way, I've got a message for you from Neil. There's a meeting in Fettes at three this afternoon that you'll want to attend.'

'Did he say what it is?'

'No; he just asked me to tell you the time, and make sure you got there.'

She turned off the motorway and headed into, then through Govan. The traffic was building, but most of it was headed for the Clyde tunnel, so there were no hold-ups. They passed through street after street of sandstone tenements until, suddenly, the river came into sight and with it a tall development of newer apartments. She turned into the car park of the third block, and tucked the Stilo into a space marked 'Reserved. 4a'. Bob took his flight bag from the boot, followed her inside and into the lift.

The flat was on the fourth floor; it was small, but the space was well planned. The living room had a corner window which looked across the Clyde, and eastwards, towards the city. 'Very nice,' said Bob, impressed.

'I like it,' Aileen replied. 'I wish the parliament was in Glasgow, then I could live here all the time.'

'You could do that if you wanted. The government cars would pick you up from here and bring you back. Like you said, it's a perk of the job.'

'My days are too unpredictable.' She smiled. 'As for my nights, there's nothing to draw me back here.' She reached up and touched his face, feeling the stubble on his chin. 'You look tired. Do you want to go to bed for a couple of hours?'

'Do you mean alone?' he asked her, with a quiet grin.

'That, sir, is up to you,' she murmured, provocatively. 'I have things to tell you, and that might be as good a place as any.'

He put his hands on her hips. 'Honest to God, Aileen, I couldn't do you justice. I'm just off the flight from hell, I've got a chin like a hedgehog, plus . . . to be honest, the time isn't right.'

She stood on tiptoe and kissed him. 'I know. But I thought I'd make the offer anyway, out of devilment, if nothing else.'

'You don't feel snubbed that I've turned it down?'

'No, honestly.' She smiled, shyly. 'I'll regard it as a rain-check. The truth is, I don't know how I'd have felt if you'd taken me up on it.' She ran her palm over his beard. 'You're right about the stubble; heavy-gauge sandpaper at the very least.'

He looked at her, his emotions churning, temptation gnawing at him, realising that he was approaching a pivotal moment in his life. He thought of his marriage, and asked himself, for the first time, whether he wanted to repair it, even if he could. 'I really would like to sleep for a bit, though,' he told her, to end the moment, as much as anything else.

She led him through to her bedroom, showed him the *en suite* shower room. As soon as she had left him alone, he stripped off his clothes, slipped under the duvet, and was gone in sixty seconds.

61

When he was awakened by a gentle touch on his shoulder, she was sitting on the edge of the bed; her blonde hair was perfectly arranged and she had changed from the casual clothes she had worn earlier into a dark business suit. She smiled down at him; for a second he was disorientated, then his eyes and his mind focused. 'Hi,' he mumbled, drowsily. 'What time is it?'

'Five to twelve.' She picked up a mug of coffee from her bedside table. 'Yours is there,' she said, nodding over his shoulder.

'Thanks.' He pulled himself up to sit beside her, picked up his mug from its coaster, and took a sip. 'Jesus, I needed that.'

Aileen laughed. 'Which? Sleep or the coffee?'

'Both.'

'How did things go in Florida . . . or don't you want to talk about it?'

'There's not a lot to talk about. Let's just say we reached some understanding of where we stand and what we really feel about each other. Before, there was anger on both sides, but I think we've worn that out. Sarah says she's going to do some thinking over the next few days. I suppose I'll do the same. I've got all sorts of worries in my head, but most of all the kids. What do you tell them at times like this?'

'The truth, I suppose, if they're old enough to understand it.'

'They're old enough to be hurt by it.'

'So are you. It's in your eyes.' She ruffled his hair. The duvet was folded back to his waist, and her eyes were drawn to a ragged scar on his side. 'What's that?' she asked.

'That? It's where I was stabbed a few years back.'

She touched his face above the nose. 'What about that? Who gave you that one?'

'Big Lenny Plenderleith; he got plenty in return, though. I think that's how I earned his respect.' He grinned at her; there was a mischief in his eyes that she had never seen before. 'How many scars do you have, then?'

She jumped off the bed, unfastened her trousers and pushed them down enough for him to see a faint line on her lower abdomen, to the right. 'Appendix,' she said, then fastened herself in again. 'When I was twelve. All the rest are on the inside.'

'I'd like to heal those.'

'Maybe you can't; maybe no one can. Just make sure you don't give me any more.'

'I promise I won't do that. So talk: these things you mentioned, tell me them.'

She drank some more coffee, then set down her mug. 'Okay,' she said, 'but first I've got a question for you. Did you know that Sir John Govan was being replaced as the First Minister's security adviser?'

She could read the surprise on his face, so she knew his answer before he spoke it. 'No, I had no idea.'

Aileen smiled. 'That's good. If you had, my next question was going to be "Why the hell didn't you tell me about it?" But you would have, wouldn't you?'

'Of course, but I'd have expected you to be consulted.'

'That's not the way our First Minister works. Tommy wants his own man, not someone with anyone else's seal of approval. He made the appointment all on his own.'

'So who is it?'

'One of your guys, Mr Jay.'

Bob sat bolt upright in bed, forgetting that he was naked. 'Greg Jay? You're joking.'

'You'll find I'm not, when you get to your office. He's full-time in post as of yesterday. But he was active before that, as I know to my cost. After our bust-up on Sunday, Murtagh had him monitor my telephone calls. He knows I called you in Florida; he knows you leaked the story to the press. He's threatened to ruin you if you don't behave, and to boot me out of the Cabinet in disgrace if I don't fall into line and go along with his plans.'

'Has he now?' Skinner growled. 'Let's see him try. It doesn't take a genius to guess who was behind the story, but let him prove it. You could stick John Hunter in the High Court and have a judge order him to reveal a source on pain of jail, and he wouldn't. If Greg Jay tried to interrogate him, he'd laugh in his face.'

'Couldn't he check your phone calls from the hotel?'

'He'd need the FBI's help, and it's no cert he'd get it; but even if he did he'd come up dry. I used Sarah's American cell-phone to call John, and he knows nothing about that.'

'Don't underestimate him. He knows a lot about us. That's why I came to pick you up this morning; it's why I wouldn't speak to you on the phone yesterday. I was afraid that someone would be listening.'

'What does he know, exactly?'

She repeated everything that Murtagh had told her about their meetings, about the Arts Club, her Edinburgh flat, the Open Arms Hotel. 'Jay must have been tailing us all along, or me at least.'

Bob took a deep breath, releasing it slowly. 'No,' he said, quietly. 'I'd have known if he was doing that. He didn't follow anyone unseen, not me at any rate; he's not that good, and I'd have known if he had used any serving officer for the job. Somebody told him about those meetings.'

'But who could have?'

'Work it out. It wasn't me, so that leaves only one person.'

Aileen's brow knitted into a frown. 'No, it couldn't be; she wouldn't.'

'Lena McElhone isn't your personal secretary, love. She's your private secretary and that's different. She's a civil servant: if she was leaned on by the First Minister or his stooge, she'd have a career choice to make. I wouldn't blame her, but I'd be careful what I let her know in future, other than your official business.'

'Those bastards!' She spat the words out. 'I can just see them doing it too. What's this man Jay like?'

'Disgruntled, is how I'd describe him. He didn't quite make it to the top, but he thought he should have. I transferred him recently, out of Leith to another division; he accepted it at the time, but I could tell that he didn't like it. I don't think he liked me either.'

'Why not?'

He chuckled. 'It's not compulsory. Greg might seem like a quiet, sober, middle-aged man, but inside that drab exterior there lurks an ego at least as big as mine.'

'How did he get the job? Murtagh said something about him having friends.'

'He does. He's got Masonic connections for a start. I guess the First Minister must have sent out scouts and his name came up. He's no security expert, but I guess that isn't the main requirement for the post any more.' He looked at her. 'This is not good. What are these plans of wee Tommy's that you mentioned?'

'He intends, and I quote, "to take a lot tighter control over the police service". He also wants me, as his Justice Minister, to go along with it. He wants you, as he put it, to "lower your profile and stop interfering". Or else.'

'He's threatening us?'

'Exactly. If we don't play ball he'll do some leaking of his own, about you and me.'

Skinner laughed. 'But he doesn't have anything to leak. Or didn't until now. Innocent we may be, but what would the tabloids do if they were tipped off that we've been together in your flat?'

'Murtagh and Jay didn't know we were coming here,' she protested.

'They didn't have to, not necessarily. Do you know how small they can make bugs and cameras these days?'

Aileen gasped. 'Jay might have bugged this place?'

He shook his head. 'Relax, I don't really think so, not for a moment. But just to be on the safe side give me a spare key and I'll have the Strathclyde Special Branch sweep it. And this . . .' He reached across her and switched on her bedside radio, pressing pre-set buttons until he found Clyde Two, then turning up the volume. 'Enjoy that, boys,' he growled.

'God,' she whispered, 'the very thought of it. Bob, I've been silly.'

'No dafter than me,' he replied. 'Besides, when you showed up at the airport this morning . . . it brightened my morning, that's all I'll say.'

'Mine too.'

They were silent for a while, avoiding eye contact, each thinking private thoughts.

'So you are going along with Murtagh's scheming?' he asked, eventually.

'It's going to happen, whether I do or not.'

'What is, exactly?'

'The First Minister is legislating to give himself the right to confirm every appointment at assistant, deputy and chief constable rank; he will also have to approve all short-lists for interview. Beyond that, he will take added powers to intervene directly and fire those whom he decides are not performing properly, or are in dereliction of their duty.'

'He's taking command of the police?' Skinner was incredulous.

'Effectively, that's what it means. He showed me the enabling bill yesterday; he's had a team of civil servants and policy advisers working on it in secret. The draft's finished, the preliminaries are under way and it'll be ready for introduction to the Parliament next week.'

'Will he get it through?'

'I'd say so. He's persuaded the coalition partners to back it; he's promised them that approvals and confirmation will be virtually automatic, and that the firing power will only be invoked in extreme cases.'

'And they believed that?'

'They believed in the additional Cabinet post he's offered them. That'll be unveiled next Monday. But it's not just them. The SSP will support it as well, I'm sure, and probably the Greens. I wouldn't be surprised if the SNP do as well.'

'Don't tell me you believe his assurances?'

'No more than you do, but the majority of my party colleagues will; those that don't will obey the whip.'

'What if ACPOS, our chiefs' association, comes out and opposes it unanimously?'

'Then I'd guess that Tommy's spin machine will portray you as self-interested storm-troopers.'

'And you're going along with it?' he asked her. 'You really are?'

'If I don't, if I resign and try to drum up opposition to it, Tommy will use every means to discredit me, but first and foremost he'll come after you. As soon as the bill's signed into law, he'll find an excuse to remove you. I'm not going to allow that to happen.'

'Maybe I would, though!'

'Listen, love, two days ago you persuaded me to stay in government. Back me up now, please. Murtagh's a shrewd wee swine; he knows we care for each other, and he knows we're both ambitious. We've got to sit tight, stay well clear of each other if that's what it takes, and appear to play ball, even if it means letting him pass his bloody law. But I promise you one thing. You keep telling me I have it in me to be First Minister myself one day: if that ever happens, and I inherit that legislation, my very first act will be to repeal it. Trust me, Bob, please.

'Tommy was right about one thing: I care about you, and I won't let you come to harm.'

He wrapped the duvet round himself and swung his legs off the bed, to sit beside her. 'I hope, Aileen,' he murmured, 'that I can make you the same promise and keep it. As long as you realise that keeping my head down under a threat from someone like your boss will be just about the most difficult thing that anyone's ever asked me to do.'

Sixteen

Mary Chambers took the folder from the envelope in which it had been delivered. She and Tarvil Singh had witnessed the autopsy on young George Regan, and so she knew that the pathologist's report she held in her hands was unsurprising.

Nonetheless, she looked through it, avoiding the photographic section, and passed it to Stevie Steele. 'Death was the result of a broken neck,' she said. 'The boy received a severe blow to the left side of the jaw, which was also shattered. Professor Hutchinson says that it was consistent with the type of injury that could be sustained as the result of a fall from a moderate height.'

'Were there any other injuries noted?' Steele asked her.

'There were superficial scratches on both his hands, with dirt and fine gravel in them; the same was found on his clothing. They could have been caused by him throwing his hands out as he fell, or by him scrambling up the banking.'

The inspector dropped the report, unread. 'It backs up the accident supposition, then?'

'All the way. There's nothing in it that takes us in any direction other than accidental death. The old prof's conclusion is that that's what it was. My view is that we have to accept he's right, and report to the Fiscal accordingly. Have we found any witnesses who can help us top and tail it?'

'None of his pals can help,' he replied. 'We're agreed that they all seemed genuinely shocked when they were told George was dead, and they all describe their last sight of him in the same way. We've found a bus-driver who remembers seeing him standing at the stop in Lothian Road, but his wasn't the route George wanted so he drove on.

He said that the boy was alone, and that none of his passengers got off at that stop.'

'So there are no sightings?'

'No, but there is one thing that might be significant. The gates to the castle rock are closed at nightfall, to keep kids out.' Steele pointed out of the window of the mobile office. 'The big one, the vehicle access over there, is padlocked and it's smooth; it'd be easier to climb the rock than that. Yet when the park attendant turned up to open it yesterday morning, the chain was hanging loose. Young Haddock and I found the guy who was supposed to have locked it on Sunday: he wouldn't admit that he didn't, but he couldn't swear that he did. He was very defensive.'

'I'm not surprised. If he was negligent, left the gate unsecured and a boy got in and fell to his death . . . It's all bloody questions, Stevie,' Chambers complained. 'No bloody answers.'

'And we've interviewed everyone we can. Mary, if this wasn't a copper's son, what would we have done right now? We'd have reported the circumstances to the Procurator Fiscal's office, giving them the pathologist's report and letting them close the book on it.'

'Actually, we'd probably have left the whole thing to the uniformed branch,' she pointed out. 'So are we agreed, then? We should wrap it up and pass the buck to the PF?'

'Almost.' Steele hesitated. 'But not quite: there's one more thing I'd like to do, for George and Jen's sake, to give them as much closure as we can. I think we should go back to basics, and make a press appeal for witnesses. I know it's quiet at that time on a Sunday, but other people than that driver must have seen George. There's the passengers on his bus for a start, and on other buses. The shops were open earlier: some of their staff might still have been on their way home. Why don't we ask them for help in tracing wee George's final moments?'

The detective superintendent sighed. 'I'll go along with it, only because I want to go the extra mile for a colleague, just like you do. I'll get Royston to lay on another press conference. You do this one on your own, though: I look bloody awful on camera.'

Steele hesitated. 'I can think of someone better than me,' he said. 'Why don't we ask George if he'll do it?'

'And his wife?'

'It only takes George to make the appeal. It would be an ordeal for Jen and there's no need to put her through it.'

Chambers shot him a grim half-smile. 'But give her the chance, Stevie,' she said, softly. 'Let her make that decision: she may feel she owes it to her son.'

Seventeen

He liked the feel of the leather against his head as he leaned back; he liked the ease with which the chair swung round, giving him a clear view down the U-shaped roadway in front of the police headquarters building in Fettes Avenue. In one of their arguments, Sarah had told him that his office was the centre of his universe. He had denied it angrily: he believed that ultimately his life was about his children. Yet he had to admit that when he was not around them, the room in which he sat was where he was most happy.

Aileen had dropped him at the foot of Orchard Brae; they had agreed that they would keep in touch by cell-phone, and that they would try to meet again in Glasgow, soon.

On the drive through, she had told him more of Tommy Murtagh's plans: his strategy of direct control went further than the police, although they were his number-one target. Education was in his sights also, with social quotas being imposed on Scottish universities and top-up fees charged to students applying from independent schools. Most serious of all to Skinner was his intention to change the make-up of the judicial appointments board, by giving it a seventy per cent majority of lay members, and by vetting lists of candidates before interviews. 'There's a word for this,' he had grumbled. 'It's called dictatorship.'

'Tommy's crafty: he puts it another way,' Aileen had told him. 'He calls it empowering the people by giving them control over the institutions and symbols of authority.'

'I know. One man, one vote, and all that; as long as he's the man and he's got the vote.'

He had repeated his promise, though, to keep his head down, and not to seek confrontation with the First Minister. 'I'm glad,' she had said, as they parted. 'I think what you need most of all right now is some quiet in your life.'

'Quiet?' he mused, as he gazed out of the window. 'That'll be the day.'

Blinking himself back to the present, he picked up the telephone and called his home number. Trish, the nanny, answered circumspectly, as she always did when neither he nor Sarah was at home. When she realised that it was him, the ever-cheerful girl sounded more pleased than he had ever heard her.

'I'll be back as soon as I can,' he told her. 'Kids okay?'

'They're fine,' she said, in her gentle Caribbean accent, 'but they've been missing you. The video calls to the computer were great, but they're not the same.' She paused. 'Do you know when Sarah will be home?' she asked. He read the unspoken 'if'.

'She'll be back well before Christmas; that's all I know for sure,' he replied, candidly. 'See you later . . . by six, I hope.'

He hung up and dialled his daughter's direct business number. 'Good afternoon. Alexis Skinner, can I help you?'

As he heard her voice, a great wave of relief swept through him, and he realised for the first time how tough the last two weeks had been and how emotionally tired he really was. 'You already have, baby,' he said.

'Pops! You're back,' she gushed. 'And not before time. I've done my best to be a surrogate mum, and so has Trish, but those kids need you. Have you and Sarah patched things up?'

'Good question, Alexis; I'm not sure that we know how. Come out to Gullane tonight and I'll tell you about it.'

'Okay, will do. Got to go now: I'm due in conference with Mitch Laidlaw.'

'Don't keep the boss waiting, then.'

He dialled a third number; Neil McIlhenney answered. 'Hi,' said Skinner. 'You in on this three o'clock shindig?'

'Yup.'

'Good. I want you to set up another meeting, somewhere nice and quiet, and well off patch. Three people present: you, me and Andy Martin, nobody else in the loop. Soon as you can.'

As he hung up, he smiled at a vision of his friend's puzzled expression.

He reached out and buzzed for Jack McGurk, his executive assistant. The towering detective sergeant appeared in his office within seconds. 'Welcome back, boss,' he said, as he laid the in-tray on his desk. Skinner was impressed by the fact that it was relatively small. McGurk was learning to filter out the most important business for his attention and delegate the rest.

'What's this three o'clock meeting about, Jack?' the DCC asked. He checked his watch: it was two forty-five.

'I don't know, sir. The chief, ACC Haggerty and DCI McIlhenney are involved in it; people from London, that's all they've said.'

'Ah,' said Skinner. 'Colleagues from another service, I suspect; spooks, to the punters. Where is it?'

'The main conference room.'

'Okay.' He rose from behind the desk. 'Thanks, Jack. Now I must have a word with Sir James.' He followed McGurk from the room and stepped across the corridor. Gerry Crossley, the chief constable's secretary, was at his desk in the anteroom that led to the chief's office. He looked up as Skinner entered, then blinked in surprise.

'Hello, sir,' he exclaimed. 'Good to see you back.'

'Thanks, Gerry, I'm not sorry about it myself.' He nodded towards the door to his right. 'Is he . . .?'

'Yes. Go on in.'

Skinner opened the door and stepped into the office. He had never coveted it: although it was bigger than his, the view was over the playing-field behind the headquarters building. The silver-haired figure behind the desk was bent over a folder, studying its contents. 'Yes, Gerry,' he murmured.

'Wrong: try again.'

Sir James Proud's eyes widened; a smile followed. 'Bob!' he exclaimed. 'Willie said that we could expect you today, but he wasn't sure when. You must be exhausted, man.'

'I'm fine,' Skinner replied. 'I managed to get my head down for a while.'

'How did things go? Did you and Sarah . . .?'

'Things are not yet resolved.' He sighed. 'In fact, Jimmy, truth be told, we're in a right pickle, and it's more my fault than hers. I'd like to talk to you about it, when we've more time.'

'Mmm,' the veteran chief constable murmured. 'Forgive me for asking this, but it's been on my mind. Do I sense a dangerous liaison in the air?'

Bob stared at him, pure surprise in his eyes. 'Has someone been talking to you?'

Proud Jimmy shook his head. 'No,' he said, quickly. 'But the new Justice Minister is a very attractive and dynamic woman, and when I saw her in your office a few weeks ago, it occurred to me that it might not have been an official visit.'

'I see. So you haven't had a visit yourself, then?'

'No. Who'd have come to see me?'

'Greg Jay, perhaps.'

'Jay?' Sir James looked baffled. 'What's he got to do with anything? He's not part of the picture any more. Since you've been away, he's taken early retirement and gone.'

Skinner grunted. 'He might have gone, Jimmy, but he hasn't retired. He's the First Minister's new security adviser, so-called.'

'Good God!' The chief slapped his desk lightly; it was as close as he ever came to an angry gesture. 'The duplicitous so-and-so! He never mentioned a word of it to me. He let me believe that he had had enough and wanted to work on his garden and his golf handicap.'

'No, he has other plans for his future. His appointment's a real bugger, too. When he was in the job, Jock Govan was a friend of ours; most certainly Greg will not be, as he's proved already. Murtagh's had him keeping tabs on Aileen and, in the process, on me.'

'And has he found anything...'

'That could damage us? If you mean real harm as opposed to some fleeting and unpleasant publicity, no, and he won't, either, because there's nothing to find. From now on, I'll be watching him even closer than he's watching us. But it's all very murky, Jimmy. Very soon you and I and all the others are going to find that we've got a new boss.'

'Who?'

'The First Minister . . . directly.'

Sir James gasped. 'But he can't,' he protested.

Skinner frowned at him. 'He doesn't have that word in his vocabulary, Jimmy,' he said. 'And people who don't, they tend to be rather dangerous.'

Eighteen

McIlhenney stared at the phone in his hand as if it was smiling at him. Finally he put it down, retrieved Andy Martin's private office number in Dundee from his index, and called it.

'How goes, big fella?' asked the Tayside deputy chief. 'Why's Special Branch calling me?'

'This isn't Special Branch,' he replied. 'This is DCC Skinner's vicar on Earth. He wants to see you and me together, on the quiet, as soon as you can make it.'

'What do you mean "on the quiet"?'

'I mean nobody else is to know about it. Somewhere off patch, he told me.'

'What's the mystery?'

'No idea. He's literally just back from Florida; one of the first things he did was to tell me to set up this meeting, but he didn't say why.'

'Just us?'

'Just you, me, and him: nobody else is to know about it. I tell you, Andy, he's got me worried. If he wants the two of us together like this it's not just for a pint: he's got something serious to tell us.'

'What's your guess?'

'I'm trying not to guess,' McIlhenney exclaimed, 'but he's fresh back from the States. Do you know what he's been doing there?'

'Trying to sort things out with Sarah, he told me. And she's been making loud noises about wanting him to quit.'

'Exactly. What if she's persuaded him?'

'Forced him to choose between the force and the kids, you mean? She's hardened a lot over the last couple of years, I'll admit, through her parents dying, then Bob's illness, and her own troubles. I could see her putting it that way. But whether he'd give in . . . that's another matter.'

'I'm not so sure: his four children are the only thing in this life he values above the job.'

'You know what you're saying there?' asked Martin. 'That he puts the job over Sarah.'

'He's proved that in the past,' McIlhenney reminded him. 'Besides...' he stopped himself short.

'What?'

'Nothing. Nothing at all. When can you manage?'

'Tomorrow, midday: let's meet in the Green Hotel, in Kinross. It's off your patch, if not mine, and about equidistant for all of us.'

'Deal. I can do that and the boss will change his diary if he has to.'

'Fine. I'll make the arrangements from here.' Martin paused. 'By the way, while you're on, have you seen your colleague Mackenzie lately? I've been expecting to hear from him about a wee bit of business we did together on Sunday.'

'You won't,' said McIlhenney. 'That's disappeared.'

'What? They were looking at attempted murder and Christ knows what else. The guy Cable bloody near spiked me.'

'And he's got the nose to prove it. Forget that one, Andy: we'll buy you a new jacket if it'll make you happy.'

'Put the old one back together: that'll make me happy. Anyway, you can tell me all about it tomorrow.'

'Maybe yes, maybe no. See you at the hotel.' He hung up and checked his watch, then pressed a button on his desk that changed the light outside his door from red to green.

Almost at once, Bandit Mackenzie stepped into the room. He glanced at his watch. 'Five minutes to three,' he said. 'Spot on. So, what am I here for? If it's to tell me that Special Branch wants to know every move that the Drugs Squad makes, forget it. I know I'm the new guy around here, but I'm in command of that unit and nowhere in my brief does it say that I report to you.'

McIlhenney smiled, affably. 'Nobody's saying it does, my friend, but you're part of a wider world, whether you like it or not, as you're about to find out. Come on.' He headed for the door.

'Where are we going?'

'To meet the Dark Side.'

He led Mackenzie out of the Special Branch suite, along a corridor and up a flight of stairs that led to the Command Corridor. As they passed the deputy chief's room, they saw that the red light was on. Jack McGurk was in his own small office: its door was open, and they could both read the nervousness in his expression.

McIlhenney stopped and leaned against the frame. 'Everything in place?' he asked.

The sergeant nodded. 'The conference room's ready. The technical people went in half an hour ago and swept it, and the Venetian blinds are closed just as you asked.'

'Who's there ahead of us?'

'Just the ACC. The chief's in Mr Skinner's room.'

'And the visitors?'

'I don't . . .' As he spoke his phone rang. He snatched it up. 'McGurk.' A pause. 'Okay, I'll collect them.' A sigh. 'I told you, Benny, they don't sign in.' The sigh turned into a growl. 'Fuck the health and safety regs: do what you're told.'

'That's the attitude.' Mackenzie chuckled as the DCC's towering assistant swept past him, the top of his head almost bumping against the door lintel.

'We'd better get in there,' said McIlhenney. 'Mr Haggerty'll be feeling neglected.'

'Are you going to tell me what this is about, Neil?' Bandit asked, as they reached the conference room door.

The big man reached for the door handle. 'I only know the part of the story involving Cable and Bell. I don't know why, I don't know what, I just know who. We're having a visit from the people whose toes you stood on.'

'Am I on the carpet?'

'No.' He stopped. 'David,' he said, 'a word of advice. Don't say anything glib in there; don't say anything at all, until you're asked. Act serious, however hard that might be for you.'

Mackenzie grinned. 'That's fine, but please don't call me David. I only get called that by my mother, or when I really am in the shit.'

They stepped into the conference room. Willie Haggerty had half risen from his seat at the conference table, but he sat down again. 'Ah, it's you two,' he grunted. 'I thought it was the serious people.' He pointed at a trolley against the wall. 'Help yourself to coffee if you want it: there'll be nae waitresses in here. Come to think of it, now that Bob's back, I don't know what I'm doing here.'

McIlhenney shrugged his shoulders. 'Duck out now, if you want, sir. I've seen the fax they sent to the chief; it didn't ask for you by name, just for relevant chief officers and Special Branch.'

'What am I doing here, then?' Mackenzie asked.

'They asked for you later, Bandit.'

'You mean after . . .'

'After your fun and frolics on Sunday: you've figured it out at last.'

'So who are they? The Scottish Drug Enforcement Agency?'

'Of course not. If you'd screwed up one of their operations, they'd have dropped in on you in person and kicked your arse.'

'The Americans?'

'We don't let them operate here.'

'So who the . . .'

The door of the conference room opened, and Bob Skinner walked in, looking not at all like a man who had just come from a day-long journey. He was followed by two men and a woman; one of the men had a heavy plaster across his nose, and his eyes were blackened and puffy. McIlhenney heard Bandit Mackenzie's soft 'Ah' beside him. He glanced at him, but saw that he was gazing intently at the newcomer.

'Good afternoon, gentlemen,' said the DCC, briskly, moving towards a seat on the same side of the table as his colleagues. 'The chief's decided not to sit in on this meeting,' he glanced at Haggerty, 'but, Willie, you should stay.' He directed the visitors to chairs facing his team, then took his own. 'Anybody want coffee?' he asked. The three newcomers all shook their heads. 'Fine,' he said. 'I've had my caffeine quota too, so let's get to it. Introductions: on our side, left to right, Assistant Chief Constable Willie Haggerty, Detective Chief Inspector Neil McIlhenney, Special Branch, and DCI David Mackenzie, head of our Drugs Squad.'

'Thank you,' said the woman, seated on his left. She was middle-aged, grey-suited and reminded McIlhenney of his wife's consultant obstetrician, as she looked across at him. 'On our side,' she began, 'I'm Amanda Dennis; my colleagues are Rudolph Sewell, and, with the facial decoration, Sean Green.'

'We've already met,' said Mackenzie, icily, drawing a warning look from Skinner.

'So I believe,' Dennis replied. 'That's prompted our visit, in fact. We are members of the Security Service, also known as MI5. That makes us colleagues, and so I want to get this briefing off on the right foot. I'll begin by offering you gentlemen the same apology that I've just made to Chief Constable Proud. It was, on reflection, wrong of us to mount an operation on your territory without advising you of the fact. Let me try to explain to you how and why this happened.'

'That should be good,' Mackenzie murmured.

The DCC glared at him. 'Bandit,' he said, softly, but with menace, 'if you interrupt once more, I'll have you measured for a uniform.' He turned to Dennis. 'Sorry, Amanda: please carry on.'

'Thank you.' She leaned forward, clasping her hands together on the table. 'I'll begin by explaining what exactly MI5 does. I apologise again if I'm telling you things you already know, but in our experience even senior police officers can have gaps in their knowledge. We are an agency charged with responsibility for protecting national security. We're not the only one, of course: we work closely with the Secret Intelligence Service, MI6, with the Government Communications Headquarters, and with the Defence Intelligence Staff, among others. Our specific roles are to gather and assess secret intelligence about threats, to advise government of them as they arise, to work with other agencies to combat them and, when necessary, to act directly against them.' She looked around the table at Haggerty, McIlhenney and Mackenzie. 'Understood?' All three nodded, unsmiling.

'Good,' she continued. 'We don't operate outside the law, whatever people may think. We're governed by statute and codes of practice, but we can do things that more public agencies can't,' she smiled, wryly, 'or at least shouldn't. We intercept all forms of communications, we plant bugs, we keep subjects under round-the-clock surveillance; most of the time we're watchers and listeners. Our active involvement depends on the threat.' She leaned back in her chair once again, sweeping aside a few strands of silver hair that had fallen across her forehead.

'Okay. What's our business? Traditionally, we've been spy-catchers: that's why we were set up. However, over the years we've become spies ourselves, in what is colourfully described as the war against terror. At first our brief was almost exclusively Irish, but modern international terrorism has changed all that. It now makes up one third of our total workload and that proportion is rising. But aside from counter-espionage, counter-terrorism and, these days, counter-proliferation, there are two other areas which, taken together, make up about ten per cent of our workload. They are emerging threats, in which my colleague Rudy, who is the assistant director general of the Security Service, is sector head, and serious crime, for which I have lead responsibility. In my area of operation, I must stress to you that we are tasked by other agencies: it's not our role to initiate or to act independently, and we'll only accept an assignment if it is the collective view of everyone involved that we can make a difference to the investigation.'

She paused. 'That's the background; now let's get to the specifics.' She looked beyond Skinner. 'Rudy, would you like to take over?'

Rudolph Sewell nodded and drew his chair closer to the table. For all that he outranked her, he was several years younger than Amanda Dennis; but he was dressed in the same Whitehall civil servant mode. His suit was dark blue, and he wore a white shirt with a crested tie that suggested a public-school background. His hair was conservatively cut and he seemed to have no distinguishing features; then he looked up, and his round, rimless spectacles made his eyes grow huge and frog-like, attracting instant attention.

'My section,' he began, 'operates in a variety of ways, across a very broad remit. We rely particularly on the co-operation of intelligence agencies from other countries, or, as in this case, groupings. Some weeks ago, the director general received a warning from NATO intelligence officers that a group of four Albanians had left their own country and were moving through Europe, heading for Britain. These were people with known criminal backgrounds, but in Albania that doesn't exactly mark them out. You'll be aware that it was the last totalitarian communist state in Europe, and that for decades it operated a policy of total isolation, from everyone except the Chinese, who, in fact, didn't care for them at all, and since they were strategically useless found them more of an embarrassment than anything else.' He allowed himself a thin-lipped smile. 'Imagine, if you will, Osama bin Laden being revealed as an Arsenal supporter: he'd be greeted at Highbury with the same warmth that Beijing showed to Tirana.' Sewell paused, as if inviting laughter, but none came.

'The old Albanian regime,' he continued, 'was so brutal and repressive that there was no semblance of an opposition voice; not a political one, at any rate. So, when it imploded, in the aftermath anarchy ruled, criminality became the norm, and the place became a magnet for all sorts of dangerous activity. The people we were warned about are right in the thick of it. They ran protection rackets, controlled prostitution, regulated the drugs trade and supplied all sorts of illegal armaments to all sorts of people, including a significant number of those against whom the war on terror is being fought.'

'Sounds like a nice wee empire,' Skinner mused aloud. 'Why did they leave it all?'

'That's what our NATO source didn't know for sure, and it's what we've been tasked to find out.'

'So what do you know?'

'We know that they left the Albanian port of Durres, crossed the Adriatic and landed in Brindisi, on the heel of Italy. From there they travelled by road to Genoa, crossed into France by hiring a helicopter, and disappeared.'

'Completely?'

'For a while, until their scent was picked up in Rotterdam: they stopped there for long enough to pull off a bank robbery in Amsterdam.'

'Risky. Why would they do that?'

'We think they needed currency; at home they deal in US dollars, and we suspect that they didn't want to flash too many of them about. Significantly, while they took euros, they also took all the sterling that the bank held.'

'A pointer, I'll grant you.'

'Eventually, after some damned good detective work based on witness descriptions, the Dutch police traced them to an address, a great barn of a place in the Oosteinde of the city. They had been living there, under their own names, for over a month, but they had gone by the time the place was raided. Their hosts were Kosovar refugees, ethnic Albanians. They were arrested and interrogated, and of course they pleaded innocence, claiming that they had only been putting up fellow asylum-seekers, and that they had no idea where they had gone. However, further enquiries revealed that one of them had a sister who lived with a Dutch trucker. Under threat of the loss of his licence, he admitted that he had smuggled them across the North Sea on his lorry, sailing out of Zeebrugge to Rosyth, in Fife.'

'What was he carrying, apart from the Albanians?' asked Haggerty.

'Flowers. He's a regular traveller on that route, well known to the Customs people. They took a look at his truck, but not close enough, apparently. However . . .' Sewell paused, his great frog eyes sweeping round the table. '. . . he was also carrying four large rucksacks, which from his description were much bigger than anything an asylum-seeker would be likely to have. These were offloaded by the Albanians when they reached their destination in Edinburgh.'

'Oh, shit,' said Skinner, quietly.

'You guess what I'm going to tell you,' the MI5 operative exclaimed. 'Further interrogation of the Kosovars in Rotterdam revealed that, after the second robbery, the Albanians had a meeting in their hide-out with a man whose description matches that of a well-known Dutch arms-dealer. The dealer can't be traced, or hasn't been yet, but we would like very much to know what they were talking about.'

'You don't know for sure?'

'No, but when my Dutch opposite numbers raided his warehouse they found that while his inventory and his stock tallied some of the recorded buyers of items did not. For example, the police chief in Amsterdam did not buy silencers with the carbines he ordered, and he only received half the number of firearms that were shown on the order. Also, the small African nation which was shown to have purchased eighteen American anti-tank missiles for its defence force in fact only received fourteen.'

Skinner shook his head. 'I really do not like the sound of that,' he muttered.

'Neither did the Home Secretary; hence the pressure of his finger on the panic button.'

'Merry Christmas, Scotland. Where did the Dutch trucker drop his passengers and their load?'

'At a car park in a shopping mall to the east of the city.'

'Not in daylight, surely.'

'No. He made some deliveries during the day, with them hidden in the truck, then dropped them off at two in the morning. They were met by a fifth man, driving a Transit van.'

'When did this happen?'

'Just under four weeks ago.'

The big deputy chief constable gazed at Sewell for several long seconds. 'And you didn't think to tell us?' he asked quietly.

'We were ordered not to,' Amanda Dennis replied. 'When our sources gave us this information, we took it to the Home Secretary.'

'The English Home Secretary,' Skinner reminded her, acidly.

'I didn't take you for a rabid nationalist, Bob,' she retorted.

'I'm not, but we do have a devolved government here, although sometimes I wonder whether you people have noticed.'

'Be that as it may,' Sewell intervened, 'we were dealing with a perceived threat to the national security of the UK as whole, and when that happens the Home Secretary is the person we consult. He consulted the Defence Secretary, then gave us direct orders to carry out a covert operation to trace and detain these men, by whatever means we thought necessary. He stressed the word "covert", and said that no other agencies were to be advised or involved, unless it was absolutely necessary.'

'Given all that, how did Jingle Bell and your man here become involved?'

'Amanda and I decided between us that Mr Bell was the necessary means.'

'He's one of my assets,' said Dennis. 'Or he's an agent of ours, if you prefer that term. He has been since the National Crime Squad caught him in Birmingham on the wrong side of a drugs operation in which we were also involved. Bob, it's our experience of these Albanian gangsters that they're incapable of behaving quietly. Wherever they go, they display an irresistible urge to muscle in on the local action. The problem is that, thanks to you and your colleagues, there isn't much local action in Edinburgh. So the DG decided that my section should create some, in the hope of flushing them out. We set Bell up to create a small drugs operation in your friend's club and in other sites around the city that he considered vulnerable. Sean, who is a member of my section, was his handling officer. The mistake the assistant DG and I made, for which we do apologise, was in interpreting the Home Secretary's order too strictly. We should have told you, or DCI McIlhenney, what was going on.'

Skinner stared at her. 'You're telling us that two of your guys were pushing hard drugs on our patch?'

'I'm afraid so.'

'Does your statutory remit cover that sort of activity?'

'That's grey, but it's another reason for our not involving you ... to avoid compromising you, so to speak.' She sighed. 'The whole thing was a misjudgement. Again, all I can do is apologise.'

The DCC frowned. 'Apology accepted, as long as there's no blame attached to my people for doing their job properly.'

'None at all; in fact we compliment them on it.'

'Speak for yourself, Mandy,' Sean Green muttered, fingering the plaster on his nose, and breaking the tension with a grin. 'I'm sorry about the blade, by the way. At first I thought your guy might have been an Albanian, but I could tell by the look of him that he wasn't, so I didn't try to stick him, honest. If I had been trying . . .'

Skinner's eyes fell on him like two blocks of ice. 'You wouldn't be here today, boy,' he said, slowly, in a voice not much above a whisper. He turned back to Dennis. 'They're out of the picture now, you know that. Too many people in the club saw him being filled in and Jingle being lifted.'

'Absolutely. I accept that we can't put them back in. That's why we're here.'

'Cap in bloody hand, eh.'

She nodded, and smiled, wryly. 'I have to accept that description.'

Bandit Mackenzie raised a hand. 'Permission to speak, sir?' he asked.

The DCC chuckled. 'Aye, go on then, as long as it's constructive.'

'It's a question really, sir, for Sean. After you and Bell were done, when we had you in the interview room, why the hell did you keep stringing us along? You must have known that it would all end up at a meeting like this and that I'd find out about you in the end. So why didn't you just switch off the tape and spill it?'

Green looked at him, through his puffy eyes. 'If it had been just you and me, I probably would have, but your sergeant was there. All due respect, but Mandy would have crucified me if I'd talked in front of her.'

'On a barbed-wire cross,' his section head confirmed.

'So,' Skinner exclaimed, 'with your team out of the picture, what are you asking of us?'

'That you take over from them: find the Albanians, determine what it is they're up to, and remove them as a threat.'

'By any means necessary?'

Dennis looked at him, but said nothing. In the silence, Rudolph Sewell leaned forward. 'It may be,' he murmured smoothly, 'that once you have secured them you would prefer to hand them over to us.'

'And it may not,' the big policeman retorted. 'I've just lost a terrorist gang, identified and arrested by my people, to the Americans; that's not going to happen again. Let's cross that one when we reach it, though. Meantime, how much scope do we have?'

'You operate under the same legislation and codes of practice that we do,' Dennis replied.

'What about electronic surveillance? We'll need legal authority for wiretaps.'

'You have it: you'll be our agents in this operation and the Home Secretary has given us blanket authorisation already.'

'How wide is the loop? Has the Home Secretary changed his mind and advised our First Minister, or his own opposite number in Scotland, our Justice Minister?'

'No, and I'm told by my director general that he doesn't plan to.'

Skinner stared across the table. 'I've got to have discretion to do that if I think it's necessary, without reference to you.'

Sewell drew in a deep breath. 'Oh, I don't know about that,' he retorted. 'We're the principals in this operation; I don't think we can delegate to that extent.'

'You weren't listening to me,' the DCC told him. 'I said that I must have that discretion. I'm not negotiating here. You may be his number two, but I know your director general; I have done for longer than you've been in post, and maybe even in the service. I make one phone call, I will get what I need and you will be overruled. Let me tell you, within these walls,' he glanced at his fellow police officers, 'why I must have the ability to widen the loop if I need to. Our First Minister has decided that he's going to take overall control of the police service into his own tight wee grasp. He's persuaded his coalition partners that it's in the public interest to give him the effective power to promote or dismiss every senior copper in Scotland, and the bill to enable that will be published very soon. Already we're coming under closer scrutiny than ever before. Mr Murtagh has appointed a former colleague of ours to be his eyes and ears, and he's making his presence felt. I don't want him blundering in on this operation by accident.'

'Would you like us to persuade the Home Office to advise Mr Murtagh and Ms de Marco?' asked Dennis.

'No. Leave it to me to tell them, if I judge it to be necessary.'

She looked at Sewell, who nodded. 'Okay, Bob,' she conceded, 'that's agreed. Do you want anything else?'

'Yes. I want you on the ground here.'

She smiled again. 'So does Rudy, but thank you for inviting me.'

'And I want the ability to call in special forces the moment that we identify an imminent threat.'

'No promises, but we'll do our best.'

Skinner rose to his feet. He looked at his three colleagues. 'Willie, Neil, Bandit, you're the lead team on this operation, reporting to Mrs Dennis and me. If you need additional personnel, use only your most trusted people, and tell them as much as they need to know, but no more. Amanda, will you be in a position to give us everything you have on these men at nine tomorrow morning?'

'Yes,' she replied.

'Excellent; we meet in this room.' He headed for the door. 'Now, if you don't mind, I'm getting out of this murky place and going home to my kids.'

Nineteen

My son was an inquisitive boy,' said George Regan. 'From his earliest years, he was always wanting to know how things worked, always with a question in waiting to follow the one you were answering.' He smiled. 'It was difficult staying one step ahead of him from time to time.' A tentative laugh rippled through the group of journalists as they faced him.

'I can't deny that he was an adventurous lad too, always up for a dare, always up for showing what he could do. My wife and I are ready to accept that his death was the result of an adventure gone wrong. While it was unusual for him to be so reckless, I can't put my hand on my heart and say that it was out of the question.'

He paused and took one more look around the room. 'But we need to know for sure about his final moments. Jen and I can't face the uncertainty for the rest of our lives. So, if there are people out there who saw wee George after he left the bus stop where he was last spotted, if anyone saw him entering the castle grounds, I ask them through you, ladies and gentlemen, and through the broadcast media, to come forward and help us to cope with what has happened to our son. Thank you.'

Slowly he rose from his chair, behind the table, in front of the backcloth embellished with the police-force crest, and walked from the room. There was no sound as he left; no questions were called after him. It occurred to Stevie Steele that he had never heard a group of journalists so quiet for so long.

He followed his colleague through the door, and back through the CID office to his own room. 'Thanks, George,' he said, as he closed the door, 'I know what it must have taken to do that.'

Regan gave him as sad a smile as he had ever seen. 'With respect, Stevie,' he replied, 'I don't really think you do. I was pleased to do it for you, though; I meant every word I said out there.'

He sat on the edge of the detective inspector's desk, all at once looking completely exhausted. 'You're going to close the book, aren't you?' he said, quietly. 'You're going to pass the file to the Fiscal and let him make the decision.' There was no rancour in his voice: it was matter-of-fact.

' 'I promise you, mate,' Steele told him, 'that Mary and I have been totally conscientious about this. I admit that we've gone as far as we can in term of witnesses; that's why we asked you to do the public appeal. But we're going to do what you'd expect of us, and what you would do yourself. We'll wait for responses to your statement, and we'll follow them up meticulously. There are no constraints on us.'

'Not even from Dan Pringle? This isn't really a CID job; we both know that.'

'Absolutely no pressure, I promise; and if there was we'd resist it. The head of CID's as gutted as the rest of us, George, believe me.'

'Ach, I do. I've known Dan for years; he's a good bloke. It's just that we're all totally bloody driven by clear-up figures these days. See public accountability, Stevie; setting targets and all that stuff. It's great in principle, but when it affects the way we do our job, or stops us doing it altogether, I wish they'd just let us get on with it.'

'So do I, from time to time,' Steele admitted. 'It's here to stay, though, and I've got a hunch that it might get worse before it gets better. I just heard something on the grapevine that set me back on my heels. A pal of mine in St Andrews House told me that the security adviser's office there has a new occupant: Greg Jay.'

'You're joking!'

'My sense of humour isn't that black. I asked the chief super if she'd heard about it, but it was news to her.'

'That'll be great,' Regan exclaimed, ironically. 'Mr Bitter and Twisted himself, whispering in the ears of the First Minister and the Justice Minister.' He glanced at his colleague. 'Although my own personal rumour mill says that someone has been whispering in de Marco's ear before him.'

Steele frowned. 'Who's that?'

'I'll do you a favour and not tell you. If it's just unfounded gossip you're best not to know.'

Between them, a silence fell; and in it, Regan's grief, from which their conversation had been no more than a moment's respite, returned in full force. 'I've got to go, Stevie,' he said. 'It was a hell of a job persuading the wife not to come here; I have to get back to her now. I'll take a couple more days' leave, yes?'

'You'll take a couple of weeks more; you'll take as long as you and Jen need. Fuck the clear-up figures, George: there are more important things in this world.'

Twenty

'Pops, there's something I have to tell you,' said Alexis Skinner.

'You're getting married.'

'No. I'm not even seeing anyone just now.'

'So you're not pregnant either, then.'

'Don't be daft. I made that mistake once; it won't be repeated.'

'What is it, then?'

'I'm a bit scared.'

Bob looked at her across the dinner table, eyebrows raised in surprise. 'You're what? You've never been scared in your life. What's the problem? Are you in trouble at work? Are you ill?' He sat bolt upright as his mind ticked off a list of crisis scenarios and stopped at the worst case. 'You haven't found a lump, have you?'

'No, Pops, it's nothing like that, none of those things. I'm fine, but I'm scared for you.'

He picked up his glass and shook his head slowly. 'Is that all? Alex, my love, you're the oldest of my children, but you're not always the most sensible. Why the hell are you scared about me, any more than you have been for the last twenty years?' He rose from his dining chair. 'Come on, let's go through to the comfy seats and you can tell me all about it.'

'Okay, but go and say good night to the sibs first.'

He did as he was told, climbing the stairs to the children's rooms. They had been all over him when he had arrived home, even Seonaid, whom he had thought too young to have noticed his absence. He had given time, and presents, to each of them in turn, explaining as best he could to the two boys why their mother had decided to stay in America for a little longer.

To his surprise, Mark had been the most anxious of the three. James Andrew and Seonaid had accepted his promise that she would be back for Christmas, but his older son had needed more reassurance. 'She isn't ill, is she?' he had asked at one point.

'No,' he had replied. 'She's been very tired, but she's okay. Mum's been through a lot this year. She's in need of a good long rest, that's all.'

He stood in the doorway of Mark's room, looking at him; as he had expected, his younger son and daughter were sound asleep. He was sitting with his back to the door at his computer, as usual, but not at a document or website. He was on-line, in the midst of a video conversation, but he wore a headset so only he could hear the incoming sound. Bob moved silently behind him to see the face on the small square in the centre of the screen: it was Sarah, and from the background he could tell that she was in the internet café they had found near their hotel. He waved at the camera. A second or two later, Mark turned, surprised and looked up at him. 'Go on,' said Bob, quietly, ruffling the boy's hair. 'Don't mind me.' He leaned over to be close to the microphone. 'Hi, Sarah, sorry to butt in. I'll leave you to it; my big kid's downstairs.' He read her lips as she mouthed, 'Okay. Good night.'

'Good night,' he replied, 'to both of you.' He closed the door behind him and made his way back to Alex.

She was sitting in the big conservatory-style sitting room on the end of the house. 'All okay?' she asked.

'Yeah, fine.' He told her about the conversation he had interrupted, and about Mark's earlier concern.

'You know why he's anxious, don't you?' she asked.

'Tell me.'

'He's already lost one mother; he doesn't want it to happen again.'

'He sees that as a possibility, does he?'

'Of course he does. You parents either have unrealistic expectations or you underrate your children. Mark's a very gifted mathematician; you're aware of that, but you don't realise how emotionally mature he is. He picks up the same vibes I do. He reads things that the other two can't see.'

Alex pulled her legs up underneath her on the big armchair she had chosen. The curtains were open and the lights were dim; through the picture windows, the moon shone on the Firth of Forth, turning the eleven-mile wide estuary into a great silver ribbon.

'How was I with you?' Bob asked. 'Unrealistic or a putter-downer?'

'Father, you thought the sun shone out of my arse but, then, you thought the same about my mother too.'

'I don't deny either of those charges. I don't regret either . . . either. Fact is, I've never changed those opinions.'

She drew him a long look, arching her eyebrows. 'Even though you now know all about Mum's affairs? Even though I aborted my fiancé's baby, without even telling him I was pregnant?'

'Even though. I'll support you in anything you do.'

'Even if it's illegal?'

'Even if. But that's semantics: you couldn't do anything illegal, unless it was for the most moral reasons.'

'What makes you so sure?'

He grunted. 'You're my daughter.'

'I'm also my mother's daughter. Does that mean you expect me to have affairs?'

'God help the guy who marries you. If genetic inheritance counts for anything, he's stuffed from both sides.'

Alex turned on him. 'You see? There you go, that's how you're scaring me. You've changed, you're not the man I've always known. You're different.'

'Nothing's changed. This is the man I've always been; if I seem different it's because I've shed my old skin. Maybe it happened when they put the pacemaker in. Maybe it was when I found out that my brother was dead. Maybe it's when I found out about Sarah and Ron bloody Neidholm.'

His daughter gasped. 'What? The man in Buffalo? The one who was killed? Sarah and he . . .'

'. . . were lovers? Yes.'

'God, Pops. I don't know what to say.'

'How about "Not again"? Before that there was another guy in the States, called Terry Carter.'

'You haven't been perfect yourself,' she reminded him.

'Of course not. I'm obsessive, I have a wicked temper, and I have an occasional tendency to follow my dick where it leads me. I suppose that's why your mother and I were soul-mates.'

'You missed out "cynical".'

'Sorry, that too. But it's a fault I've acquired only recently.'

'Pops, what's brought all this on?'

'Like I said, I don't know. All I do know is that suddenly I've become completely self-aware, and with it self-critical. All my life, Alex, I've had a great big ego; I've believed in my own public image, and, I confess, I've even pandered to it from time to time. I just didn't recognise the fact until now. Maybe it was the heart scare; maybe when it stopped, then started to beat again, I came round as a different guy. Certainly, from around that time I've seen things, and myself, completely differently.'

'Are you saying you've lost your self-belief?'

'I don't think so. Truth be told, when I'm not with you, and them upstairs, I'm happiest doing my job. That's why I fought so hard when it was under threat. That's the main reason why Sarah and I are in the trouble we're in right now.' He looked at her, suddenly, sharply. 'Who's the most important person in your life?'

'You are.' Her reply was instant.

'Good. Next.'

'James Andrew, because he's special; he's my blood and he's you, scaled down.'

'Then if anything happens to me, you raise him, and make him different. Instil some humility in him; my dad tried it with me, but he failed . . . possibly because he wasn't very good at it himself,' he added.

'Nothing's going to happen to you for a very long time,' she said, 'so let's not even go there. What's the point of your question?'

'My point is that if I made the same list, totally honestly, the names on it, in order, would be you, the Jazzer and Seonaid, my blood children, first equal, then Mark and then me. Sarah would follow on somewhere.'

'I see. Not a good basis for a sustainable marriage, is that what you're saying?'

'Unless you both think the same way, and you realise it and accept it.'

'And what if that special person comes along?'

'I think Ron Neidholm may have been that special person for Sarah.'

'And what about you?'

His mouth fell open slightly with surprise as he looked at her. 'God, don't you know that? I met her long ago. She died long ago.'

'Mum.'

'Of course.' He felt his eyes mist over, and turned his head away so that she would not see. 'I have never got over your mother's death, Alexis. I've put it away in a box inside me, like that box of hers I hid in the attic in the old cottage, but the hurt has always been there. It always will be. You have no idea how much I miss her.'

'Maybe I do,' she whispered, with a catch in her voice, but he did not notice.

'There is no day goes by without me thinking of her and feeling the pain of her loss. Tell me, did you assume that if I had found out about her infidelities when she was alive I'd have divorced her?'

'I suppose I did.'

'Well, you're wrong. I could never have done that because I loved her with all my being, and she loved me in the same way. Okay, I was arrogant and driven and consumed by ambition, and she was manipulative, immoral and ruthless. Those guys of hers: they thought they were using her, and all the time it was the other way round.' He laughed. 'There we were, the two of us, the *Guardian* couple of the month, Gullane edition, all of it a front. And yet behind the secrets and lies, when it came to it we were like twins, conjoined at the heart and at the very soul.'

'Pops, you've had twenty years to think about this. If you'd found out at the time . . .'

'I'd have felt the same. I'd have forgiven her, like she forgave me once.'

'Jesus, this is confession time! When was that?'

'When we were engaged: I had a heavy thing for a while with someone else.'

'Someone she knew?'

'No.'

'And is she still around, this person?'

'Very much so, but keep it to yourself. It was Lou Bankier; we were at university at the same time. At the end of the day, I chucked her and went back to Myra; told her about it.' He chuckled. 'At the time I thought she took it very well. Eventually I found out why: she'd been doing the same with my best pal!'

He turned to face his daughter once again. 'Am I making sense?'

'Yes. I'm just astounded by it all.' She looked at him, her eyes big and earnest. 'Pops, you and Sarah: you've both got all this baggage. Couldn't you just put it down and get on with your life together?'

'Settle for what we've got, you mean? That's the decision we have to make.'

'It's not that difficult, is it? With trust and honesty on both sides, couldn't you give it a try?'

'If there were no other issues, we could.'

The big eyes narrowed. 'What sort of issues?'

'Female.'

'Oh, shit. Are you seeing someone else?'

'I wouldn't put it like that, certainly not in the sense you mean, but there's someone I like very much.'

'It's not Lou again, is it?'

'Wash your mouth out, girl!' he said, indignantly. 'She's married, and to my friend at that; I've got a scrap of personal morality left! Does the name Aileen de Marco mean anything to you?'

'Sure does. I should be shocked. Why am I not?'

'Because she's a very compelling and charismatic woman.'

'That's certainly how she comes across on television,' Alex conceded. She picked up her wine-glass from the floor. 'Bloody hell, Pops. What are you going to do?'

'What I always do . . . until Sarah comes home, at least. Get my head down and lose myself in my job. God knows, right now it needs my full attention.'

Twenty-one

'Can I ask you something, Neil?' said Bandit Mackenzie.

'You already did.'

'Eh?'

'You asked if you could ask me something. That, of itself, constitutes a question. The answer is "yes". However, there is no guarantee that you will get a reply.'

'I'll take my chances. Do you always look this knackered in the morning?'

McIlhenney grunted. 'It shows, does it? My wife's pregnant; it's like sleeping with a chorus line.'

'Ah, I know that one. Commiserations, pal. How long does she have to go?'

'Quite some time yet; about four months.' He was glad that Mackenzie had bought the lie. The dream had recurred the night before, even more vividly: it was not something he wanted to be drawn into discussing. For all Lou's reassurance, he had found it profoundly disturbing.

Their conversation was interrupted as the door of the conference room swung open, and Amanda Dennis entered, followed by Bob Skinner, Willie Haggerty and Sean Green. She was carrying a bulky folder, which she laid on the table.

'Good morning, gentlemen,' said the DCC. 'Let's get this going.' McIlhenney looked at him and moaned inwardly: he was sharp-eyed and focused, as if jet-lag did not exist for him. Suddenly the day promised to be very busy. 'Amanda.'

She nodded and opened the folder, then took four brown foolscap envelopes from it and handed one to each of the police officers. 'Inside

98

these,' she began, 'you will find photographs of our four targets and intelligence notes on each.' She took a photo from her folder and held it up. 'Naim Latifi.' It showed a clear colour image of a swarthy, moustached man, with a thick mop of grey-flecked hair.

She laid it down and selected a second shot. 'Fadil Ramadani.' The photograph was less sharp than the first, as if it had been taken from a greater distance and enlarged, but the sharp, foxy features and V-shaped hairline were recognisable.

She held up a third. 'Samir Bajram.' The subject looked younger than the other two, and bigger, more muscular. His head was shaved and he wore a gold ring in his ear, with a crescent hanging from it. He was smiling at the camera.

'The other two are surveillance shots,' Skinner observed. 'How was this one obtained?'

Dennis looked at him. 'It was taken by a member of the German security service who infiltrated the gang as part of an operation against organised car theft. A few days later, he was compromised; his body was dumped on the steps of the police headquarters building in Tirana, with some important parts missing.' She held up the last photograph. 'Amet Ramadani, brother of Fadil.' The features were identical, although the younger Ramadani had more hair and appeared to be bigger. Again, the shot had been posed. 'This was taken by the same unfortunate officer, at the same time as the other.'

She gathered the images together and replaced them in her folder. 'These are not nice people,' she said. 'They're typical of a hard core that exists in modern Albania, which the police and the military cannot control because they simply do not have the firepower.' She looked at McIlhenney and Mackenzie. 'Do you know much about Albania?'

'I'd an uncle who went on a package holiday there about fifteen years ago,' Bandit replied. He grinned. 'He was a bit tight: it was the cheapest deal he could find. He told me that when he was there, they had a bit of student unrest; nothing major, just disobedience. The army rounded them up and strung up the three ringleaders from lamp-posts. They weren't bothered about the tourists seeing it, either.'

Dennis nodded. 'That was fairly routine behaviour for the regime at that time. And the fact is that although the system may have changed the people haven't. I know about that incident you describe: it's in the files on Naim and Fadil. Although they were all masked, as was usual, it was said that Latifi was the officer in charge of the detail that executed those young people and Ramadani was one of his men.'

She took a document from her folder. 'This is a run-down on Albania. You'll find it in your envelope. To summarise it, the place has a pretty tragic history. It was ruled by the Turks for four hundred years, until it finally won independence in 1912. For about half of the time since, it lived under xenophobic Communist rule. Since that collapsed around twelve years ago, it's been trying to introduce multi-party democracy, but it's been a struggle. The early governments were corrupt, and allowed the gangsters to take effective control; that still exists, although there are signs of progress . . . it is said.' She raised a disbelieving eyebrow.

'The country's infrastructure is appalling. Paradoxically, it has decent mineral resources, and yet it's the poorest nation in Europe. It can't produce enough energy to sustain itself, there's one telephone to fifty people, and there's less than three and a half thousand miles of proper road in the entire place. The population is predominantly Muslim, but there is little sign of fundamentalism. As always, the gangsters' true religion is money. The black part of the Albanian economy is far and away the strongest. Another paradox is that proportionately there are more Mercedes owners there than anywhere else in the world; they're stolen in Germany by Albanian gangs and sold in Durres. That's why the unlucky German came to be where he was. They will traffic in anything: arms, cigarettes, general contraband, people, you name it. But, as always, drugs top the list. It's an active shipment point for Golden Triangle heroin, hashish and cannabis coming into Europe through the Balkan route. Some South American cocaine also makes landfall there.'

She continued, 'However, it is more than a staging post. It grows its own opium and cannabis, and in recent years ethnic Albanian narcotics organisations have expanded rapidly in mainland Europe.

My gut feeling is that our four subjects have come to Scotland to extend that growth.'

'What about the arms-dealer in Rotterdam?'

'Oh, they may have used some of the proceeds of their robberies to buy modern weapons, but these people are criminals, not terrorists. We're guarding the airports as a precaution, that's all. I think they're here to move drugs. That was my bet when we sent Sean and Mr Bell in to flush them out.'

'Then why aren't you talking to the Scottish Drug Enforcement Agency?' asked Mackenzie.

'Because I was ordered not to: too many people would know and the operation would become too obvious. My director general sent me here to brief Mr Skinner and seek his co-operation; they've had dealings in the past.'

What she stopped short of saying was that he had had active involvement with MI5 in the past and continued to be consulted by them. 'Kind of him,' he growled. 'I'll co-operate on one condition, that when the situation is resolved, if this is a drugs operation, the DG explains to the commander of the SDEA why he cut him out.'

'He anticipated that, and he promises to do so.'

'Fine. Now tell us about these four guys.'

'I will. As the assistant DG said yesterday, they are at the heart of much of the criminality in Albania. They are not overlords, but they are powerful and feared, strong men among other strong men. As I indicated earlier, Latifi and the older Ramadani brother were officers in the army under the old regime. When it collapsed, they kept much of their unit together and went into business. Samir Bajram and Amet Ramadani weren't soldiers . . . they were too young when the Communists fell . . . but they were brought in as added muscle and to strengthen the family influence. They're all closely related: all four of them had the same grandfather, Shaban Latifi, who was the second most feared man in the country in his time, after the dictator Enver Hoxha himself.'

'Is it possible that these guys are just on the run from Albania?' asked McIlhenney. 'Maybe there's been some gang warfare and they're the losers.'

Amanda Dennis shook her head. 'Naim Latifi is not a loser. My information is that if there had been a gang war it's more likely that the other side would be dead or on the run than that he would. But there have been no such indications. The Latifi family operations are continuing unfettered in the boss's absence; there are other cousins.'

'Do we know if they're travelling under assumed names?'

'They didn't as far as Rotterdam, but they may have false papers now; in fact, I'd guess that they do. They hadn't changed their appearance when the trucker dropped them off, but they've had time to do it since. The Dutchman said that Samir had grown some hair, so don't go looking for a skinhead.'

'Do we have a description of the fifth man, the guy who met them when the trucker dropped them off?'

'Not much; he was the same height and stocky build as Naim, but that was all the driver told us. He couldn't get close enough. He said that when he stopped, he opened the back of the truck. Naim got out of the cab and went across the car park towards the man with the Transit. They hugged like long-lost friends, then Naim waved to the others and they joined him. The trucker said that he got out of there as fast as he could. He was afraid that they might not want any witnesses.'

'Why would he think that?' Skinner asked. 'Did he know something about them that put him in danger? Did they say anything in front of him?'

Dennis frowned. 'They spoke in Albanian among themselves in the little time he was with them. When they spoke to him it was in English . . . good English, incidentally. We certainly know that Naim is fluent. However, as we told you, the driver has a Kosovar Albanian girlfriend, so he understands a few words. When they spoke among themselves, the name "Petrit" was used quite a lot; it's a common Albanian male forename. Apart from that, the one word he overheard that struck him as odd, was "Saviour". He said that Naim used it several times to the others, with emphasis.'

'Saviour,' McIlhenney repeated. 'What the hell can that mean?'

'Maybe they've converted,' said Mackenzie, cheerfully. 'Maybe they've come over to start a Christian mission. God knows, we could use it here.'

'If they have, it's a front,' Dennis replied, tersely. 'Don't take the communion wafer or you could be high for a week.'

'I don't suggest that you begin your search with the churches,' Skinner grunted.

'How about the Salvation Army hostel, sir?' asked Mackenzie. 'Could they have meant that?'

'Don't be bloody silly, man. There is only one thing these people will do, and that is to disappear into the local ethnic community. Agreed, Amanda?'

'Absolutely, and that is another reason why we should have been allowed to involve you from the start, and why we need you now. You have established links with that community. We don't: we only spy on them from time to time.'

'If I was an illegal Albanian immigrant,' Haggerty interposed, 'I'd go to Glasgow, not Edinburgh: there's more of them there, so it would be easier to hide.'

'Granted. But these people wanted to come here,' Dennis countered. 'The Dutch driver made several calls in Glasgow during the day. He could have dropped them off there, but he didn't, because they asked specifically to be brought to Edinburgh.'

'That's next to bugger all to go on,' said Skinner, 'but at least it's a start.' He turned to the ACC. 'Willie, we have established relationships with the ethnic communities, and we also work closely with voluntary organisations. I think we should put them to use. Without compromising the secrecy of this investigation, let's see if we can try to establish where Latifi and his friends are most likely to be hiding.'

'We'll try,' said Haggerty. 'Not all the Kosovar refugees went home after 1999; that'll be a good place to start.'

'Yes, but gently. We want to find them, not just to move them on.' He paused. 'There's one other thing: the fifth man, the guy who met them. I know we've got little to go on, but let's start by guessing that he's the "Petrit" the Dutchman heard them speak about. Let's see if we can find anyone of that name in this area.'

He turned to the two chief inspectors. 'Neil, Bandit, I don't discount Amanda's original hypothesis, that these are highly illegal people and that their visit here may well be drug-related. So keep an eye on the clubs, and be sensitive to any signs of new players on the scene.'

'Personnel?' asked McIlhenney.

'What do you need? We don't want to start speculation that something might be up.'

'I'd like to bring Mavis in on it,' said Mackenzie. 'She's already speculating why we had to spring Sean and Jingle Bell.'

'You trust her to maintain secrecy?'

'Absolutely.'

'Then brief her. Anyone else?'

'Alice Cowan?' McIlhenney murmured.

Skinner nodded. 'I thought you'd ask for her. Sure, you can have her; she's proved herself in Special Branch by now. Will that be enough?'

'On top of our normal operations,' Mackenzie replied, 'it will.'

'What about Sean?' asked Dennis. 'He's available to you.'

'We can't put him into another club,' Skinner told her. 'He's already been there, and very visibly too. I think it's best if he's at Willie's disposal for now.' He looked at Green. 'Are you okay with that?'

'Fine by me, sir.'

'Good.' The DCC stood up, picking up his envelope from the desk. 'Go on then, plunge into the haystack and find these five bent needles.'

He left the conference room and walked along the corridor, back to his office. Once inside he switched on the red 'busy' light outside the door, retrieved a number from his palm top and dialled it, using his secure phone.

'Hello, Bob,' said a familiar voice. 'And what fooking crisis has fallen on your old grey head this time?'

'Less of the old, you cheeky little bastard,' Skinner grunted. 'And what makes you think there's a crisis? Can't I call an old mate for a chat?'

'You've never called me just for a chat in your fooking life, so what's up?'

Major Adam Arrow held a senior and sensitive post within the Ministry of Defence, in its great grey headquarters in the heart of Whitehall. The two men had been in some dangerous situations together; indeed, they had survived one of them by the skin of their teeth. The little soldier maintained an amiable front, but behind it he was disciplined, resourceful, reliable and absolutely deadly.

'Maybe nothing,' the DCC told him. 'I've had a visit from the spooks, that's all. They want me to run an op for them.'

'Five?'

'Yes. Amanda Dennis and one of her boys, overseen by a guy named Rudolph Sewell. I've never met him before.'

'I'm not surprised: until recently he's been in the background . . . even by their standards . . . but he's highly rated and his star is on the rise. He's the next DG, or so they say.'

'Who says?'

'The creatures who prowl the murky corridors in which I walk, mate. You could join us, you know.'

The remark took Skinner by surprise. 'What do you mean?' he asked, warily.

'I mean what I said. You're rated down here, Bob. You've worked with Five, and have a reputation there; the DG would have you in his team in a minute, and pretty near the top too. I wouldn't be surprised if he created another assistant post for you, at the same level as Sewell, or maybe even above him.'

'He's never said anything to me about it.'

'That's not the way it works. You have to make the right noises.'

'What? Put in a job application, you mean?'

'No. Just pick up the phone and tell him you'd like to step into the darkness.'

Skinner drew a deep breath. 'But I wouldn't, Adam. My life's dark enough as it is. Right now, I'd welcome a little more light.'

'Winter blues.' Arrow chuckled. 'Anyhow, what can I do for you?'

'Right now? Nothing. Just tell me what you know about Albanians.'

There was a pause, as the soldier considered the question. 'Very little,' he answered, eventually, 'beyond the stereotype; they're virtually lawless, clannish, very big on blood feuds and into illegality in a big way. Why? Are you thinking about employing one?'

'No, we're having a visit from some, I'm told.'

'They'll be moving dope, then,' said Arrow, firmly.

'That's what Five think.'

'And they'll be right.'

'Would it take four of them to do it?' asked Skinner.

His friend laughed. 'They'll be moving a lot of dope.'

Twenty-two

Stevie Steele was poring through the papers on his desk when he heard his door open. He glanced up, expecting to see the massive, shirt-sleeved figure of Tarvil Singh filling the frame, but instead he saw a much smaller, slighter form, in uniform.

'Not interrupting, am I?' Maggie Rose asked, as she closed the door behind her.

'No.' He grinned. 'But you're a chief superintendent: you can interrupt me any time you like.'

'Does that never get to you, me outranking you?'

'It will,' he replied, cheerfully, 'when you start wearing your uniform in bed, but until then, no, not a bit. Would it get to you if I was the chief super and you were the DI?'

'No.'

'Well, stop getting sexist on me. What can I do for you, ma'am?'

'I was wondering how the response to George's appeal had gone, that's all.'

The smile left Steele's face. 'Poor,' he told her. 'Piss-poor, in fact. We'd one extremely nasty call saying that he was a copper so who cares, and a few from well-meaning people who couldn't tell us any more than we know already. Otherwise there's been nothing. And since it's in the nature of these things that all the response comes in the immediate aftermath of the telly appearance, I think we have arrived, very quickly, at the dead end we feared.'

'So what are you going to do?'

'First off, recommend to the Fiscal that he release the body for burial; second we're going to submit our report and let him decide whether he wants a formal fatal-accident inquiry.'

'Which he won't.'

Stevie shrugged his shoulders. 'I doubt it very much.'

'Why don't I think you're entirely happy with that?'

He smiled at her once more. 'You know me that well already? Maybe it's just that I knew the boy and know his parents, but my nose is twitching, that's all.'

'You know, you sounded just like Bob Skinner when you said that.'

'I'll take that as a compliment. Speaking of the DCC,' he asked cautiously, 'is he back from his break?'

'Yesterday. Jack McGurk called me this morning, looking for George Regan's home address; he said that his boss wanted to visit him and Jen.'

'And did he come back alone?'

'I'd hardly ask Jack that, would I?' she said. 'However, an observant if not too discreet sergeant under my command did let it slip that he saw him being dropped off near Fettes yesterday by a lady who did not look at all like Sarah.'

'Bloody hell!'

'Just what I said to Sergeant Evesham. That's a piece of information he'll be keeping to himself from now on, as, my darling, shall we.'

'Too right: I don't want to get anywhere near that situation. I've been too close already.'

Maggie grinned at him, eyes flashing with mischief. 'Come on, the boss's wife had a crush on you. Most guys would be secretly flattered by that . . . especially if she looked like Sarah Skinner.'

'If she wasn't that particular boss's wife, maybe, once upon a time, I would have been. But that was then, and this is now.'

'So what's different?'

'Stop fishing for them.' He chuckled. 'You're the difference and you know it.'

'Sure, but I love to hear you say it.' She paused. 'Will you be free for lunch?'

'God and Mary Chambers willing. Canteen?'

'Hell, no. Pub snack at Ryrie's: there's some stuff I want to tell you away from the office.'

'Can't it wait till we get home tonight?'

'Yes, but I don't see why it should. See you at one.'

Twenty-three

Skinner and McIlhenney had crossed the Forth Bridge and were heading along the M90 for Kinross before the silence was broken. The chief inspector had insisted on driving: he knew that his friend must still be tired from his long journey, but there was more to it than that. His recurrent nightmare had left him with an irrational unwillingness to sit in the passenger seat.

They had paid an awkward, painful visit to George and Jen Regan, offering what condolences they could, before leaving and heading almost gratefully out of the city.

The DCC had indeed nodded off almost as soon as the Vectra had turned on to the Queensferry Road, but he woke when they pulled up at the toll booth. As they sped away, McIlhenney muttered his usual imprecation about having to pay for driving on the public road. Skinner grinned: he had heard it all before, and as a long-term property owner in Spain he was used to paying road-toll charges.

'What do you think, then?' he asked, out of the blue, as they passed the exit that led to Deep Sea World, the giant aquarium to which he had promised to take his children on the following Sunday.

'About what?'

'About the bloody Albanians, what else?'

'Honestly? Until I see the original intelligence reports on them, I think the Home Secretary has his knickers in a twist. So four gangsters disappear from their home base and are traced to Britain. The best way to find them is by involving all the agencies with an interest in what they might be doing, not by handing it over to the spooks and having them screw it up by running covert operations with unreliable bampots like Jingle Bell.'

The DCC nodded. 'I agree with you, up to a point. Telling them not to advise or involve anyone else was a mistake, but that's what can happen when politicians start taking operational decisions. When it comes to intelligence reports, if Whitehall hasn't learned by now to treat them with the utmost caution, then it never will.'

'You can say that again, gaffer. Do you think they're telling us everything they know?'

'I think they are. At the very least, they're telling us everything we need to know.'

'What about Green?'

'I don't know about that lad: he was a bit glib about pulling that knife on Andy, and that begs the question nobody's asked him yet.'

McIlhenney's eyebrows rose slightly. 'You mean what would he have done if Andy hadn't been there, when Jingle called him in as back-up?'

'Exactly. Would he have carried on in his Richard Cable mode, and would he have carved up Mackenzie?'

'That's a question that hasn't occurred to the Bandit boy yet. When it does, I hope our Sean has a convincing answer.'

'A good reason why they shouldn't work together in this operation. Make sure it doesn't happen, will you?'

'As far as I can; but what if the ACC throws them together? I'm reporting to you and him, remember.'

'No, you're reporting to me. Willie's role is to talk with the Scottish refugee charities and the other public bodies; yours and Bandit's is to keep an eye on the underworld; and mine is to keep an eye on everything. So you come straight to me. I'm sorry: I should have made that clear.'

'No matter, I know now. What do you think our chances of tracing these guys are?'

Skinner frowned. 'I expect you to trace them, if they're still here. I've got no doubt that you will. The question is, can you do it before they attempt whatever stunt they've come here to pull?'

'Let's hope so.' Suddenly McIlhenney chuckled. 'Hey,' he said. 'A thought occurs. What if those four big rucksacks the Dutch guy described had golf clubs in them? Maybe they're just here on a golf tour.'

Skinner laughed with him. 'If they are . . . well, I've seen bigger gangsters than them as visitors to my home village. There's nothing better than a golf tour for bringing out the worst in middle-aged men.' He paused, looking out of the window as they passed the turn-off for east Fife. 'When are you going to ask me, Neil?'

'You mean why we're heading for Kinross to meet Andy? No point, you'd only have to repeat it once we got there.'

'I didn't mean that. When are you going to ask me about Sarah and me?'

'I'm not. I'm going to wait for you to tell me, in your own time.'

'And what if I tell you that we're finished?'

The chief inspector concentrated even harder on the road ahead. 'Then I will be very sad,' he replied, slowly, 'for both of you, because you're both very fine people. But I'll be sadder for your children.'

'So will I, but if it isn't right for us, can it be right for them?'

'There's no simple answer to that. So, are you telling me that you're finished? Can't you save it? The fact that you came home alone might say as much.'

'No, I'm not saying that, not yet; but I'm having trouble finding anything to save, other than friendship.'

McIlhenney sighed. 'I've never been in that situation, so I can't offer anything. Can I chance my arm and ask you one thing, though? Does this have anything to do with Aileen de Marco? When the Justice Minister calls me on my private line and asks if it's okay if she picks you up from the airport rather than me, it's liable to make me a bit inquisitive.'

'Touché,' said Skinner. 'I might be deceiving myself here, Neil, but I honestly don't think it has. Aileen's . . . a friend; but if she didn't exist, Sarah and I would still have this trouble. There are issues between us that can only be resolved by one of us capitulating. I won't; I've told her so. Now she's got to decide how to deal with that.'

'I see.' The DCI drove on in silence for a while, until the exit for Kinross came into sight. As he drove off the motorway, he glanced across at his friend. 'Good luck, Bob,' he murmured. 'That's all I can say.'

'It's enough; thanks.'

They followed the road off the roundabout that took them into the small county town, and drove along its leafy main street until, on their left, they came to the Green Hotel.

Twenty-four

George Regan stood in his kitchen, looking through the open door at his wife as he made another pot of tea: he thought that it was the fifth of the day, but in truth he had lost count. Jen was staring at the wall, at the same spot that had held her attention since the call had come about their son.

Finally, they were alone. Mary Chambers had just left, having come to tell them in person, rather than by phone, that the Procurator Fiscal had agreed to release George junior's body for burial. If such news could be described as good, it was, for at least it would give them something to do, something on which to focus for the next few days. After that they could both go back to work, him to the force, and Jen to her secretarial job with an accountancy firm.

Bob Skinner had called in too, with his Special Branch sidekick Neil McIlhenney. They had been *en route* to a meeting somewhere; Regan had found that a blessing, since both men were imagining all too obviously their own horror as parents at such a loss.

Before them there had been the grandparents, Jen's mum and dad and his own father, come as a group for no obvious reason. There was no consolation. The fact was that their visits, and those of their brothers and sisters, wee George's cousins, their colleagues and their close friends, only served to make the loss even less bearable. Each one brought their own grief, adding to the sum total in their quiet, still sitting room, and there had come a moment when George had wanted to scream, 'Please, thank you, whatever, just go and leave us to our private sorrows,' and another when Jen had run weeping from the room at the strident sound of the doorbell's ring.

In fact, that had not been another caller but another Interflora delivery. The house was full of flowers, more than they had vessels to contain them. They had been forced to borrow vases from the neighbours, and now the latest bouquet was displayed in an old ice-bucket that George had recovered from the garden shed.

As he dropped two Scottish Blend tea-bags into the green ceramic pot and poured in boiling water, he found himself wondering what it was that made people send flowers on every one of life's milestones: birth, marriage, anniversaries and most of all bereavement. He had been told, and maybe he would take Jen to see them, that dozens of floral tributes had been laid already at the spot where their son had died. But why? Was it an instinctive human reaction, or simply the result of subtle marketing?

Whatever it was, it was bloody good business for somebody, judging by the number of those cooler trucks from Holland that seemed to be about the city these days. He even remembered seeing one a few weeks back, parked at Fort Kinnaird at two in the morning. He and Jen had been on their way back from a party in Musselburgh and they had passed the bastard, parked on a public road for the night, skimming his expenses, no doubt, instead of taking a room in the King's Manor, less than a mile away. With a few cans under his belt, he had been for getting out his warrant card and rousting him out of his sleeping-bag, but Jen had refused to stop and driven on.

That party: high-flying Brian Mackie's promotion do, celebrating his elevation to command of the City Division, or the 'special forces', as George had christened it, another coppers' get-together. He thought of the guest list, trying to remember civvies who had been there. The only two he could recall were Brian's brother Rab, and Sheila's divorced sister Magdalena; they had made eyes at each other all night, until finally they had disappeared into the upper reaches of the house. The rest, though, had all been coppers.

He knew he wasn't the first to ask the question, and he wouldn't be the last. How many friends outside the force does your average police officer have? Damn few, was his answer. Inevitable, he supposed, that police people, being authority figures, should stand apart from the rest and group together socially, professionally, and even, in some cases, Masonically. It was getting worse, too. Now, with the increase in the number of female officers, more and more coppers were marrying other coppers. Look at Maggie Rose, for Christ's sake: she packs up with Mario McGuire and then she shacks up with Stevie Steele, swaps one CID suit for another. Not that George had anything against her, though. He liked Maggie, and Stevie too; a good lad and a lot safer bet than big McGuire. There was something about that one that said 'danger'. He was one of only three guys on the force, maybe anywhere, who were capable of scaring DS Regan, and the other two were not long gone from his house. Skinner himself, he was another example; his wife might not have been a cop, but she'd been a police surgeon when they had met, and his two closest friends were big Neil, and Andy Martin, who, come to think of it, also came into the 'scary' category . . . and who had married a detective sergeant.

'Should I chuck this job?' he mused aloud, as he poured the tea into two chunky mugs and added a dash of milk, no sugar, to each, not noticing that Jen had come to stand behind him.

'Why would you do that?' she asked.

He turned, surprised, spilling a little tea from one of the mugs as he picked them up. He kept that as his own and gave the other to his wife. 'Sorry, love,' he said. 'I was just talking to myself.'

'Sure, but when you do that it usually means something. Are you thinking of chucking the police?'

'If I did, maybe we'd get a life.'

'We've got a life, George. It's been torn apart for the moment, but you and I remain. We could even have another child.' Her chin seemed to quiver for a second. 'I'm not too old.'

'As the minister pointed out to us so directly, and so tactlessly. The way I see it, Jen, the loss of one child is the worst possible reason for conceiving another. We'd be making comparisons from the cradle, especially if it was a boy. Let's discuss that in six months, if you want, but please, not now. As for me and the police, I don't suppose this is the time for me to be making career decisions either. I'll let that sit on the shelf for a while too. I've got things to do in the meantime.'

'Things?' Jen sipped her tea. 'What things?'

He leaned back against the work surface. 'I've got to do something, love. I know that Mary and Stevie and the lads have done everything they can, and for the last couple of days I've sat back and let them get on with it, as the book says I should. But no way am I going to sit back and let our son's death be signed off as accidental without doing everything I can, myself, to find out for sure what happened to him.'

'How will you do that?'

'I don't know yet, but big Tarvil's bringing me a copy of the completed report this afternoon. Once I've seen it, and seen exactly what they've done, I'll have a better idea.'

'You're not saying they've been lax, are you?

'Not for a second. Think of me as an outside consultant, brought in to run a fresh eye over things. I won't see anything they should have done that they haven't, but there may be some things I can do differently.'

Twenty-five

Deputy Chief Constable Andy Martin was waiting for them in the hotel foyer. Skinner looked at him and saw a change; for the first time he noticed the network of lines around his friend's vivid green eyes, and the streaks of curly hair around his temples that had made the short transition from blond to silver.

He was dressed casually, in black slacks and a very conservative sports jacket, worn over a pale grey roll-necked sweater. 'Welcome to Kinross,' he said, as he shook hands with both of the newcomers.

McIlhenney looked around their comfortable surroundings. 'The inspector in charge of the local nick must have a nice life,' he commented.

'He doesn't complain about it, that's for sure,' Martin agreed. 'There are worse places I could send him. You wouldn't be after an inter-force transfer, would you, Neil?' He paused. 'Ah, but you're a chief inspector, aren't you?'

'There's a few would take a drop in rank for that posting.'

'Where do we go?' Skinner asked, as if he was impatient to get down to business.

'I've booked a small meeting room, with a coffee and sandwich lunch for the three of us.' He caught McIlhenney's wince. 'What's up?'

'I don't eat bread,' the DCI told him. 'And I don't drink coffee.'

Andy Martin laughed out loud. 'Jesus,' he said, 'you used to start the day with three bacon rolls and a pint of Nescafé. What's happened to you?'

'I used to be three stone heavier and a bag of twitching nerves too.'

'Fair enough. Ham salad and fizzy water okay?'

'Fine.'

'I'll fix it. Bob's paying anyway; I got the impression that this wasn't something I could put on my force's tab, or on yours, and since he called the meeting . . .'

'If you'd told me that,' Skinner growled, 'we'd be having more than bloody sandwiches. Where's this room, then?'

'Just a minute.' Martin walked across to the reception desk and spoke to a young man behind it. He came out and led them through the hotel to a light, airy room with a conference table that could have seated up to a dozen.

'I'll serve lunch now, shall I, gentlemen?' the manager asked. Skinner nodded, and the man left.

The two visitors looked out of the window across the hotel's attractive gardens. They were in winter mode, befitting the approach of Christmas: the day had dawned crisp and clear and had stayed that way, although it had grown colder through the morning. Kinross was in for a hard frost that night, and maybe snow was not too far away. McIlhenney felt himself shiver.

As Skinner surveyed the grounds his eye fell on a woman pushing a pram or, rather, a modern multi-position device designed for the carriage of small children. 'Hey,' he exclaimed, 'is that Karen out there?'

'Yes,' said Martin, with a sudden dazzling smile and a look in his eyes that McIlhenney had never seen before in him but which he recognised as the pride of the new parent. 'I decided that I'd take the day off and bring her and Danielle down with me. When you two have gone we're going to have a swim in the hotel pool.'

'How's she liking being up here?' asked McIlhenney.

'Ah, she's loving it.'

'Do I detect from your tone that you might not be?' Skinner murmured.

'I'm enjoying my job very much, Bob.'

'That's not an answer.'

'It's the best one I can give you.'

'You know that the chief constable job in Dumfries and Galloway's coming up?'

'I don't have the experience,' said Martin, quickly. 'Why don't you apply for it?'

'That'll be bloody right!'

'There you are, then.'

'Okay,' Skinner admitted. 'I know that job's not for you, but there'll be fall-out from the appointment when it's made . . . and it could be made soon, for reasons I'll explain shortly. When it's advertised, I'll bet you that a certain stocky Glaswegian ACC, whose office is only a few yards from my own, will be among the applicants.'

'Interesting,' Martin agreed. 'And if Willie gets it there will be a vacancy at Fettes. That's what you're hinting, is it?'

'It's more of a forecast than a hint. Willie's been told to apply for the job, by the outgoing chief, no less.'

'But if he left, you'd promote from within, wouldn't you?'

'Who fills the bill?'

'Brian Mackie?'

'Too new in his present job.'

'Maggie?'

'Likewise; and within these walls I don't fancy any of our other chief supers moving into the Command Corridor. So if and when the vacancy arises, there will be an outside appointment. You want it, you got it, son; it's as simple as that.'

'Food for thought,' Martin mused. He glanced out of the window at his wife and baby daughter. 'I'll keep it to myself for now, though.'

There was a knock on the door; it opened and a waiter appeared pushing a trolley, laden with a large plate of sandwiches, an attractive salad topped with several slices of thick ham, a pot of coffee and two large bottles of mineral water.

As he left, slightly enriched by a tip from Skinner, the three men took places at the table. At first they concentrated on lunch, since they were all hungry, but eventually Martin pushed his plate to one side. 'So, Bob, what's this about?'

'I'm worried,' Skinner replied. 'I think we have something nasty and potentially very dangerous to our service on our hands. What's the respective role of chief constable, board and ministers, in the simplest form?'

'Chiefs are responsible for policing,' Martin shot back, instantly, 'the board for equipping, and the Secretary of State, or First Minister now, for enabling.'

'Perfect. That's how it's always been and how it should be. The problem is that we have a First Minister who wants to change all that: he wants to emasculate the boards and take control for himself. He wants to approve every appointment at our rank, and have the power to fire us, personally, at will.'

'He can't do that!'

'Oh, no? The bill's already drafted. He's sweet-talked his coalition partners into going along with it on the basis that the powers it gives him are for use in extreme cases only. It's as bad in its own way as the Americans' Patriot Act: the law that gives the US Attorney General the right to decide who's a terrorist and who isn't. I suspect that our beloved leader Mr Murtagh might just be a bit of a Fascist, but in rose-red clothing.'

'Have you seen this bill?'

'No, but a friend of mine has and described it to me in detail.'

'What about the new Justice Minister, de Marco? I thought she was supposed to be pro-police. She made her feelings plain on Monday about those people being packed off to Cuba.'

Skinner looked at him and picked up another sandwich. 'She's the friend,' he replied, and took a bite. He let the silence linger until he was finished, reading all the questions in his friend's eyes as he did. 'Aileen didn't make her feelings plain directly; I did it for her. Now she's been coerced by Murtagh into appearing to go along with it, and we've agreed that she should acquiesce for now. The guy thinks he's got me by the balls too, and I plan to let him go on thinking that.'

'So are you going to sit on your hands and let the bastard get on with it?' Martin demanded, as angrily as he could ever sound.

'I'm going to appear to do that. He'll be watching me like a hawk or, rather, his newly appointed Himmler will.'

'Who?'

Skinner raised his eyebrows. 'You haven't heard that Jock Govan's been booted as security adviser? Jimmy Proud told me he'd let all the other chiefs know.'

'It's news to me, but Graham Morton was away yesterday and Monday. I haven't seen him this week. Who's the new guy?'

'Greg Jay.'

Martin gasped. 'You have to be joking.'

'Am I smiling?' Skinner retorted. 'Officially he retired from us last week, but unofficially he's been working for wee Tommy for a while. He's even been checking up on Aileen and me … not that there was anything for him to check up on, in the sense you're thinking.' He caught a flicker of McIlhenney's right eyebrow, but no more.

'He's made his presence felt with other people too. I spoke with Niall Foy, the Chief Inspector of Constabulary this morning. He's absolutely livid, because apparently Jay's been saying that he'll be allowed to conduct private investigations into individual officers and report directly to his boss about them. Again, Murtagh's saying that it would only be in the most sensitive and exceptional circumstances, but if you believe that…'

'This is appalling,' Martin exclaimed. 'What do you think, Neil?'

The chief inspector smiled. 'Just between you and me, Andy? Personally, I think Jay should have been sent home to his garden a while back, when he crossed my friend McGuire, but I wouldn't have dared say it to the boss, would I?'

Skinner grumbled, 'No, but maybe Dan Pringle should have.' He paused. 'Is there anything you wouldn't dare tell me about him?'

'As head of CID,' McIlhenney replied, 'Dan was a man for his time. Now that time's nearly up. There's other things I could say as well, but I'm not going to dig that up.'

'No, best not to. Anyway, back to the pressing matter. I wanted to see you guys today because I want to ask you to put your careers on the line. I want to get that little bastard Murtagh and I want you to help me do it. He is just too bloody slimy to have no skeletons in his closet. I want to find out whose they are, or what they are, and I want to make their bones rattle until they drive him out of office.'

He looked at Martin once again. 'Murtagh may be Edinburgh-based now, but he has a Dundonian background. I want to know all about it. I want to know who his pals were when he was here, whether he preferred women to sheep, where he worked before he gave it up and became a politician. I want schoolfriend anecdotes, office gossip . . . did he ever feel the typists' bums, that sort of stuff . . . any weapon you can find me, and as many of them as you can.'

He turned to McIlhenney. 'Neil, I want you to do a vetting operation on him in Edinburgh. I've already had a conversation with Amanda Dennis. She understands what's at stake and she'll help you in any way she can. I know I'm piling a lot of responsibility on your shoulders, with the other thing on the go, but I have to assume that I'm being watched myself. I won't forget it, don't worry.'

'I never have,' said McIlhenney. 'What about Jay?'

'Jay is a minion.' Skinner spat the word out contemptuously. 'If you think about it, you and I both know already how we can bring him into line. But I will choose my moment. Who knows? Maybe I can turn him into our best weapon against Murtagh.'

He winked at his colleagues, at his friends, and picked up yet another sandwich.

Twenty-six

I like this pub,' said Maggie, as she looked around the old tavern, strategically placed beside the railway station on the five-pointed Haymarket junction. 'I came here when I was little more than a girl, and it's barely changed since.'

'Unlike too many of them,' Stevie Steele commented. 'I don't like designer boozers, converted banking halls, that sort of thing, but I really hate it when places like this are revamped and modernised just for the sake of it, when a coat of varnish is all they really need.'

'This one's survived, at least.'

'But for how much longer?'

'As long as it makes a nice profit.'

He laughed. 'And serves a nice pie.' He looked at her as he sprinkled vinegar on his chips. 'So, love, what's so important or enticing that couldn't wait till tonight?'

Maggie slipped her arms out of her overcoat and let it fall behind her over the back of her chair. She still wore her white uniform shirt, but she had removed the black and white checked cravat and epaulettes. Police uniforms always drew stares in pubs; without the tell-tale neckerchief, she might have been a bank clerk.

'I had a letter from my lawyer in the mail this morning,' she said. 'He's agreed the financial settlement with Mario's solicitor and it's ready for us both to sign. I'm getting the house free and clear, as Mario promised, and everything in it.'

'That's good,' Stevie replied, quietly. 'But it's no surprise, is it? You didn't expect him to go back on his word.'

'No, of course not, but it's still nice to know that the formalities are done with. Once it's signed it'll just leave one tie to be cut between us, the marriage itself.'

'Divorce, you mean? That'll happen the year after next, won't it, once you've been apart for two years?'

She nodded. 'It would do, if we followed the simple procedure and divorced on the ground of irretrievable breakdown. But if I sued Mario for divorce on the ground of adultery, it could happen virtually right away.'

' Stevie's eyebrows rose. 'Would you do that?' he asked.

'I don't know. I don't feel vindictive towards him, or even towards Paula. It depends.'

'Depends on what?

'Depends on whom: it depends on you. Would you like me to be single as soon as possible?'

Stevie stopped in the middle of cutting a segment out of his mutton pie. He frowned, looked at the ceiling for a few moments, then took a mouthful from his pint of orange squash. Finally he looked back at her. 'As in free to marry?' he asked.

'I wasn't implying anything like that,' she answered quickly.

He smiled into her eyes. 'I don't care what you were implying. Whether it was a back-handed proposal or not, the answer's yes. I want you absolutely free and clear from Detective Superintendent McGuire at the earliest opportunity, and I want to marry you. But will it be that easy? Big Mario might not care to be branded publicly as an adulterer.'

'Big Mario does not care. Big Mario told his lawyer to tell mine that if that's what I want to do then it'll be fine by him and Paula, as long as I keep her name off the petition.'

Stevie's smile spread from ear to ear. 'Bloody hell!' he exclaimed. 'That's a twist.'

'But it's not unexpected by me. Mario and I weren't very good at being husband and wife, in any sense, but if either of us needs something from the other, it's as good as done.'

'Should I worry about that, long term?'

'No. Not any more. There's nothing tying us together.' She paused. 'All the bodies have been buried, and all the evidence burned.'

He laughed. 'There's nobody better at a cover-up than a copper. Are you going to do it, then, go for an immediate divorce?'

'Yes. You've just made my mind up for me.'

'I'm glad. Now make me even happier and eat your lunch: it's getting cold.'

They concentrated on their pies, their chips and their beans until they were finished. When they were, they piled their plates one on the other and picked up their drinks. Stevie shook his head, a slightly bemused grin on his face. 'Let's go to Laing's on Saturday,' he said. 'You'll have to steer me: I've never bought an engagement ring before.'

'I'm glad to hear it, but you're forgetting something. I haven't said "yes" yet.'

'Well, will you?'

'Let me tell you something else first,' she replied. 'Then you can ask me again, if you want. My letter arrived okay, but a few days ago, something else didn't.'

'Uh?'

'Do you know the last time I missed a period, Stevie?'

His eyes widened. 'I wouldn't, would I?' he whispered.

'The answer's never since I started having them. Regular as clockwork, on the dot; you could set your watch by me. Until this month.'

His mouth fell open; he stared at her, idiotically. 'You mean . . . Have you . . .'

'I'm going to give it another day or so, and if nothing's happened, I'll get a kit and do a test. If I am, how do you feel about it? Would you be upset?'

'Upset?' he gasped. 'Think of me waking up as chief constable, us winning the lottery and you being pregnant. That's my wish list, in ascending order.'

'Really?'

'Couldn't be more real. I'll ask you again: will you marry me?'

To his surprise, she blushed bright red, her face in vivid contrast to the white of her shirt. 'I guess so,' she replied.

Twenty-seven

Mario McGuire put the phone back in its cradle; he wondered when, or even whether, he had heard Maggie sound so happy, and the thought sent a sudden feeling of sadness through him. It passed quickly, though, and he smiled. 'By God, young Steele,' he murmured to himself, 'you make a better go of looking after her than I did, or I'll make sure your life will be hell on earth.' She had told him only that she wanted the quickest divorce possible, so that she and Stevie could marry. He had taken her word at face value, but inwardly he wondered whether there might just be more to it.

He picked up the phone once more and called Paula Viareggio at her office. 'Hi, kid,' he said, when she answered. 'You're listening to a soon-to-be-official adulterer.'

'She wants it, then?'

'Yes, and she can have it, as long as you're not named on the petition, which you won't be.'

'That's fine,' said Paula, not quite as unconcerned as she had meant to sound. 'It won't make any difference to us, will it?'

'Not a bit.' He laughed. 'We'll still go on being Leith's favourite casual couple.'

'Yeah? You won't start feeling fancy-free all of a sudden, will you?'

'Don't be daft. I'm happy as we are; never been more so, just like my soon-to-be-ex-wife.'

'In that case,' she told him, 'I'm cooking osso bucco alla Milanese tonight; bring a nice bottle of Barolo with you.'

'One of Nana Viareggio's recipes?'

'Truth? No, I got it off the internet.'

'Ah,' he laughed. 'The modern Italian woman. Are Neil and Lou still coming?'

'Of course.'

'Maybe I'll bring two bottles.'

'You'll drink most of them yourself, then: Neil's driving and Lou won't want much, in her condition.'

'I wonder if it's infectious?' Mario muttered.

'We don't need to worry if it is,' Paula countered. 'You've had the vaccination.'

He let it pass. 'See you later.'

'About seven thirty. Bye, lover.'

He hung up and went back to his paperwork, reports from his CID team on current investigations. He noted, with some satisfaction, a significant drop in reported petty thefts within his division, wondering whether it might have less to do with his arrival than with the disappearance of a certain Moash Glazier.

He was still pondering the fate of the missing thief, when his door swung open. Annoyed by the absence of a knock, McGuire looked up to see a tall, slim, middle-aged man with muddy grey eyes slide into the room, and take a seat facing him. 'Greg,' he exclaimed. 'I heard you'd taken the pension. What the hell are you doing back here? Did you leave something behind when you left this office?'

Jay gave a thin smile. 'Nothing I had any use for, Mario. How are you settling in behind my old desk?'

'The desk's fine, thanks; the chair's clapped out, though. I've asked for a replacement. As for the job, I like it here; livelier than the Borders division, that's for sure.'

'And you're doing very well, I hear. Meeting your targets right across the board, so Pringle told me: you'll be after his job next.'

McGuire felt his hackles start to rise. 'I've never been after anyone's job in my life, Greg, not while they were in it at least. I heard you took the hump when you were shifted out of here, but that had nothing to do with me. I didn't ask Dan or anyone else for a move and I certainly didn't ask to be transferred here.'

Greg Jay raised a placatory hand. 'Don't get excited, Mario, I'm not saying you did. I know who was behind the moves, all right. The mighty Mr Skinner: who else? He calls all the shots on this force. If your face fits with him, you're made. You and your ex are classic examples of that. I've got nothing against you, though; don't think that for a minute. I'm happily out of it now, just an interested observer on the sidelines.'

He shot a crafty glance across the desk. 'Have you heard any rumours about Skinner?' he asked.

'For fuck's sake, man,' McGuire exclaimed, 'there are always rumours about Bob Skinner. One minute he's going to the top job in the Met, the next he's taking command of Interpol. They're all balls, every one of them.'

'I didn't mean rumours about his career moves. I was talking about his private life. I heard his marriage was up the spout, and that he had a new lady-friend.'

'I don't go in for that sort of gossip. I've been the subject of it myself, just recently. If you want me to pass on any crap about the boss, you'll be waiting a long time.'

'Mmm. Time is something I now have plenty of, my young friend. How is Paula, by the way?'

'Very well, thanks.'

'A very interesting lady, I've always thought, from a very interesting family. I remember your grandfather very well: he was a classic of his type, wasn't he, a real old-school Italian? He could have stepped right off the pages of a Puzo novel.' Jay laughed. 'I suppose you could too, come to that.'

McGuire's eyebrows lowered. 'Greg, what is this? Why the honour of this visit?'

'Just a social call, son, honestly. Tell me, don't you ever find it difficult, being a serving copper and chairing your family business?'

'No more difficult than you found working here and being Right Worshipful Master of your Masonic Lodge. I don't have an executive role, as you know very well; I have a lawyer who advises me on all the important decisions, and who has power to act for me.'

'And not just any lawyer either, I hear, but Miss Alexis Skinner, the sharpest young solicitor in town.'

McGuire's anger rose, its flames showing in his eyes. 'Who the hell told you that?' he snapped.

'That's not important. Why are you so tetchy anyway? Was that supposed to be a secret?'

'No, but it's my private business, and I don't like it being ground in your gossip mill.'

'Sorry, if I upset you. That temper of yours, Mario, it's awfully near the surface these days. I hear you've been showing it to some old friends of mine, too.'

'Such as?'

'Malky Gladsmuir, for one, the manager of the Wee Black Dug pub. I'd a pint in there at lunchtime, and he mentioned that you'd been in to see him. You know, I think you scared the poor chap. I never thought anyone could do that, but you seem to have managed it. He's a valuable informant of mine, is Malky, so I'd appreciate it if you eased up on him a bit.'

'He's a devious bloody scammer and he always has been. You missed a hell of a lot that went on in that pub in your time here, my friend. And what do you mean "is" a snout of yours? You're gone, Greg, remember?'

'Not gone, Mario; "translated" would be a better word. Clearly the news hasn't filtered down to your level: I've got a new job.'

'What's that? Security at the docks?'

'A little more important than that, and a little more sensitive. Ask your friend McIlhenney next time you see him. He'll know about it, I'm sure; the Great Man will have told him by now.'

Jay pushed himself to his feet. 'I'd better be going. Wouldn't do to interrupt the fight on crime any longer than necessary.' He walked to the door. 'By the way,' he said, 'I hear there's a new regulation in the pipeline. It's going to require complete disclosure by police officers of all business interests, whether direct or through their wives and families. It'll cause quite a stir, I reckon. Where something's deemed unsuitable, the officer involved will be given a straight choice between giving it up or leaving the force.'

'Oh, yes?' McGuire growled. 'And who's going to do the deeming?'

'My new boss, actually . . . acting on my advice, of course. Be seeing you again, I'm sure.' He opened the door and stepped outside.

McGuire snatched the phone from his desk and buzzed the CID office. Detective Sergeant Sammy Pye answered at once. 'Sir?'

'Sam,' he exclaimed, 'that bastard who's just come out of my office: Jay. Have him followed; in fact, do it yourself if you're clear. I want to know where he goes.'

Twenty-eight

George Regan stepped out of the Castle Terrace car-park office. The manager had been annoyed at another police visit, but eventually he had co-operated and given him a rundown of his regular customers, those whom he knew and their usual times of coming and going. Most of them were office employees, professionals from the impressive new buildings that had sprouted in the city's West End during the last decade of the millennium, but several were shop-workers, with differing hours and shift patterns that involved them sometimes in weekend working.

He checked his watch: it showed twenty past six. Normally most of the shop people would have been gone by that time, but in December their hours tended to stretch a little. He looked around level five of the well-lit car park: it would have been full during the day, but most of the cars had gone. Still, there were enough around to make his trip worthwhile.

He heard footsteps behind him, and turned to see a woman trot down the stairs and hurry across to a small blue Citroën hatchback. He moved towards her, taking out his warrant card. 'Excuse me, madam,' he called out. 'I wonder if you can help me. I'm a police officer.' She turned, startled; she was mid-forties, with brown, well-cut hair, and she would have been attractive but for the sharp suspicious eyes that seemed to drill into him. He held the card up high, for her to see more clearly, and she peered at it carefully.

'What can I do for you?' she asked, in cultured, clipped tones.

'I hope you can be of assistance,' he told her. 'Are you a regular user of this car park?'

'Yes, I'm here every day during the week.'

'How about weekends?'

'Not normally, but on occasion I come into my office out of normal hours.'

'By any chance were you here last Sunday?'

She frowned, as she scanned through her mental diary. 'Yes, I was, as it happens, but not at work. There was an evening carol concert in St John's Church.'

'What time did it finish?'

'Seven o'clock.'

'And when did you leave the car park?'

'I'm not sure, but it must have been after eight. They had mulled wine and mince pies afterwards, and I stayed around.'

'When you left, which exit did you use: top or bottom?'

'The lower exit,' she said. 'I always go out on to King's Stables Road; it's easier for my route home.'

Regan felt a burst of optimism surge through him, and tried to keep it from showing on his face. 'Would you think very carefully about this, please, ma'am?' he asked. 'When you turned out of the car park and into the road, did you see anyone?'

She looked at him; as she did, the suspicion left her eyes and her tight mouth seemed to soften a little. 'This is about that poor child, isn't it?' she asked. She stared at him even more closely. 'And you're his father, aren't you? I saw you on *Reporting Scotland*, I'm sure.'

Embarrassed, Regan nodded.

'Oh,' she said, 'I'm terribly sorry, for you and your family, but I really can't help you. When I saw your appeal on television I did think about it, but I can't recall seeing anyone, least of all a small boy.'

'He wasn't that small. He was thirteen.'

The woman shook her head. 'No, I'm sorry,' she said. 'I'd love to help you, but I really can't remember there being anyone in the street at all.'

She was so definite that the detective felt the candle of hope within him flicker and die. Nevertheless, he took a business card from the breast pocket of his jacket and handed it to her. 'Those are my office and mobile numbers,' he said. 'Please keep them, Mrs . . .'

'Miss,' she said, as she took the card. 'Miss Bee, Betty Bee. I'm sure

I won't recall anything that will be of help, but if anything at all does occur to me, I will get in touch, I promise.'

He thanked her, holding the door of her car open for her as she climbed in. 'Thank you,' he said, as he closed it gently. He watched her as she drove off, then leaned his head back and closed his eyes. That had been pure luck, he knew: he would not find many more potential witnesses so easily. He had to try, though. Slipping his warrant card into the pocket of his overcoat, George Regan made his way down to the barrier that controlled the exit to King's Stables Road, and settled down for a long evening of questioning drivers, even though in his heart of heart he knew that it would be fruitless.

At least he was doing something.

Twenty-nine

'What's up?' Lena McElhone blurted out the question as she stood with her hands in the sink, washing the pan in which she had cooked the spaghetti that she and Aileen de Marco had shared.

'What makes you think that anything is?' her boss, friend and tenant replied.

'I know you well enough by now to read the signs. You hardly spoke last night, and just now it was like eating in a public library: no talking, please. Did something happen to upset you when you stayed in Glasgow on Monday?'

'Yes and no. But my problem is, Lena, that I can't talk to you about it. In fact, I think I might have to move out.'

The other woman gasped and her face went chalk white. 'But why? What's happened?' she demanded.

Aileen looked down at the tiled floor, then turned and led the way through to the flat's small living room. She had hoped to avoid a confrontation, but finally she recognised that it had to be. 'This arrangement of ours,' she began, 'my living here: it's unique, as far as I know, for a minister and her private secretary to share accommodation. A few of my colleagues, and yours too, I guess, think it's weird, that there's something improper about it.'

'You mean they think we're gay?'

'Some probably do, but that doesn't matter. The point is that my sharing your flat is convenient for us both, and it works, because it's built on trust.' She looked Lena in the eye. 'I have to ask you something. Have you been talking about me?'

'You mean have I been gossiping about you? Absolutely not! Do you actually think I would?'

'No, that's not what I mean, not at all. Have you been asked about me professionally? Have you been asked about my movements, for example, and my meetings with Bob Skinner?'

The private secretary's face went from pale to crimson in a matter of seconds. 'Oh, no,' she whispered; her shoulders shook and she began to weep. 'He couldn't have.'

'He could,' Aileen replied, gently. 'Calm down and tell me about it.'

She waited until Lena's sobs had subsided. 'It was last Friday,' she began, when she could. 'When you were in the Parliament, I was asked to go to see a man in an office on the fourth floor. He told me he was the First Minister's security adviser, that his name was Mr Jay and that he needed to talk to me. When I got there, I found that he wanted to talk about you.'

She gulped. 'He said that part of his job was to vet all new members of the Cabinet, and that since you had been promoted only recently, you had to be put through the process. He told me it was routine, nothing to worry about, it happened to everybody, even the First Minister.' Aileen choked off a retort. 'I told him that I didn't think it was right for me to discuss your business, but he said the whole thing was totally confidential, and that nobody would know. When I said that I was still reluctant, he got a bit nasty and said it wasn't a request it was an order, and that if I liked I could have it from the First Minister himself, but if it came to that it would have an "adverse effect", as he put it, on my career.'

'So he blackmailed you?'

'I suppose you could put it that way.' The civil servant looked at her plaintively. 'I'm sorry, Aileen. He promised me it would be okay.'

'I'm sure he did. Go on.'

'I showed him your diary,' said Lena. 'I went and got it from the office. But he wanted to know more than that. There was a note in it about your first meeting with Mr Skinner, when you took him to dinner at the Arts Club. He asked me if that was the only time you'd met. I told him it wasn't, that you'd seen him here, and in his office, and that he'd returned your hospitality with lunch at the Open Arms. He asked me about your meeting with Mr Laidlaw, and I told him about that. Then he asked me more personal stuff about you, whether you had a steady boyfriend, whether you ever brought men back to the flat. I said you hadn't, and that if you had that sort of a private life you conducted it well away from me.' She drew another deep breath. 'And that was it. He was very nice after that. He laughed and said it all sounded very respectable and very responsible, and that there was nothing untoward. He told me I should discuss our meeting with nobody, and that I should forget it. Aileen, I'm so sorry,' she protested. 'I trusted the man when he said you'd never even know about it, that it was a purely routine piece of security. How did you find out?'

'It's been used against me,' the Justice Minister replied. 'And not just against me.'

She picked up her mobile phone from the sideboard, and selected Bob Skinner's number. When he answered, she could hear the sound of children in the background, and felt a sort of regret that there was a part of his life she might never know. 'Hi', she murmured, her back turned to McElhone so that she could not hear. 'It's me.'

'Yeah,' he drawled, 'so my clever phone told me.' He sounded tired, as if the jet-lag was giving him another jolt. 'What's up? Do you want company?'

'That would be nice, but we can't. I want to ask you something. You told me that you did the security-adviser job for a while, didn't you?'

'Yes,' he replied, 'until the Secretary of State of the day got so far up my nose that I had to blow him out. Jock Govan took over after that.'

'When you were in post, did your duties include the vetting of ministers, interviewing their staff about their public and private lives?'

'Of course not; that's all tosh. Why?'

'Because that's the story Jay spun Lena to find out about you and me.'

'Bastard,' Skinner hissed. 'That goes on his tab as well.'

She read meaning in his tone. 'Bob, are you up to something?' she asked.

'Me?' He managed to sound offended. 'Did I promise you I'd keep my head down?'

'Yes,' she admitted.

'Trust me, then.'

'Sorry.'

'Forgiven. I've got some good news for you, by the way. Your flat's clean as a whistle, certified bug-free by Strathclyde Special Branch, so no one'll be playing us any doctored tapes.'

'I'm glad to hear it, but how can I be sure that it'll stay clean?'

'I asked them to leave a scanning device in your top kitchen drawer.'

'That was thoughtful. Do you plan on coming to test it?' The question was out before she could stop herself.

'Maybe, but not for a while and certainly not this weekend. My rambunctious younger son has threatened to head-butt my kneecaps if I don't take him to Tynecastle on Saturday, and then on Sunday we're going to look at some sharks. But I would like to think that a return trip to Glasgow might happen some time.'

'I hope so too.' She moved further away from Lena. 'I think I may have to go back through there full-time.'

'Is that wholly necessary?'

'Not completely. I'm sure that Lena really was conned, or coerced.'

'Then think before you jump. If you move out, Jay will know, and he'll guess why. You won't be doing the girl any favours.'

'I see what you mean,' she mused. 'She and I were just about to discuss that, in fact.'

'Do it, then. Good night, Minister.'

'You too, Deputy Chief Constable.' She ended the call, and turned back to Lena. 'Okay,' she said. 'Here's what we're going to do about Mr Jay.'

Thirty

'Do you think you'll ever go back to your career?'

Louise McIlhenney smiled. 'That depends,' she replied. 'It depends on my husband, it depends on Lauren and Spencer's needs, it depends on my health, it depends on me getting any offers to go back, but most of all it depends on how I feel after I'm a mum. I know the modern trend is to leave it late before starting a family but I'm an extreme case. I'm over forty: at an age when some women are starting the menopause I'm having a baby.'

Paula Viareggio shivered, sending her silver hair rippling across her shoulders. 'Rather you than me,' she said, 'at any age. But you don't look forty plus, you look younger than me, for God's sake.'

'No, I don't. I've been an actress for twenty years, so I'm good at makeup. You might accentuate your hair colour, but that's all you do. Where I see a sign of grey, and there's plenty under this lot, I cover it up. I don't let Neil see my hairdresser's bills: he'd have a fit if I did.'

Her husband laughed. 'I know who your hairdresser is,' he exclaimed. 'That's enough.'

'Come on,' Paula retorted. 'Don't try and kid me that men's hairdressers are cheap.'

Mario McGuire held up a hand. 'There's a guy in Leith, near the docks, who'll still cut your hair for a fiver; and it's two quid for OAPs.'

'And would you go to him?' his partner challenged.

'Not even if I was stone bald,' he admitted, cheerfully. 'But by the same token, neither would I dream of going to a barber who drives a Ferrari, the kind that you girls are talking about.'

139

'Charlie Kettles does not drive a Ferrari.'

'Charlie's pals would laugh him out of town if he did, as you well know, but there's others who do.'

'So? They run successful businesses. So do you and I, and we're not ashamed of it.'

Mario's smile vanished for a moment. 'There are times when I'm embarrassed by it. It's not something that I chose; it was wished on me by my grandfather and latterly by my mother, when she decided to retire to Italy. But the businesses employ a lot of people, and I feel responsible for them. Okay, we're planning to change things, but when we do, I only hope I don't have Papa Viareggio haunting me.'

'Me too,' Paula agreed. 'But you handle things the way they are just now; having Alex Skinner act on your behalf wherever possible is a good idea.'

'It is for her firm; it costs plenty.'

'What does Alex drive these days?' asked McIlhenney, casually.

'A nice wee yellow two-seater, last I saw,' Mario told him. 'Nothing flash. But speaking of Alexis, her name came up in conversation this afternoon.'

'Oh, yes?'

'I'll tell you later.'

Paula frowned and leaned across the dinner table. 'Is that our cue to withdraw to the drawing room?'

Mario looked around him. 'This place is open plan; we're in the bloody drawing room. But there is something I want to talk to Neil about.' He paused. 'We could always go to the pub, I suppose.'

She rose to her feet. 'Indeed you will not! Come on, Lou, let's retire to the kitchen for our port and cigars. Better still, we'll load the dishwasher and open that second bottle of Barolo.' She began to place the dinner plates and cutlery on a tray, while the two men took their glasses and walked over to the armchairs in the opposite corner of the big loft.

'What's up, then?' Neil asked quietly as he sat down. 'Who was talking about Alex?'

'Greg bloody Jay, that's who. He swanned into my office this afternoon, like the Archangel Gabriel on an undercover mission for God. I don't know what he was trying to do, impress me, threaten me, warn me or what, but what he did succeed in doing was piss me off. He went on about some new job of his . . . that my best pal knows about, apparently, but hadn't got round to telling me about . . . and then he told me to give Malky Gladsmuir a wide berth. He thinks Malky's his snout, not mine.'

'And will you?'

'Like hell I will. Malky's in for a personal visit tomorrow; in fact he'd have had it by now if you and Lou hadn't been coming for dinner. Anyway, once Jay left, I had Sammy Pye tail him. You know where he went?' Mario paused in his tirade. 'But then I suppose you do know.'

'St Andrews House?'

'Got it in one.'

'What's he doing there?'

'Whatever Tommy Murtagh tells him to do: he's replaced Sir John Govan as security adviser.'

'How long have you known this?'

McIlhenney glanced at his watch. 'For approximately nine hours; I haven't had a chance to tell you since then.'

'Apology accepted.'

'I didn't know I'd offered one.' He took a sip of San Pellegrino. 'Do me a favour,' he said. 'Don't go off at half-cock over this. For example, don't do anything too painful to Gladsmuir.'

'Why not? I'm not having the bastard thumbing his bloody nose at me.'

'Maybe not, but just hold off for a wee while, okay?'

'Are you up to something?' McGuire growled.

'Let's just say that the Jay problem is being addressed. If you think that Jay pissed you off, you have no idea what he's done to Bob Skinner.' McIlhenney leaned back in his chair and watched a wicked smile cross his friend's face.

'Is that so?' Mario mused. 'In that case, far be it from me to get in the way of his vengeance.'

'Good. I was hoping you'd see it that way.'

'I'm not daft. I want to hold on to my ambitions, for a while at least.'

McIlhenney was taken by surprise. 'You? Ambitious? I thought that all your Christmases had come. You're in the division you've always wanted, you're in a relationship that's exactly right for you, with neither you nor Paula making any demands of each other. On top of that, you're got the option of buggering off to run the family business any time you like. What the hell more do you want?'

'I want Dan Pringle's job when he goes.'

'Mmm. You do, do you?' McIlhenney murmured. 'I've wondered, but it's the first time I've heard you come right out and say it. What about Alastair Grant? He's got seniority now that Jay's out, and Maggie's back in uniform.'

'I'll take my chances; but in the meantime I won't do anything to undermine them, don't worry.' McGuire glanced up, quickly. 'Enough about me, though: how about you, pal? Are you all right?'

'I'm fine. Why do you ask?'

'I thought you were looking knackered, that's all.'

'Ah. I haven't been sleeping too well, if you really want to know. I think I must be worrying about Lou and the baby. Plus, I've got a lot on my plate.'

Mario laughed. 'Pull the other one,' he said. 'I've done the SB job, remember. I'd have thought you'd caught your quota of terrorists for the year. It's not your fault that Murtagh gave them away.'

McIlhenney scowled at him. 'I wish I had performance targets like you divisional guys. Just when you think you've pulled yourself out of the morass, something grabs your ankle and you're back in there.'

'Something I should know about?'

'Something I can't tell you about, officially.'

'Unofficially?'

'Not in detail.'

'Spooks?'

'No comment.' McIlhenney fell silent for a few seconds, then looked up once more. 'What do you know about Jay's connections?'

'What kind? Masonic?'

'Maybe, but I was thinking political. I mean, the guy walks out of a successful but unspectacular thirty-year police career, one of a hundred or so across the country, with no flair and no distinguishing features, yet next day he's in an office at the heart of the Executive with a lot of real power in his hands. Clearly he didn't apply for the job; he was put there. It would be good to know how that happened.'

'I'll ask around, but don't expect much. He didn't leave too many friends behind when he was transferred out of Leith.'

'Ask quietly.'

'Of course.'

McIlhenney nodded. 'While you're at it, there's something else.'

'There always is. Go on.'

'Albanians.'

'Balkan gangsters; terrible football team. Do I get any points for that?'

'That's just your starter for ten. I'm looking for some.'

'Is this what you can't tell me?'

'Could be. Let's just say there are four of them, and there are a lot of soiled underpants around down south.'

McGuire let his head fall against the high back of his armchair and raised his Barolo to his lips as he gazed at the loft's vaulted ceiling. 'Albanians,' he whispered. 'They're not exactly thick on the ground around here.'

'I didn't think they would be.'

'But there is one.'

McIlhenney sat a little more upright. 'Yes?' he murmured.

'There's a restaurant, in Elbe Street; it hasn't been open all that long. It's called Delight, would you believe? and it's supposed to be Turkish. The guy who owns it has a funny name: he's called Peter Bassam. One of my people was there for a meal a few weeks ago, and she got talking to him. She'd just been to Turkey on holiday, and she asked him what part of the country he was from. He said that although he'd lived in Ankara for many years, he was from Tirana. He laughed and said that he'd opened a Turkish restaurant because he didn't think he'd have any customers if he put "Albanian" over the door.'

'Have you been there?'

'No. She said it was okay, but not exceptional.'

'What wasn't?' asked Paula, walking towards them with Lou. In her left hand she had a bottle of mineral water, which she gave to Neil as she topped up Mario's glass with her right.

'The Turkish place in Elbe Street.'

She shuddered. 'Sheep's eyeballs and all that! No wonder it's only the Turks who eat there.'

Thirty-one

Willie Haggerty normally prided himself on his focus and his powers of concentration. Yet as he waited in the outer office of the Castle Street basement, listening to the secretary's fingers clattering on her keyboard, he found his mind wandering.

He had had his eye on the Dumfries and Galloway job for a while. It, or something like it, had definitely been part of his career plan. Yet now that the moment might be drawing near, and the finger of opportunity was being flexed, ready to point, he found himself strangely torn.

He had come to Edinburgh with mixed feelings, lured by Jimmy Proud and Bob Skinner, when his instincts had told him that he would find the place an alien environment after half a century of childhood, adolescence and an active police career in his bigger, and more dynamic native city.

And yet he had been proved wrong. He had enjoyed it from the start. The Edinburgh force was not small by Scottish standards, yet it was dwarfed by its monolithic Strathclyde neighbour, which was second in size in the UK only to the Met. Where he would have been struggling to know half the officers under his command in an ACC post in Glasgow, Haggerty had settled in far more quickly than he would have believed, and had built good working relationships with all the ranking men and women in the uniformed divisions that reported to him.

He had been looking forward to a couple of years more in post, before going for a top job, and so when the call had come from Geoff Dees, the Dumfries chief, giving him advance warning of his departure, he had struggled to sound enthusiastic at the pointed hint that went with it. Still, very few police officers enjoyed the opportunity

145

that was before him now and he knew that he owed it to himself, and to his wife, to go for it.

He was mentally planning his tactics at the interview, when the door opposite him opened, and a middle-aged man, dressed in a check shirt and faded jeans, beckoned to him. The secretary carried on typing as if nobody else was in the room. 'Sorry to keep you waiting,' he said, without sounding as if he meant it. 'I'm Tom Herron, the director of this organisation. Come on in.' The man looked harassed, and Haggerty found himself wondering what had made him that way, as he followed him into his office. It was furnished as shabbily as its occupant was dressed; its barred windows faced out on to a tiny courtyard, above which the policeman could see the grey stone buildings on the other side of Castle Street.

'What would they call all these places if there was no bloody castle?' he asked aloud.

As they settled into their respective chairs, his host gave him a look that questioned his sanity. 'Pardon?'

'Ach, don't mind me,' said the ACC. 'It's just the Glaswegian in me. Thanks for agreeing to see me, Mr Herron.'

The man nodded; his manner was suspicious, if not hostile. 'I don't have much time,' he said, 'so let's get on with it. How can Refuge Scotland be of help to the police?'

'I hope we can be of help to each other. We live in a changing world, even in Scotland, and even in Edinburgh. It's important that we keep up with events, so that our policing strategies are always relevant to the actual needs of the community.'

'Very praiseworthy, I'm sure, Mr Haggerty, but what does that actually mean?'

'Boiled down, it means that we need to know what's going on, all the time.'

Herron swung round in his wooden swivel chair; it was old, and it squeaked. 'I see, so I guessed right: this is a spying mission.'

'Not at all!' Haggerty protested. 'Why the hell are you folk in the voluntary sector always antagonistic towards the police?'

'Long experience.' The man pointed to the pile of papers on his desk. 'See that lot? A significant amount of that correspondence involves complaints against the police, or other public authorities. Asylum-seekers in this country are hustled around from pillar to post. Do you know that you can't seek asylum in Scotland any more? You have to go to Liverpool to do it, but the government won't help with your travel costs. That's one reason why organisations like mine exist.'

'You've heard this before, I'm sure,' the ACC retorted, 'but we don't make the law, we just enforce it. I'm not aware of a significant number of complaints against our force. Give me some examples.'

Herron bridled. 'Okay, let's look at people arrested on suspicion of theft. They're held in custody for hours, often for far longer than they should be.'

'I'm sorry, not often. We've had seven cases in the last year of asylum-seekers being arrested on suspicion of shop-lifting or other petty thefts . . . that's seven among many hundreds. If anyone was held for longer than normal it was because an interpreter was needed . . . an interpreter whose costs are met by the police service. I'm sorry, I'm not going to buy that one. I'm not here to antagonise or persecute anyone. I just want to pick your brains about what's going on out there.'

'Couldn't the Home Office tell you?'

'Do you trust information from the Home Office?'

The director swung back to face him, smiling for the first time. '*Touché*,' he said. 'Okay, pick away.'

'Thanks. I know that we have fewer asylum-seekers than they do in the west of Scotland, but we still have some arriving here. I'm interested in where they're coming from.'

Herron shrugged. 'My information is that most of them are from the sub-continent and Afghanistan. We have a well-established Asian community in the Edinburgh area, and it's natural that they should be drawn to cultures similar to their own. There are Iraqis, of course; Saddam drove a fifth of his population into exile, and they haven't all gone home. There are quite a few Turks as well; in fact, in Glasgow there are more Turkish refugees than from any other ethnic group. Then there are Somalis, Congolese, and people from several other African nations.'

'How about the Balkans?'

'It's got a lot quieter there in recent years. We took a quota of

Kosovars during the crisis, as you know, but most of them have been repatriated since the fall of Milosevic.'

'Albanians?'

'The Kosovars were ethnic Albanians.'

'I know, but I mean home-based Albanians.'

'They're negligible in Scotland as far as I know. There are some economic refugees from Albania, of course: it's a very poor country unless you're part of its Mafia. But as far as I know, most of them head for Germany.'

'Are there any here that you know of?'

'I don't know of any specifically, but if you ask some of the other charities, or even the local social-work department, they might be able to tell you. In any event, there won't be enough of them to require a separate strategy on your behalf.'

'So any that did show up here would tend to stand out?'

'I suppose they would, unless they blended with the Kosovars who are still here, or with another ethnic grouping; the Turkish community would be the likeliest, I'd say.'

'Mmm,' said Haggerty. 'That's very useful, thanks. I won't take up any more of your time.' He stood, watching his host raise himself carefully from his unstable chair.

'There's one thing I forgot to ask,' Herron murmured, as they moved towards the door. 'What is your rank, Mr Haggerty?'

'I'm an assistant chief constable.'

The director stopped and looked at him. 'That either makes you a very unusual copper,' he said, 'or it revives all of my suspicions about your visit. I've been around the police for quite a few years now, and I've had a few of your colleagues in this office. None of them ranked higher than sergeant. I've never known an ACC who did his own leg-work, and certainly not for a piece of routine fact-finding.'

Thirty-two

'How did you know about Jay's appointment?' asked Dan Pringle. 'It isn't the sort of thing that's put on the bulletin board. The command corridor's absolutely livid about it, I can tell you.'

Mario McGuire chuckled. 'I'll bet they are.'

'Even the chief, and it takes a lot to rile Proud Jimmy. So how did you find out?' The head of CID paused. 'Of course,' he exclaimed. 'Your big pal Neil: he'll have told you.'

McGuire caught the subtle change in Pringle's tone: he and McIlhenney were not bosom companions. 'Wrong,' he said. 'Someone beat him to the punch: I had a visit from the man himself yesterday. He sat right where you're sat now.'

'I hope you had the bloody seat sterilised,' the chief superintendent growled. 'I don't particularly mind him getting the job, but it's the way he went about it. Now he's gone and he's not under my command I can tell you that I never liked the man. He's as slimy as they come.'

'He worked for you in Division, didn't he?'

Pringle nodded. 'Aye, he did, briefly. When I took over as head of C division, CID, he was my second in command, but he got his own promotion and the move to Leith not long after that.'

'Who promoted him?'

'The head of CID of the day, Alf Stein. And do you know who he moved into Greg's job?'

'No.'

'Bob Skinner. He'd been Drugs Squad commander, but Alf wanted him back in mainstream CID. It was easy to see why: he was only there for eighteen months, then he was given Western division, and leapfrogged over us all when Alf retired, me, Greg, Roy Old, John

149

McGrigor. The rest of us could see it coming, but Greg was livid. He and Alf were Masons together and he'd thought the job was his.' He tugged at a corner of his moustache. 'So why did he come to see you?'

'I'm not sure. Maybe it was just to wind me up; if it was he succeeded.'

'I hope that's all it was,' said Pringle. 'He came to see me as well, yesterday morning, to introduce himself in his new role, so he said . . . although I don't recall ever having a visit from Sir John Govan when he was in that post.'

'What did you talk about? Old times?'

'Not for long. Your name came up pretty quickly. I don't know why, but he's got it in for you, son. He was asking about your split from Maggie and your relationship with Paula. Whether the second caused the first; you know.'

'I hope you told him to mind his own damn business.'

'I did, but I also told him what Maggie told me, that you and she had come to the end of the road, and that she bears Paula no grudges. It didn't stop there, though: he asked me about your business interests. I told him that as your line commander I'm happy with the arrangements you've made and, more than that, I know that the DCC and the chief are too. Did he raise any of this with you?'

McGuire nodded. 'The business part, yes; if he'd raised the other I'd have thrown him through the nearest window. He dropped some hints that I didn't like.'

'Such as?'

'Well, for a start, he said . . .' He paused as Pringle's mobile phone chirped a few familiar bars of the William Tell overture.

The head of CID grunted his annoyance as he took it from his pocket. 'Yes,' he barked.

As McGuire looked at him across the desk, he saw a sudden and awful change. His colleague's face grew ashen white, and he seemed to collapse into his chair. His mouth moved as if he was speaking but no sound came out. He tugged again at the corner of his moustache, but this time it was as if he was trying to rip it from his face. 'Yes,' he croaked at last. 'I'm still here. I can hear you. I just don't believe it, that's all. Yes, yes,' it came out as a moan, 'I'll be there.' He took the phone from his ear and jabbed at it as if to cancel the call, but his fingers were trembling. It slipped from his hand and fell to the floor.

'Dan!' McGuire exclaimed. 'What's up? What is it?' The man stared at him helplessly; tears filled his eyes and his mouth hung open. 'What is it?'

At last he responded. 'I've got to piss,' he mumbled, then jumped from his chair and rushed out and through the CID office.

McGuire followed him, ignoring the curious looks of his team. He pushed open the door of the male toilet; he found him standing in a stall, urinating, his shoulders shaking. A bell seemed to ring in his head, and he remembered the moment when he had been told of his father's death. He waited until Pringle was finished, and until he had washed his hands. 'It's family, isn't it?' he asked quietly.

'It's Ross, my daughter,' Pringle blurted out, choking back a sob. 'She's in a student flat on the Riccarton campus. They said something about a faulty gas fire. They said they couldn't revive her; the paramedics took her to the Royal. I've got to go there, Mario.'

He headed for the door, but McGuire blocked his way. 'I'll take you.'

'I'll drive myself.'

'You'd be a danger; I'm taking you, and that's it.'

Thirty-three

'Before I accepted this job,' said Bandit Mackenzie, 'I asked my wife if it was okay with her. She said that it was, not for the pay rise, but for the chance to move to Edinburgh. She thought that running the Drugs Squad here would be like running the marriage-guidance office in a convent. It hasn't taken long for her to know different.'

Neil McIlhenney laughed. 'What is it with you Weegies?' he said. 'There's a lot of money in this city; crime follows money, especially the drugs business. The profile might be different here . . . more coke-sniffing yuppies than in Glasgow . . . but it's active and it's profitable. Some very good coppers have had your job over the years and none of them have managed to shut it down completely. There's always someone new appearing on the streets.'

'That's what my wife's finding out.'

'Is she giving you a hard time?'

'The beginnings of a hard time. When we were wrapping up Jingle Bell's operation I had a few late nights. Now we're on this operation, I can see a lot more stretching out before me. I got in at three thirty this morning, and she was awake and waiting for me. Thank Christ we're living through here now, or it would be even worse. As it is, it's a matter of time before she starts to suspect that I'm porking Mavis.'

'Why would she think that? Have you got a track record?'

'No, but I might as well have. My wife's a very suspicious woman; she was sure I was having it away with Gwen Dell, my sergeant through in Lanarkshire. She was always dropping hints about us. Eventually I got fed up with it, so I bought a pair of very flimsy knickers off a stall at Barrowland market and left them under the passenger seat of my car. They were gone inside a week; she never said another word about it after that.'

'Jesus, that's a high-risk strategy.'

'It would have been, if I hadn't written "I love you, Cheryl" on them with a red marker pen.'

'What's your wife's name?' asked McIlhenney, casually.

Mackenzie opened his mouth to reply, but caught on, and laughed. 'Nice one,' he said.

'Have you got kids?'

'Three; two girls, and a boy in the middle. You?'

'Two and a half; Lauren's twelve, and Spencer's ten. The third one's due around next Easter.'

'How did they take to your new wife?'

'Great, especially Lauren. It's nothing to do with having a famous stepmother either. It gave her a chance to get her childhood back. After Olive died she decided that she had to look after me; that meant doing everything for me, except for the ironing. She was smart enough to let me do that. As for Spence, he's your average action man, a friendly, open kid. He accepted Lou from day one, and that was that.'

'It must be terrible to lose your wife so young. I don't know if I could cope with it.'

'You would, because you wouldn't have any choice, but I hope you never have to.' He leaned across Mackenzie's desk. 'Did you get any leads last night?'

'Nah,' his colleague replied. 'Not a sniff. We went to three clubs, but they were all quiet. We saw a deal go down in one of them, but we let it pass. It was small-time stuff, a bit of hash, and Mavis recognised the dealer. We can go back and get him any time.'

'Or trace him back to his supplier?'

'We know who that is already: it's an Irish team through in the west. If the Albanians had muscled in on them, we'd have found some bodies by now, or noticed a couple of people missing. How about you? Have you picked up anything?'

McIlhenney hesitated for a second. 'Maybe. We had dinner with Mario and Paula last night, and he mentioned somebody. There's no reason to doubt that the guy's legit, but I've got Alice checking him out. If it's worth following up, I'll take it to the boss.'

'Haggerty?'

'I don't report to him. Besides, he and your pal Green have got their hands full going round the charities and the social workers.'

'Rather them than me: it's like getting blood out of a stone, persuading the do-gooders to talk about their punters . . . sorry, their clients.'

'Willie Haggerty can be more persuasive than he looks.' He stood up. 'I'd better be getting back to my place. Are you and Mavis out on the razzle again tonight?'

'I'm afraid so.'

'Don't be afraid. There's worse ways to spend a night than clubbing with a big leggy female. You could be on the pandas in Muirhouse.'

Mackenzie sighed. 'Cheryl would prefer it I was,' he said. 'At least then she'd know when I was coming home.' He looked up. 'Where's the best place in Edinburgh to buy sexy knickers?'

'Wouldn't know, pal,' McIlhenney replied, cheerfully. 'I don't wear any.'

Thirty-four

Mario McGuire had done a police driving course early in his career. It showed as he carved his way through the traffic, along Seafield Road and then into Sir Harry Lauder Road, heading for the Jewel and the Edinburgh bypass.

Dan Pringle sat beside him, staring straight ahead but seeing nothing. 'They said they couldn't revive her,' he whispered, as they roared on to the A1. 'What does that mean, do you think?'

'They probably needed more equipment than they had in the ambulance,' McGuire suggested lamely. 'Don't worry, Dan. They'll have given her oxygen and everything.'

'Oh, Christ, I hope so.'

'Who was it that phoned you?'

'Ray Wilding, my assistant. There was a general 999 call; one of the officers who responded realised that it was my daughter. There was a photo on her desk and when they gave her my name as next of kin, he twigged who I was and called my office.'

'So nobody's called your wife?'

'I don't suppose so. Do you think I should?'

'It might be wise.'

Pringle took out his mobile and selected his home number; McGuire concentrated on the road, trying not to listen, but he found it impossible.

'Elma, hello, it's me. I'm on my way to the Royal. No, I'm fine, but there's been an incident with Ross, at the university. No, no, don't panic now; I'm just calling you because I thought you'd want to know. Aye, okay, if you want to come that's fine.'

'Tell her you'll have a car pick her up,' said McGuire.

'What? Aye, okay. Elma, just you wait there. I'll get a panda to pick you up. It won't be long. See you there; and don't worry.' He ended the call and looked round, helplessly. 'Who'll I call, Mario?'

'Wilding. Just tell him to fix it; nearest available car to your house, pronto, then to Accident and Emergency.' He braked, and swore, as he saw that the lights at Sheriffhall roundabout were at red, and that there was a small queue of traffic.

Fortunately it took less than two minutes to clear the junction, for Pringle was almost jumping out of his seat in his agitation. 'Nearly there, Dan,' Mario told him, as they headed through Gilmerton, ignoring the speed limit.

At last, the road signage told them that they had reached the new Royal Infirmary complex. They took the second entrance, and headed straight for the A&E unit, ignoring the car park signs. McGuire jerked to a halt a few yards away from the entrance, on a yellow line.

'You can't park there, Jimmy,' a security guard called out to him, before he had time to close the car door.

'Police,' he snarled, fixing the man with a glare that made him decide that he had more pressing priorities in his life. When he turned back towards Pringle he saw that he was gone, running past an ambulance that stood there, reversed into the wide doorway. It had no crew but its engine was still running.

He broke into a trot to catch up, reaching his colleague just as he arrived at the admission desk. 'Ross Pringle,' he heard him bark at the receptionist. 'She was brought here. Where is she?'

The young man looked up at him. 'Ross Pringle? We havenae had any guys brought in for a while. There was a girl just now, but that's all.'

'Where did they take her?'

'They just rushed her straight through to the emergency room.' He pointed towards a doorway facing the entrance. Pringle turned and ran towards it, with McGuire at his heels, ignoring the receptionist's shout: 'Hey, yis cannae go in there!'

They burst through the double door as if it was made of paper. The area beyond was divided into a number of cubicles. Three were occupied by patients whose injuries were visible and superficial; they were all unattended. The curtains were drawn across a fourth; from behind them, they heard the sound of quiet voices.

The realisation came to McGuire that they should hold back, but it came too late. Before he could stop him, Pringle stepped forward and swept aside the curtains.

Six faces turned to stare at him, but he was unaware of any of them: all he could see was the slim figure lying on the table. She had dark hair, close-cut in a page-boy style. She was barefoot, and wearing pyjamas. The jacket was open; her small breasts were uncovered and several coloured stickers were attached to her chest, leading to a monitor, on which a fluttering heartbeat showed. They could not see her face, for most of it was covered by an oxygen mask.

Nobody spoke. The medical staff continued to stand there as if frozen, gazing at the newcomers. If Pringle was aware of their presence, he gave no sign of it. His eyes were fixed on the table, and on his daughter.

And then he seemed to slump into himself; his knees buckled, and he might have fallen if McGuire had not caught him by the elbows and supported him. 'Come on, Dan,' he murmured. 'Let's just go next door and take care of you.'

Pringle said nothing, for he was incapable of speech, but he allowed himself to be steered into the next, empty, cubicle and sat down on a chair. A white-coated doctor followed. 'The father?' he asked. McGuire nodded. He leaned towards the shocked, ashen figure. 'It's not good, I'm afraid,' he said gently. 'She had a cardiac arrest as she arrived here. We've managed to resuscitate her, but by the time she was found her body had been almost completely starved of oxygen. I wish I could tell you that she'll be all right, but I can't.'

Pringle blinked and looked up at him. 'What? Eh? Aye?' he mumbled. He turned to his colleague. 'Mario, she's not going to die, is she?' He was begging for an answer that could not be given. McGuire, big and hard as he was, found that he could not bear the weight of those eyes on him. A lump came to his throat; he gazed up at the ceiling, fighting to keep his own control as he heard the first sobs.

'What am I going to tell Elma?' Dan Pringle moaned. 'What am I going to tell her mother?'

Thirty-five

'Have you heard?' Bob Skinner asked, as McIlhenney came into his room, but the sight of his friend's expression gave him all the answer he needed.

'About Dan's daughter? McGurk told me just now. She's in a deep coma, he said. Bloody awful isn't it? Just turned twenty apparently. The big lad out there's in a terrible state. He was friendly with the Pringles, and so he knew the girl very well. Gas, was it?'

'So Jack told me. Ray Wilding said something about a faulty room heater.'

'She was in student accommodation, wasn't she? Surely these things have to be inspected annually.'

'I've no doubt they are. The university'll be all over it, but I've told Jack to get one of the technicians from our forensics lab out there to examine it.'

McIlhenney sighed. 'What a bloody week we're having,' he exclaimed. 'First George Regan's lad, and now this.'

'I meant to ask Dan about the Regan investigation this morning. I'd better give Mary Chambers a call instead.'

'She'll tell you that they're ready to send the file to the Fiscal as an accidental death. At least that's what Maggie told Mario yesterday.'

'Mmm,' Skinner murmured. 'I'm glad that's sorted. I'm desperately sorry for George and his wife, but a formal verdict is probably the best way for them to get closure. That could be a long way off for Dan and Elma, though, I reckon.'

'Maybe, but I'm not so sure he'll recover as well as George Regan. He's older, and he's tired, plus…'

Skinner nodded. 'I think I know what you mean. Dan's quite a volatile guy under the surface and, let's not mince words, we all know he likes a drink.' He frowned. 'Neil, if it comes to it, you know about bereavement counselling; could you give him any advice?'

'If I thought he'd take it from me, sure, but given that he and I aren't close, it might be better if you suggested it to him . . . and to George, for that matter. There's an organisation called Cruse; it's national, but it has branches here. All its people are trained to a pretty high standard.'

'Do they help?'

'They helped me.'

'Give me the details, and I'll pass them on.'

'You could get the human-resources people to do it,' McIlhenney suggested.

'I know I could, but there are some things I don't delegate.'

'There are many things you don't delegate.'

'So it's been said,' the DCC admitted, with a brief smile. 'Anyway, you wanted to see me. What's up?'

'It's the Albanian thing, and it might be as well if Amanda Dennis was here.'

'She and Green are using a room along the corridor. I'll ask her to join us.' He made the call; the two men sat and waited for around a minute, until the door opened and the MI5 officer stepped into the room.

'Thanks, Amanda,' said Skinner, once she was seated. 'Neil's got something for us. Fire away, Chief Inspector.'

'Yes, sir. My wife and I had dinner with Mario McGuire...' he looked at Dennis '. . . he's a friend of mine, a detective superintendent in Leith . . . and Paula last night, and he and I had a private discussion. Don't worry,' he said hastily, 'I didn't spill all the beans, but I did ask him if he knew of any contacts. He gave me a lead, to a bloke who runs an allegedly Turkish restaurant down in Leith, only he's not Turkish by birth, he's Albanian. He goes by the name of Peter Bassam.'

'Indeed?' He had Dennis's attention. 'Have you had him checked out?'

'First thing this morning. Alice Cowan ran him down with the DSS and the Home Office immigration section; she found out that he's here because he's got a German passport, thanks to his grandfather, an SS officer who deserted to Albania from Greece when the Germans got out of there, and sired his mother. He applied for citizenship through the German embassy in Turkey four years ago and it was granted.'

'So he's legit: he has a right to be here?'

'Yes, he's a European Union citizen.' McIlhenney smiled. 'But there is one thing about him that caught my attention, thanks to young Alice, who dug deep enough to find it. He calls himself Peter Bassam, but that's not the name on his passport. His given name is Petrit Bassam Kastrati.'

Skinner chuckled. 'Is it indeed? I can understand why he doesn't use his surname, but why did he change the other, I wonder?' He looked at his colleague. 'Sounds as if he bears investigation. Any ideas?'

'I've got one. While Alice was doing her research, I took a run down to Elbe Street and checked out his place. It was closed, of course, but he's got a sign in his window saying that he's looking for a waiter.'

'And you were thinking?' Dennis asked.

'I was wondering, to be more accurate, whether Sean Green has any experience in that line of work.'

She looked at Skinner. 'Sean's experience is pretty broadly based. He's been under cover in pubs before now; I'm sure he'd be prepared to play the waiter. Is this a formal request?'

The DCC considered the question, then nodded. 'I reckon it is. Do you have to clear it?'

'Only with Sean; I never force people into undercover assignments.' She smiled, fondly. 'He's never turned one down, though.'

'Okay, ask him. He'll need a new identity, references, and the ability to back them up. How long will that take?'

'That can be in place tomorrow. But what about the state of his face? Won't that invite questions?'

'Sure, but that won't be difficult. Couldn't you build it into his cover story, as a reason for being sacked?'

'Screwing the chef's wife at his former place of employment, for example? Good idea: he could certainly pull that off. It would be quite in character in fact. My only small doubt is that he's been exposed in this city only recently.'

'We can take that chance,' said McIlhenney. 'Clubbers don't eat Turkish in Leith. They hang out in the yuppie bars in George Street and go on from there.'

'In that case, I'm convinced. We'll give him a hair-dye job and spectacles as added cover, just in case, but let's go. He'll need an address, but I can do that. Let's just hope that sign hasn't gone from the window by tomorrow.'

Thirty-six

Andy Martin had the greatest respect for his chief constable. Graham Morton had been in post for almost as long as Sir James Proud, although he was still a few years short of the compulsory retirement age, and he was regarded as one of the leading figures in the Association of Chief Police Officers Scotland.

Nevertheless, Martin was cautious as he faced his boss across the desk of his office in Dundee. 'What line do you think that ACPOS will take over the First Minister's new appointment?' he asked.

Morton leaned back in his chair, scratched his square, bald head and considered the question. 'I think that at the next meeting there will be a lot of huffing and puffing. I expect that Dees will lead the charge: he says that the moment he heard about it he decided to retire.'

'And do you believe that?'

'Not for a minute.' The veteran chief constable chuckled. 'Geoff told me in private six months ago that he was planning on spending Easter with his son in South Africa, and maybe not coming back till the summer. His resignation's been in for a fortnight, and he's persuaded his board, which does not have a Labour majority, to fill the post as soon as possible.'

'I'm told that Murtagh's planning to take a greater interest in the police service,' said Martin, 'and that this appointment's just an opening shot.'

'It wouldn't surprise me. Even when he was on the council here, wee Tommy was a bit of a control freak.'

'You know him well?' asked Martin.

'Well enough; I was in post all that time, remember. I confess that I was quite relieved when he left to become a Westminster MP for a constituency over in Fife.'

'What sort of man is he?'

'Take the following three words: cunning, ambitious and bastard. They just about sum him up.'

'You missed out "talented".'

'So I did,' the chief constable admitted, 'and I should have included it. I can't deny him that. Mr Murtagh has a talent for climbing. He started off as a labourer on a building site, and in no time at all he was a general foreman.'

'A wee chap like him? Building sites can be hard places.'

'Don't let his size fool you, Andy. He's as hard as nails; the legend was that a big brickie had a go at him one day and wee Tommy laid him as broad as he was long. Real foreman material from the start, you might say. Anyway, he gave that up pretty soon and went to Dundee University as a mature student; he did a degree in politics and economics. He was elected to the council in his final year, and when he graduated he went back to work for his old firm, Herbert Groves Construction, with the title of contracts manager.'

'And did his firm win many council contracts?'

'They got their share, but Tommy always declared an interest at every stage, and the officials always noted these in the minutes. But the fact was that he didn't need to vote in the debates: the council was heavily Labour, and his colleagues voted the right way. To be fair, most of them were competitive tenders and Groves came in with the lowest quote.'

'Insider knowledge?'

'There was never any evidence of that, and none of the unsuccessful firms ever complained.'

'What was Councillor Murtagh's lifestyle like?'

'Pretty decent, but the company was successful. So why did he give it up to become an MP? That's what you're going to ask next, isn't it?'

'I suppose so.'

Morton smiled. 'He never said, but we all just assumed he'd out-grown Dundee. I wasn't sorry to see him go; there was talk of him becoming chair of the police authority, and I did not want that to happen. You see, he was anti-police even then, Andy.'

'Why?'

The chief constable raised his eyebrows. 'I'm damned if I know.' He paused. 'I do know this, though: you've been picking my brains.'

'No, I haven't, Graham,' Martin protested. 'We've been talking about something that concerns you as much as it will everyone else. What I began by asking, if you remember, was what you think ACPOS will do if he comes after us. You still haven't answered.'

'You're right, I haven't. Okay: ACPOS will talk around it behind closed doors and then we'll decide to do nothing at all. I had Jimmy Proud on the phone this morning, dropping the same hints you are, and trying to talk me round to the view that we can't afford to have a public fall-out with the First Minister.'

'And did he succeed?'

'Of course he did, because he's right. I don't trust Tommy as far as I could chuck you, but he's a persuasive wee sod, and he knows which of the public's buttons to push, and when. We might not like him, but we can't oppose him overtly. I suspect that you know that too.'

It was Martin's turn to grin. 'And that's why you were feeding me all that information about him?'

'Was I? And here was me thinking we were just passing the time of day.'

'Of course we were, Graham. Is there anyone else I could pass the time of day with, anyone who knew him better than you in the old days?'

The chief constable paused for thought. 'His worst enemy on the council was Diana Meikle, the Tory leader. She's out of politics now, like most of the rest of the Tories, but she's still around. She lives up in Broughty Ferry, if you want a chat with her.'

Martin nodded. 'Thanks.'

'And then there's Roy Greatorix. Our head of CID's been around for as long as I have, and there's nobody has his ear closer to the ground. It'd be worth talking to Roy, but . . .'

'But what?'

'But be very careful, and trust no one. I can read what's going on,

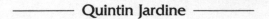

and I can guess who's behind it. Just remember, the guy's network is everywhere, and it's still at its strongest here. You've got a fine career ahead of you, son, even if it's not going to be on Tayside in the long term, or maybe even in the short term. I'd hate to see your head being one of the first that Mr Tommy Murtagh sticks on a pole.'

Thirty-seven

Willie Haggerty liked being home. As he drove along Argyle Street the old song rang out in his head: 'I belong to Glasgow, dear old Glasgow town . . .' He did too. He had been born in Rotten Row, the city's bizarrely named maternity unit, and brought up in a council house in the Garngad, a part of the city that spawned few policeman.

Leaving the place had been a wrench, but he had spent his career waiting for an offer he could not refuse, and when the ACC job in Edinburgh had been offered to him on a plate, he had gone for it in an instant. Truth be told, it was not the attraction of working with Jimmy Proud and Bob Skinner that had lured him across the country. No, it was the fact that service at command rank in another force would make it easier for him to achieve his dream, his ultimate ambition, to command the Strathclyde Police Force, Britain's second largest after the Met. It was still a long shot, he knew, but the Dumfries and Galloway post, if it came off, would take him one step closer. Service at chief constable rank was a prerequisite for the top job, and with a couple of years under his belt...

Haggerty thought through his rivals and came up with only two names, both of whom he knew well: Skinner himself, and Andy Martin. Yet he had heard Bob mutter often enough that he had no ambition to be sidelined, as he put it, into a chief's office. As for Andy, if he was ever to land the Strathclyde job, given his age it would almost certainly be after his own turn had come and gone.

There was something else. He had been sanguine about his chances of landing the post . . . two of them, slim and none, as Muhammad Ali had said famously . . . but the events of the current week had made him think again. At first he had been as outraged as Skinner and the chief when he had been told, in confidence, of Tommy Murtagh's plan to take effective control of the police, until another thought had come to him.

Was the First Minister a politician? Yes. Did politicians, by the very nature of the word, love populist gestures? Yes. So how much more populist could you get than by appointing a boy who had escaped from the war-torn Glasgow housing schemes as head of the city's police force?

It was a thought that he had kept to himself, yet it was preying on his mind.

He pushed it away as he swung into Kelvinhaugh Street, then took another turn to his left a little further along. It was still there, and as he had suspected it had not seen a lick of paint in the three years since his last visit. The Argyle Kebab Parlour stuck out on the corner of its neglected street like the last tooth in a derelict's mouth. Haggerty wondered if the doners were still as good as he remembered.

He parked his car directly outside the scruffy shop . . . so that it would always be in his sight . . . and walked inside. He smiled as he looked at the posters on the wall; they were a mix of Galatasaray and the Turkish national squad, revered in some parts of Scotland since their baiting of the English side in a European qualifier. It was well before noon and so there were no customers, just a young man behind the counter firing up the gas jets below the great roll of meat, on its vertical spit, the trademark of Turkish takeaways. The boy, who was no more than seventeen, turned and stared at Haggerty, as if he resented his intrusion. 'Can ye no' read?' he asked. 'It says on the door we're no' open till twelve.'

'I can read, Bulent,' the police officer replied. 'That's why I'm here now. Is your father in?'

The question was barely finished before a bead curtain at the end of the counter was roughly parted; an older man appeared, shaking off its fronds as he stepped into the front shop. 'I thought it was you,' he said. He was built like a beer barrel with short limbs and a round head. In contrast to his son, who spoke pure Glaswegian, his accent was still heavy and redolent of his native land.

'How goes it, Rusty?' Haggerty greeted him, as the two shook hands.

'Same as ever, as you can see,' replied Rustu Kerimoglu. 'How goes it with you? I thought we'd seen the last of you, since you became a great man in Edinburgh.'

'You thought wrong, then. You know what they say: they can take the man out of Glasgow . . .'

The Turk finished the homily for him. '. . . but they can't take Glasgow out of the man. No, they can't, can they? Someone should develop a vaccine, maybe.'

'None of us would take it.' He glanced at the younger Kerimoglu. 'Isn't that right, Bulent? Once a Weegie, always a Weegie.'

The boy gave him a small grin. 'Maybe,' he murmured.

'So what brings you back?' asked Rusty. 'Don't tell me you missed our kebabs: they're not so good that a man would drive fifty miles for one.'

'They're not bad, though. You get that spit fired up, son; I'll maybe have one before I leave.'

'Come on through the back,' said the older Kerimoglu, turning and parting the curtain. 'Bulent,' he called back over his shoulder, 'you keep an eye on Mr Haggerty's car, now.'

The two men stepped into a back room that was part store, part kitchen, part sitting room. Rusty had been preparing salads on a big well-scrubbed table. This struck Haggerty as odd. 'Where's Esra?' he asked. For as long as he had known the Turk, in all the twenty-five years and more since he had opened his shop, his wife had done that job.

The man smiled. 'She's retired, Willie,' he replied. 'When the boy left school a year ago, I decided that she'd spent long enough cooped up in here. It only takes the two of us to run this place, so now, with our Mata coming in to help out when I want a break, she's completely a lady of leisure. It's great, I tell you; for the first time in our married life I get something other than kebab or pizza for my dinner. She's been going to cookery classes. And,' he added with pride, 'she's learned to drive. We even went up to Oban last weekend.'

'Was there anything to do there?'

Kerimoglu's face split into a broad smile. 'As it happens, no, but it was a nice drive.'

Haggerty gave a small shudder. 'You'll not be doing that this week-end,' he muttered. 'From the look of the weather we're in for snow.'

'Good. It'll keep our customers here.' The Turk paused. 'So, my old friend, what can I do for you?'

Haggerty grinned. 'Probably nothing, Rusty,' he said. 'Remember a few years back, when I was in Special Branch, and I used to pick your brains about things that were happening in the Muslim community? Well, it's a bit like that again.'

A look of alarm crossed Rusty's face. 'Al Qaeda? You don't suspect that those guys are still active here, do you?'

'No, we're pretty confident that we've seen them off. But there's more than them in the field. For example, there are Albanians.'

'More's the pity.'

'You don't like Albanians?'

'I don't like any I've ever met. Why? Are you looking for some?'

Haggerty nodded. 'As it happens I am. A guy in Edinburgh said I should look among the Turkish community: you know more about that than anyone else, hence this visit.'

'Any names?'

'None they'll be using. Are there any around in Glasgow that you know of?'

'There are some who made their way over among the Kosovar refugees, but very few. Most of them are old, or they're professional people looking to retrain over here. But you're an Edinburgh police-man now. Why do you come looking in Glasgow?'

'We're looking for these people everywhere.'

'Are they very bad?'

Haggerty took an envelope from his pocket and handed it to Kerimoglu; he watched as he slid it open and looked at each of the four photographs inside. The Turk winced as he finished. 'They look bad, that's for sure. Can I keep these?'

'No, I can't let you. It wouldn't be wise, or safe.'

Rusty held out a hand. 'Let's have another look, then.' He took the envelope as it was handed back and spread the images on his table. He was standing over them, peering intently, when Bulent pushed his way through the curtain.

'Who are those guys?' he asked. Instinctively, his father tried to put his body between him and the table, but the young man shouldered past him.

'You don't need to know,' said Haggerty. 'Just . . .'

'Aye, but I do know him,' Bulent exclaimed, pointing eagerly at one of the photographs.

The stocky policeman's eyes narrowed. 'Are you serious?' he snapped.

'Sure, Ah'm serious.' The boy picked up the print and held it up: it showed the smiling face of Samir Bajram. 'He was in here the other day with two other guys; they bought four doners and a pizza.'

'You're certain it was him.'

'Dead certain. He was wearing an Ajax baseball cap . . . you know, the Dutch fitba' team . . . and he still had thon earring in. He's got a fair, fuzzy beard now, like bum fluff, but it was him, Ah'm telling ye.'

'Okay, I believe you, son,' said Haggerty. 'Now, what about the people he was with? Do you recognise any of them there?'

Bulent leaned over the table, and looked at the three remaining photographs for around half a minute, before glancing up at Haggerty and shaking his head. 'Naw,' he announced, 'they're no' there. But I knew one of them, mind. We call him Frankie Jakes, but he's a Macedonian. He's a hood; he deals smack and tabs in Partick; drinks in a pub called the Johnny Groat.'

His father stared at him, appalled. 'How do you know these things?'

The boy smiled indulgently. 'Ah went tae school in Partick, Dad, remember? Plus Frankie's brother, wee Bobby, plays fitba' wi' us in the Tuesday half-day league.'

Rusty turned to Haggerty; the policeman could see the concern on his face, and knew why it was there. 'Okay, Bulent,' he said. 'Now listen to me. You've never seen that man before in your life. You've never heard of him, you've never heard of me, and I was never here. Understood?'

The smile was gone. 'Clear as day.'

'Next time you see wee Bobby, you do not go and ask him about his brother or his mates. Understood?'

'I get the picture.'

'No, you don't, and you don't want to know what's in it.' Haggerty turned to his friend. 'Rusty, I'm out of here. I'm sorry I parked my car outside. What I just said to Bulent . . . it goes for you too.'

The Turk nodded. 'Sure, Willie. And not for the first time either: it's been a long twenty-five years. Next time, just come for a take-away.'

Thirty-eight

Neil McIlhenney smiled as he stepped into All Bar One; for the first time in days he felt refreshed. The dream had not returned the night before, and he put it down to Lou's excellent consultation with her obstetrician, the Amanda Dennis lookalike, who had told her that all was well with her pregnancy and that she could look forward to delivering a healthy child in a few months' time, wiping away her last concerns about becoming a first-time mother at forty plus.

But there was more than that behind his grin. His lunch date had made him think about where he stood in his career, and he felt good about that too. In his early years as a policeman, his service had been solid but not spectacular. He had been like a stereotypical cop, overweight, a shade heavy-handed and more than a little cynical about the character of his fellow man.

It had taken Bob Skinner to look into him and see what else was there. Under his tutelage he had developed both as an officer and a man. At first he had wondered why he was being favoured, but as he had come to know the Big Man, he had come to realise also that he surrounded himself with people whose values reflected his own.

Now he was prepared to admit to himself, and to anyone else who asked, that in his early years he had been freewheeling, holding down a nice cushy job which, with his late wife Olive's teaching salary, had given them a comfortable if not opulent standard of living. It had taken Skinner, then head of CID, before his move to the Command Corridor, to draw out his best and largely untapped qualities, identifying him and his mate McGuire . . . known to most of their colleagues in those days as the Glimmer Twins, for their joint love of a bevvy and of the Rolling Stones . . . as two under-performers with much more to offer the force.

Mario's special gift, apart from sheer innate ferocity when in a threatening situation, was a cool analytical brain, inherited from his mother and his grandfather, Papa Viareggio, who had founded the family's small business empire. His had been the ability to size people up and to know instinctively who was a straight-shooting, valued contact, and who was simply shooting the breeze.

His lunch companion had arrived before him. She was sitting at a table, away from the other diners, in the furthest corner of the restaurant; it was a converted banking hall, as were half of the other eating places in George Street. She was in her forties, plump, with shiny black hair that was swept back and held in a short pony-tail, and she wore a dark, heavy sweater and a long grey skirt. She glanced up as he approached. 'What happened?' she asked. 'You're ten minutes late. Couldn't you find a parking place?'

'As it happens you're right,' he told her. 'It's a real bugger in the Christmas period, even at lunchtime.'

'I thought you guys didn't have to worry about yellow lines.'

'Tell that to the Blue Meanies,' he retorted. 'We hate them just as much as you civvies do. One of them put a ticket on the chief constable's car a few weeks ago, even though he had left his uniform cap on the steering-wheel.'

'Did he pay it?'

McIlhenney nodded. 'The chief is like that.'

'Is the guy still in a job?'

'That I do not know, and I don't want to.' He settled into the seat facing her.

'I've ordered lunch like you asked,' she said. 'Soup of the day . . . it's minestrone . . . and a chicken salad. Are you sure you want salad? It's December, Neil.'

He patted his stomach. 'Why get fat just because it's winter?'

She shuddered. 'God, you self-control freaks! I remember you when you were a porker. You weren't sanctimonious then.'

It was true, he conceded to himself. He and Debbie Wrigley did go that far back, to the days when he had been a beat cop and she had been an assistant manager in the Clydesdale Bank. He had taken a statement from her after a bungled robbery . . . as most of them were . . . and they had struck up an instant friendship.

They had both moved on since then, he through the ranks and into the Special Branch office, she to the National Mutual, where she was a general manager with responsibility for the private-client division.

'Did you order us drinks?' he asked her.

She nodded. 'A glass of red wine for me, and a spritzer for you.' She pulled a face. 'A spritzer, for Christ's sake! What happened to the three or four pints of lager? Are you up yourself, or what? Is this what happens when you marry an actress?'

He grinned. 'No. It's what happens when you decide that you'd like to live to see your kids grow up, and maybe even your grandkids.'

As he spoke, their first courses and their drinks arrived at their table.

'So what's the honour?' Debbie asked, as she picked up her fork to attack her calamares Romana. 'It's got to be serious if you're paying.'

'It is,' he said, testing the temperature of his minestrone. 'I'm doing a heavy vetting job on one of your clients. I want to know everything about him without him or anyone else finding out.'

She whistled. 'You don't ask small favours, do you?'

He smiled at her, cheerfully. 'No, I only give them.'

She looked him dead in the eye. 'I take it this is in the national interest.'

'My colleagues and I think it is.'

'So who's the client?'

McIlhenney waited until she had forked a large piece of battered squid into her mouth. 'Tommy Murtagh,' he murmured, then smiled as her eyes bulged and her round face reddened.

'To…' she gasped. 'How did you know that he was a client of ours?'

'Your manager in Dundee was best man at his wedding; call it an educated guess. Will you do it?'

'Are you serious?'

'Never more so.'

'I'd be putting my arse on the line, never mind my career.'

'They'll both be in good hands.'

She looked at him, for a long time. 'Well, you make damn sure you don't drop them,' she said.

Thirty-nine

Excitement and Willie Haggerty did not go hand in hand, yet as he stood in the DCC's office, the assistant chief constable looked about to burst. Skinner could not keep his amusement from showing. Even Amanda Dennis was smiling.

'It's great when we get a result, Willie, isn't it? I heard an author say once that the best bit about his job comes when something appears on the page as he's writing it that not even he expects. It's the same for us detectives. When we walk into an interview and something happens that we weren't looking for at all, we get a buzz like . . . Ah, you know what I mean.'

Haggerty beamed. 'It's even better when the guy who gives you your break isn't even in the interview in the first place. If young Bulent hadn't come into the kitchen for the salads when he did, I'd never have known any better.' He paused. 'How do we find out about this Frankie Jakes character?'

'Not through the SDEA, that's for sure,' Skinner replied. 'They'd want to know why we were asking, and since we've agreed to keep them out of it, that could be awkward. I've got a contact in the National Criminal Intelligence Service; I can try her in confidence. If he's a small-change guy, though, they might not know too much. While they're looking, let's ask nearer home.' He picked up a phone on his desk and dialled a number. 'Bandit? You're in, good. This is the DCC; come up to my office, now.'

The three waited. 'I heard about Pringle's girl,' Haggerty said eventually, breaking the silence. 'How is she?' he asked Skinner.

'Gravely ill, and unlikely to get any better. I checked with the hospital just before you got here. The consultant's due to meet with

Dan and Elma any time now, to give them a full rundown on her condition.'

There was a rap on the door, and then it opened: Bandit Mackenzie breezed into the room. 'Yes, sir,' he exclaimed, then saw the others. 'Sorry, sirs and ma'am. What can I do for you?'

'Do you still have friends in Glasgow?' Skinner asked. 'By that I mean do you have friends in the CID at street level, that you can trust to be discreet?'

'One or two, boss. Gwennie Dell, my old sergeant in the northern division, works out of Baird Street now. Why?'

'I want background on someone, a bloke who goes by the name of Frankie Jakes. He's a dealer who works around Partick, in and around a pub called the Johnny Groat.'

'Why are we interested in him?'

'Because we've got a confirmed sighting of Samir Bajram in Jakes's company,' said Haggerty, with a hint of pride.

'Where did this come from?'

'You don't need to know that.'

'Do you know Jakes yourself, Bandit?' asked Skinner.

'Never heard of him, sir.'

'Do you know or are you known in the pub I mentioned?'

Mackenzie shook his head. 'I've never worked in Partick, and I sure as hell wouldn't drink there out of choice.'

'Good, because I want you to start now. Use your contact through there to get info on Jakes and known associates, and get her to show you mug-shots if they have them, so you'll recognise them.'

'What do I tell her if she asks why I want this?'

'Tell her more or less the truth, that something's come up in Edinburgh that Jakes is linked into and that it's very hush. What you don't tell her is that you'll be hanging about the Johnny Groat this weekend, waiting for Samir or one or more of the others to show up again.'

'Alone?'

Skinner almost replied, 'No, I'll be with you.' It was on the very tip of his tongue. Then he thought of promises made, of a football match, of Deep Sea World, and he had a vision of a small boy's hurt if they were broken. He frowned. 'Your wives will both hate me for it, but you'd better take Neil with you. I reckon that Mavis might attract too much attention in a boozer like that. Besides, if you do get into bother . . .'

'He can handle himself, then?'

'You'd better believe it. But he can also shoot straight. We have to assume that the Albanians will be armed, so you guys will be too.'

Bandit grinned. 'If we have to shoot somebody that'll kind of blow our cover, won't it?'

'You let me worry about that. But please, try not to. If Samir shows up, do no more than tail him; if all of them appear, get word to me, or to Amanda, but otherwise do nothing without further orders.'

The DCC saw Haggerty's frown. 'What if they do get rumbled, Bob, and all the team are there?'

'Why should they?'

'I could go too.'

Skinner chuckled. 'Willie, I've seen you at firearms practice. If you fired a warning shot in there you'd miss the ceiling. Besides, your mug's well known in Glasgow; you've probably lifted half the guys in that pub in your time.'

'Could we get a few SAS in there in plain clothes?'

'Maybe we could,' Dennis conceded, 'but do you really want to fill the place full of strangers?'

'Maybe not,' the ACC conceded.

'Plus, it would be overkill,' said Skinner. 'Let's be clear this will be an intelligence-gathering operation, no more. If these guys have jumped to Glasgow, against expectation, the objective is to find out where they're based. Once we know that, we can take them out at a time of our choosing, hopefully when we've identified the fifth guy.'

'Frankie Jakes couldn't have been the fifth guy, could he?' asked Mackenzie.

'Unlikely. If it was him, why did he come to Edinburgh when they could have jumped off the flower truck in Glasgow earlier in the day?'

'Granted.'

The DCC raised an eyebrow. 'Thank you, Chief Inspector. Okay, time's pressing. Call your contact through in Glasgow and get what you can from her. If you need to go through there to meet her, do it. I'll brief Neil when he gets back from his lunch date. On your bike.'

Mackenzie nodded and left, with Haggerty at his heels. Dennis remained behind. 'I could have a detachment of special forces close by, just in case,' she said.

'Too many people on the ground, and unnecessary at this stage,' Skinner maintained. 'Look, if things really do look like going pear-shaped, we can have a Strathclyde armed-response team there pretty fast. But somehow I don't think they will. Frankie Jakes is supposed to be Macedonian, according to Willie's contact. Maybe he's just another cousin, and Samir went to look him up. This investigation is full of maybes.' He looked at her. 'How are you coming along with Sean Green's new identity?'

'It's done. This afternoon he'll be ready to call Bassam and ask for an interview for the job. After that we trust to luck and Sean's persuasiveness, which can be pretty effective, I assure you.'

'Good. Maybe this weekend we'll find out what we really need to know . . . what the hell these guys are doing here.'

As Dennis nodded agreement, the phone rang on Skinner's desk: his direct line. He picked it up, his mind still on their discussion. 'Yes?' he exclaimed, not realising that he sounded irritable.

'I'm sorry,' said Sarah. 'Have I called at a bad time?'

'No, no,' he assured her quickly, then put a hand over the mouthpiece and turned to Dennis. 'I have to take this,' he told her. She nodded and left.

'Sorry,' he said, as the door closed. 'I had someone with me.'

'Something important?'

'Very.'

'Another shitty fan, eh, Bob? That's the story of your life.'

'I wish my life was that simple. Where are you?'

'I'm still in Key West, but not for long. I'm about to check out.'

'You're coming home, then?' Part of him wanted to add 'please', yet the rest felt ambivalent.

'Not straight away. I'm going back to Buffalo; I've made some decisions and I need to be there to put them into effect. I'm going to sell all the property there, both my parents' house and the up-state lakeside cabin; the cars as well, the furniture, everything. I'm finished with that city, Bob.'

'And once you've done that?'

'Once I've instructed estate agents, and all the other people I need to see, I'll come back to Scotland to you and the kids.'

'Still in time for Christmas, though?'

'Of course.'

'And after that?'

'I'll tell you when I see you.'

He felt his stomach flip. 'Not "we'll talk about it"? You'll tell me?'

'I'm sorry: that was badly put. When I get back we'll sit down and have a discussion and compare our respective ideas about the future. How's that?'

'Come on, Sarah,' he said. 'What do you mean by that?'

'Leave it. I'm sorry I said it. I'm not going to discuss the state of our marriage over the phone. How are things with the Justice Minister, incidentally?'

In spite of himself, he bridled. 'You can leave that out, too. You're the one living in the . . .' He stopped himself before 'glass house', but she caught his meaning. There was a long, expressive silence.

'How did we get like this?' she murmured, eventually.

'We've just lost the plot, honey, that's all,' he replied, wearily. 'Can we pick it up again?'

'I don't know. That's what I don't want to discuss at long distance. I'll see you in a few days.' She hung up, leaving him staring out of his beloved office window on to a world that was in danger, for the first time in his adult life, of moving out of his control.

Forty

As soon as she stepped through the front door Maggie kicked off her heavy black shoes and climbed the stairs to the bedroom. Twenty minutes later she had showered, towel-dried her thick red hair and changed into a sweatshirt, jeans and slippers.

As she stepped into the big kitchen she glanced at her watch, wondering what had delayed Stevie, until at that moment she heard his key turn in the Yale lock. She was there to kiss him as he stepped through the door. 'Hi, boy,' she greeted him. 'What kept you?'

'Mary,' he said. 'She wanted to fill me in on the latest about Ross Pringle.'

'Mmm,' Maggie murmured. 'That's terrible, isn't it? How is she? What did Mary say?'

'She's still unconscious, and nobody's taking any bets that she'll ever come round. Apparently Dan's just devastated. He collapsed completely at the hospital. They had to sedate him, then Mario took him and his wife home. He wouldn't let her hand go, apparently.'

She frowned. 'The whole thing's tragic,' she said. She led him into the kitchen and poured him a large glass of red wine from a bottle that had been left over from the previous evening, then went to the sink and drew herself a large glass of water from the tap. 'I'm not surprised that Dan's taken it like that. It's in contrast to the way George Regan's handling his loss, but they're very different people. Dan's emotions have always been closer to the surface.'

'Plus, he's older,' said Stevie. 'He probably figures he owes it to his wife to be with her.'

'I doubt it. Elma's always struck me as the stronger emotionally of the two of them. I'd guess that he needs to be with her.'

'Are there any other kids?'

'They have a son, Samuel. He's at least ten years older than Ross, maybe more than that; he works in Hong Kong with a merchant bank. I don't think he and Dan got on: he never talked about him much.'

'They'll have to get on now.'

'It might not be as easy as that. Closeness between parents and kids isn't something that can be switched on at will.'

He sipped his Coronas. 'You sound bitter when you say that. Personal experience?'

She nodded, looking at her glass. It was empty, so she refilled it. 'Yes. My mother and I never got on; it wasn't my fault, at least I don't think it was. There was no bond between us, that's all.'

'And your father? You realise you've never talked about your parents?'

'My father's dead. I've never talked about him because I don't want to, don't want even to think about him, ever again. Does that shock you?'

'No. If he makes you sound like that, I don't want you to think about him. I'll never ask you again, I promise.'

Her smile returned. 'You know, Stevie Steele, you can be a real love sometimes.'

He chuckled. 'Only sometimes?'

'Okay, all the time. But some times even more than others, like yesterday, when I told you my news. Honestly, I wasn't sure how you'd take it, with us still being so new to each other. But you looked so happy, you made me want to cry.'

'If you're right, I'm still just as happy, I promise you. You're still sure, are you?'

'Yes, but I'm a copper, so I need evidence.' She reached into her handbag, and held up a package wrapped in paper. 'I can't wait any longer. I left a bit early today so that I could go into a chemist where nobody was likely to know me, and I bought this. It's a testing kit.'

He laughed out loud. 'I wondered why you were drinking all that water.'

Maggie patted her stomach. 'It's having its effect, too.' Still holding the kit, she headed for the door. 'I won't be long . . . at least I don't think I will.'

'Do you want me to come with you?' He was joking, but for a second she took him seriously.

'I know how to aim, thanks,' she retorted. 'Shut up or I'll use your beer tankard for the sample.'

He watched her as she climbed the stairs, then drained his glass. As he poured himself a refill, he realised that his hands were trembling and that his heart was beating fast. He walked to the window and looked out into the night. The weather had become progressively colder, and he thought that he could see a few snowflakes in the beams of the streetlights. He smiled as he dreamed of building a snowman in the garden.

He was lost in his thoughts and so he did not hear her come back into the kitchen, until she coughed quietly behind him, to attract his attention.

He turned. Her face was impassive, and her hands were behind her back; and then a grin turned quickly into a beam as she held up a white plastic strip. 'I got a black dot,' she said. 'Congratulations, Dad.'

Forty-one

Bob Skinner felt a pang of shame as he stepped through the front door: he had never set foot in the Pringles' house before, something that he regarded as a major sin of omission, since he was on calling terms with most of his senior colleagues. And beyond his guilt, he felt a great weight upon his shoulders. It was Friday morning; he tried to recall a more stressful week in his professional or his private life, and found it impossible. There was the time he had been stabbed, of course, but he had been out of it for the worst of those days.

Elma stood aside to let him in. 'It's good of you to come, Bob,' she whispered, making him feel even worse.

'No,' he replied, automatically. 'It's the least I could do.' He followed her into the living room, and recoiled slightly at what he saw. Dan Pringle sat slumped in an armchair; he was wearing a heavy cardigan over a white shirt; it was open at the neck and he saw the flesh hanging loose and flabby. His face was streaked and his eyes were red. He clutched a glass of whisky in his right hand, and Skinner guessed that it had just been refilled.

The chief superintendent looked up at him; for a second his eyes were blank, then as recognition set in, he made to rise, until the DCC waved him back into his chair. 'I'm sorry, Dan,' he said, as he sat on the couch to his left. 'I am so sorry.'

'Aye, Bob.' The words cracked in his throat. He picked up a glass of water from a small table at his side, and drank from it. 'It's a terrible thing to lose a child,' he went on, his voice steadier. 'I never thought it would happen to us.'

'Come on, now,' said Skinner. 'Ross is still alive; there's hope.'

'Since when were you a neurologist?' Pringle snapped at him, rejecting what they both knew was a platitude. 'She's in a deep coma. They say that if she does come round, she'll be seriously brain-damaged. That's what gas does to you.'

Skinner was aware of Elma, taking a seat on the couch beside him. 'They're not giving us any hope at all, Bob,' she said quietly, more in control than her husband. 'The doctor we spoke to said that there are only minimal signs of brain activity. They're going to observe her for a wee bit longer. Then, when we've all had time to reflect, they're going to talk to us about what her future might be. At least, that's how they put it.'

The DCC thought of Alex: she was only a few years older than Ross Pringle. 'Jesus,' he whispered. 'They haven't pulled any punches with you, have they?'

'We wouldn't want them to. Dan and I find that it's better to face the truth from the start than to have the rug jerked out from under us later.'

'Have you thought about what you'll do?'

She nodded. 'Yes, we have. Whether we'll be able to do it when the time comes, that's another matter, but we've reached a decision, one that we believe Ross would support.'

'Have the crime scene people finished?' asked Dan, abruptly.

'Yes, they have. In part, that's what I came to tell you. Arthur Dorward told me that the supply pipe to the heater was loose. There was enough getting through to make it function, but some gas leaked very slowly into the room. It built up over a matter of hours, until it reached lethal levels.'

'Was the room not ventilated?'

'Yes, but the vent was closed. It's winter and the things can be draughty, so they're often slid shut. To be honest, mine often are at home, the way the wind comes off the river sometimes.'

'The pipe was loose? How could that happen?'

'More easily than you'd imagine, according to Dorward. The two sections were linked by a bolt, and it's probable that it was accidentally kicked loose. A bump against it at the right angle might have been enough.'

Elma sighed. 'By what a fine thread a life can hang. We are all clinging to the planet by our fingernails, when you think about it.'

'Maybe it's best not to think about it,' said Skinner, quietly. 'If we did, we'd never get up in the morning, and we'd never let our kids outside.'

'George Regan will be wishing he hadn't,' Dan muttered morosely.

'No,' the DCC countered. 'George will not wish that. He let his boy grow up in the real world, and he didn't try to stop him being all the things a boy is. Suppose wee George had been locked in every night, likely he'd have found a way out. Give them freedom you're giving them respect, and respect is what you get back.'

'So what made him try to climb the castle rock by moonlight?'

'The romance of it, puberty . . . who knows? It beats me. But he did, that's all there is to it. What made Ross, or one of her pals, bump against that bolt and loosen it? Fate, Dan.'

Pringle gave a huge sigh. 'I suppose,' he exclaimed, glancing at Skinner. 'Do you ever worry about your own kids?'

'All the bloody time, man, in every way. My five-year-old son beat up two kids at his school not so long ago for calling him a copper's bastard or some such. My older one's so mathematically bright I fear it might consume everything else in his life. My younger daughter would stick her finger in an electric socket to see how it worked, if her nanny didn't watch her constantly. And even my older daughter isn't immune to trouble, although she seems to be living a very quiet life since her engagement broke up.'

'That won't last,' Pringle growled.

'Probably not.' He paused. The conversation was beginning to unsettle him. 'Listen,' he said, 'back to you. Is there anything, anything at all, that we can do to help you? Transport to the hospital, for example: just call the office and there'll be a car here for you. If things go better than you expect, and you need advice on care of the disabled, that sort of thing, ask and we'll arrange it.'

'That's good of you, Bob,' said Elma Pringle, evenly, 'but there's really only one thing you could do for us. Would you please process Dan's retirement as quickly as you can? We've discussed this over the last few hours, and we're agreed. However it goes with Ross, even if there's a miracle, I want my husband at home with me, for his own good and mine.'

Skinner looked from one to the other. 'Are you sure?' he asked.

'Dead certain,' Pringle replied. 'I'm sorry if it causes problems for you; I know you were looking to me to stay the course until you had an obvious successor ready, but the truth is, man, I'm done. I know what you're going to say. You're going to tell me to wait until I'm less emotional, then think it through again. I'll do that if you insist, but I tell you now, the decision will be the same. Guys like you and me, we evolve backwards, Bob. Alongside these young guys, I feel slow, I feel tired, and I struggle to keep up with them, let alone command them. I wasn't always one, but now I've become a dinosaur, and I know it. So's Jimmy Proud, only it hasn't dawned on him yet. You should watch for the signs yourself . . . they might be a few years off yet, but you'll see them, and when you do, you'll know, if you're honest with yourself, that your time's up too. So let me go now, eh?'

The DCC looked down at the carpet, then back at the head of CID. 'You want it, Dan,' he told him quietly, 'you've got it. Give me a formal request to retire when you feel like putting it on paper; meanwhile I'll get it under way.'

'Thanks, Bob,' the veteran replied. 'I'm sorry I barked at you earlier on. You know, even when you were working for me and I was giving you a chasing, I always knew that you were a good guy.' He forced a smile. 'And there's one good thing. At least you won't have Greg Jay lobbying you for my job.'

Skinner would have laughed, but in that room of mourning he found himself unable. 'As if I'd ever have listened to him,' he said, as he rose.

Forty-two

'Delight' was pitching it a bit strong, Sean Green thought, but overall the place was not too bad. The furnishings were reasonably comfortable and, from what he had seen on his way through to the small office behind it, the kitchen looked clean.

'Hello,' said the bald, thick-set man behind the desk, as he rose to his feet, 'I'm Peter Bassam. You're the guy who phoned about the job?'

'That's right,' he said, extending his hand. 'John Stevenson.'

'Do you have references?' Bassam's English seemed impeccable, although his accent reminded Green of a Turkish villain in an old James Bond movie.

'Sure.' He took an envelope from his jacket and laid it on the desk. 'Plus there's a list of the places I've worked.'

'Where are you from? You don't sound Scottish.'

'Neither do you,' he responded, with a grin. 'I'm from Sussex originally; I came to Scotland a couple of years ago.'

'Why?'

'Girlfriend. I met her in Brighton, and followed her up north. She lives in Stirling so I took a job there.'

'Why are you moving on?'

Green fingered his nose, tenderly, under the new, plain-glass spectacles. 'Because her husband found out.'

'Ahh,' Bassam exclaimed. He grinned, and Green knew in that instant that he had the job. 'Always a risky game, my friend. What did the husband do?'

'He was a wholesaler; only a little guy, but he knew a couple of big guys.'

'This place you worked in Stirling, what was it?'

'Asian.'

'And before?'

'In Brighton? Asian again, but before that a couple of Cordon Bleu places, the kind where you're embarrassed about the size of the portions you're bringing to the table.'

'You won't have that problem here, I promise.' Bassam opened the envelope and slid out five sheets of paper, all different colours. 'These are all glowing, I take it,' he said.

'They're all honest. You'll find addresses and phone numbers on every one. Please, check me out.'

'I will, don't worry.' Somehow Green doubted that he would phone them all, but if he did, each call would be switched to an operative who would endorse the testimonial. 'When will I hear from you?' he asked.

'Where do you live?'

'I've rented a place in the West Port.'

Bassam glanced at his watch. 'That's good. Get yourself home and make sure you've got the proper dress for the job. My waiters are all expected to come to work in a clean white shirt, black trousers, black shoes and socks; we supply the red tie. Come back for six this evening, John, and I'll give you a trial.'

Green smiled. 'Thanks very much,' he said, meaning it. He shook Bassam's hand again as he rose.

'Just one thing,' said his new employer, with a raised eyebrow. 'If you ever meet my wife, don't get any ideas. The people I know break much more than noses.'

Forty-three

Andy Martin had passed through Broughty Ferry only once or twice since his move to Tayside, and he had never stopped there. It was not the type of place to give the police any trouble, and so there was little reason to go there other than to show the flag and keep its people content that they could sleep safely in their beds.

Councillor Diana Meikle, retired, slept safely in hers, that was for sure, thought Martin, as he approached her house, in a leafy street a few rows inland from the esplanade. Two large alarm bells were fixed to the facade of the detached villa, one above the garage, the other above the front door, and a sign on the wall advised that the premises were monitored by a security company. Since the house was probably listed, the policeman wondered if it had occurred to Mrs Meikle to seek planning permission for the installation, but he dismissed the idea as none of his concern.

The front door was opened by a maid attired in a black uniform. Andy remembered his father telling him, long ago, about an old doctor he had known whose household had a domestic servant, but he had supposed that, in urban Scotland at least, those things had died out with the tramcars.

'Who shall I say is calling, sir?' asked the woman, who looked not far short of sixty.

'Deputy Chief Constable Martin,' he told her. He had come in plain clothes, not wanting to advertise his visit. 'Mrs Meikle is expecting me.'

Clearly, the maid had known this all along, but she had been following the routine of a lifetime's service. 'Come this way, sir,' she said, 'and I'll announce you.' Stifling a smile, he followed.

He was shown into a conservatory, a great solid construction that had probably been built with the house itself, rather than one of the mass-produced extensions that the previous owners of his own home had added. Diana Meikle was pruning a bush as he entered. He had no idea what it was: he left gardening to Karen. The former councillor turned to greet him. 'Mr Martin,' she boomed, extending a hand in a way that seemed to invite either a kiss or a handshake. He chose the latter. 'Thank you, Gretchen,' said Mrs Meikle, dismissing the maid. He noticed, near two wicker armchairs, a table set for afternoon tea, complete with an old-fashioned cake-stand, adding to the impression that he had stepped back into his grandparents' time.

'Come and sit down,' his hostess instructed. For all the trappings around her, she did not seem in the least old fashioned. She was not much older than her maid and was dressed in slacks and a light blouse that had probably come from Marks & Spencer. 'Find me odd, do you?' she asked, reading his mind. 'Don't blame you. My late husband, God bless him, was quite a bit older than me, and I was middle-aged myself when we married. Gretchen was his maid; he was in shipping, and it was the norm in those circles. After he died I kept her on because I knew that's what he would have wanted. When you've been in domestic service for as long as she has you can't just go and work in a shop, can you?'

She poured two cups of tea and offered one to him. He took it, adding a little milk, but no sugar. 'Cake,' she offered, 'or a meringue?'

'No, you're quite right,' he said, helping himself to a plate, and a chocolate éclair.

She smiled at him as she sank into her chair and he perched uncomfortably on his, balancing the crockery. 'So, Deputy Chief Constable,' she began, 'what brings you here? When Graham Morton called to arrange your visit, he said there were a few things you wanted to discuss with me, but he wasn't specific. He did, however, use the word "discreetly". That suggests that you want me to spill some beans. Since there's nothing in my life of any interest other than my days on the council, I assume that's what you want to talk about.'

'Correct,' said Martin, laying the plate on the floor while he sipped his tea. 'You were a regional councillor rather than city, yes?'

'Indeed; and I still think that abolishing the regions was a great mistake. I served for ten years till the electors bumped me off. The Tories are an endangered species in most of Scotland; here we're pretty much extinct.' She looked at him sagely. 'I suspect that doesn't bother you.'

'It does, though,' he countered. 'How I vote isn't relevant; I believe that there should be the widest possible choice.'

'Say no more,' she announced. 'You're a Liberal.'

'Whatever I am, don't hold it against me, please.' He was warming to the woman.

'I promise you, it's nothing to me,' she said. 'Politics are a thing of the past for me; I often wonder why I became involved in the first place. Because of my husband, I suppose: he talked me into standing for the council. Now he would have held it against you. He hated the Liberals; he was very proud of the fact that his father was active in the defeat of Winston Churchill in Dundee in the 1922 election.'

'Churchill was a Conservative, surely,' Martin exclaimed.

'Only when it suited him, my dear. But you didn't come here for a history lesson, did you?'

'Not that far back, no.' He looked at her. 'Mrs Meikle, can I count on your absolute discretion?'

'When you can't I'll stop you,' she promised.

'Fair enough. In that case, what can you tell me about Tommy Murtagh? I gather that you and he were on the council at the same time.'

'That odious little man!' she exclaimed. 'Yes, we were, more's the pity. If the people of his ward had seen through him thirteen years ago, the first time he stood, we might have been spared a lot. You'll be familiar with the phrase "something of the night". When I sat opposite him in the council chamber I found it difficult to see anything of the day in Mr Murtagh. It simply appals me that he's now our country's First Minister. I argued long and hard against devolution, and I was in the foreground of the "No" campaign in the referendum. I warned that something like this would happen and now I've been proved right.'

Martin waited for the storm of her indignation to subside. 'I gather that Murtagh had a meteoric rise though the local Labour Party,' he said. 'Do you know if he had any particular mentor at the time?'

'Brindsley Groves,' she said at once. 'Old Herbert was still around when Murtagh was a youngster, but he spent most of his time on the golf course by then, or at least in the bar. His son ran the firm with very little input from him. It was pretty well known that there was something between him and Murtagh's mother, and that Brindsley made him a foreman because of it, helped him through university, then gave him a management job afterwards.'

'Did Groves benefit from it?'

'Council contracts, do you mean? Of course he did, but we could never prove it.'

'How did he take it when Murtagh opted for a parliamentary career?'

Diana Meikle looked down her nose, as if she was inspecting one of her potted plants. 'He engineered it; at least that's what I heard. There was another runner for the seat, but he decided to pull out at the last minute. The word was that he had something nasty in his past involving little boys, and that the people behind Murtagh had unearthed it.'

'The mother's dead now, isn't she?'

'Yes. She lived long enough to see her son elected to Westminster, and died the same year. Tommy told me, in one of the few civil conversations we ever had, that she had chronic kidney disease, and it affected her heart.'

'Does he have any other family in Dundee? His father, for example?'

'No, Tommy's parents lived in Derbyshire when he was born. The family, or at least he and his mother, moved up here when he was four.'

'Why Dundee?'

'I have no earthly idea.'

'Why didn't the father come north with them?'

'He was dead by then. He was a motor mechanic; the story was that he was killed in a work accident when Tommy was a baby. The mother took a job as a clerk in Herbert Groves's office; that's where she met Brindsley. He'd have been in his mid-twenties at the time; he's late-fifties now.'

'She was a widow, and yet you're saying their relationship was a secret?'

'It was from Celia, Brindsley's wife.'

'Ahh.' Martin chuckled. 'They must have been married young.'

'They were.' She gave a wicked smile. 'Contraception was much less reliable in those days, you know. The pill wasn't as readily available then as it is now.'

'How many children do they have?'

'Two; a boy and a girl. The son runs a tea-importing business; he and his father fell out years ago, and have barely spoken since. The daughter married a doctor and moved to London. They're not the happiest of families, although Brindsley and Celia are still together.'

'Murtagh doesn't have any siblings as I understand it.'

Diana Meikle frowned. 'Who told you that?'

'I've read his official party biography: it says he's the only child of George and Rachel Murtagh.'

'Maybe so, but he's not his mother's only one. She had a daughter when Tommy was about ten. She took her mother and brother's surname, of course, but all the gossip said she was Brindsley's. This is Dundee, though: the talk never got to where the rich people live.'

'Where's the daughter now?'

'I have no idea.'

'Do you remember her name?'

'Funnily enough I do: she was called Cleo.'

Forty-four

'Your source is secure, is it?' Skinner asked Bandit Mackenzie. 'She's not going to talk to a pal about your visit?'

'Gwennie? No, she'll keep it tight. I trusted her with a few things when we worked together, and she did likewise.'

'I won't ask.'

'Nothing too serious, I promise. The main thing is that she won't let me down.'

Skinner looked at the photographs on McIlhenney's desk. 'These are originals. What if someone notices they're missing?'

'They won't: Jakes isn't top priority just now. But if someone did ask, Dell would just roll her eyes and look innocent.'

'She takes chances for you, this girl.'

Mackenzie grinned. 'She has an extra incentive.'

'What might that be?'

'She fancies a transfer to Edinburgh. I told her you could swing it for her.'

The DCC laughed at his sheer audacity. 'And she believed you?'

'Of course, because it's true. You can do that, boss ... you did it for me.'

'Hah! You flatter yourself: I brought you through here to take a load of trouble off the hands of my chief officer colleagues in Strathclyde. I was doing them a favour, not you.'

'That's not what my ACC said when he approved my transfer; he called you a thieving bastard, sir, as I recall.'

Skinner grunted. 'Ungrateful sod. She's good is she, this DS Gwen Dell?'

'I rate her.'

'Tell her to apply for transfer, then. I'll keep my hands off it, though; I'll arrange for the new head of CID to process it.'

'Eh?' Neil McIlhenney exclaimed, sharply.

'Within this room for now, please, till there's an official announcement.' Skinner told the two chief inspectors of Dan Pringle's decision. 'I have to respect his wishes,' he said. 'I thought about trying to talk him out of it but, honest to God, he's a broken man.'

'So who . . .?'

'I haven't had time to think about that, Neil. It's an appointment I didn't think we'd have to make for another year or two. For the moment, I'll do the job myself, till the present crises are over.'

'What?' Mackenzie intervened. 'We've got more than one?'

'Always,' Skinner shot back, covering his slip of the tongue. 'Did you think you'd come to a cushy number?' He leaned on the desk. 'Let's concentrate on this one for now, though. Frankie Jakes.' He jabbed a finger at one of two images on the desk: it showed a man with dark, scowling eyes, a low forehead, and a scar on his stubbled chin. 'This ugly boy. What did Dell tell you about him?'

'Age twenty-nine, or at least that's what his asylum documents said. They also gave his real name as Branko Janevski, and his home city as Skopje. He was granted asylum five years ago, on the ground that he'd been ethnically cleansed, but the view in Strathclyde CID is that you couldn't cleanse Frankie with a high-pressure hose.'

'Do they know of any Albanian connection?'

'That's why he was allowed to stay. A lot of Macedonians have ethnic Albanian origins; when things went nasty in the break-up of Yugoslavia, they were persecuted. A lot were killed; the younger guys like Frankie got out any way they could and headed for Calais.'

'What about his criminal activity?'

'Small time; that's what I was told. He's suspected of dealing, as we knew already, and of being hired muscle for gangs across the river. His name was mentioned in connection with a shooting in Paisley a while back, but only in the passing, and he wasn't even interviewed. He has a couple of arrests on his record, but no convictions. The closest shave he had was two years ago, when he was caught with a supply of ecstasy tabs. He was going to be charged with possession with intent to supply, but the drugs got nicked from the evidence room before he got to court.'

Skinner tapped the other photograph. It showed a much younger, less menacing man, clean-shaven with slightly frightened eyes. 'Who's the other guy? "Bobby Jakes", it says here.'

'That's right; his real name's Bobi Janevski, Frankie's wee brother, said to be nineteen years old. He came over with him, and he's never far from his side. They share a flat in Dumbarton Road. He was lifted along with Frankie on the ecstasy thing, but that's the closest call he's had.'

'Okay, those are the guys; what about the pub?'

'The Johnny Groat's an old-fashioned boozer in Cameron Street, not far from where they live. The owner has half a dozen small pubs, with a manager in each. He lives in Skelmorlie and he doesn't give a shit about them. It's run-down and shabby and so are the punters. The local CID look in every so often, but they can't be everywhere, and there never seems to be much happening.'

'What's your cover story when you're in there?'

'If anyone asks, we're night-shift porters at the Western Infirmary,' McIlhenney told him. 'We've just been transferred from the Royal; that's why we're not known around there.'

'Sounds okay,' the DCC conceded. 'So, when will you be in there?'

'Tonight. I've got someone to see here, and then we'll be off.'

'Have you told your wives what you're doing?'

'No detail, obviously. Stake-out is near enough to the truth.'

'How did Lou take it?'

'She didn't press me on it, but I can tell she's worried.'

'How about your wife, Bandit?'

The chief inspector shot him his most disarming grin. 'Her exact words, boss? "Jesus Christ and General Jackson, David, not another weekend up the bloody spout!" She's well used to it by now.'

Forty-five

Andy Martin had respected Rod Greatorix from their first meeting in his own early days as head of CID in Edinburgh. They had both been detective chief superintendents then, opposite numbers in their respective forces, and he had found his colleague to be a ready and valuable sounding board.

If Greatorix had ever resented the younger man's appointment to the Tayside deputy chief constable post, he had kept it to himself, and their good working relationship had continued in their new circumstances. Thus when Martin invited him to lunch with him in his office, there seemed nothing unusual about it.

As they ate, their conversation across the table had been restricted to golf, and to the unlikelihood of either being able to play that weekend as the weather closed in. It was not until they had reached the coffee stage that the DCC turned to what was on his mind. 'How long have you been in post, Rod?' he asked.

'Twelve long bloody years, Andy. Your old colleague, Dan Pringle, is the same age as me, to within a month, and he's only had his job since you left it. Are you going to tell me I've been in it too long?'

The question took Martin by surprise. 'God, no!' he replied. 'You're one of the biggest assets this force has got. The chief and I are only sorry that you can't do another twelve long bloody years.' He paused. 'You should be sitting in this office, you know. It didn't occur to me when I applied for the job that my conscience would bother me after I got it.'

'Then let it rest in peace. Nobody was ever going to appoint someone my age to chief officer rank, and you know it.'

'Maybe I do, but maybe also I don't agree with that, as a matter of principle. You earn things in this life. You earned the silver braid on your hat and the lift in your pension. It's not your fault that my predecessor was only a couple of years older than you and chose to sit out his career here until the last possible moment.'

'There was nothing to be done about it, though, was there? And anyway, it was my own fault: I could have had an ACC job in Inverness ten years ago, but my wife didn't want to move up there. So don't you worry about that; I'm content.'

'I'm glad for you,' said Martin, 'for I'm not.'

Greatorix was taken aback. 'Why the hell not? You're on a fast-track to the stars, son. What have you got to be worried about?'

'The future, Rod; not mine in particular, but everybody's in this service. Have you heard any talk about a new bill that's coming up in the Parliament?'

The older man chuckled. 'I'm long past bothering about those things. Let them get on with it, I say.' He sipped his coffee. 'But I thought this new Justice Minister was supposed to be a good act. With her in post, why are you concerned?'

'Because she's not calling the shots. This new bill, Rod, it'll be introduced next week. Let me tell you what it does.' As he explained the powers that the new measure would confer upon the First Minister, he watched Greatorix's expression become more and more sombre.

'Surely he's not going to use them,' he argued. 'When he says they're only for extreme situations, shouldn't we believe him?'

'Rod, when this becomes law, all promotion short-lists at assistant chief rank will be referred to him automatically. If he's not going to look at them as a matter of course, why do it at all? The betting is that he will use the powers. He's already made one private threat to a senior officer who crossed him. You were here before Tommy Murtagh, and you were in a position to watch him operate as a councillor. You tell me that he can be trusted with overall command of the police.'

The chief superintendent sat silent for a while, gazing through the window at the grey day. The snowfall of the previous evening looked to be on the point of returning. Finally, he gave a great sigh. 'I can't tell you that, Andy. The fact is that he's one of the last men I'd trust in that position.'

'When he was a councillor, was he ever under investigation?' asked Martin.

'Informally, yes. A council employee once came to a colleague of mine, a guy who's retired now, and complained that Herbert Groves Construction had insider knowledge in three successive contracts. He pointed out that their bids were submitted last, in each case, and that they were lowest, in each case, by only a few hundred pounds.'

'Who signed them?'

'Brindsley Groves.'

'And the investigation?'

'I didn't involve myself, but it was abortive,' said Greatorix, wearily. 'My colleague had a quiet word with the chief executive, behind Tommy's back, but there was absolutely no evidence of a fiddle.' He paused. 'Listen, Andy, if you're looking to dig up dirt on Murtagh, you're not going to find it in the council. In fact, I don't think you're going to find it at all. I've never seen anyone who can cover his tracks better than him.'

'What about Groves?'

'If you want my advice, be very careful around him.'

'Funny,' Martin mused. 'The chief told me to be careful as well.'

'Take heed, then. Brindsley's smart, and if he twigs what you're up to he'll be on to Tommy like a shot.'

'What sort of a man is he?'

'Dynamic would be a good word for him. He's not a bit like his father, young Herbert, was.'

'Young Herbert?'

'Aye, he was the second generation. His father founded the firm and he was named after him. The business was solid, but getting stagnant, until Brindsley took over control. When he was at university, he used to work on projects in his vacation. He studied every trade, until he could judge the quality of every piece of work on a job. After he graduated, he went into management straight away; in theory he was assistant to his dad, but after only a couple of years he persuaded him to take a back seat. He took accountancy in his degree, and one of the first things he did was to retire the finance director, and replace him with someone who knew what he was doing. By the time he was thirty, he'd taken Herbert Groves Construction from being a cosy wee Dundee company, and turned it into one of the most successful building contractors in Scotland.'

'And somewhere along the line, he took Tommy Murtagh under his wing.'

Greatorix smiled. 'Who else have you talked to about this?'

'Diana Meikle.'

The smile became a chuckle. 'She'll have marked your card, then. She hated Brindsley from the off. She reckoned that he supported Labour for business purposes, and that he sponsored Tommy for the same reason. She was bloody right, of course. I suppose she'll have told you about Brindsley and Rachel Murtagh too.'

'Yes, and about their daughter.'

'Ouch! That was naughty of her.'

'You seem to know a hell of a lot about Brindsley Groves,' said Martin.

'I should do,' Greatorix murmured. 'He's married to my sister.'

The deputy chief constable gasped in amazement. 'Jesus, Rod,' he exploded, 'you might have told me that earlier.'

'And spoil my big moment? Never!' He chuckled. 'Don't worry, Andy. None of this'll get back to him. I'm as worried as you at the idea of wee Tommy with all that power over the police.'

'I guess that when Graham warned me to be careful, he meant in speaking to you.'

'I guess; he probably assumed you'd know that Brindsley and I are related. To tell you the truth, I'm surprised that you've never met him. He's a pretty noticeable guy in Dundee. It's time I fixed that for you: come with me to the golf club tonight when we finish. He's always in the bar with his pals from about five thirty on; I'll introduce you.'

'You're on. I'm curious to meet this guy now. Tell me, does he still have Murtagh in his pocket?'

'He never did,' said Greatorix. 'Their relationship benefited them both. It wasn't just a case of Tommy using him as a ladder. As far as I can tell that's all in the past. Each one's served his purpose for the other, so they don't see each other at all now, or at least hardly ever.'

'And what about Cleo, the daughter? Where is she now?'

'I don't know, Andy, and I don't want to. I don't believe that my sister has any idea of her existence, and I want it to stay that way. She left Dundee long ago, and I've no idea what happened to her.'

'Did Brindsley acknowledge her at all?'

'From what I heard, he did; he provided for her, sent her to a good school and then to university. I wish he'd been as kind to my niece and nephew. Young Herbie can't stand him and Rowena couldn't leave home fast enough.'

'From the sound of things, you're not all that keen on your brother-in-law.'

'Frankly I'm not: to me, he was always a cold fish, and he's got worse in recent years. I think that Rachel Murtagh was maybe the only person he ever really loved.'

Forty-six

Paula Viareggio usually lunched alone, in her office, so Mario's call suggesting that they meet in a restaurant near his office had taken her by surprise. The place had looked unimpressive from the outside, but the food, if not delightful as its name suggested, had been good, and value for money too.

'So what prompted this?' she asked, as they sipped the incredibly strong Turkish coffee.

'Nothing,' her cousin-lover replied. 'Somebody at work mentioned it, and I thought it was time we gave it a try, that's all.'

'Who owns it?'

Unobtrusively he pointed a finger at a bald, stocky man standing behind a tiny bar in the far corner of the dining room. 'He does, or so I'm told.'

Paula glanced around her. 'It's just as well his kitchen's better than his décor,' she muttered. The restaurant's predominant colour was red, with garish flock wallpaper that might have come from the seventies, and a thick acrylic-fibre carpet. Even the two overworked waiters wore red ties and aprons.

'You should offer to give him a make-over.' He chuckled. Paula had been mulling over the idea of backing an ambitious young designer in the start-up of an interiors business.

'Ah, but could he afford us? The place is busy, sure, but he's not making much from the lunch trade. Still, I suppose the idea is to entice people like us into coming back at night.'

'Which we're not going to do; I was curious about it, but I won't rush back for a proper meal.' Mario finished his coffee and signalled for the bill. 'Don't base your business plan on it, love,' he advised her.

'Whatever your bright girl advised him, he'll always want this place looking like a harem.'

'You're still not sold on the new venture, are you?'

'If you've got your heart set on it,' he told her, 'I'll go along with it, but it's against my instincts, and Alex Skinner's advice. It's not a natural expansion for the Viareggio group, in that it bears no relation to our existing areas of business. You ask yourself, what would your father or our grandfather have said about it?'

'Nothing,' she conceded glumly. 'They'd just have laughed. Okay, I'll drop it as far as the group's concerned, but . . . I might put some of my own money into it.'

'Fine, you've got enough since you sold those saunas.'

'Not all that much: your mother had an interest too, remember.'

'That is something I'd rather forget.' He slipped two ten-pound notes into the folder that held the bill, and accepted their overcoats from the owner.

'Thank you, sir,' the man said. 'Are you in business around here?'

'Yes, we are.'

'Then maybe we'll see you again.'

Mario smiled at him. 'That could happen,' he replied.

He held the door for Paula, and they stepped outside into Elbe Street. Snowflakes were drifting gently to the ground, a sign of worse to come, according to the morning's weather forecast.

Her car was parked outside; she offered him a lift back to his office, but it was no more than a quarter of a mile away, and so he chose to walk. 'Are you going out with the boys tonight?' she asked, as she fastened her seatbelt.

'I was, but Neil's working somewhere so he called off. He's asked me if I'll take Spence to the mini-rugby tomorrow.'

'If it's on,' she pointed out. 'They won't let the kids play in the snow, will they?'

'Probably not. But I've thought of that, and if it happens, I've got a fall-back plan for him, and Lauren too if she wants.'

'But you're not doing anything tonight?'

'No, so I'll make dinner at my place, yes?'

She smiled. 'And breakfast.'

She drove the short distance to her office, and parked in her allotted space in the reserved section, on ground that the Viareggio Trust owned. Officially, she and Mario were joint trustees, but in practice they ran the family's enterprises as if they were directors of a conventional commercial group.

She hurried out of the snow and took the lift up to the third floor, stepping out into the small reception area that doubled as her secretary's work-station. Danni was at her desk as usual, but she was not alone. A slim man, with muddy grey eyes, was seated on the couch reserved for visitors; he rose as she entered, stretching out to his full height. 'Hello, Paula,' he greeted her. 'Nice to see you.'

She frowned at him. 'Mr Jay. This is a surprise. What can I do for you?'

'A word in private would be good.'

Paula made no attempt to hide her irritation at his presence. She looked at the wall clock and said, 'I can give you fifteen minutes. I have some important calls to make this afternoon.'

He laughed. 'Come on, lass, you can spare me more than that. I'm important too, you know.'

'Fifteen minutes,' she repeated harshly, 'and you're using them up. Come on through.'

'Would you like coffee?' asked Danni.

'No thanks. I've just had some and Mr Jay won't have the time.' She led the way into her newly redecorated office; it looked out on to the Scottish Executive office building and, from a certain position, to the new Ocean Terminal complex. As she settled behind her desk, she saw that the snow was starting to fall more heavily.

'What do you want?' she snapped, as Jay settled into an easy chair, one of two selected by her designer *protégée*.

'Don't be so tetchy, lass.'

'Don't call me lass.'

His false smile vanished. 'Very well, Miss Viareggio, if that's the way you want to play it. I'm concerned about your relationship with Detective Superintendent Mario McGuire.'

She started out of her chair, but with supreme self-control, settled back down, fixing the man with a glare that would have chilled the snow outside. 'And what Goddamned business is that of yours?'

'As I said, I'm concerned about it.'

'In what respect? Are you jealous?'

'If I was younger I might have been, but that's a side issue. What you and McGuire do under the duvet doesn't bother me; it's what you do in business that I'm worried about.'

'I'm sorry,' said Paula. 'I think I'm missing something here. Why should I care what you're worried about, and why should my business be any business of yours?'

'Your father didn't teach you much in the way of respect, did he? Whenever I called on him he welcomed me with a smile and a glass of Amaretto ... I'm very fond of Amaretto.' Suddenly the muddy eyes seemed to grow hard. 'He certainly had more sense than to talk to me like that.'

She held his gaze, unflinching. 'And what of my grandfather? Think back twenty years, to when you were a sergeant or whatever, and ask yourself if you'd have traipsed in here then, when he was sat behind that big old desk of his.'

'You're right; I was a sergeant, and I can tell you this too. If I'd called on your grandfather I'd have been accompanied by at least one other officer and probably by people from the Inland Revenue, with a search warrant in my pocket to back me up. Your grandfather's connections don't bear close examination, any more than his tax returns did.'

Paula felt her control slip away. 'Right!' she shouted. 'Your fifteen minutes are up. Get the hell out of here, or I'll call a real policeman to remove you.'

Jay remained seated. 'I'll go when I'm good and ready, and I'll be back before too long. When I come, it'll be with specialist officers from another force, and we will go through the records of your businesses with the finest-toothed of combs. And I don't mean just the last couple of years. We'll go back all the way to the old man. When we're done, there will be no way your beloved can stay in the force. Who knows? We might even have the two of you in court before we're done. It won't stop there, though: Mario's been advanced pretty rapidly in the force.

I doubt if someone who'd made such an error of judgement could survive either.'

He pushed himself slowly to his feet. 'It's been a pleasure to see you again . . . lass,' he said. 'But I'm going to enjoy my next visit even more. Goodbye for now.'

Paula stared at his back as he turned it to her; she stared at the door as he closed it behind him. And then she picked up the telephone and called Mario.

He could almost hear the rage build up within him as he listened to her story, without interrupting her once. Even after she had finished, he stayed silent for a while.

When he did speak, his voice was soft, the way she knew it could sound when someone was in the worst trouble of his life. 'That's it,' he murmured. 'I was asked to take it easy on Jay, and I agreed. But now all deals are off. Before I've done with him, I'm going to see that bastard shivering in his own piss.'

Forty-seven

In the circumstances, there was no question of Neil McIlhenney visiting Debbie Wrigley in her office. Instead, he accepted her suggestion that they meet in the John Lewis cafeteria, where they were least likely to be spotted by anyone either of them knew.

This time, he was first to arrive: he found a space in the NCP car park beside the department store and took the lift up to the fourth-floor restaurant, where he bought a cappuccino, a bottle of sparkling water and two pieces of a thick fudge cake, took a table at the window and sat down to wait.

He looked out over the city, down Leith Walk and across to Calton Hill, cursing quietly to himself at the change in the weather, anticipating the drive through to Glasgow with Mackenzie with no pleasure at all. He had never liked stake-outs even in his younger days, and found the prospect of an evening's bogus conversation with the Bandit to be almost more than he could bear. He found himself praying that the Johnny Groat pub had a television, even if it was tuned to *Coronation Street*.

'Cheer up, Neil,' said his banker friend, as she slid into the seat facing him. 'You're supposed to like the snow at Christmas. It's meant to fill us all with seasonal joy.'

'Bugger that for a game of soldiers,' he grunted. 'All I see is traffic chaos, and all I hear is my son moaning because his rugby's been cancelled.'

'Let me cheer you up, then.' Wrigley sipped her coffee, nodding approval. 'You can't have been here long. This is almost warm.'

'Try the cake,' he urged. 'That's real comfort food; should suit you a treat.'

She looked at him over the top of her spectacles. 'Good job we're old friends,' she muttered.

'So what have you got for me, friend?'

'Nothing on paper,' she replied at once. 'I couldn't take the chance of being seen photocopying. You'll have to make notes . . . that's assuming that policemen still carry notebooks and pencils.'

'This one does, although the pencil's a shade up-market.' He took a pad and a Mont Blanc ballpoint from his pocket. 'Birthday present from my wife,' he explained.

'Very nice.' Wrigley attacked her fudge cake. 'So was that,' she added. 'Now to business.' She checked that the booth behind her was still empty and that nobody else was within earshot.

'Your subject is comfortably off,' she began. 'His salary goes in every month, like anyone else, and it is his principal source of income. However, it is not the only one. There are small payments made to him every six months; I've checked them back and found that they are dividends paid through a blind trust, which looks after his private shareholdings and any other investments.'

'That's standard practice for . . . people in his position.'

'Yes, dear, I know. I administer several of them. There's nothing out of the ordinary in that at all. However, he has other income which is not quite so orthodox. He receives monthly payments of two and a half thousand pounds, transferred from an account held in the Dundee branch of my own bank. I traced that back also; what I found might interest you. It is the working account of a discretionary trust set up more than fifty years ago to benefit members of the Groves family.'

'Who the hell are the Groves family?'

'They own a large construction company in Dundee. The trust was established by Herbert Groves senior, and his heirs and successors have benefited from it ever since.'

'He's getting thirty grand a year from a builder?'

'No,' Wrigley exclaimed. 'The trust exists entirely separately from the company. It is not required to declare its beneficiaries, other than to the Inland Revenue, and before you ask, your subject is not evading any taxes.' She finished her cake, and then eyed McIlhenney's, which was untouched; he pushed it across to her.

'I've also checked the register of MSPs' interests,' she told him. 'Your subject declares among his assets a shareholding in Herbert Groves Construction, plc, and in a number of quoted companies. He doesn't declare the trust income, because he doesn't have to: it isn't remunerated employment.'

She ate the second piece of fudge cake, slowly and with relish. 'There,' she announced, when she was finished, with undisguised self-satisfaction all over her face. 'The people who set you on this errand will be happy. You can go back to them and report that while the man appears to have a background which is at odds with his,' she glanced over her shoulder again, 'political philosophy, he is, legally, squeaky clean.'

Forty-eight

Malky Gladsmuir did not have the sunniest of dispositions at the best of times, and his mood was never improved by a visit from the police. So when Mario McGuire shoved his way through the heavy swing doors and into the Wee Black Dug, he was greeted with the scowl that he had expected.

The detective superintendent glanced around as he shook the snow from his jacket. The looming weather had taken a drastic toll of the evening turn-out: only two drinkers leaned against the bar, while another sat at a table in the furthest corner of the saloon. The assistant barman, with little to do, fixed most of his attention on a snooker tournament on television.

'What can I do for you?' asked Gladsmuir, with a degree of belligerence that almost brought a smile to McGuire's face.

'Your office: now.' He stepped behind the bar, as the pub manager shrugged and opened a door behind him.

'You're not to bother me,' he protested. 'Did you not get told?'

'Sit down, Malky.'

'Ah'll stand if I want.' Gladsmuir backed towards his desk, reaching behind him with his right hand and picking up a heavy glass paperweight.

'Okay, if that's how you want it.' He took half a pace forward; the cornered man swung at his head, hard and fast, but the detective simply smashed aside his assault, sending the weapon flying into a corner of the room, then hit him, once, hard, in the middle of the forehead. The publican's eyes glazed, his legs turned to jelly and he slumped semi-conscious into the chair behind him.

McGuire grinned. 'I told you to sit down.'

He waited until Gladsmuir's eyes began to focus once more, then pulled up the small office's other chair and sat facing him. 'That's the second time we've done this dance in here, Malky,' he said. 'When's it going to dawn on you that it'll only ever get you hurt? Or did your talk with Greg Jay make you think you were safe from me? Tell me something, my friend, which of us really scares you the most? Me or Greg?'

'You don't scare me,' Gladsmuir retorted; but his tone branded him a liar. 'Mr Jay never threatened me; he never came in here looking for trouble.'

'Neither did I; all I wanted was a conversation. It was you who took a swing at me, remember? But, Malky, did you really think that you could just go whining to Greg and that he'd warn me off, tell me to let you carry on with whatever sleazy understanding you and he had? I've told you before and I'm telling you again: I know that in his time this place was a police-free zone, but those days are gone.'

'I don't know what you mean.'

McGuire laughed. 'Don't give me that! Of course you do. What I want now is for you to tell me how it operated, what sort of stuff you were feeding him to make it worth his while. It doesn't show from my divisional records, that's for sure. I've been talking to my guys as well. None of them could recall a single arrest that was made on the basis of a tip from you. All they said was that Greg let it be known that you were his. I'll say this for him, he kept your cover bloody well. Come on, what did you give him?'

'Stuff,' the publican mumbled.

'What you mean "stuff"?'

'This and that, just wee things I heard in the pub.'

'Such as?'

'I can't remember.'

'You'd better start, pal. While you're thinking about it, tell me how you came to complain to Greg about me.'

'Ah didn't, honest. He came in here to see me. It was him that asked me how things were going wi' you. I told him the truth, that you wanted me to keep on feeding stuff to you, but that there were to be no more scams going on in here.'

'Is that you admitting that there were, and Greg knew about it?'

'I'm admitting nothing.'

McGuire leaned forward and stuck out his chin. 'Take another swing at me, Malky, go on.'

'Naw! Why? Are you daft?'

'No, I'd just like another excuse to get your attention, that's all. I'll ask you again. Was something happening here, and did Greg Jay know about it and turn a blind eye? I want the truth, or you and I are going to my office, and very publicly too, for as long as it takes. Now, give me a one-word answer within the next five seconds. One . . .'

He had reached 'three', when Malky Gladsmuir muttered, 'Yes.'

'That's good,' said the big detective. 'That's the first sensible thing you've said to me since I walked in here. Now we've made this breakthrough, let's have the rest, all of it.'

Forty-nine

Stevie Steele had never found it more difficult to concentrate on the job. Fortunately his workload was light and he had been able to afford himself the luxury of dwelling upon a turn in his life that would have been astonishing only a month or two earlier.

The night before, he and Maggie had celebrated with a bottle of cava from the fridge, and a home delivery from Pizza Hut. They were still shell-shocked from their discovery, and had ended the evening in helpless laughter at the prospect of a pregnant chief superintendent in uniform.

Although a smile was never far away, he had managed to keep a straight face at the office for most of his shift, even in the face of the apprehension of a thief in a Father Christmas suit who had tripped over his own hem when running out of the Cameron Toll shopping centre with a snatched handbag.

However, his new-found contentment was swept to one side when his door opened just after five fifteen, as he was finishing his paperwork and making ready to leave. He had expected Mary Chambers, calling to wish him good night, or perhaps to ask him what had made him so bright and breezy. Instead, George Regan stepped into the small room.

A glance at the sergeant's face told him that the reality of his loss had begun to catch up with him. His eyes were hollow and his hair, normally impeccably groomed, was untidy. Instead of the usual grey suit, he wore a heavy jacket over a sweatshirt, jeans and trainers.

'Hello, mate,' said Stevie quietly. 'How goes?'

'Bloody terrible, thanks. I'd to get the doctor to Jen yesterday afternoon; she broke down completely and he had to sedate her. She's on industrial-strength Valium now; walks about like a zombie for most of the time.'

'And you?'

'I'm trying to stay off the helpers, other than the odd beer or two.'

'Want one now? I'll come to the pub with you, if you like.'

'Cheers,' said Regan, gratefully, 'but I'd better not. I don't want to be away too long. I just called in to tell you that we've arranged the funeral. It'll be next Wednesday; twelve noon at Warriston Crematorium. Family flowers only, by the way.'

'Can we make a donation to charity instead?'

'If you want; something that benefits children would be nice.' He sighed. 'I'm done, Stevie,' he murmured. 'Looking at Jen, I just feel so bloody helpless; I don't know how to stop her crying, man.'

'Maybe if you joined her, George, just for a while.'

Regan looked at him. 'If I start to cry, I might never stop; that's what scares me.' He slumped into a chair. 'I've tried everything else, mind. I even pulled your report from big Tarvil and staked out the Castle Terrace car park for a couple of nights, with the daft notion that I might find someone who'd seen something on Sunday. I'm not implying that you didn't do a proper job,' he added quickly. 'I suppose I just hoped I'd get lucky.'

'Of course you did. I told Tarvil he could give you the report. No joy?'

'Of course not. I found a couple or three people who'd been there around that time, but none of them had seen a damn thing … because there was nothing to see. The silly wee bugger just tried one of his stunts, Stevie, that's all there is to it, and broke his parents' hearts in the process.'

Fifty

The signs for Hawthorn Moor Golf Club had occasionally caught Andy Martin's eye as he commuted from his home in Perth to his office in Dundee, but he had never followed them until Rod Greatorix directed him into the car park outside the clubhouse. It was an old building that had been adapted and greatly expanded to fit the purpose, clearly chosen for its location. It was dark and so Martin could see nothing of the course, but it was clear that during the day the members' lounge offered a panoramic view.

'Nice,' he muttered to his colleague. 'I take it that outside it's covered in hawthorn bushes.'

'The title doesn't mean a damn thing,' Greatorix told him. 'That's just a marketing name the investors or their PR men dreamed up. It used to be farmland, until the owner moved with the times and put it to other use. It's a limited company; Brindsley's a shareholder, of course. And guess who built this clubhouse? Of course you can.' He pointed to a group of three men seated round a table in the window. 'As expected, that's him holding court over there.'

As he led the way across the spacious room, one of the trio noticed them and muttered something inaudible. The man in the centre turned to look over his shoulder, then stood up. 'Here comes the filth,' he said, in a gruff, cultured accent, with just a trace of Dundonian, as he extended a hand to Greatorix. 'Brother-in-law, how are you? Come and join us.'

'I'm fine, thanks,' said the head of CID, 'and we were planning to.'

'Who's your friend?'

'This is the deputy chief constable, Andy Martin. I didn't realise till lunchtime that you and he hadn't met, so I thought I should do something about it.'

'Giving me my place in the community, you mean?' He and Martin shook hands. 'Hello, good to meet you. I'd heard about you, of course, from Graham Morton. He and I are brother Rotarians.' Without being asked, his two companions moved their chairs round, making room for the newcomers at the table. Groves glanced in their direction. 'These two codgers are Jack, on the left, and Archie. They're golf addicts, I'm afraid; no hope for them.' The two, who looked to be in their late sixties, nodded happy agreement, then turned to their own conversation.

Without being summoned, the bar steward appeared beside them. 'What can I get you, gentlemen?'

'I'll have a pint of orange squash,' Martin replied.

The man turned to Greatorix. 'Large whisky, please. I'll catch a lift back with you, Brindsley.'

'Sure.' Groves turned to Martin: he was a big man, an inch or two over six feet, and looked considerably fitter than his brother-in-law, even though the two had to be around the same age. 'What do you think of Tayside?' he asked.

'I like it very much.'

'Won't stretch you very much, though, given where you've come from.'

'My previous force was bigger, that's true, but in manpower terms as well as area. So the two jobs are pretty well commensurate, in terms of being stretched.'

Groves jerked his thumb towards Greatorix. 'I suppose you're this guy's boss now?'

'My management portfolio includes CID, that's true, but no way would I interfere with Rod. He has twenty years more experience than me, and he's a better detective than I ever was.'

'That's not what I heard,' Groves said grunted, oblivious to the implied slight. 'I was told that you had a formidable reputation, and that you've been in some real scrapes in your time. Even shot a couple of people in the line of duty, isn't that right?'

The question took Martin aback; fortunately the arrival of his drink gave him time to react. 'It's not something I dwell on, and it's certainly not something I talk about.'

'I can see why you wouldn't. Still, you can't blame people for wondering about it. I can't imagine what it must be like to kill another man, or woman, as the case may be.'

'I'm happy for you in that case. It doesn't bear imagining.' Abruptly he changed the subject. 'You've spent all your life in Dundee, Rod tells me.'

'Apart from the year I spent doing my post-graduate qualification. These days you can do an MBA by correspondence; I had to go away for mine. Don't think too harshly of me, though: our city is a very interesting place, as you'll discover if you spend long enough among us.'

'I'm prepared to concede that already. It has to have something; after all, it's given Scotland its current First Minister.'

'Ah, Tommy,' he murmured, pausing. 'Yes,' he continued, 'give him long enough and he'll be regarded as our most famous son.'

'Who's the current holder of the title?'

'Oor Wullie, I believe.'

Martin smiled. 'Yes, it's a unique claim to fame, having a cartoon character as your top citizen. I can't knock it, though. I'm a Glaswegian and ours are all footballers . . . most of them dead footballers, at that.'

'We have something in common, then: we're both sons of cities that are music-hall jokes.'

'Don't tell too many Weegies that.' He sipped his orange squash, noticing that Groves was drinking what appeared to be cola. 'How long have you and Rod been in-laws?' he asked.

Groves frowned. 'Since God was a boy, it seems. Celia and I were married when I was still at university, and before you ask, our son was born six months later.'

'Is he a member here too?'

'No.' It was as if the question had thrown a switch, turning off the man's amiability. 'Rod,' he said, sharply. 'It's time to go, the snow's bad enough as it is, and from what I can see out there it's getting worse. Just as well I brought the Range Rover.' He pushed himself to his feet, looking down at the policeman. 'Good evening to you. We'll meet again, no doubt.' Turning on his heel, he walked out of the lounge.

The two golf addicts turned towards Martin. 'So, young man,' the one named Archie began, with an impish grin, 'what's your handicap?'

Fifty-one

It was happening too often for his liking: once again, Bob Skinner was taken by surprise. He had waited late in the office, after everyone else had gone for the night, but the visitor he had been expecting was not the Justice Minister.

Nevertheless, he was pleased. He had wanted to see Aileen again over the weekend, but his need to spend quality time with his children had ruled that out. 'Bring her up,' he told the security officer who called to announce her arrival, trying to keep the eagerness out of his voice.

'Hi,' she said, quietly, as she stepped into the room.

He smiled and pointed to the low couch against the far wall, out of sight of the window. 'Hi to you,' he replied, as they sat together.

'I hope you don't mind me dropping in unannounced, Bob.'

'I should mind? You're a minister: it's an honour. Besides . . .' He leaned over and kissed her on the cheek. 'I've found myself wanting to see you.'

'Me too; that's why I called in.'

'Where are you headed?'

'Through to Glasgow: there's a party meeting tomorrow, and before that I have a constituency surgery in the morning.'

'I wish I was a patient.' Bob chuckled.

'I wish you were too.' She looked into his eyes. 'I'm trying to fight what's happening to me, you know, before I put myself at risk with you.'

'I won't let that happen, I promise. To tell you the truth I'm not trying to fight anything. I'm concentrating on doing what's right, in the right order and at the right time.'

'Do you always manage to do that?'

'I have to confess to a conspicuous record of failure in that department,' he told her.

'Have you heard from your wife?' she asked, tentatively.

'Yes. She's still in the US, but she's coming home soon.'

'And what will happen then?'

'I haven't a bloody clue; all I hope is that whatever way it goes, it's best for the kids.'

'I'm sure you'll manage that. My one big fear is that if you did split, I'd be seen as the scarlet woman who caused it. Murtagh would have a field day if he chose and, knowing him, he would, especially as I'll have served my purpose by then.'

'I promise you, Aileen, you won't be involved if it goes that way. Things were going wrong between Sarah and me long before I met you. But I hear what you're saying and, yes, we need to be discreet. What we have at the moment is a strong friendship, and we mustn't give anybody the chance to misinterpret it . . . any more than we have already. For a while, when we meet, it's either official or it's in Glasgow.'

She nodded. 'We could call this official. As well as wanting to see you, I've got news for you about the bill.'

'Tell me he's going to drop it.'

'Fat chance. No, the First Minister has told me that he's giving me the honour of introducing it in the Parliament next Tuesday. The statutory three-week study period will be up on Monday and the Presiding Officer will clear it for presentation and publication. Tommy's decided that it isn't going to be his sponsored legislation but mine, even though I'm opposed to it and had no hand in its preparation. Do you still think I should stay in office?'

Bob whistled. 'He is boxing you in, and no mistake. If you introduce the legislation, then even if you do succeed him at some time in the future, you'll look an idiot if you try to repeal it. Should you quit? If your conscience demands it, I suppose you should.'

She reached out and laid a fingertip on his chest. 'If I do, Tommy's machine will leak the story that you and I are having an affair and that you talked me into it. He told me that, flat out, this afternoon. If I let that happen, how would your wife react to it? She'd be as humiliated as you and me.'

His face twisted into something close to a snarl. 'How the hell did a nasty little bastard like him ever come to lead this country?'

'Or lead my party for that matter,' Aileen added.

He reached out and cupped her face in his big hand. 'I'll make you a promise,' he said. 'I'm going to have him; maybe not before next Tuesday, but before too long. When I bring him down, they'll hear the crash all over Scotland.'

'You be careful,' she warned him.

'I am being careful, so much so that I'm going to chuck you out now. You've walked into the middle of something you're better not knowing about until after it's done.'

He rose, and led her to the door. When he opened it, she saw, waiting outside, a big, heavily built man with black hair and flashing eyes. 'My next meeting,' he said. 'Aileen, let me introduce Detective Superintendent Mario McGuire.'

Fifty-two

In his student days, when his world was young and he had dreamed of becoming a broadsheet journalist, uncovering hidden truths and holding them up for the world to see, Sean Green had bridged the gap between malnutrition and comfort by working as a waiter, five nights a week, in an Indian restaurant in Oxford.

There had been a customer, a regular, a bookish man with big thick-lens spectacles that from certain angles made him look like a frog. He had been a good tipper, always cash too, rather than credit card; naturally, the staff had paid him special attention. He was a visiting lecturer, or so the student waiter had come to understand, at Exeter College. Their paths had never crossed outside the restaurant, since Sean was enrolled at Balliol.

And so it came as a surprise when, in the week in which he had completed his final examinations, the man gave him a business card and an invitation to lunch in London a week later.

The 'lecturer' was Rudy Sewell, and two weeks later, to his complete amazement, Sean Green had found himself a member of the Security Service, MI5.

It had come full circle, he reflected, as he laid two bowls of *iskembe* before a man whose demeanour shouted 'police officer' and a woman who was clearly not his wife, wondering if they knew that they were about to consume a traditional Turkish hangover cure. Ten years on he was carrying plates once more, only this time the pay was much better and the job description much more interesting.

He was aware that Peter Bassam was watching him, but he felt relaxed in the knowledge that it was only his waiting technique that was under scrutiny. He had no worries about not completing his trial successfully, especially when he compared himself with his colleagues, who seemed barely competent. One was Asian, and the other looked like a reincarnation of his old student self.

Already he was able to judge that the Delight's reputation was built on the reliability of its kitchen, rather than front-of-house slickness. Diners did not go to Elbe Street to be astonished by the skills of the waiters: they went for the food, which was consistent if not spectacular. The chef was an evil-tempered man called Sukur, but unlike Bassam he was one hundred per cent Turkish, and seemed very proud of both his nation and his work. He ran his kitchen with a mouth that was as foul as his disposition, but he filled his orders on time.

Green nodded to his boss as he emerged from the kitchen with a plate of *orkinos* and *mercimek*, tuna with lentils, and another of *sucuk* and *balka*, sausage and beans; Bassam smiled back. '*No worries*,' he thought.

He did not expect that his assignment would produce results. He regarded it as a long shot, no more than a line cast into a very large lake in the hope that its one and only fish might bite. So what if Bassam's origins were Albanian? The fact that he had anglicised his forename and chosen to serve Turkish food indicated, if anything, that he was trying very hard to distance himself from his homeland, and from its lawless reputation.

He knew that the man had a wife and family: their photograph was pinned to the wall, beside the till, and they lived in Northfield. He could tell, from one night's work, that the business was profitable. So, he asked himself, would he put it all at risk by harbouring a bunch of gangsters? Not that he had seen any sign of the Albanians during his first hours on the job.

However, he knew that Amanda Dennis would not be interested in his opinions, only in his findings. His thoughts were private and would be kept to himself until he was asked to voice them. In the meantime, he would keep his eyes open and try not to drop any plates.

Fifty-three

Thankfully, there was a television set in the Johnny Groat. Bandit Mackenzie smiled when he saw it, even though it was tuned to an English second-division football match.

'What gives me the idea that you would watch anything on the box?' asked McIlhenney.

'I wouldn't,' his colleague replied amiably. 'But it means that I won't have to talk to you all night.' He rapped on the bar and waved to the fat, middle-aged barman, who had seemed to be doing his best to ignore his two new customers as he leaned on the counter in conversation with a blowsy blonde woman. 'Pint of IPA and a pint of lime and soda, when you've a minute,' he called out.

The steward scowled at him, but picked up two glasses and began to pour. 'Four pound twenty,' he announced, curtly, as he placed the drinks in front of them, managing to spill a little of both.

'Jesus,' Mackenzie muttered. 'Bloody dear lime and soda that!'

'This is a pub, pal, no' a café,' he retorted, as he took the detective's ten-pound note.

'Are those pies hot?' McIlhenney asked, pointing to a food-display unit at the back of the bar.

'They will be after a few turns in the microwave.'

'Let's have a couple, then. Take them off his tenner.'

'The bridies is better,' the blonde called out. 'The pies is shite.'

'I was hoping they were mutton,' McIlhenney replied. 'Make it bridies instead,' he told the barman, 'and give the lady another of hers.'

'Gin and tonic, thanks.' She slid off her stool and made her way round towards them. 'Havenae seen you two in here before.'

Looking at her, Mackenzie decided that he preferred the view from a distance. 'If you had,' he told her, 'you'd be psychic. We've never been here before.'

'What brings you now here, then?'

'We like drinking in middens.'

She glanced around the shoddy bar. 'Aye,' she agreed, 'it could do with a lick of paint. Still, there's worse; try south of the river.'

'We're not that stupid,' said McIlhenney.

'Are yis workin', like?' she asked.

'Right now, no,' the detective lied. 'Later on, we will be.'

'Where?'

'The Western.'

Her painted eyebrows rose. 'Are yis doctors?'

Mackenzie laughed. 'Aye, brain surgeons.' He lifted his pint and took a drink. 'Cheers.'

'We're porters,' said McIlhenney, dourly.

'In that case, they'll be no use to you, Dolly,' a guttural voice exclaimed from behind them. 'Porters no' make enough to spend on gettin' their hole. You better look somewheres else.'

The two detectives turned, and looked into dark eyes, scowling from beneath a low forehead. A younger man stood behind him, shifting nervously from one foot to the other. 'Do you mind fucking off?' said Mackenzie, casually. 'We were talking to the lady.'

'Not any more.' The woman called Dolly had returned to her former position in the corner of the bar. 'Did you think you charmed her, man?' Frankie Jakes sneered. 'It's twenty quid in her place upstairs. If I'm wrong and you got twenty quid, go ahead. Your pint won't even be flat by the time you're back.'

'Are you guys her minders, then?' asked McIlhenney.

'I look after her, Mr Porter, if it's any fockin' bizniz of yours. I keep her safe from creeps. My wee brodder here, he have trouble mindin' his own cock.' He switched his scowl to the other detective. 'You new in here, so I make allowances, but next time you tell me to fock off, you in big trouble.' He hitched his shoulders, like a movie gun-fighter; one or two people looked in his direction, as if the scene had been played out before. 'Maybe you better fock off.'

Mackenzie smiled. 'What I'm going to do, pal,' he replied, evenly, 'is finish my drink, maybe have another couple, and then me and big Mac here are going to work. You enjoy your night and we'll enjoy ours.' He patted his colleague on the shoulder. 'Because, believe me, you wouldn't fancy trying to make him fuck off.'

'Leave it, Davie,' said McIlhenney, quietly. 'The guy's done nothing. Don't make him lose face in his own boozer.'

Jakes looked at him for a while, before coming to the conclusion that he might be on the verge of making a large mistake. 'Okay,' he muttered, eventually. 'You just remember what I tol' you.'

Fifty-four

It was just after midnight, but Bob Skinner was still awake. He was in his armchair in the conservatory, listening to REM in the background while trying to concentrate on a novel. He had finished *Alarm Call*, and gone back to *Blackstone's Pursuits*, having decided to read the series in chronological order.

He laid the book aside as the CD reached the almost unbearably sad live version of 'Country Feedback', which he regarded as Michael Stipe's finest hour. It was only halfway through when the phone rang. He had been expecting the call, but he swore nonetheless, before pausing the track and answering.

'Boss, it's Neil.'

He had known that it would be. 'How went it on your night out?'

He heard a chuckle. 'It was interesting. We started off by meeting a nice person called Dolly.'

'As in Dolly the sheep?'

'As in Dolly the hooker; Frankie runs her. You know, that Mackenzie is a bloody lunatic: we'd hardly got a foot in the door before he picked a fight with the subject.'

'For Christ's sake!'

'It worked out all right, though: we wound up drinking with Jakes and his brother, and they swallowed our porter story all the way. When you think about it, what undercover cop in his right mind is going to tell the guy he's supposed to be observing to go and fuck himself?'

'In his right mind, indeed,' Skinner growled.

'Sure, but it worked. Frankie's our pal now. Do you know, the cheeky bastard actually asked us if there was any prospect of us nicking some diazepam from the Western? He said he'd cut us in if we did.'

228

'What did you say?'

'We told him that we'd just been transferred from the Royal, so we were new there, but we said that we'd suss it out and let him know if there was any chance.'

'There was no sign of Samir Bajram, though?'

'No.'

'Did he mention him?'

'Not by name. When he asked us about the drugs, he did say that he had another deal going down, but that it wouldn't get in the way of anything we could do for him. He could have been talking about the Albanian, or all of them for that matter.'

'Let's see how it plays out,' said Skinner. 'Keep on with the operation, but watch it. Tell Mackenzie from me that he's taken his last risk in there.'

'I will, but he'll probably tell me to fuck off too; he's the same rank as me, remember.'

'That may change soon. Listen, I got that report you left me, and I shredded it afterwards, like you asked. Your contact is right, Murtagh hasn't broken any laws, but that trust income is very interesting. I'll mention it to Andy next time I see him.'

'You won't...'

'Of course not. I won't compromise your friend in any way.' He paused. 'There's something else that's happened since you left for Glasgow. I'm going to take down Greg Jay.'

'When?'

'Monday. I can't leave it any longer: the bastard went to see Paula Viareggio this afternoon, and threatened to bring in a team from outside the force to go through all her books and records. Mario was going to kill him there and then, but I calmed him down.'

'Have you got the means to bring him down?'

'I have now, but I want some extra insurance. There's something I want you to do for me tomorrow, before you head back to Glasgow. I want you to pay a call on our friend Joanne Virtue. She told us something off the record once; tell her that it's time for her to make it official.'

Fifty-five

Spencer McIlhenney had thought that his weekend was ruined; most ten-year-old boys would have been pleased to see the December snow, but to him it was an enemy. It had wiped out his rugby session for that weekend, but worse the impending holiday break meant that he had played his last game for the year. He lived for rugby: his coach had told him that he showed real promise, and that if he grew to be as big as his dad, he might play at a decent level. Privately, Spence hoped that his growth would slow. His favourite position was fly-half, and he could not think of a single international Number Ten who was as bulky as that.

The boy was gazing morosely out of his bedroom window when he saw the car pull up outside. Several others were parked in the street, but there were no fresh tyre marks in the snow; even those his dad's car had made were almost covered over. He had tried to console himself with his PlayStation, but he knew all the games too well for them to be any real challenge. His dad had gone out too, on one of his mysterious missions, and Lauren and Louise, his stepmother, were closeted together somewhere. He liked Louise, and was still a little in awe of her, because of her former career, but not even she had been able to break his mood.

There was only one person he could think of who was capable of doing that; by some miracle, he climbed out of the Toyota that drew up at his front door. He jumped from his perch and crashed downstairs, opening the front door before the caller was halfway up the path. 'Uncle Mario,' he called out, then yelled over his shoulder, back into the house, 'hey, Lauren, it's Uncle Mario.'

'Hush, kid,' McGuire grinned, 'don't tell the whole street. This is an undercover operation.'

He stamped the snow off his feet and wiped them on the mat before stepping into the house. Louise was in the hall to greet him. 'I thought you weren't coming,' she said. She ruffled Spencer's hair. 'But I know someone who's glad you did.'

'I take my godparenting very seriously,' he told her. 'I couldn't let the day be a total write-off.'

'Where did you get the car?' Spence asked him. 'It's a Rav 4, isn't it?'

'That's right. It's Paula's; she made me bring it rather than mine, since it's got four-wheel drive. I have to say, it handled like a dream on the way up here. Fancy a drive in the snow?'

The boy's face lit up. 'Yeah!'

'How about you, Lauren?'

'Yes, please. Can Louise come?'

Her stepmother laughed. 'That's nice of you, dear, but Louise is quite happy in front of the television. Besides, I'm expecting your father home in an hour or so.'

'That's sorted, then,' said Mario. 'Kids, do your ski boots still fit you?' Both children nodded. 'And have you kept your skis in good order, like you should?'

'Of course we have,' Lauren replied, severely.

'Right, dig them all out, and your suits, then change into warmer clothes. We're off for an afternoon on the ski-slope at Hillend.'

Spencer gazed up at him as if he was a god descended from Olympus: his weekend was saved.

Fifty-six

Dan and Elma Pringle were in a place that had been beyond their reach or their worst imagining, but which they had reached nonetheless.

They sat side by side in the small office in the Royal Infirmary. Their surroundings might have been brighter and more modern than in its predecessor, the vast Victorian village where Ross had been born and where Elma's father had died, but they noticed not at all. Wherever they were, they would simply have held hands and stared at the wall.

The door behind them opened. Neither turned; they sat and waited as the consultant took his seat behind his desk. His name was Lewis Curry, and they had seen him before, on the day of their daughter's admission, when it had been his duty to tell them that the best they could hope for was that she would live the rest of her life in total helplessness, with no idea of who they were or of what she had been or might have become.

'Hello again,' Mr Curry said quietly. 'Have you been to see Ross?'

'We looked in on her before we came along here,' Elma replied. She had taken on the role of spokesperson. 'She looked very peaceful; it doesn't seem so bad when you see her asleep like that. Who knows? We're expecting her brother back from Hong Kong tomorrow. Maybe she'll just wake up and it'll be all right.'

The consultant looked down at his hands. 'No, Mrs Pringle. She will not awaken tomorrow, or the next day, or the day after that. I wish I had grounds for offering you a different prognosis than at our last meeting, but I don't. The fact is that things have resolved themselves since then. Your daughter seems so peaceful for one reason: there is nothing going on inside her head, no dreams, no reaction to light or sounds around her, nothing at all. What little brain activity we were able to detect following her admission has disappeared; only the vital centres continue to function, because of the ventilator. In my opinion and in that of my colleagues, she is clinically dead.'

Elma was struck dumb; her mouth fell open. Dan's eyes flickered, then his head dropped, and his shoulders began to shake.

The consultant had seen it before, all too often. Even in the strongest, most confident and most intelligent of people, there was always an element of denial. It was worse for them in a way: when the truth eventually hit home, it hit harder. 'Would you like to see someone?' he offered. 'We have a hospital chaplain and he'll be pleased to talk with you.'

'No,' Elma whispered. 'We don't know him and he doesn't know us. Anyway, he couldn't change what you've told us. What happens next?' She asked for Dan's sake: they both knew the answer for they had discussed the question, but she felt that he needed to hear it from Mr Curry.

'At the moment,' he said, 'the machine is keeping her breathing, and her heart beating. You may continue that, or you may ask us to switch it off.'

'And if we did, what would happen?'

'If the brain is dead, the body must follow. If she can't sustain respiration on her own, her heart will stop.'

'So if we ask you to switch the machine off, we're taking a gamble that she'll be able to breathe on her own?'

'I wouldn't call it a gamble.'

'Can we have a few minutes alone?' Dan mumbled, from somewhere down in his chest.

'Of course.' The consultant rose and left the room.

The Pringles sat there, still hand in hand. Eventually Dan lifted his head and they gazed at each other. Neither spoke, but he gave a single tiny nod, then looked away.

Mr Curry returned a little later. Elma looked up and him and whispered, 'Yes.'

He led them along to the small one-bed room where Ross, their only daughter, lay; the electrodes they had seen earlier had been removed from her head, but the thick tube was still in her mouth. There was a chair on either side of the bed, as if she had been expecting them. Her father sat on her right, her mother on her left, and each took one of her hands in theirs. When they were settled, Lewis Curry reached across and withdrew the tube, then signalled to his registrar, who switched off the ventilator.

If they had looked up at the monitor at the bedside, Dan and Elma would have seen the steady peak of her heartbeat grow irregular, until it stopped and became a straight line on the screen.

Fifty-seven

However hard he tried not to, George Regan could not help thinking back to the previous Saturday afternoon. His son had pleaded with him to take him to Easter Road, but he had been tired, and in any event the prospect of Hibernian battling it out with Aberdeen did not excite him. So, in the end, he had given him his bus fare and his ticket money and had let him go on his own. He knew as he gazed idly and unseeing at the television that he would regret that piece of selfishness for the rest of his life.

Saturday was the worst day so far: it was the weekend, and the house should have been full of George junior, of his noise, his boisterousness, his vibrancy. He had never known such quiet. He closed his eyes, but that was worse: he imagined himself in the coffin with his boy, and the vision made him wrench himself from his chair.

He strode through to the kitchen: Jen was cooking, her usual response to times of crisis. It was her hobby, the thing that made her happiest. 'What are you doing?' he asked her.

'I'm making a beef casserole. It'll be more than we'll eat ourselves, but I'll put it in the freezer so that it'll be done if we have visitors. After that I thought I'd make a rhubarb crumble.'

'Fine, love, but before you do that can we get the hell out of here? This place is doing my head in.'

She looked at him, her eyes slightly heavy, the effect of her sedatives, he guessed. 'Mine too,' she admitted. 'Maybe things will be better after the funeral.' He knew that they would be worse, but he let her have her illusion. 'Where do you want to go?' she asked.

'Uptown?'

'In that snow?'

'It'll be okay. The main roads are cleared, and the traffic won't be as bad as usual.' He had a sudden, positive thought. 'I'll tell you what. Let's go to a travel agent and book a break for Christmas. I don't fancy spending it here, so let's go somewhere with a bit of sun.'

'Are you sure? He'll be with us, George, wherever we go.'

'Aye, but at least the wee bugger'll be warmer.'

She sighed. 'If that's what you want, let's do it. Give me a minute, while I change and put a face on.'

George knew that it would take more than a minute, but he smiled and nodded. As Jen went upstairs, he pulled on his rubber boots and went outside to scrape the snow off the driveway as best he could, and to start the car, so that the heater would be effective when they were ready to leave.

He had just cleared the last of the tarmac when he heard his mobile ring. He patted his waxed cloth jacket, looking for it in one of its deep pockets, until he remembered that he had left it on the kitchen table. He bustled back to the door, risking Jen's wrath by bringing snow into the house, as he grabbed the phone and pressed a key to receive. 'Yes,' he barked.

'Is that Detective Sergeant Regan?' a prim female voice asked.

'Yes, who's this?'

'It's Miss Bee, Betty Bee. If you remember, we met in the car park the other night, although I'm sure that I'm only one among many people you've spoken to.'

'I remember you. What can I do for you?'

'You can accept my apologies, for I believe they're owed to you. Normally I have excellent recollection; I don't know what came over me this time. I can only suppose that I took your question too literally. You asked me, if you recall, if I had seen anyone in the street after I drove out of the car park. I told you that I hadn't, and that remains the case. However, I've just remembered something else that might be of interest to you. I'm only sorry that it didn't come to me sooner.'

Out of the corner of his eye, Regan saw Jen, standing in the kitchen door. She was looking at him curiously, and seemed about to ask who was on the phone, until he put a finger to his lips. 'What was it?' he asked.

'It was a man. He wasn't in the street, though; he was in the car park itself. I was on the last of the down ramps, close to the barrier, when he came running up towards me. I really do mean running, as if someone was chasing him, only there wasn't anyone else, there was just him.'

'How close did he get to you?'

'Not close enough for me to be able to give you a detailed description, I'm afraid. I caught him in my headlights for an instant, but he swerved off to the side, into the dark.'

'Was it your impression that he didn't want to be recognised?'

'Mmm.' Betty Bee paused. 'That might have been the case.'

'Can you tell me anything about him, race, size, age, even if they're approximations? Could he have been a teenager?'

'Definitely not. His clothes were wrong for one thing: he wore a long overcoat, hardly a young person's garment. I only had the most fleeting glimpse of his face, but I don't think he was that young. He was a white man, dark-haired and solidly built. That's all I could swear to.'

'In the circumstances, that's pretty good. Thank you very much.'

'Does it help?' she asked.

'Honestly, I don't know. But it's interesting. How can I get back to you if I need to?'

She recited a mobile number; he wrote it down, then read it back to confirm that it was correct. 'Thanks again,' he said. He ended the call, staring out of the kitchen window as he pondered its potential significance.

'What was that?'

He looked across at Jen. 'Maybe nothing, but it's got my brain working again. If you don't mind, darling, I'm going to postpone that trip to the travel agent till later. First, I want to talk to my boss.'

Fifty-eight

Thanks to a sperm count that was much closer to twenty than the twenty million regarded as a marker of fertility, Mario McGuire knew that his chances of having children of his own were of the same order as those of a single tadpole trying to swim the Atlantic. Since he had made the discovery, early in his marriage to Maggie Rose, he had been philosophical about it, but he had taken particular pleasure in the company of Lauren and Spencer all through their childhood.

He was godfather to them both, and took his responsibilities seriously; their first communions had each brought a tear of pride to his eye.

The big detective's soft centre would have come as a surprise to the many villains he had terrorised over the years, but it was in evidence as he pulled his borrowed car into the park at the Midlothian Ski Centre. It had been known as Hillend when he had first brought the children there four years earlier, and he doubted that many of the citizens of the Edinburgh area were aware of the name change. When first he had looked out on to the morning, he had been concerned that it might have been closed because of the severity of the overnight snowfall, but a phone call had reassured him that it was operating normally.

Its beauty was that it had artificial runs, and was floodlit; it was in use all year round, apart from the two weeks in June when it was closed for maintenance. Both Lauren and Spencer had taken naturally to the sport, and after four years had reached expert status and had graduated to the most severe runs. They donned their ski-suits and boots eagerly; when they were all ready, Mario bought them each a strip of tickets, and they set off for the lift to the top of the slope. He let Lauren go in front, but kept Spencer beside him.

When he stepped out of his seat, he realised that they were almost alone. He felt himself frown, wondering if the sport was on the wane.

'Is this as good as Italy or Switzerland, Uncle Mario?' Spencer asked him. He had learned the basics of skiing in the Italian Alps, on holiday with his parents. He smiled as he thought of it: his dad, big Eamon, had been absolutely useless, but fortunately he had inherited his mother's eye and sense of balance.

'It's not the same thing at all,' he replied. 'What you have to remember is that this is an artificial slope. It's very good, and it's a far more reliable place to ski than any of the Scottish resorts, just because it doesn't need snow, and has the lights, but don't think for a minute that it's anywhere near as good as the Alps.'

'I want to be a downhill racer when I grow up,' the boy said.

'I thought you wanted to be a rugby star?'

'Maybe I'll be both.'

'I don't think you'll manage that, kid. If you play top-class rugby, they won't be keen on you skiing. There's too big a risk of injury.'

'Maybe I won't tell them. Will I be as good as you one day?'

'You're as good as me now. This slope is just about the best I can do these days, and you two handle it easily.'

'It's great to be on snow,' Lauren exclaimed, 'and not just the artificial.'

'So enjoy it, then.' He watched as she set off, gliding carefully but gracefully down the run. Spencer set off after her, and soon overtook her.

'Hey, no racing,' Mario yelled after him.

They made run after run, staying on the slope for over an hour, until there was hardly anybody else there, and their passes were almost used up. 'Two more runs each and that's it,' he said, as the slope's only other occupant, a bulky figure in a white suit and heavy goggles, a designer skier if ever Mario had seen one, made his way to the lift. He paused. 'Tell you what, you two go up on your own this time. I'll watch you from down here and see how your style looks. And remember, Spence, no racing!'

As he spoke, he was aware of the snow beginning to fall afresh. 'Get up there: if this gets any heavier, that'll be us for the day, for they'll close the slope.'

Handing two tickets to the attendant, the youngsters poled across to the lift, jumped on and headed for the top once more. When they were a little more than halfway up, Mario felt a pang of concern: the snow had thickened and they were out of his sight. He waited for a few minutes, his unreasonable anxiety growing, until finally he saw Lauren's red suit as she slalomed her way downhill.

She was smiling as she reached the foot, turning to look at her brother. But Spencer was nowhere to be seen. 'Where is he?' she asked. 'He was ready to come after me; he said he was going to race me anyway.' She raised her goggles and he could see the alarm in her eyes. 'Maybe he fell,' she ventured.

'Maybe,' Mario conceded. 'Let's go up and find him … although if the wee sod skis past us when we're on the lift I'll kick his arse for him.'

They made their way across to the lift, but it had stopped. 'Closed,' the attendant said, firmly. 'The snow's too bad.'

'Start it up,' the detective ordered. 'The boy's still up there.'

'He'll ski down; I watched him, he's good.'

Mario raised his goggles and looked him in the eye. 'I'm a police officer,' he told him, more calmly than he felt. 'Start it up and that's an order.'

The man caved in and switched on the continuous belt. Mario settled himself into a support, only to see Lauren jump on board beside him.

'Hey, you stay here,' he told her.

'Like hell I will,' she replied, sounding exactly like her mother.

They rode the lift peering through the ever-thickening snow, but seeing nothing. The journey seemed to take an eternity, but at last they reached the top. There was no sign of the boy.

'Spence!' the detective roared, anger overcoming him. 'Stop messing about, kid, or there'll be no rugby for six months. And that's if your dad lets you off lightly.'

As he gazed around, he felt a tug at his sleeve. 'Uncle Mario,' Lauren exclaimed, pointing. 'Look, those are his skis.' He followed her finger and saw that she was right: they were lying side by side; through the snow that was gathering on them he could see the maker's name. He traversed across towards them, and then his anger left him, to be replaced by fear. Beside them lay another pair, larger, adult size. And then he remembered the man, the would-be Franz Klammer in the designer gear, who had gone up on the lift before the children, but who had not come down.

He looked more closely at the ground and saw tracks, not clear footprints, but clear signs of someone climbing sideways over the hill, and perhaps of someone else being dragged. Trying not to let the panic show on his face, he ripped off a mitt, and searched inside his suit until he found his cell-phone. He found a stored number and set it up to be called, then handed the Nokia to Lauren. 'Take this,' he said, 'and call that number: it's the control room at police headquarters. Tell them that you're Chief Inspector McIlhenney's daughter, tell them where you are and that you're with me, and tell them that I want police here right away, equipped to climb the hill. Then you ski down and wait for them. Understood?'

Neil had told him in the past that her mother's death had made part of the girl into a woman overnight, but until he looked into her eyes, Mario had not understood fully what he meant. She looked back at him with calm, steady eyes that could have been Olive's, and nodded. 'Yes,' she said. 'Now you go and get him!'

He kicked himself free from his skis and headed off across the slope. At once he realised that he might have an advantage. He was strong and very fit, yet it was hard going for him . . . and he was not dragging a struggling boy. He pressed on following the tracks: the snow was heavy towards the top of the hill and it had begun to cover them already.

He glanced at his watch, and estimated that he had only another hour left of daylight, such as it was. He picked up the pace, until he achieved what for most men would have been impossible and broke into a run up the incline. His lungs burned with the effort, but he drove himself on. His legs felt that he had run a mile and more, and yet he knew that he had come only a couple of hundred yards. He paused to yell once more across the hillside. 'Spence! Spence!'

And on the wind, he thought he heard a faint reply: 'Uncle Mario!' a cry choked off.

He broke into his painful trot once more. His eyes were swimming, but he could still see the tracks, following them as they headed into the cleft at the top of the hill. He ran on, until ahead he saw a high outcrop of snow-covered rock.

Spencer was there, in a heap, trying to get to his feet. Mario started towards him . . . and then the snow seemed to move alongside him. He saw a white flash through the blizzard, he heard his godson cry out a warning, then lights exploded inside his head, and he knew no more.

Fifty-nine

Bob Skinner was happy. He had spent his morning watching cartoons with Seonaid, and playing video games with Mark ... without winning once. After a hamburger lunch round the kitchen table he had spent two hours watching James Andrew hit orange-coloured golf balls in the snow on the children's course outside the Mallard Hotel. When they were finished, he had taken him into its warm, stone-floored conservatory, sat him down, and bought two pints, one lager, the other orange squash, and two packets of salt and vinegar crisps.

He looked at the bright face of the youngster, as he clutched his glass in both hands, and felt as if he was in another world, one without death, danger, sorrow, one full of optimism and bright dreams. It was a place he enjoyed. 'Sorry about the football, son,' he said, not for the first time that day, 'but it's not safe for the players in the snow.'

'I'd play in the snow,' Jazz replied.

'Sure you would, and I'd play with you if you wanted, but it couldn't be a real game, because nobody would see the lines, so they wouldn't know whether the ball was in play or not.'

'We just played golf in the snow.'

'Not quite: we hit some shots, but we didn't putt; you can't putt through it.'

'I don't like putting. I only like hitting shots.'

Bob laughed. 'You and me both, kid, but if you want to play well, you'll have to practise chipping and putting for just as long as you practise hitting.'

'Will you practise with me, Dad?'

'Whenever I can, son, I promise.'

'It's a pity Mark doesn't like golf: he could practise with us too.'

243

'One day he will. Once I can persuade him that there are mathematics about golf, he will. Right now, he's only interested in playing it on a computer screen.'

'And Seonaid too.'

'No reason why not: she's in the process of mastering walking right now, but once she's done that, we'll try her out.'

'And Mum?'

Bob paused, and smiled. *You sneaked that one up on me, you little so-and-so,*' he thought. 'If she wants,' he replied. 'Mum hasn't played golf for a while; I think she might be going off it.'

'Will she be home soon, Dad?'

'Yes, she will. She called me the other day and promised that she would. She has some business to do back in America and then she'll be home.' He glanced out of the conservatory windows, up towards the Smiddy and across the main street, where three new homes had replaced the old filling station and garage. Gullane was changing, but slowly, at its own pace.

The street-lamps were starting to shine bright: the short afternoon had become evening already. 'Come on, son,' he said. 'Time we went home.'

'Can we watch *The Lion King* DVD?'

'Again?'

'Please.'

He grinned. 'We'll put it to the vote.'

'That's all right, then: Seonaid'll do what I tell her, so I'll win.'

Bob was still smiling as he took their empty glasses and the crisp wrappers back through to the bar, and as he walked with his son up East Links Road and across the Goose Green playground. He was still smiling as he reached home, going in by the utility-room door where they discarded their snowy footwear and jackets. 'Go on, then,' he told James Andrew, 'you see what's on telly, while I check on the other two.'

The youngster ran off, and he stepped into the kitchen. Trish was there, preparing the children's supper. Seonaid was on the floor, happily making a mess with some flour and a mixing bowl. 'Teach them young,' the cheerful nanny said.

'You'll be teaching her to knit next.' He chuckled.

'No, sir. I'll be teaching her to shop!' She looked at him. 'Two messages for you; just as well you left your mobile at home. One was from Mr Pringle, and the other was from Sergeant McGurk.' In her Bajan accent, she pronounced 'McGurk' without the r. 'The numbers are there, on that notepad.' She nodded towards the telephone. 'Oh, and Alex called too: she said the buses are running so she'll be out for dinner.'

'Thanks, Trish,' he said. 'I'll call them back from my bedroom; there'll be a row if I tell the boy to turn down the telly.'

He took a Budweiser from the fridge, uncapped it, and made his way upstairs, looking in on Mark; his older son was playing chess on his computer. He frowned, and made a mental note to show him the relationship between mathematics and golf, as soon as he had worked out what it was.

He sat on the bed and dialled Dan Pringle's mobile number, the one that he had left. He did not expect good news, and when his veteran colleague answered his call, he could tell in an instant that there was none. 'She's gone, Bob,' he said. 'Peacefully, this afternoon. Her mother and I were with her when they . . . when it happened.'

'I can't tell you how sad that makes me, old friend. My condolences to both of you. I'll call on you soon, once you've had some time to grieve together.' He replaced the phone in its cradle. He was back in the real harsh world, ripped away from the happy island that his day with the kids had been. 'Maybe Sarah's right after all,' he whispered to himself. 'Maybe I should turn all this in.'

He pushed the notion away and dialled McGurk. 'Hi, Jack, it's the DCC. Have you heard from Dan?' he asked at once.

'Yes, sir,' the sergeant replied, quietly.

'It's just too bad, isn't it? And her just a kid too. Was that what you called to tell me?'

'Not that alone, sir; there's something else. About twenty minutes ago, the control room at Fettes had a call from a kid. She told them that her name was Lauren McIlhenney, and that she was calling from the top of the ski slope at Hillend. She said that she was with Detective Superintendent McGuire and that someone had abducted her brother. Mr McGuire had set off in pursuit and wanted snow-equipped officers there, pronto.'

Skinner could barely take in what he was being told. 'Jesus!' he whispered. 'What did they do?'

'They took her at her word. They had caller ID; it was the superintendent's phone she was using. The duty inspector in the control room ordered all available units to the scene.'

'Good. And Neil? Have you, has anyone, called Neil?'

'I vetoed that, sir, until I'd spoken to you. I hope my judgement was right, but I didn't want him charging up that hill like a one-man army.'

'Your judgement was spot on, Jack. Having Mario there is enough; my main worry is that if he catches the abductor, they'll have to scrape him off the hillside. Leave Neil to me. I'll call him, and while I'm doing that I want you to get a car to pick me up from Gullane and take me to the scene. I'd drive myself, but I've had a couple of beers.'

'Very good, sir. Er, you'll let me know how it turns out, will you? With the boy?'

'Sure.' He hung up once more, and took a deep breath; when he was ready he dialled McIlhenney's cell-phone number.

'Yes?' Skinner could tell by the background noise that his friend was on the road.

'Neil, it's me. Where are you?'

'We're on the M8, just short of Livingston, heading for Glasgow. Bandit's taking me to his favourite curry shop before we go to the pub.'

'Forget it for tonight: your stake-out has been cancelled.'

'By whom?'

'By me, for fuck's sake! Isn't that enough?'

'Sure. Sorry, boss. What's up? Is the situation resolved?'

'No, and it won't be tonight either. Who's driving?'

'I am.'

'Well, come off at the first exit, head back to Edinburgh, check in your firearms, drop off Mackenzie and go home. Understood?'

'Yes, but . . .'

'But nothing; that's a direct operational order, so obey it, please . . . to the letter.'

Sixty

George and Jen Regan were the last people Stevie Steele had expected to find on his doorstep when he answered the ringing of the bell.

He and Maggie had made no announcement in the office of the fact that they were living together, although their relationship was known to Mary Chambers. She had her own reasons for discretion but, grapevines being grapevines, they had assumed that sooner or later it would become common knowledge. Still, there was a moment's awkward silence when he saw them, ended the instant he realised that they might misunderstand the reason behind it. 'Hey,' he exclaimed, 'this is a surprise. Come on in.' He led them up the stairs to the hall.

'I hope we're not interrupting anything,' said George.

'Not at all. We're in the play-room, where we keep the music and the telly.'

'We?' Jen quizzed him. 'Have you got a new girlfriend, Stevie?'

'House-mate, actually.' He stood to one side. 'Go on in and say hello.'

For the second time inside two minutes there was a period of stunned silence, until Maggie broke it. 'You mean you didn't know, George?' she asked, with a smile.

'Well . . . no, I didn't. I knew you two were friendly, but . . .'

'Not this friendly? We've been living together for a few weeks now. The bosses all know about it, so that's okay; we just haven't put it on the Torphichen Place notice-board, that's all.'

George looked from one to the other as he struggled for words. Eventually Stevie let him off the hook. 'Mags, get some glasses. I'll get a bottle of something from the rack.' He disappeared into kitchen, returning with a bottle of Bornos, a Spanish *sauvignon blanc* that they had found on a website. He filled the glasses and handed them round. 'Grab a seat,' he told their visitors. 'Saturday tends to be a chill-out day with us. We do all the domestic stuff on a Sunday morning.'

'I'm amazed,' said George, finally, 'about you two. I won't say I hadn't wondered, but I never suspected that you were . . .'

'Shacked up?' Stevie suggested.

'If you want to put it that way, yes. You've covered your tracks well.'

'The remarkable thing is that we haven't covered our tracks at all,' Maggie told him; she dug Stevie in the ribs. 'It makes me wonder about the efficiency of our divisional CID.' She paused. 'But enough about us: how are you two getting along?'

The question seemed to bring a cold draught into the room. 'As well as we can, Maggie,' Jen replied. The two women knew each other, having met at several social events. 'We've tried to keep busy; it's only since we've run out of things to do that we've really hit the wall. Neither of us can get our heads round it yet: it's all a bad dream, only we know we're not going to waken up.'

'Have you been sleeping?'

'The doctor had to knock me out eventually. The Valium, they keep it at bay . . . until they wear off, that is.' She looked at her husband, in a chair opposite hers. 'As for him, he's had his own form of therapy.'

'I know,' said Stevie, looking at his colleague. 'He told me about it.'

'And that's what brings us here,' George announced. 'Out of the blue, I had a call this afternoon, from a woman I spoke to when I went to the car park. She remembered something, and phoned to let me know about it.' He repeated Betty Bee's story in every detail, laying particular emphasis on the time of her encounter with the running man. 'What do you think?' he asked. 'I need an objective view on this. Does that witness statement alone offer sufficient grounds for keeping the investigation open? If it was Mr and Mrs Joe Public's son, not ours?'

Stevie looked at the ceiling, his eyes tracing the line of the fine plaster cornice. 'Do you mean will I take it to Mary Chambers?'

'I suppose so.'

'Yes, I will.'

The room seemed to brighten as a wave of hope swept across George Regan's face. 'Thanks, Stevie,' he sighed, with pure relief in his voice. 'I was afraid you'd say I was grabbing at moonbeams.'

'No way. Sarge, you've forgotten something: you're a bloody good detective. For as long as we've worked together, I've always trusted your instincts.'

'Well, that's good, because I'm going to fly another kite at you. Our son dies in a freak accident. A few days later, another policeman's child is as good as killed by a dodgy gas fire. Coincidence?'

'Bob Skinner once told me,' said Maggie, quietly, 'that he flat out does not believe in coincidences.'

'Let's try it on him, then,' Stevie declared. 'I'll talk to Mary Chambers first, as I must, since she's our boss; if she clears it, I'll take Miss Bee's story to the big man himself, and see if he lets me run with it.'

Sixty-one

'Uncle Mario! Uncle Mario!'

The voice was that of an angel. Everything around him was white; he was floating on a cloud. '*I am dead*,' he thought. '*And there is another side, even if it is bloody cold.*'

'Uncle Mario!' The angel's call sounded again, but closer this time. But then he felt a slap across his face and a blinding pain shoot through his head, advising him forcefully, that alive or dead, he was not in heaven. Since the alternative was not to his liking, he pulled himself to a sitting position and rejoined the real world.

Lauren had been four years old when last he had seen her in tears. She was on her knees beside him, her right mitten clutched in her left hand, the other red from hitting him.

'Hey,' he muttered, his voice weak, his breath forming a cloud in the snow. 'I'm all right, kid.' He tried to wink at her and the flash of agony returned, drilling a hole in his head behind his right ear, to make it clear to him that he was not.

'What are you doing here?' he asked. 'I thought I told you to ski down.'

'There was too much fresh snow,' the girl replied. 'It looked too dangerous, so I followed you instead. What happened to you?'

The memory came flooding back, and with it the fear, renewed. 'I was ambushed,' he told her. 'Whacked on the head.' Shakily, he pushed himself up, finding a precarious footing on the hillside. 'Did you make the call?'

'Yes. They said they would do what you said.'

'Good. This time I really do want you to wait here.' He looked around, trying hard to focus. There were more tracks on the ground, heading into the gloom. The snow had eased to little or nothing, but it was almost dark. In the distance he could see the glow from the floodlit slope and, beyond, the orange halo that covered the night city, offering the false illusion of safety. 'I'm going after them again. You should hear policemen soon. When you do, yell for all you're worth. You're good at that.'

He turned and headed after the tracks once again, but much more slowly this time. His legs were trembling under him, and the pain in his head would not abate. He drove himself on, though, ready in his heart to kill his attacker with his bare hands when he found him again. But if he did not find him again...

He did his best to banish his worst fear and pressed on. Gradually the light changed before him, and the landscape changed with it. He realised that he had come to the edge of a plantation of trees, and that the tracks led inside. He closed his eyes and prayed.

When he opened them again, a cloud had cleared away and the scene was moonlit. He looked into the forest. It would be impossible to follow the tracks; from that point on it would be guesswork. 'Please, Spence,' he murmured, 'please be alive.'

He stepped into the wood, knowing that there was no finer place for another ambush. At once it grew pitch dark; a branch slapped across his face, and round the right side of his head, setting a new fire burning within it. He stopped: a few yards in and he was totally lost. He was effectively blind: there was no way forward.

And then he heard a sound; distant at first then louder, coming towards him. He backed away, retracing his steps without turning, his eyes on the direction of the crashing din. He wondered whether there were deer that high up, in such weather.

Before he could dwell further on the question, the noise was upon him, a small dark bundle, running for his life, scraped and cut by the lashing branches, but safe, crashing into his arms. 'Spence!' he cried, a sob choking him. 'Are you okay?'

Without waiting for an answer, he turned towards the light and to the way out of the woods. The snow had turned heavy once again, although not as bad as before. He looked at the boy and realised that his weather-suit had gone. 'How did you get away?' he asked.

'He had a strap attached to me,' Spencer told him. 'In the dark he couldn't see me unfasten my snowsuit. When I had it done, I fell over, rolled out of it and ran away.'

'Is he coming after you?'

'I don't know.'

Mario's head swam. He knew that he was concussed, and that flight was beyond him. And so he stripped off his own suit and made the boy climb inside it, then turned, shivering already in sweater and jeans, but more than ready to face the kidnapper, should he be foolish enough to risk his wrath.

Sixty-two

Alex heard the front door open; a few seconds later, her father appeared in the doorway of the sitting room. She checked her watch. 'It's nearly nine. What sort of time is this to be crawling in at?'

'Stop it,' he pleaded. 'You sound just like your mother when you say that.' He walked towards her. 'Have you eaten?'

'No, I waited for you. I've got a table booked at the Golf Inn, if you want. They said as long as we got there before nine thirty they'd feed us. Don't worry, I'm paying.'

'Trish is in?'

'Yes, her boy-friend's working tonight.'

'Come on, then. I'll change my shirt and we'll go.'

As he stepped into the light of the hall she saw him more clearly. 'God,' she said, 'you look bushed. Are you sure you want to go? I can always whip something up.' And then a memory came back to her. 'Oh, shit, I forgot: Stevie Steele called earlier. He said he needs to talk to you.'

'It had better be urgent,' Bob growled. 'Bugger the shirt, they can take me as I am. Come on, I'll phone him from the restaurant.' He fetched a heavy leather jacket from the cloakroom off the hall, and they headed for the door.

The restaurant was a few hundred yards away from the house; in less than ten minutes they were seated at a corner table, and Alex was ordering wine from the extensive list. As soon as the waiter had gone her father took out his phone and dialled Steele. It was Maggie Rose who answered. 'Hold on, I'll get him,' she said.

'Thanks, Mags. Oh, and before I forget, I want to see you in my office next week, as soon as we can both fit it in.' He waited, until her

253

partner came to the phone. 'You wanted me,' Skinner grunted.

'Yes, sir. I'm sorry about the timing, but I don't think it can wait. I've spoken to Superintendent Chambers and she agrees. I want to reopen the investigation into George Regan's son, and link it with DCS Pringle's daughter's so-called accident.'

'Her death, you mean. Ross passed away this afternoon.'

He heard Steele's gasp. 'Sorry, sir, I didn't know that.'

'No matter. What's prompted this?'

'George has found a witness, a woman who saw someone legging it into the lower entrance to the car park at around the time the pathologist reckons the boy died. She described him as running away from someone, only there was nobody chasing him.'

'That's your link?'

'It's enough for me, boss.'

'And me, Stevie. Given what happened to young Spence McIlhenney, I've been kicking myself all night for not pursuing the theory, even with no evidence to say so, that the two events might have been linked.'

'What happened to him?'

'You don't know? Call Neil, and he'll fill you in. I'm on-side with you on this; this is your investigation. You're detached from all other duties and you report directly to me. Here's where you start. I want you to identify every investigation where Regan, Pringle and Neil McIlhenney worked together, plus I want a list of all the other officers involved with them. That's a priority: I don't want any more tragic so-called accidents. Get moving on it first thing tomorrow. If you find you need help, then co-opt Ray Wilding from the head of CID's office, on my authority. He'll be sat on his hands for a while anyway.'

He hung up just as the waiter appeared with Alex's choice of wine, and with a pint of lager. 'You look as if you need that,' she told him. 'I'll let the Faustino breathe for a bit.'

He picked up the tall glass gratefully, and drained almost half of it in one gulp.

'That sort of day?' his daughter asked.

'Since about four o'clock.'

'What was that about Neil?'

'Someone tried to snatch Spencer, his boy, at the top of the Hillend ski slope.'

'My God,' she gasped. 'You mean a perv, a paedophile?'

'I don't think so. Did you read about George Regan's son being killed, and Ross Pringle being gassed in her room on the campus?'

'Yes.'

'Well, this may have been the third in a series . . . in fact, I'm bloody sure it was.' He stopped as the waiter approached. 'I'll have the black-pudding starter, then venison,' he said, then turned back to Alex. 'A year ago, kid, I would have made that assumption on day one. I don't care how clearly accidental they looked, I would not have bought that coincidence.'

'Pops,' she told him, 'you can't do the thinking for the entire force.'

'Why not?' he shot back at her. 'I'm the highest-ranking CID officer. I'm not supposed to make mistakes, especially not one that put a kid's life at risk. I have not had my mind on the job, daughter. I have been so bloody preoccupied with my domestic life that my performance is suffering. I wouldn't take that from a junior officer, so I sure as hell won't take it from myself. I have to get my eye back on the ball, or kick the damn thing into touch.'

'Shape up or ship out, you mean?'

'That's about it.'

'And which will it be? No, forget that: it was a damn silly question.'

He forced a grin. 'I had a moment of weakness this afternoon,' he confessed, 'but that's gone. My decision's made: it's not a matter of choosing job or family. How many men have to do that? No, it's a matter of finding the proper time for both and giving both my total attention.'

'And what about this woman you told me about? Is there room for her too?'

'She's as committed to her job as I am. We have common interests and we like each other; that's all there is to it. Aileen's not an issue; Sarah is, and the future of our marriage.'

'Well, sort it out, Pops, please, for I do not like to see you like this. I'm going to have serious words with my stepmother when she gets back.'

'You will not. Don't get involved, and don't take sides.'

'I'm promising nothing; I'm on your side, damn it, and that won't change.' She rapped the table. 'Now, enough of that and tell me what happened to Neil's son. You said "tried to snatch him", from which I take it that he's okay.'

'He's got some cuts and bruises, and he's shaken up, but he's all right. Mario McGuire's not so good, though. He's in the Western.'

'Mario?'

'He took the kids skiing. At the moment the best guess is that the kidnapper was watching the house, and tracked them to the centre. We know that he hired skis and boots there, and bought a snowsuit and goggles . . . paid cash, God damn it, so there's no card to trace. He grabbed Spencer when he was isolated from Mario, and Lauren was on her way down the slope, The big fellow worked out what had happened and set off after them, but the guy lay in wait for him and whacked him with a rock in a sock: they found it at the scene.'

'How bad is he?'

'He'll live. The doctor who examined him at the scene reckoned concussion and maybe a hairline skull fracture. They're keeping him under observation to make sure there's no inter-cranial bleeding. He was hit pretty hard, but not hard enough to stop him picking himself up and heading back up the slope to where he and Spence found each other. When our officers got there, he was standing guard over the kid and ready to slaughter anyone who touched him. He decked two constables before they calmed him down.'

Alex gazed at him in horror. 'That's awful,' she exclaimed. 'What about Lauren? She must have been hysterical.'

He surprised her by laughing. 'The words "hysterical" and "Lauren McIlhenney" do not go together. Neil was in a far worse state than she was when I told him what had happened.'

Sixty-three

Detective Inspector Arthur Dorward was used to out-of-office calls, but Stevie Steele's Sunday-morning visit took him by surprise. He and his wife had only just finished breakfast when he arrived.

Dorward, who ran the scene-of-crime unit, was universally regarded as one of the most competent men on the force. When he heard the story, he needed very little guidance on what was required. 'I'll pull my best team together,' he said. 'We'll get back out to the campus and go over that room again, and again, and again, until we can prove someone sabotaged that gas fire. I can only hope that it hasn't been compromised since we were there.'

'I called the university last night. I told the security staff to seal the room, but they said they were pretty sure that nobody's been in it since your lot left.'

'That'll be a break if it's true. Don't worry: if there's anything there we'll find it, now we're treating it as murder and not a simple accident investigation.'

'There's something else,' his colleague told him. 'When you get to the lab, you'll find a sock with a rock in it waiting for you. Right now, it's being shown to the pathologist who's being asked to say whether it could have caused young George Regan's fatal injury. When you get it, I want you to go over the boy's clothing to see if you can find any fibres that match it.'

Dorward smiled. 'This sounds like a fun day.'

'It would be, if it wasn't so bloody serious.'

Steele left him on his doorstep, and drove for twenty minutes until he reached Neil McIlhenney's house. The chief inspector opened the door for him before he had time to ring the bell. He still looked grim and shaken.

From the kitchen, they could hear the children. 'How are they?' Stevie asked.

'Fine, thanks, all things considered. Spence has got an eye on him like he's been in with George Foreman, but otherwise he's okay. He's quite proud of the shiner, actually. Lauren's her usual controlled self. They're both more worried about Mario than they are about each other.'

'How is he?'

'He's okay. I called the Western this morning and they let me speak to him. He's still a bit woozy, but he's sounded like that on many a Sunday morning.'

'You don't blame him for taking the kids up there?'

McIlhenney looked at him as if he had suddenly grown a second head. 'Why the hell should I?' he exclaimed. 'If this guy was going to follow them, I'd rather he did it when Mario was there than when he wasn't. McGuire's Rambo act is something to be feared; it's as well for you he's on-side about you and Maggie.'

'So I've been told,' Stevie conceded. 'Can we sit down?' They were still in the hall.

McIlhenney looked contrite at once. 'I'm sorry,' he said. 'I'm forgetting my manners.' He led the way into the living room. 'Would you like a coffee? A croissant?' He grinned. 'Christ, man, would you like breakfast? Lou's feeding the bears, I'm sure she could knock something up.'

'That's very kind of you, sir, but I'm fine.'

'Sir, is it? This is starting to sound formal ... which, I suppose, it is. The boss called to tell me you were carrying the ball on this investigation.'

'Plural.'

'Pardon?'

'Investigations: we're linking the attack on your son with the deaths of George Regan junior, and Ross Pringle.'

McIlhenney nodded, to himself rather than to his colleague. 'Of course you are.'

'There's a witness in the Regan case; someone who reported seeing a running man.'

'He'd better keep on running.'

'Let's hope he does, but we'll still have to catch up with him. Sir…'

'Neil, for God's sake.'

'Neil, then; I'm starting by looking for links, between the three attacks and between the victims.'

'You mean between their fathers?'

'Exactly. I need to know about every investigation where DCS Pringle, DS Regan and you all worked together. I'm going to ask all of you for your recollections. You can see why it's important; we've got to find out if other officers' families might be at risk.'

'Absolutely.' McIlhenney smiled. 'The sun is starting to shine on you, Inspector. I've been thinking about that too, and I reckon I can cut your workload. There was only one single investigation on which I worked with George Regan and Dan Pringle.'

Steele straightened in his chair. 'Are you sure about that?'

'One hundred per cent. I was a detective constable then, and I was drafted in from my own division because Central CID was short on manpower. Once the case was closed, I went back to Western.'

'And were there other officers involved? Do you recall that?'

'Not on the CID team. There were a few uniforms, but they wouldn't be identifiable. Dan, George and I were the police witnesses in the High Court.'

'What was the investigation?'

McIlhenney stood. 'First, let me get you a coffee. You're showing signs of zeal, the mark of a man with Bob Skinner on his tail.' He left the room, to return carrying a mug and a glass of orange juice.

'Thanks,' said Steele, as he took the mug. 'Don't you drink this stuff?'

'No. I guess that makes me an unusual copper, doesn't it?'

'I can't think of another.'

The chief inspector settled back into his chair. 'I wasn't always, though. Back then I was a real archetype. I drank eight mugs a day, minimum. I smoked, ate anything deep-fried in batter, went for a few pints after work, all that stuff. I was like a younger Dan Pringle, you might say.'

Steele detected an edge of bitterness in his tone, but did not pursue it.

'The investigation you want to know about took place ten years ago. It involved a girl called Patsy Aikenhead; she was only a kid, twenty-one years old, married to a guy called Chris Aikenhead, aged twenty-six, as I remember. They had a big flat in Marchmont. He worked offshore on an oil-production platform, making good money. She was a qualified nursery nurse, so they adapted the flat and set her up in business as a child-minder. She had a nice wee life, until one of the kids in her care was admitted to the old Royal Infirmary with convulsions. The baby died . . . Mariel Dickens, aged one year and one month . . . and the post mortem revealed cerebral haemorrhage as the cause of death.'

'Who called the ambulance?'

'Patsy did, at fifteen minutes after one. The child had been delivered to her care at half past eight that morning, and the pathologist reported that the injury was sustained between one and a half and two hours before she arrived at the hospital.'

'Where was the husband at this time?'

'On his platform.'

'Did she work alone?'

'No, she had an assistant, a Spanish girl called Magda Vilabru. George and I interviewed them, under caution from the start: they were both terrified, and they both denied harming the child. We interviewed the mother, Jocelyn Dickens, and the grandmother, who was living with her at the time. They both stated that Mariel had been happy and healthy when she was dropped off at the nursery.'

'How did you proceed,' Steele asked, 'if neither woman accused the other? Did you charge them both?'

'We didn't have to. We took each of them through their morning, and found out that at some point . . . neither could be specific about when that was . . . they had run low on disposables and baby food, and that Magda had gone to get some. We interviewed the woman in the corner shop that she used, and she told us that the girl had arrived there just before half past eleven. She was a regular customer, so she and the shop assistant chatted for ten minutes, Magda made her purchases and walked back to the nursery. We had a woman officer replicate the journey, several times; it took a minimum of sixteen minutes. That meant . . .'

'That Magda couldn't have been there when the child was injured.'

'Exactly,' McIlhenney affirmed. 'Enter Detective Superintendent Pringle.' He looked at Steele. 'I know you worked with Dan, but I'll be frank. He was a good officer, no question, but to my mind he had two weaknesses: he was too quick to judgement and he liked to be in at the kill.'

'I can't argue with that,' the inspector admitted. 'I've noticed the same. What did he do in this case?'

'He marched in and took it over. George and I had done all the work, and he told us to back off, that we were being too soft and that he was going to interview Patsy Aikenhead. I sat in on it, under orders not to say a word. Honest to God, Stevie, he terrorised the girl. She had no lawyer, no nothing, as he lashed into her. She was in tears inside five minutes. Inside fifteen minutes, she had admitted that she'd been in a foul mood because one of the babies was cutting back teeth and upsetting the others. Inside an hour, she had signed a statement admitting that she might have thrown Mariel into a cot and banged her head on the bars. Dan wrapped it up at that, and charged her with culpable homicide.'

'It went to trial, though? You said you were all witnesses.'

'We were. The defence withdrew the statement, but they couldn't deny that it had been made. The case hinged on that time period when Magda was away from the nursery, and the shop assistant confirmed the statement that George and I had taken from her at Torphichen Place. Magda wasn't in court herself, by the way, she'd gone back to Spain, and refused to come back to give evidence. It didn't matter, though. Juries always want to convict someone in dead baby cases, and they found Patsy guilty; unanimous verdict. The judge remanded her in custody for reports, as he had to since she was a first offender facing a jail sentence, but he warned her that he had it in mind to make an example of her, as I recall it, "to those who take responsibility for the care of other people's children". Yes, that's how he put it.'

Stevie frowned: something was beginning to niggle at the back of his mind. 'Should I remember this case? I was on the beat out in West Lothian ten years ago, just about to transfer into CID.'

'Maybe you should. Maybe you should remember the appeal too. The trial took two days; that was all. The first day was mostly medical evidence; the second day was when the key stuff happened, when we were in the box, and the shop assistant. After the verdict had been handed down, there was a full report in the *Scotsman*. Guess what? No, if you don't remember, you'll never guess.'

McIlhenney smiled, but there was a sadness about it. 'The next morning, Dan had a call at the office from a member of the public who'd read the paper. The woman insisted that she had to see him, so he took Regan and they went to her house. Dan came back with a face like thunder. I asked what had happened, but he wouldn't speak to me; George had to tell me about it afterwards. It was surreal, Stevie. The new witness was a customer in the corner shop. The baby died on the last Monday in October. What happens on the last Sunday in October?'

Steele felt his eyes widen. 'The clocks go back!' he said.

'Every year, without fail; but in that shop, the owner hadn't got round to changing his. The shop assistant was too thick to realise it, and we didn't interview her on the premises, so we never actually saw the bloody thing. It changed everything: it put Magda Vilabru right back in the frame, but she was in Algeciras, from which safe haven she couldn't be extradited in those days.'

'So was the case reopened?'

'Of course. The defence appealed formally against conviction and the Crown didn't oppose. The Advocate Depute told the court that he could no longer rely on the testimony of a key witness; that was all. The investigation was reactivated, but without the Spanish girl there was nowhere to go. And suppose we did bring her back now, we'd never get a conviction. Her being there only meant that she could have done it, not that she did it.'

'What if Patsy Aikenhead gave evidence against her?'

'We'd need to reconstitute her ashes for that. She hanged herself in her cell on the night of her conviction.' The big chief inspector looked at his colleague. 'It all happened ten years ago this month,' he told him. 'If I was you, I'd be wanting to know where Chris Aikenhead is right now.'

Steele returned his gaze. 'But you're not me, Neil,' he replied. 'So promise me that you won't try to find him yourself.'

Sixty-four

Skinner had expected to find Mario McGuire's head swathed in bandages, but the only dressing was a plaster covering a cut on his forehead. In fact, the detective superintendent looked remarkably normal as he sat up in bed in the small hospital room. 'Hello, boss,' he said. He sounded in good shape too.

McGuire looked at the tall figure, at the two boys who flanked him, and at the little girl he carried in the crook of his right arm. The older of the boys was slim, with a serious expression, while the younger was sturdy, a strikingly handsome child with clear blue eyes and tousled blond hair that was starting to darken. The girl, although only a toddler, was on course to be a stunner, with auburn hair and a friendly smile. 'I didn't expect to see you today,' he went on, 'especially not mob-handed. Mind you, I don't remember a great deal about seeing you yesterday.'

'We're on a trip across the river,' Skinner explained 'How's the head?' He directed his question towards Paula Viareggio. 'I'm asking you, because I want the official version.'

'He'll live, this time at least,' she replied, with obvious relief in her voice. 'They did another scan and an ECG this morning, and they were both absolutely clear. There's no fracture either; this man has a seriously hard head. We were having an argument just before you arrived about whether he goes home today or stays for another night under observation.'

'Would it help if I ordered him to stay … or tried to?'

'It's okay,' McGuire told him. 'You don't have to. I've given up arguing with Paulie, about the non-business things at least.'

'That's good, because I want you rested and fresh tomorrow. If they let you out, and assuming you feel fit enough to come in, I was hoping you'd be able to join me when I have my conversation with Mr Jay.'

'I'd join you for that, boss, supposing I was in a wheel-chair.'

'Two thirty p.m., then; in my office.'

'Excellent. I'll be dancing by that time.' His eyes left Skinner and moved to the door. 'Christ,' he laughed, 'it's getting crowded in here.' The DCC turned to see Maggie Rose and Stevie Steele come into the room. He glanced at Paula, looking for signs of tension between the two women, but found none. Maggie smiled at each of the boys, and made a fuss over Seonaid, amusing her father, who had never seen his former assistant in this light before.

'I'll relieve the crush in that case,' he said. 'Come on, boys and girl: we're off to the aquarium.'

The quartet watched them leave, James Andrew closing the door carefully behind them. 'You're looking unscathed,' Maggie told Mario.

'I've been worse.' He grinned.

'I know,' she said. 'I was there.'

He glanced around the room. 'The accommodation's better this time.' He nodded to Steele. 'Hi, Stevie. Is this social or professional?'

'Both. I'm running the investigation so I need a description, if you can give me one.'

McGuire winced. 'He was dressed in white gear, he wore a woolly hat and wrap-round goggles. I took him for your average punter who watches *Ski Sunday* and thinks that's how you have to look. Height? Hard to tell with the boots on, but as tall as me, I'd guess. I'm sorry, pal, but that's the best I can do.'

'I appreciate that. Spencer told me much the same thing, and he was with the man for a while. The person who supplied him with the ski equipment couldn't help us either: he just picked it out and handed over the money. No conversation, no eye contact; clean shaven, and not a youngster, that was all the kid could tell us. But there are other things you might have picked up that could help me, like a better feeling for his age, for one thing.'

'He has to be a fit bloke, Stevie. He was able to control Spence, which is not as easy as it sounds, even if he is only ten. He was able to keep ahead of me on the way up that hill, and I know what I can do.

Plus, he was able to get the drop on me and knock me spark out with whatever it was he hit me with.'

'A sock.'

'A sock?'

'With a bloody great lump of rock in it.'

'Ouch! You're bringing my headache back.'

'Sorry, but all that helps, Mario. We're talking about a mature man with a pretty high level of fitness, somebody maybe in his thirties.'

'Did Spence hear him speak?'

'Not at all: he didn't say a word.'

McGuire's face grew grim as he relived the scene. 'Jesus!' he whispered. 'You know, Stevie, if Lauren hadn't come up after me . . .' He shuddered at the thought. 'Did they find any trace of the guy afterwards?'

'They think he made it down the side of the hill, and they think they know where he parked his car, but that's it. There's no physical evidence to take us forward. It's as well we've got the link.'

'What's that?'

'The thread that ties Dan Pringle, George Regan and Neil McIlhenney together: the Patsy Aikenhead investigation.'

McGuire gave a long whistle. 'Oh, my,' he murmured. 'That's what it's looking like, is it? It'll hit Neil hard, that will. Even though he didn't do anything wrong, that case has always preyed on his conscience. It was Dan Pringle who ordered George and him to have that witness brought in, rather than interview her on-site where they might have seen the clock for themselves. It was his mistake, but the guys covered up for him. That's the real reason for the famous coolness between Neil and him, whatever else might have happened since.'

'It's all history,' said a voice from the door. Mario, Paula, Maggie and Stevie all turned to see McIlhenney standing there. 'As will be the guy who took Spence when we find him: a bad memory locked up for good.'

He looked at the trio standing by the bedside. 'Would you please excuse me for a moment?' he asked. 'I'd like a private word with my friend.'

'Of course,' Maggie answered, for them all.

The two men looked at each other, hearing rather than seeing the door close.

'I'm sorry, man,' Mario said, hoarsely, on the verge of tears.

'Don't be daft,' Neil told him gruffly. 'I'm here to thank you, not thump you. My kids could never come to any harm while they're with you: I've always known that.' He sat on the bed. 'Sunshine, do you believe in things beyond our ken?'

'No. I have to see reality to accept it.'

'Well, I do. I've seen the paranormal, I've experienced it, and I accept it.' He told his friend the story of his recurring dream. 'I thought it was me, and that it was a warning of impending death. But now I know different. It was you, and it wasn't Olive driving you on, but Lauren, her double. Wherever it came from, it was a message that, although something bad was going to happen, in the end it would be all right.'

Sixty-five

Bob Skinner had been on a guilt trip all weekend; as soon as he stepped inside Deep Sea World he was hit by another wave. Mark and James Andrew had been nagging him for a year and more to take them there, but he had always found an excuse for delaying the adventure. And even now, when the moment finally had come, there was, if not an ulterior motive, a secondary purpose to the family trip.

The aquarium itself was a fantastic experience. The boys were consumed by it, and Seonaid squealed with excitement as they made their way through the exhibits: the touching pool, where youngsters were given hands-on experience of fish, the interactive displays and, most impressive of all, the underwater safari, where visitors were conveyed on a moving belt inside the vast aquatic wildlife park itself.

They spent two hours there, before Bob announced that it was time to go for lemonade and biscuits and, in his case, a cappuccino.

The café was busy but he found a table, leaving Mark and James Andrew to watch their sister as he made selections for them. He had just returned and was sipping his coffee, when Jazz shouted, 'Hey, Dad, there's Uncle Andy.'

He turned, to see Andy and Karen Martin approaching, pushing the infant Danielle in her chair. 'Fancy seeing you here,' Andy exclaimed, with more than a hint of a laugh. Bob pulled up two more chairs, making sure that one of them was next to his own.

'What do you think of the aquarium?' Karen asked Mark, and the two of them embarked on a discussion of its high points and other merits.

'How are you doing?' Bob asked Andy, as they sat together.

'I've been getting an idea of the life and times of Tommy Murtagh. He's a creepy bastard, but we knew that.' He took his friend step by step through the First Minister's meteoric career, from the shop floor to the power and trappings of high office, and through his family background.

'Brindsley Groves, eh?' Skinner mused as he finished.

'Have you heard of him?'

'I've heard of the firm, but not him: Dundee's a closed book as far as I'm concerned. The *Courier*, the Discovery, and that's all I know about it.'

'There's more to the city than that.'

'Maybe, but let's concentrate on Mr Groves. Have you met him?'

'Thanks to Rod Greatorix, I met him on Friday evening. Mrs Groves is Rod's sister.'

'Is that awkward for you?'

'No. They're not bosom pals.'

'What's he like?'

'He's like a lot of rich men, amiable as long as you know your place with him, but his kids didn't stick around long, so there must be another side to him. He's fifty-eight, so Rod said.'

'And he was banging Murtagh's mother, while she worked for him?'

'So the great Dundonian rumour mill has it.'

'Maybe more than the rumour mill.'

'What do you mean?' Martin asked, intrigued.

'Did you know that there's a Groves family trust in existence?'

'No, but it wouldn't surprise me. There has to be a hell of a lot of money there.'

'There is. Now guess who one of the beneficiaries is.'

The younger man's green eyes gleamed. 'The man himself?'

Skinner nodded. 'There's nothing illegal about it, in that it doesn't require to be declared on any public register, but it's a fact. We can't use the information in any way, because that would probably betray the source, but it begs a few more questions.'

'Damn right it does. It's time I took a closer look at Tommy Murtagh's antecedents . . . beyond the official biography.'

Sixty-six

It would have been wrong to say that Neil McIlhenney was nervous as he drove through to Glasgow, with Bandit Mackenzie in the passenger seat of his car. He knew that his family could not be safer: they were being guarded round the clock by an experienced police team, and the children would be taken to school in the morning by detective escorts. Despite all of that security, he would rather have been with them.

In fact he had been offered the opportunity, but he had declined. To pull out of the stake-out would have been to leave his colleague exposed, and he could not contemplate that. So he pressed on with the assignment, hoping that Samir Bajram would show himself, that he would lead them to his three companions and that they could wrap the whole thing up.

Bandit was quieter than usual on the drive through. Although legal constraints had prevented the press from using Spencer's name, the incident had been reported, and word had spread rapidly through the police ranks that he was the child involved. However, the link to the two earlier deaths had not been picked up.

'Is your kid all right?' Mackenzie had asked, as they left Edinburgh.

'Yes, thanks, but I don't want to talk about it. I want to stay focused on tonight's job.'

'Have they got any leads?'

'Yes. Now shut it, please.'

They listened to music for the rest of the journey, until finally they arrived in Partick. McIlhenney parked under a light in the next street to the Johnny Groat, and they walked the short distance. The pub was quiet as they arrived: Dolly was either occupied, working elsewhere or taking a night off for her corner of the bar was empty.

They ordered their drinks and settled down for a night in front of the television. Adept though he was at nursing a pint, Mackenzie was on to his second before the door swung open and the Jakes brothers appeared. Bobby looked as edgy as ever, but Frankie smiled as he walked across to them. 'Hello, boyz. Night shift again?'

'Afraid so,' McIlhenney grunted.

'You have a chance to think about that thing we talk about the other night?' he asked.

'Give us time. It might be possible, but we'll need to be sure that no fingers get pointed at us. We'll let you know in a few days whether we're up for it or not.'

'Okay, I stay patient. You wanna drink?'

'No, thanks,' said Mackenzie, 'we've just got them in.'

'Ah,' grunted Frankie, accepting a pint from his brother. He glanced up at the television set above the bar. 'Anything on?'

'The usual Sunday-night shite.'

The Macedonian laughed. 'Could be worse. You could be working already.' He turned as the door opened again, and his ugly face split into a huge grin. 'Sammy!' he exclaimed.

Samir Bajram looked just like his photograph. Even without the crescent earring the two detectives would have recognised him. It was his eyes that were compelling: they were a deep brown colour and they seemed to sparkle, radiating danger and an eagerness to do harm. The beard they had been told about was still there, but it was so fair that it was almost invisible.

He embraced the Jakes brothers. Frankie turned towards them. 'Boyz, this is my cousin Sammy. He's visiting for a while. Sammy, this is Mac and David, I might do some bizniz with them.'

The dark eyes fell upon them in a silent challenge. McIlhenney guessed that this was how he greeted all strangers. He longed to hold his gaze, to send him a message, but he resisted the temptation. 'Hello,' he murmured, picking up his glass.

'Pleased meecha,' the Albanian replied.

Frankie took him by the arm. 'Boyz,' he told them, 'Sammy and us got to talk bizniz. See youse later.'

The two brothers and their cousin turned their backs on them and walked to the far side of the bar, taking a table behind Dolly's empty corner, where Bobby ordered another pint of beer. McIlhenney and Mackenzie turned their eyes back to the television, but listened elsewhere. From time to time, a buzz of conversation drifted across to them in a strange language. They waited: their cover story would allow them to stay until ten thirty at the latest. If necessary, they agreed, they would go back to the car and wait close enough to observe Samir leaving, then follow him.

They were almost ready to go when the three stood up. The bar had filled up by that time, and they eased their way through the drinkers, Frankie greeting those he knew and shouldering past the rest. 'So long, boyz,' he called out to them, as the trio left.

'Count to twenty,' said McIlhenney. 'Let's give ourselves long enough to make it look as if we drank up before we went, rather than that we followed them straight out. We'll cop where they're going and take it from there.'

Mackenzie counted off the numbers slowly and quietly. Finally he whispered, 'twenty' and they rose.

Once outside the pub, they glanced left and then right. Fifty yards away, three figures slouched along, backs towards them. 'You wait here; I'll bring the car.' Mackenzie nodded agreement, and stepped back into a close, making himself invisible to their targets, but keeping them in sight.

As he watched, they stopped beside a car. Frankie bent over beside the driver's door, as if to fit the key into the lock, then the doors were opened and all three stepped inside.

'Get a move on, N—' Mackenzie began, and then the street erupted in a great orange glow, engulfing the car and the three men. The noise of the blast assaulted his ears a millisecond later.

Instinctively, forgetting McIlhenney, he jumped from his cover and pounded down the street. Flames were erupting from the mangled vehicle; as he drew near, there was a second, smaller explosion, which radiated searing heat, stopping him in his tracks. He stared in horror, until McIlhenney's shout, from just behind, interrupted him.

'Get in.'

Without thinking about it, he obeyed. He jumped into the Vectra; even before his door had closed, it was roaring away from the scene.

Sixty-seven

It was a quiet night in Delight, inevitably, because it was Sunday, and because the snow was still thick on the ground. Nevertheless, there was still a full staff complement, and Sukur the chef was still ranting and raving in his kitchen, terrorising his underlings.

Sean Green was on time as usual: he had passed his audition with flying colours, so much so that he had been designated head waiter by Peter Bassam, and presented with a black dinner jacket that almost fitted him. 'It's a job I've been wanting to fill, John,' the owner told him. 'I didn't want to advertise it as such, that's all.'

To his surprise, he had actually been pleased, not just to be so solidly embedded in the restaurant but that his skills had been recognised. There was an extra bounce to his step in the restaurant that night; he knew it, and he made no attempt to hide it. If the other waiters resented him, they gave no sign; he guessed that they were simply glad to be in a job.

The evening started out as if it would be busy; by seven o'clock, there were seven tables occupied. However, as time went on, no new customers appeared, and Bassam appeared to grow more and more edgy. Finally, just after eight, he beckoned Green across. 'John,' he said, 'I'm going to go out for a while, maybe have a meal in someone else's place for a change. You're in charge: look after the till, keep it smooth out front, don't let that crazy chef kill the dishwashers, and I'll see you later.'

Green nodded, thinking that he might take up this line of work permanently.

His sudden elevation did nothing to attract business. At nine thirty the restaurant was empty; just after ten three couples appeared, taking a table for six. At ten forty-five two men entered, but one was so blatantly drunk that Sean told him, quietly but firmly, that the kitchen was closed.

The sextet lingered on: each had three courses, and they drank four bottles of wine. As they sipped their coffee, the new head waiter and acting manager told the kitchen staff and one of the waiters that they could go home.

Finally, at eleven forty, the six paid their bill and left: Sean told the last remaining waiter, who had been looking after their table, that his night was over. He was alone, an opportunity that he had not expected.

Quickly, he went through to Bassam's office. He was still convinced that the restaurateur was clean, but he had a job to do. He fanned quickly over his boss's desk, but saw nothing out of the ordinary. A quick check of the drawers told the same story. He was on his way back to the restaurant, through the tiny bar, when his eye was caught by something that had actually been there all night.

The corner of a piece of paper protruded from under the till, as if it had been shoved in there hastily. Taking care that it would not catch and tear, he withdrew it. He frowned: it was a street map of St Andrews, golfing capital of the world. He struggled to think whether he had ever heard of a Turkish golfer, but could not come up with a single name. But St Andrews was not built on golf alone, he reminded himself. It was a holiday resort, he was sure. In all probability Bassam had been planning a weekend break for his wife back in the summer; the thing could have been there since then for all he knew. Idly, he folded the map and shoved it into his trouser pocket.

He stood there, the man in charge, surveying his empty empire. He had begun to doubt long before that his boss was coming back at all that night, and wondered whether he should leave himself, until he realised that that would leave him with the keys in his possession. Of course, he could always come in early in the morning…

As he weighed his choices, the door opened: there stood Bassam, behind him the flash of something white moving away from the pavement outside.

'John,' he called out. 'It's like a grave in here.'

'It was like a funeral for most of the night,' Green replied. 'Not many punters.'

'Is everybody gone?' The owner stepped over to the bar.

'Yes, long gone. Time I was off too: I've got a bus to catch.'

'Ahh, have a drink with me before you go. I'll give you a lift. Gin and tonic?'

'I'd prefer Bushmills, straight, no rocks,' Sean told him honestly.

Bassam poured him a double and took a Cognac for himself. 'So how do you like my restaurant?' he asked.

'Very much, Mr Bassam; it's a good place to work.'

'Call me Peter, man. I'm pleased with you too. It's good to have someone here at last that I can trust to take the weight off my shoulders.' He finished his drink. 'In fact, I'll show you how much: I'm going to give you a bonus, cash, so you don't need to declare it.' He headed for his office. 'Come on through,' he said, over his shoulder. 'I keep some money in my safe.'

He stepped into his office. Amused, and wondering whether he would declare his windfall to Mandy Dennis, Sean followed.

Before he had taken two steps into the room, two men appeared from either side of the door. His arms were seized and pinned to his sides, a hood was pulled over his head, and everything went dark.

Sixty-eight

'We must stop talking like this,' Bob Skinner chuckled, as he answered the phone just after midnight, 'Trish will get suspicious.' There was no laugh from the other end of the line. 'What's up?' he asked suddenly serious.

'Samir Bajram is,' McIlhenney replied, tersely. 'Him and the Jakes brothers; I'd reckon they're about three miles up by now and heading for orbit.'

'They're what?'

'As far as we could see it was car bomb. Sammy showed up in the pub. Frankie introduced him to us as his cousin, then the three of them went to the other end of the pub. They had a drink, went outside, got into a motor and were blown to smithereens.'

'Were you close?'

'Not close enough to get hurt, although the Bandit nearly got his eyebrows singed.'

'What did you do?'

'We got the hell out, as fast as we could. Since we weren't supposed to be there in the first place, I didn't reckon you'd want us giving witness statements.'

'Too damn right. We'll leave it to Strathclyde, and maybe the SDEA to clear up. You are sure it was Samir?'

McIlhenney growled. 'I won't dignify that with an answer, boss.'

'Okay, sorry. Did you get any idea what he might have been up to?'

'Frankie said that they were doing some business . . . or bizniz, to use his word. I guess it was that other thing he was talking about.'

Skinner frowned. 'Given his background that must mean drugs.

Could that be all there is to these guys' presence here after all, a drugs shipment?'

'Maybe, but if so, where were the other three? No, I don't think so.'

'No, that's true.' He sighed. 'It's a bugger, though: I was counting on Samir to lead us to the rest; now we're back to scratch. Plus, it leaves us with another question. Who did the three of them in, and why?'

'The way I see it, Sammy was in the wrong place at the wrong time. It looks like a Glasgow gang hit, with the Jakes boys as the target. I could understand Frankie pissing somebody off badly enough.' He laughed, softly. 'He was an annoying so-and-so.'

'You sound as if you'll miss him.'

'Strangely enough, I will. I actually liked the ugly wee bastard. Whoever did him just joined the long list of people I'd like to meet.'

'Chances are you never will, Neil. Good night.'

Skinner replaced his bedside phone in its cradle, and picked up his book. He looked at the page, but the letters were blurred. The day was coming, he knew, when he was going to need help for night-time reading. But it was not his late-forties vision alone that made him unable to focus. At the back of his mind, a disconcerting scenario was taking shape.

He thought about it for a few minutes, then reached a decision. He climbed out of bed, picked up his personal directory from the dressing-table and, holding it directly under the light so that he could see clearly, looked through it until he found Amanda Dennis's mobile number.

She was fuzzy with sleep when she answered. 'Yes?' The word was slow and heavy.

'Amanda,' he snapped, urgently. 'It's Bob. I want you to pull Sean Green out of his waiter job, right away. I'm probably being alarmist, but he could be in danger.'

Sixty-nine

Andy Martin worked assiduously in his Dundee office for two hours. When he was finished he had read through all the papers in his in-tray, scribbling notes on those that required action on his part, and he had dictated six letters. Satisfied, he took the tray and his electronic notepad through to his secretary and left her to do her part.

Back in his office, he switched on the 'engaged' light above his door, hung his jacket over the back of his chair, settled down and switched on his laptop computer. He could have used the terminal on his desk, but that would have left a record of his activity, and that was something he did not want.

He waited for the machine to power up, then went on line, using his private account with AOL. Opening the powerful search engine, he entered three words, 'Herbert Groves Construction', then sat back, gazing at the screen, until a range of options appeared.

The firm's website was top of the list: he chose it and watched as the home page appeared, as fast as his computer would allow. It was a professional job, one befitting a major business, and it offered an extensive menu, offering history, services, projects completed, current projects, financial performance, employment opportunities and, finally, the element he had hoped to find, biographies. He selected it, and images of the company's senior executives appeared before him, with that of Brindsley Groves at the top. He clicked on the smiling face and waited.

A page of text assembled itself on his screen: the life story that he had hoped to find. He began to read, silently.

Brindsley Groves, BA, MBA, is chairman and managing director of Herbert Groves Construction. He is fifty-eight years old, and has been chief executive of the company for thirty-one years, since succeeding his father Herbert Groves II. He was elected chairman of the company on his father's death.

He was educated at Strathallan School, and at Aberdeen University, from which he graduated with honours in accountancy and economics at the age of twenty-one. Before taking up a position with the company, he studied for a further year at the University of York, obtaining a Master's degree in Business Administration. Under his guidance the company has risen to become Scotland's second largest construction group, with annual turnover in excess of £300 million. Mr Groves is a member of CBI Scotland, and of the Caledonian Home-builders Association. He is also a non-executive director of four other Scottish companies.

He is a keen sportsman, and represented Scotland at cycling. His other major interests are equestrianism, golf and horology. He is a member of the Antiquarian Horological Society.

Brindsley Groves has been married to the former Celia Greatorix for thirty-seven years. They have two children, Herbert Groves III, and Rowena Groves.

'He's been a busy guy,' Martin murmured to himself, then focused on the period of his life that interested him most.

Seventy

In Edinburgh, Stevie Steele had one thing on his mind: the whereabouts of Chris Aikenhead. He had completed all but one of his list of informal interviews; the last, with Dan Pringle, he feared would be the most difficult. He had served under the outgoing head of CID at divisional level, and for all his acknowledged weaknesses, he had admired him as the type of detective that he hoped to be himself.

He knew that, like most detectives, Pringle hated offences against children more than anything else, and so he was not surprised that he had gone for Patsy Aikenhead in the interview room, given the evidence that he had had before him at the time.

He told him as much, as they sat in his drawing room.

Pringle exploded in his face. 'Are you digging that thing up again?' he shouted, his bushy moustache quivering. 'I'll tell you this once, Stevie, and once only. That bloody shambles had nothing to do with me. It was all that arrogant bastard McIlhenney's fault. He sent a uniformed officer to bring the Yasmin Khan woman to the office for her interview, rather than getting off his fat arse and going to talk to her on-site.'

Steele had experienced his former boss's temper before: he knew that the one thing he could not do was bend before it. 'That's not George Regan's recollection, sir. He told me, without even being directly asked, that the order to bring her in came from you.'

Pringle's eyes blazed. 'If George said that McIlhenney must have put him up to it.'

'If McIlhenney had done that, sir, then surely he'd have told me that story himself, but he didn't. The only thing he said to me that was critical of you in any way was that he thought you went too hard against the girl.'

'Maybe I did, son.' Steele was surprised by the concession. 'But there's one thing you and everybody else seems to have forgotten about her. That balls-up over the time didna' prove she was innocent, it just meant that the Spanish girl, Magda what's-her-name, could have done it too. Only she didn't, Stevie: Patsy Aikenhead was guilty. She did what she confessed to doing: she threw the kid into the cot in a temper, and the poor wee thing banged her head on the bars and died from it. I know that, I heard her say it, and for all her hysterics I bloody know she was telling me the truth!' He was breathing hard. 'Did you ask McIlhenney if he thought she was innocent?' he barked.

The inspector felt his own temper rise. 'It doesn't matter what McIlhenney thinks!' he barked back. 'It doesn't matter what you think. I haven't been asked to investigate the conduct of the Aikenhead case. I've been asked to find links between you, Neil and George because of what's happened to all your children. I've been asked to protect any other coppers' kids who might be at risk. So will you please drop the outrage and the protests and co-operate with me?'

It was as if Steele's sudden anger had blown out Pringle's fire. The older man seemed to sink into himself. 'She did it, Stevie, that's all,' he said, quietly, as he slumped into his armchair.

'Okay,' his colleague murmured as he sat opposite him. 'Okay. Now, can I get down to the things I need to ask you?'

'Aye, go on.'

'First, do you agree that there are no other possible links between the three of you? This is most important.'

'Yes, I agree. McIlhenney was on temporary secondment to my division. Maybe our paths crossed once or twice after that, I'm not sure, but certainly never with George involved.'

'Good. That's a weight off my mind. The other questions I want to ask you are about Chris Aikenhead. At any point in the investigation did you interview him?'

'No. He was away; it was only after we'd charged the girl that her solicitor got in touch with him and he came back. He came to see me then, but it was all wrapped up and the girl was on remand by that time. With hindsight, I shouldn't have let him anywhere near me, but he made such a fuss in the station, it was either that or have him arrested for breach of the peace.'

'Why didn't you?'

'I felt sorry for the boy. He hadn't killed the baby; he was just reacting like any husband might have in the circumstances.'

'How did your discussion go?'

'As you'd expect; he yelled at me that his wife would never do something like that, and I told him that she did and that she'd admitted to it. He said that it must have been the girl Magda; I told him that we knew for sure it wasn't, although I didn't tell him why.'

'Did he make any threats?'

'He got steamed up about the Spanish girl, until I told him that if I caught him within a mile of her I would have him arrested on the spot.'

'Can you remember enough about him to give me a description?'

Pringle nodded; he closed his eyes, as if it made it easier to form a picture in his mind. 'Big bugger,' he murmured, as if he was describing it, 'about six three, maybe, sun-tanned, brown hair, don't know about the eyes. Very fit; a strong-looking boy, but you'd expect that with him working on the rigs.' He blinked and looked across at Steele. 'That was ten years ago, mind. Can you not get a photo?'

'I'm trying, but no luck yet; he's never been arrested, and he doesn't have a photographic driving licence. Was that your only meeting with him?'

'Not quite. I saw him again at the trial, then afterwards, when the whole thing had blown up in our faces. He asked to see me again, and I agreed. He was very quiet this time, very controlled; he asked me if the inquiry would be reopened, and I had to tell him that while it would, there was no prospect of progress as long as the other girl involved refused to come back from Spain, and that even if she did, the prospect of a guilty verdict against her was remote.'

'How did he react? Do you remember?'

Pringle closed his eyes again. 'Oh, yes, I remember. He looked across the desk at me and he said, "However long it takes, Mr Pringle, we can only hope that justice will be done." And then he said, "Of

283

course, sometimes it needs help." He was calm, though, not threatening in any way; he just sounded sad.'

He shifted in his chair. 'He was right, and all, Stevie. It needs help when buggers like us are involved. I'm sorry about my tantrum earlier. You see, it was no surprise your coming to see me. I've been expecting it, ever since I heard about the McIlhenney boy, and I've known what we would wind up talking about. I canna' bring Ross back, but I truly hope we're all wrong about this, and that her death was a one-in-a-million accident. For if it wasn't, I don't know if I'll be able to live with the knowledge that it was caused by something I did. You were spot on, son: whether I was right or I was wrong doesn't matter a toss. My daughter will still be just as dead, and so will George's son.'

Steele rose, and Pringle showed him to the door. 'There's an extradition agreement with Spain now,' he said. 'D'you think this might lead to us trying to get the Magda girl back over here?'

The inspector frowned. 'There wouldn't be much point. That's the one thing I've learned for sure, this morning. She died in Algeciras, five years ago, from a drug overdose.'

Seventy-one

When Maggie Rose arrived at police headquarters for her lunch date with Bob Skinner, she discovered that they would be eating in private and not in the senior officers' dining room as she had thought.

A table had been set up in the deputy chief constable's office, and a bottle of sparkling water was cooling in an ice bucket.

Skinner was on the phone when Jack McGurk showed her in: he had his back to her and was speaking quietly so she could hear nothing of what was being said, but when he ended the call and turned to her she could see a concerned expression on his face. 'Problem?' she asked.

'I hope not. There's someone we've been trying to contact all morning, without success.'

'One of our people?'

'No, a friend. It relates to something we have on the go just now.'

By telling her next to nothing he had told her a lot: somewhere within their territory, or sphere of influence, an operation involving another organisation was under way, one of sufficient sensitivity for him to be unwilling or unable to divulge its details. He knew that she would realise this, but he knew also that she would put the moment out of her mind as soon as she left his room.

'Sit yourself down,' he invited, ushering her to one of the two chairs at the neatly set table. 'Would you like a sherry before we eat?'

She declined. 'No, thank you, sir. I drove myself down from the office.'

He grinned. 'I didn't mean a whole bottle, but as you wish.' He took the silver covers from the two plates that lay already on the table, revealing a starter of avocado and prawns, then opened the mineral water and filled two glasses. 'I hope I've remembered your tastes from when you worked on this floor,' he said.

'This is a good start,' she told him, as they picked up their cutlery and began to eat.

'Are you enjoying being back in uniform?' he asked her.

'As much as any of us does,' she replied, candidly. 'But I really am enjoying the job that goes with it.'

'Even when you're out in the rain doing crowd control at a Hearts home game?'

'Even then. Divisional command's made me think in a different way than before, and see the wider picture again.'

'Plus, you get to deal with people who aren't criminals; that's how Willie Haggerty put it to me when I asked him the same question.'

'He's right. I feel that I'm part of respectable society, rather than just the underbelly. Didn't you feel the same when you reached command rank?'

Skinner grinned. 'Maybe, but I like being part of the underbelly. Sure it's a multi-faceted job, but I'm the sort of cop who joined up to put away the bad guys, and I always will be.'

'Speaking of which, do you know how Stevie's getting on with his investigation? I haven't spoken to him since breakfast this morning.'

'I had a report from him half an hour ago. He's got a firm line of inquiry, and a man in his sights.'

'A suspect.'

'Let's just say it's someone who'll have to have a good story when we speak to him.' He laid down his fork. 'Can I turn it around? How are you getting on with Stevie? That's a purely personal question, by the way, nothing to do with the job.'

'I know, and I'm touched that you ask it. The answer is that we're fine. To be honest, boss, I am truly domestically happy for just about the first time in my life, and it feels great. I enjoy waking up in the morning, I enjoy going to sleep at night, and I enjoy all the bits in between.'

'That's great,' he said, sincerely. 'A lot of people who know you both will be pleased to hear that.'

'As far as the job's concerned,' she continued, 'I don't have a problem working in the same place as him. If you were wondering, that is.'

'I wasn't, but again, it's good to know. Still . . .'

There was a knock on the door. 'Okay!' he called out, and Maisie, the dining-room waitress entered, pushing a trolley.

'Beef olives for two,' she announced. 'Chips and carrots.'

'As requested,' said the DCC, watching as she served them.

'You were going to say,' Maggie ventured, as she left. 'There was a "Still . . ." hanging in the air.'

'True. I was going to add . . . that shouldn't close your mind to other situations. Hell, I'll get to the point. Dan Pringle's going; understandably, after the tragedy, he wants to devote all his time to Elma. So I'm looking for a new head of CID. I've made no decisions yet, indeed I've been too busy to give it much thought, but I want to know this. When I consider the candidates for the job, do you want your name to be on the list? I know you're new in divisional command, but you're an experienced and very talented detective officer. If you tell me you're interested, I'll consider you with the others.'

She stared at him, across the table. 'You still have the power to surprise me, boss. I thought you had invited me here to tell me very politely that you were going to move either Stevie or me to a different station.'

She gulped. 'I don't know how to tell you this, and I'm very grateful that you would think of me for one moment as Dan's successor, but I have to decline. There's the practical, personal point that Stevie's career is clearly CID, for a while at least. I would feel awkward living with him and commanding him, but also, although you're right, I am new in my present job and I could go somewhere else without creating too big a gap, I feel that I've made a commitment to the post, and I want to see it through to its conclusion.' She stopped for a moment, then continued, nervously, 'There is one other thing: I am not sure that you would want a head of CID who's hardly in the office before she goes off on maternity leave.'

Skinner stared at her across the table, before exploding in a laugh. 'That guy Steele,' he bellowed. 'I should put him on a disciplinary for interfering with executive planning. Oh, Mags, congratulations, that's terrific. Bugger the job, it's secondary. I'm as happy for you, my friend, as you are for yourself.' He rose, walked to the small fridge beside his desk and took out a half-bottle of champagne. 'Sod the iced water. This has to be toasted.'

Seventy-two

The van was like any other old Ford Transit, big and chunky, a commercial work-horse. It had seen better days, and its white-paint job was not the one with which it had left the factory. A keen-eyed observer who looked closely enough would have made out the words 'Stuart James Heating Engineer' beneath the new skin, and perhaps another layer below.

It was parked in the yard of a building-supplies company in a small estate just off Newcraighall Road, and it had been there all morning. The warehouse manager had no idea who owned it, and as Monday was always a slack day, he had not been too concerned about the space it took up.

However, as the hours ticked by, and more trade customers appeared, its presence began to annoy him. 'Does anybody have any idea whose that bloody Transit is?' he called out to the stock controller as he passed.

'I thought it was young John's,' the man replied.

'Naw. John's was pale blue, and anyway he got rid of it three months ago.'

'In that case, I've no idea. Is it bothering you?'

'It's takin' up space.'

'In that case call the police and have it towed.'

The manager allowed the van's owner another half-hour's grace, until finally his patience was exhausted. He took his friend's advice and called the Craigmillar police station, the closest at hand. He made a formal complaint that a vehicle appeared to have been abandoned on his premises.

The constables who arrived were rookies; he could tell that at a glance. The pink-cheeked boy could not have been any more than twenty-two or twenty-three and the girl, an Asian, looked even younger. He began to feel his age.

'Are you sure it doesn't belong to one of your employees?' the woman officer asked him.

'We don't have that many, miss. If it did, I'd have found him by now. The thing was here when I got on this morning, it's taking up space in my park that I need for customers, and I want it moved.'

'We should try and trace the owner first, and make sure it hasn't been reported as stolen.'

'Do whatever you have to do. Just make it go away.'

She walked over to her colleague. The manager saw him speak into his radio and heard him read the registration number. 'The sergeant says we should see if the keys are in it,' he called to her. 'If they are we've to drive it back to the station.'

'I'll have a look,' she said.

As she headed for the van, the manager turned and went back to his business. He was completely unprepared for her scream. When it came, he almost jumped out of his Hush Puppies. He ran out of the warehouse.

'There's someone in there,' he heard the girl cry out to her colleague.

'It'll be a dosser,' he called, taking pity on their youth. He walked to the back of the Transit, thinking that he should have done it a few hours earlier, took hold of the handles, twisted it and wrenched the door open.

She had been right: there was a man in there. He had been wrong: it was no dosser. He could tell that from his bulging eyes, his purple face, and from the red tie, knotted tight around his throat.

Seventy-three

Mario McGuire was early for his appointment in the deputy chief constable's office. He arrived just after two twenty, but Skinner was free and ready for him. 'How are you feeling?' he asked, as the superintendent entered, and they shook hands.

'Fine, thanks, boss. I've still got a bit of a headache, but nothing that a couple of codeine doesn't put away.'

'When did they let you out?'

'My consultant came in at nine thirty this morning. He started to say something about another night, but I told him he'd have to tie me down or drug me for that to happen, so he let me out, on condition that I take at least three days' sick leave.'

The DCC laughed. 'So what the hell are you doing here?'

'This doesn't count as work. Dr Moores told me to go home and relax. I've been home and now I'm relaxing. I'm looking forward to this.'

'I shouldn't really admit this, but so am I. While we're waiting…' He glanced at his watch as he led McGuire over to the informal seating. 'Jay will be late, I'll bet. I told him two thirty, but he'll keep me hanging about for ten minutes or so, just to make the point that he's an important man. So let's use the time. I had Maggie in for lunch earlier; I wanted to sound her out about becoming head of CID. I didn't offer her the job, you understand; I only asked her if she wanted to be a candidate.'

'Did she turn you down?'

'She did, as a matter of fact. You're not surprised?'

'No. She likes her new job, and she likes her new home life. Plus, she likes being well away from me. If she became head of CID I'd have to report to her.'

'She didn't offer that as a reason, I have to tell you.'

'Maybe not, but it would be in her mind, for sure.'

'Would it have been a problem for you?'

'Not at all, but it might have been awkward round the table for the other divisional commanders, knowing our personal history.'

Skinner scratched his chin. 'I suppose so,' he admitted. 'But it's not going to happen, so that's that. It leaves me with one less candidate, though.'

'Is this where you tell me I'm not on the list, boss? Because, honestly, I don't expect to be.'

'You're either kidding me, Mario, or you're underrating yourself. Of course you're on the list, you and two others. But this is where I tell you there's a condition attached.'

McGuire frowned, then winced as if the gesture had been painful. 'What's that?'

'I want you out of your family business, completely. I can live with your involvement at the moment, just, but if you were in line for a step up, I'd have trouble persuading the chief that it would be appropriate, and make no mistake, he will have to approve the final choice.'

'Boss, I'm only there because my grandfather's will and my mother's retirement put me there.'

'I know that, and I appreciate what you've done by having a lawyer stand between you and hands-on involvement … even if I was slightly embarrassed when you appointed my daughter.'

McGuire's eyebrows rose sharply; he winced again. 'I didn't appoint Alex directly; I appointed her firm because they're the best, and they nominated her.'

'Understood; that's why I let it happen. But listen, Mario, I don't care what your grandfather's will says. This force can't have a head of CID who is a director of a large commercial company; if we did there are people on the joint advisory board who'd be all over us like a rash. The Viareggio businesses would be subjected to more scrutiny than any other in town.'

The big superintendent laughed, if a little gingerly. 'Your kid really is discreet, you know.'

'What do you mean?'

'She's been working on getting me out of it for the last three months. It's complicated and all the family members have to sign off on it, but basically what's going to happen is that we'll convert from our present status and become a public limited company, with those of us who are beneficiaries at the moment becoming shareholders. Our first act will be to have a general meeting where Paula will be appointed chair, with Stan Coia, her brother-in-law, as the other executive director on the board. My mother's agreed to be a non-executive director, as long as it doesn't involve her in too many meetings. Alex will become company secretary.'

'She's discreet indeed, Mario. She's never mentioned a word to me, or even dropped a hint.'

'The main thing is I'll become an ordinary shareholder: that's as far out as I can get.'

'That will be okay. Christ, I own shares myself in half a dozen companies, and in God knows how many more through some bond investments that I have.' Skinner nodded. 'That's good, Mario; you've taken a load off my mind.'

'Will there be formal interviews for the job, boss?'

'What would we ask you that we don't know already?'

A phone on his desk sounded, once. Skinner looked at his watch again, and smiled. 'What did I tell you? Ten minutes late.' He picked up the handset. 'Jack? Yes, bring him up, please.' He went to the door and waited, until his assistant appeared at the top of the stairs, leading a tall grey-suited figure. He stepped forward and shook his hand, vigorously. 'Greg,' he exclaimed, 'how good of you to find the time to see me. Come in, and tell me all about your new job.' He looked at McGurk. 'No interruptions, please.'

Jay followed him into the wood-panelled office, and stared in surprise when he saw McGuire. 'What the hell is this, Bob?' he demanded, as the door closed on them. 'What's that man doing here?'

'He may be putting his health at risk, Greg; his consultant would shit fireballs if he knew he was here. But he insisted on joining us. Have a seat . . . no, not on the comfy stuff, sit there.' He pointed to the straight-backed chair facing his desk, then walked round and settled into his own leather swivel. 'Tell me about the job, Greg; tell me how you got it.'

'I sense an interrogation here,' Jay protested. 'I haven't come for that.'

'No,' said Skinner calmly, 'you haven't, have you? I apologise, that was unnecessary . . . I know how you got it.'

His eyes locked on to Jay, and held him in a steady gaze that brooked no interruption. 'There is a man called Albert Trumble; he is a senior member of the Labour Party and has been for donkey's years. He's one of their king-makers, old Labour in a new Labour suit, although he hasn't held office since Fife Regional Council was disbanded. If you don't have Albert's support, you'll find it difficult to advance through the ranks. If you do, you'll find it easy. Twelve years ago, he met a young man from Dundee at a gathering of regional councillors. This lad had just been elected, but he impressed Albert. A few years later, a vacancy arose for a seat in the House of Commons, in a constituency where he had a lot of influence. He put the word about and, after a local rival had been disposed of, his *protégé* was selected as the Labour candidate. Naturally, since it was in Fife, he won. When devolution came, the young man chose the Scottish Parliament ahead of Westminster. He became a member of the cabinet, on Albert's recommendation to the founding First Minister, who was an old council buddy of his. When the top job itself became vacant a year or so back, well, Tommy Murtagh was more or less anointed, wasn't he? Thirty-five years old, and at the head of the Cabinet table, a great achievement by him and a monument to Albert Trumble's influence.'

He paused. 'That's not news to you, though, Greg, is it? Some of it you could even have read in the papers. But there's something about Albert that's never been reported. He's a fairly rare beast, a Labour Party grandee who is also an active and senior Freemason. As a matter of fact, Greg, you and he have both been masters of the same lodge, over in Fife. You've known each other for twenty years.'

Skinner broke off, glanced at McGuire and laughed. 'Here, this is just like *This Is Your Life*, isn't it? I'll bet you're half expecting Albert to come out of my bathroom and give Greg a hug.'

The visitor made to rise. 'I'm not staying here to have the piss taken out of me.'

'Sit down!' The DCC's sudden shout slammed him back into his seat, as surely as if he had reached out a hand and shoved him. 'That's better,' he said, calm again in an instant. 'Now where was I? Oh, yes. Not so long ago, Tommy Murtagh told Albert he was looking to replace Jock Govan as security adviser with someone . . . a little more hands on, let's say. He didn't give it a second thought: he said that you were the man. True?'

Jay glared at him.

'You don't need to answer for I know it is, from an impeccable source. One thing that maybe you didn't know about your friend and patron is that he isn't just a member of your lodge. He belongs to another, in Edinburgh, a very select body with a very limited membership. I'm going to tell you a secret, knowing that you as a good Freemason will not divulge it to anyone, and that Mario, who values his career, won't either. The present master of that most exclusive chapter is none other than Sir James Proud. He asked Albert if he'd put you in post and he told him that he had.'

Skinner swivelled round in his chair. 'That was very silly of Albert, you know. Maybe he thought that Jimmy wouldn't pass it on; if he did, he failed to realise that his first loyalty is to the police service, and that if its integrity is under threat he will do anything to protect it. I don't think I need to tell you, Greg, how embarrassing it would be for the First Minister if the connection that led to your appointment became known, since his party's last manifesto in Scotland promised to root out, quote, "the last remaining influences of Freemasonry on the Scottish police service". Tommy's really going to be pissed off at you.'

'Are you trying to threaten me?' Jay asked.

'Not yet. This is just the warm-up. But if you want me to get to the heavy stuff, I will.' He glanced at McGuire. 'My colleague is present, Mr Jay, because this is about to become an official interview, at which certain allegations will be put to you.' The ex-detective's face took on a shocked expression as he was read a formal caution. 'Mario,' said Skinner, when it was done, 'would you like to carry on, even though you are officially on the sick?'

McGuire rose from the couch and walked over to take the other straight chair, turning it to face Jay. 'Last Friday,' he began, 'Detective Sergeant Sammy Pye and I took a statement from Mr Malcolm Gladsmuir, licensee and manager of a pub called the Wee Black Dug in Leith. Mr Gladsmuir alleged that over a period of several years, he made you regular payments, in return for an understanding that there would be no CID surveillance of activity in his pub. However, the money did not come from Mr Gladsmuir directly but from his three employers. They hide their property holdings behind a limited company, unsurprisingly, for one of them has a conviction for armed robbery, while the other two also have records. All three are thought to be currently involved in organised crime. Do you deny the allegations?'

'Of course I do,' Greg Jay blustered. 'You're not going to take that seriously, are you?'

'I wouldn't have interviewed Gladsmuir in the first place if you hadn't warned me to lay off him, and if you hadn't then visited my cousin at her place of work and threatened her, an act I interpret as a further attempt to put me under duress. You ask me if I take it seriously. Too right I do.'

'Then there's this,' said Skinner, taking a folder from his drawer. 'It contains a statement from a former prostitute named Joanne Virtue, claiming that at an earlier period in your career, when your duties included control of vice in the Leith area, you regularly elicited sexual favours from her, in return for a blind eye being turned. She directed us to three other street women who made similar allegations. Under a strict interpretation, coercing women into sex could be construed as rape.'

'You're accusing me on the word of hoors?' Jay murmured.

'These are sworn statements, man. Why shouldn't a prostitute's word be as good as a priest's?'

'I want a lawyer. You will never prove any of that in court.'

'Don't get ahead of yourself, Greg. If I have to, I will arrest you and hold you in custody, while the experienced officers from another force, with whom you threatened Paula Viareggio, go through your financial affairs. They will look at every penny you've ever spent and link it to every pound you've ever earned. Unless you've buried that money in your garden, and maybe even then, for if we have to we'll dig up every square foot of it, we will prove Gladsmuir's statement beyond any reasonable doubt. If at that point you plead guilty, I won't humiliate your wife by producing the women. If you force me to, I will.'

He stood and walked to his coffee filter in the corner, filled three mugs, added milk and handed McGuire and Jay one each, then took his own back to his desk.

'That's what you're looking at, Greg. I'd reckon it will be worth between five and seven years, given your rank at the time.'

The former superintendent was convinced at last. He sat, broken, as his former colleagues looked at him sternly. 'Is there a way out?' he murmured.

'There might be, for all of us,' Skinner replied. 'I don't give a stuff about you, but I don't want to embarrass this force or the honest men and women who work in it, any more than I have to. My problem is that Mario and I are police officers, and we've got an allegation of corruption before us: we couldn't ignore it even if we wanted to. However, if you make a full statement and admit to receiving payments from Gladsmuir, I won't arrest you, at this stage at any rate. I'll talk to the Crown Office, and we'll see what sort of a plea bargain they'll tolerate. Dig your heels in and I'll bury you. Accept, and once you've made your statement you can walk out that door.'

He locked his eyes on to Jay once more. 'In return for that leniency I want only one thing: a full account of every order you've ever been given by Tommy Murtagh and of everything you've ever done for him.'

As the cornered man nodded, the phone on Skinner's desk rang. Frowning his annoyance he picked it up. 'Sorry, sir,' said Jack McGurk, 'but DCI McIlhenney's here, and he says that he has to speak to you at once.'

A sense of foreboding gripped Skinner, and a fear that he had tried to push aside returned. 'Tell him I'll be there in a minute.' He hung up and turned to McGuire. 'No conversation till I'm back.'

McIlhenney was standing in the corridor outside McGurk's office as the DCC approached, with Amanda Dennis beside him, looking distraught. 'Green?' he asked.

The chief inspector nodded. 'A white Transit van, registered owner Petrit Kastrati, has been found, abandoned, outside a warehouse in Newcraighall. There's a body inside. The officer who reported it says it looks as if he's been strangled. Divisional CID were on their way, but I stopped them. I thought you'd want me to.'

'Good thinking, Neil. Tell them to go to Bassam's restaurant instead, not that there's a cat's chance he'll be there, but clear the place anyway. I want it torn apart. Meanwhile take Mackenzie and go to the warehouse yourself. Confirm the identification, then act as you think fit. I'm in some heavy business here. When or if I can I'll join you.'

'I'll go with them,' Dennis declared.

'You will not, Amanda.' He turned and leaned into McGurk's office. 'Jack, I want you to call Alice Cowan in Special Branch, tell her to come up here and take charge of Mrs Dennis. She is to be held incommunicado, and she is not to be left alone.'

'Bob,' the MI5 officer protested, tears in her eyes, 'this is outrageous.'

'Maybe so, but it's necessary: you of all people should know why. Stay with DS McGurk, then go with DC Cowan. I'll speak to you later.'

He walked back towards his own room, motioning McIlhenney to follow.

'What was that about?' the DCI whispered.

'Coincidences. Samir Bajram wasn't the victim of a gang hit, like the tabloids are inferring. That's far too neat and convenient. We had a lead to him and he was killed to close it off. The same with Sean Green; someone told Bassam what he was. Within the very small group of people who know about this operation, Neil, we've got a leak, and the finger points at Amanda Dennis.'

Seventy-four

Willie Haggerty liked to think that he had a bit of cunning about him. He picked up the telephone in his office, trying to stop himself wondering why Bob Skinner had greeted Greg Jay like a bosom buddy, and why he had even let him into the building in the first place, and dialled a Glasgow number from a list on his desk. 'Max,' he said, as his call was picked up, 'how are things in Strathclyde CID?'

'Is that you, Willie?' Detective Chief Superintendent Max Allan replied. 'I thought you'd forgotten about us.' Not so long ago, Haggerty had sat in Allan's chair, as the senior crime-fighter in Glasgow. He had enjoyed the job, and had achieved considerable success in it.

'How could I do that, Maxie, when you're all over the front pages every day?'

'You can talk. What the hell went on up at that ski centre on Saturday? Would I be wrong, or did I read between the lines that it was a policeman's kid the guy tried to snatch?'

'If you did, you shouldn't have been able to, but you're right. It was Neil McIlhenney's son; our head of Special Branch.'

'Good God! Was it political?'

'We don't think so, but it could be connected to his service. Bob Skinner's detached one of our best DIs to run the investigation; I hear he's got someone in his sights already.'

'Glad to hear it; I hope you nail the bastard good. Now, are you going to tell me what you want?'

'I'm on the scrounge, as usual. We've got a couple of openings coming up through here, at sergeant level, and we're always out to strengthen our team. I was wondering if any of your people had itchy feet.'

'There's always some, Willie,' Allan conceded. 'Are we talking CID?'

'Among other things, yes.'

'Specialist?'

'Not necessarily.'

'I'll look into it, see who's applied for transfer lately and let you know.' Haggerty heard Allan chuckle. 'Here, talking about transfers, how's Bandit Mackenzie getting on through there?'

'He's settling in fine, as far as I know. He reports to Bob, not me. You sound as if you might have been glad to get rid of him.'

'Well, I'll say this: we sleep easier in our beds knowing he's with you. He's some boy, the Bandit. He always sailed closer to the wind than any other officer we had. You must remember that, surely, from your time here.'

'I remember his clear-up figures . . . they were bloody impressive.'

'Maybe so, but there was always that terrible fear that he'd become a statistic himself one day. Here, that reminds me: his old sergeant, Gwen Dell, put her name in for a move last week. I'm not keen to let her go, though. She's a good operator, and a lot less reckless than Mackenzie.'

'That wouldn't be hard. If you do decide to go along with her request let me know and we'll see whether she fits what we've got. Now I'd better let you get back to work and catch those bombers of yours. We can't have the druggies blowing each other up: they could hurt too many innocent people.'

'How did you know they were druggies?' Allan asked. 'We didn't release that.'

'Do me a favour. Who do you think you're talking to?'

'Point taken. You're right, of course: three victims blown to bits. We've identified two of them as Frankie and Bobby Jakes, former asylum-seekers, and now former everything. We haven't a clue who the third guy was, although the barman in the Johnny Groat, where they'd been drinking, said he sounded foreign. Whoever he was, we found his arse in the car . . . a big flashy American thing, it was. The rest of him was all over the place and what was left was pretty well crisped, but the pockets of his jeans were crammed full with what had once been white powder.'

'Supply cut off at source, you might say. At least that's a bonus for you, if not for them.'

'Mmm,' DCS Allan muttered, 'but there's a downside. We're not telling anyone this either, but it wasn't a bomb that blew them up. My ballistics guys have been working all night on it, and they tell me they're pretty much certain that it was a missile, an American Javelin anti-tank weapon, they reckon.'

'Bloody hell!' exclaimed Haggerty. 'I've never heard of them in Partick before.'

'Me neither. But at least we've got somewhere to start looking. There were two guys in the pub. They'd been seen talking to the Jakes boys, and when they left, this pair went out just after them. They were seen making a very sharp exit from the scene just after the explosion. We reckon they might have fired the missile from their car.'

Haggerty felt his scalp tingle. 'How do you know they weren't just punters?' he asked.

'We know for sure they weren't. They were heard telling Jakes, and a woman, that they were porters at the Western. Only they're not. The hospital's never heard of them. We reckon that they were the hit team, and right now, finding them is our absolute top priority. We're putting E-fit pictures out on television tonight. Hopefully, they'll lead us to them.'

Seventy-five

The two officers who had found the body in the Transit were still there, but a uniformed inspector had arrived from divisional headquarters in Leith and taken charge. McIlhenney eyed the two youngsters. A tight lid would have to be put on the situation; he wondered whether they could be trusted, and how strong their loyalty to the force was.

Dottie Shannon, the inspector, saw them as soon as they stepped out of Mackenzie's car, which he had parked in the roadway outside the warehouse. She was a contemporary of the Special Branch commander, and he had no worries about her discretion.

'No press around?' he asked.

'Not a sign. We've made as little fuss as possible, as you asked; I've even let the warehouse stay open. You'll see that the vehicle was left well away from the business entrance, so we've cordoned it off and let them carry on as usual, in the meantime at least.'

'That's fine.'

'The only thing that concerns me, Neil, is that we don't have a medical examiner here.'

'Is he dead?'

'Oh, yes, he's dead all right.'

'In that case, unless you can find me one who specialises in resurrection, we don't need a doctor. Dot, I don't need to spell anything out here, do I?'

The inspector looked up at him from under her cap. 'You've done that already.'

'What about the kids over there? How much have they seen?'

'Hardly anything: the girl looked in the van but from what she says,

302

she didn't hang around to see much detail. The other officer wasn't that curious; he took the word of the warehouse manager and called it in.'

'Do you know them?'

'Yes. They're both sound; they'll accept what you tell them.'

'Do they know who I am?'

'No.'

'They don't need to find out, then. Tell them that this is a suicide, that the guy's a copper from another force, and that there is to be no talk about it. I'll deal with the manager.' He turned to Mackenzie. 'Bandit, let's take a look.'

The two chief inspectors walked round and into the car park. 'Hey, Neil,' Mackenzie said quietly, as they approached the van, 'something's just occurred to me. Shouldn't Amanda Dennis be here? This is her guy, after all.'

'She's otherwise engaged.'

They reached the Transit: a foul odour wafted out to greet them through the rear doors, which lay very slightly ajar. McIlhenney glanced around to make sure that they could not be seen from the road outside the compound, and opened them to their full width. He sensed his colleague flinch beside him as he saw Sean Green's purple face, and his dead bulging eyes. 'Easy now,' he murmured. 'He might look scary, but he's not going to bite you. Poor guy: he paid a heavy price for chibbing Andy Martin's jacket.'

'I'm supposed to be the flippant one around here,' Mackenzie reminded him. 'We knew this man. How can you talk like that?'

'I find that it helps.' He gulped a lungful of relatively fresh air then squeezed himself up on to the platform of the van, for a better view. He saw that Green was wearing what he assumed was his waiter's uniform, black trousers and a white shirt. It was buttoned all the way up to the neck, as if his tie had been ripped off and used to strangle him.

'Was he killed in the van?' his colleague asked.

'I don't think so. Sean would have been trained to handle himself, and the space in here is limited. My bet would be that it happened in or near the restaurant, given that he's still in his working clothes.'

'What do we do now?'

'You call in for a black van to take him to the city morgue. I'll check to see if there's anything on him that might help us.'

A little gingerly, he reached inside Green's right trouser pockets; he found a wallet and withdrew it. On flipping it open he found that it contained thirty-five pounds in cash, two credit cards and a photographic driver's licence, all in the name of John Stevenson. He handed it to Mackenzie, who stared at it, looking puzzled. 'They didn't take it?'

'They couldn't have needed thirty-five quid,' McIlhenney replied, tersely.

The left trouser pocket held a small cell-phone. He withdrew it and tried to switch it on, but was asked for a passcode. He slipped it into his own pocket, for the technical people to explore, then bent over the body again, and rolled it on to its side. There was a back pocket on the right-hand side of the slacks. Even more gingerly, since Green had soiled himself in death, he felt it from the outside, then reached in with two fingers and slipped out a folded sheet of paper.

He opened it, carefully, and could just determine that it was a map, a street plan of the town of St Andrews. He frowned, peering at it, but it was dark inside the Transit and so he jumped out, back into the grey afternoon, where there was just enough of the fading daylight for him to see.

In fact it was only a section of a map, a graphic guide to the north end of the town. Landmarks and prominent buildings were shown in miniature and a seagull flew over St Andrews Bay. Lines across the top and bottom told him that it had been downloaded from the internet, then faxed. 'Why?' he asked himself, as his colleague joined him, looking over his shoulder. 'I doubt if he was planning any sightseeing while he was up here.'

'What are those marks on it?' Mackenzie asked, pointing.

McIlhenney followed his finger and saw that two circles had been drawn on the page. One was round the Sea Life Centre while the other encompassed a tiny illustration of St Salvator's College and its quadrangle. They were linked by a line, running along a street called The Scores. On the map, there was a cartoon of a boat in the bay, heading out to sea. It, too, had been circled.

The chief inspector cleared his mind and concentrated, the page hanging loosely in his fingers as he thought. And then he gave a long, soft whistle. 'Salvator,' he murmured, 'Salvator. Bandit, what was the Albanian word the Dutch lorry drive overheard? Remember?'

'Saviour, wasn't it?'

'That's right; probably what you'd come up with if you were translating Salvator into Albanian.'

'Yes, so?'

'David, my friend, what's St Andrews famous for, apart from golf?'

'Dunno.'

'The university, that's what. And who's its most famous student?'

Mackenzie's mouth fell open. Before it had closed, McIlhenney had his phone in his hand and was calling Bob Skinner.

Seventy-six

Stevie Steele had been expecting a report from Arthur Dorward, not a personal visit, so he was surprised when his red-haired colleague walked into his office. 'Hello,' he exclaimed, 'I didn't think that you Howdenhall lab guys could find your way to divisional offices any more.'

'We get precious little thanks when we do,' Dorward answered, 'so these days we only deliver the good news in person.'

'Good news? You bear good news?'

'I do indeed, my son. A double helping, in fact.'

Steele leaned back in his chair and smiled. 'Let me have it.'

Casually, Dorward tossed an envelope on to his desk. 'It's all in there, but this is what it says. First, the sock: as you suggested, we had another look at wee George's clothing, and knowing what we were after made all the difference. We took several fibres from his jacket; they were an exact match for the cotton in the sock that socked Mario McGuire. We checked the garment too. That wasn't difficult: it's a Marks and Spencer product, fits size eight to ten shoe, and it's from a range that was withdrawn only six months ago. Before you ask, it could have been bought in any of their stores but, still, it's a big step forward.'

'True. It eliminates half of the male population and one or two large females as well.'

'Get away with you. It changes your report on the boy's death entirely, and you know it. Would you like to know about the rock?'

Steele chuckled. 'I can hardly wait. Did you put your top geologist on it?'

Dorward looked down his nose. 'Naturally. It's a lump of grey granite from the north-east, the stuff that Aberdeen and a few other

306

places are built out of; very hard, much tougher than sandstone. The interesting thing about it is that it's been machine cut. Superintendent McGuire must have a seriously hard head to have got up after being whacked with that.'

'He has, take my word for it. He'll be out of hospital by now.'

'He's lucky he's conscious by now,' the inspector said. 'If that weapon is what was used on young George Regan, the kid didn't have a chance.

'Now, the other. We went back to Ross Pringle's room, and we dismantled that heater. I put my best girl on it, and on one side of the loosened socket that caused the leak, she found a clear right thumbprint. We had to fingerprint Ross's body, I'm afraid, which I didn't like doing, but it allowed us to eliminate her. We took the lock on the door apart too. There were scratches inside it that my specialist thinks would have been made by a skeleton key. He also . . . and this is where he got really clever . . . found traces of two different types of lubricant inside the lock, which led him to speculate that the skeleton might have been oiled to make it work better.'

'Whose speciality would that be?'

'Apart from a locksmith? A joiner? A mechanical engineer? A policeman? We're scientists, Stevie, we only go in for guessing when it's founded on something concrete.'

'Have you eliminated the engineer who did the last service on those gas appliances?'

'Gimme a break! Of course we have. Match that print and you've got your man.'

There was a knock at the door. Steele looked up and saw, through the glass, Detective Sergeant Ray Wilding. He beckoned him in, as the smiling Dorward stood. 'When we catch this guy, I'll buy you a beer, Arthur. So will George, Dan and Neil, I'm sure.'

The two officers passed in the doorway and Wilding took the seat that the inspector had vacated. Steele had taken up Skinner's sug- gestion that he bring him into the investigation and had found him only too willing. 'You're looking pleased with yourself too, Ray,' he said.

'So will you be in a minute, Stevie. I've found Chris Aikenhead for you, and he's right on our doorstep.'

'Yes!' Steele hissed.

'I read through the file on the investigation, and I found a reference to him, saying that he worked off-shore with a Scottish-owned company called Oriental Petroleum, so I checked with them. He still does. He worked on their platform in the North Sea at the time, and for three years after his wife's suicide, until he was moved to an installation off Venezuela. He remarried out there and stayed until September, when he came back to a job in the Edinburgh office as development manager. The personnel officer was very co-operative: she gave me his address.'

'Hold on, Ray. What if she tells him that the police have been asking about him?'

'I asked her not to do that, in case she alarmed him unnecessarily. I told her that something had arisen that related to his late wife's case, and that we wanted to advise him of it. She promised me she wouldn't say anything to him.'

'Let's hope she's as good as her word. Where does he live?'

'In the Buckstone area.'

'Christ, that's close to Neil, and Dan Pringle.'

'And the ski centre.'

'It gets better. What was his trade on the rigs?'

'He was an engineer.'

'It all fits. We pay a call on him, Ray, but first we get a warrant. We might need to search his house for a sock that's in want of a partner.'

Seventy-seven

Skinner was turning into Elbe Street when his cell-phone sounded in its hands-free socket in his car. He hit the answer button.

'Boss,' Neil McIlhenney exclaimed. 'Got you at last. I tried the office, but Jack said you'd gone. This is the third time I've called your mobile.'

'That's the trouble with technology,' the DCC grumbled. 'It never works when you need it. What's up? Are you still at Newcraighall?'

'Yes.'

'It was Green, then?' The question was tinged with resignation.

'Yes, but there was never any doubt about that, was there? Are you on your way here?'

'No. I decided that I'd go to the restaurant instead. I'm just pulling up outside in fact.'

'Good, I didn't want you driving when you heard this. We've found something on Sean's body that might be the answer to everything.'

As McIlhenney described the map of St Andrews, Skinner, for all that he had seen and done in his career, felt his blood chill. 'What do you still have to do there?' he asked.

'Nothing. The van's just arrived to remove the body, and we've spoken to everybody we need to. We've managed to convince the warehouse manager that it was a suicide, and that Sean managed to strangle himself with his own tie.'

'Okay. I want you to get Bassam's address, and go there. No chance he'll be there, but check it out, and then come here, as fast as you can.' He switched off the cell-phone, took it from its holder, and jumped out of his BMW.

A uniformed constable was guarding the door of the restaurant. For a second he moved to bar Skinner's way, but recognised him just in time and stepped aside.

There were no diners inside, only DS Sammy Pye and two other CID officers, four very confused staff members and one angry chef. 'Who you?' he demanded, before the door had even closed behind Skinner.

'Deputy chief constable,' he replied. 'Now who are you?'

'I Sukur. I cook here. We have customers; no boss, no head waiter, but we working still, then you people come and tell us we have to close. When Mr Bassam come back, you hear about this, I tell you.'

'Where is Mr Bassam right now?' Skinner asked him.

'I no' know.'

'Has he been in at all this morning?'

'No, but I have keys. Usually I open up.'

'Did Mr Bassam lock up last night?'

'How should I know? I go after we serve the last people. He no' here then, though. New head waiter say I could go.'

'Who was here when you left?'

'John, the new guy, and him.' The chef pointed to one of the two waiters, the Asian.

The man nodded. 'But I left after that,' he said, quickly.

'So John was alone?'

'Yes.'

'Where was Bassam?'

'I don't know.'

The DCC turned back to the chef. 'Do you?'

'No' here,' the truculent Sukur grunted. 'He went out before that.'

'When?'

'Earlier on.'

'Don't try my patience,' Skinner warned him. 'At what time?'

'I dunno, maybe eight, maybe earlier.'

'Did he tell you where he was going?'

'The boss no' tell me anything. He just leave me to run the kitchen.'

'But you knew he had gone. Does that mean you saw him leave?'

Sukur nodded. 'I see him through kitchen window. He get into van.'

'What van?'

'Mr Bassam's van: an old thing he uses to go to the cash and carry. He keep it at his house and sometimes he bring it here. It was here last night, parked out back. He get into it with the other guys.'

Skinner's eyes narrowed. 'What other guys?'

'I no' know who they are; they friends of his, though. Not Turkish, but then neither is he.'

'What do you know about them?'

'Nothing. They been living upstairs, but they don't come in here, ever.'

'What's upstairs?'

'The boss have a flat upstairs; he used to stay there, till he bring his family over and buy his house.'

'Do you have keys for it?'

'No. The boss keeps those.'

'How long have these people been there?'

'I dunno; not long, a few weeks maybe.'

'Come on,' said the DCC, 'show me where this place is.' He turned to Pye. 'Sam, with me.'

The chef, still scowling, led them through the kitchen, and out into Delight's back yard. A flight of stone stairs, on the outside of the building, led to a green-painted door. 'There,' he grunted.

The two police officers climbed the worn steps, coming to a square landing on top. Skinner tried the door handle, then, finding it locked, kicked it open effortlessly with the sole of his right foot.

'Sir,' Pye exclaimed.

'It was stuck: the wood must have been warped.'

'Yes, but . . .'

'Ah, you think they might be in there, do you, Sam? Not a cat's chance, but there's one way to find out.' He stepped into the flat.

All four doors off the hall were open: two led into bedrooms, each with twin beds, a third to a bathroom, and the last into a large living room, with a kitchen area against the far wall. The place was a mess: discarded cigarette packets, bottles and food wrappers lay everywhere.

'Not exactly *Good Housekeeping*,' Pye muttered.

'Looks a bit like your wife's desk from time to time.' The DCC chuckled. The sergeant was married to Ruth, his secretary. He walked over to a small dining-table positioned at the window. It was strewn with crumpled sheets of paper, which seemed to have been torn from a pad. He picked one up, and saw a few words jotted down. Whatever the language was it was unknown to him.

'Sir.' Skinner glanced across at Pye. He was standing by a small side table, looking at a heavy black machine. 'It's a fax,' he said.

'Do you think it might have been used?'

'If it has, it might have a log that tells us.'

'Try it.'

The sergeant bent over the device, pushing a button repeatedly as he read the menu. 'Got it,' he whispered, finally, then straightened as a humming sound began, and a sheet of paper started to emerge from a slot below the key-pad. He caught it before it could fall to the floor, and handed it to the DCC.

He read it, his eye scanning down a list of numbers and dates. Only two entries had any currency, and both showed messages received from the same number. 'Oh two oh seven,' he murmured. 'Thanks, Sam,' he said. 'That was good thinking. Now go back to the restaurant, please, and wait for DCIs McIlhenney and Mackenzie. When they arrive, send them up here.'

As soon as he was alone, Skinner took his palm-top computer from his pocket and turned it on, using a security code. He opened his personal directory and chose the letter 'A', quickly finding the phone number he sought.

He switched on his mobile and dialled. His call was not picked up directly; instead he heard a click and the dialling tone change pitch. At last a voice answered. 'Yes, Bob,' said Major Adam Arrow.

'Are you on a cell-phone?' he asked his friend.

'I'm in the field at the moment. What can I do for you?' There was none of the customary profane banter that was his usual trademark.

'Is this secure?'

'All the way, don't worry.'

'I need a number checked out.'

'Have you thought about Directory Enquiries?' The question reassured Skinner; it was more like the usual Arrow.

'For about a nanosecond: remember those Albanians I told you about?'

'Yes.'

'I've found them. I'm in a flat on my patch where these guys have been living since they pitched up here. They've been under the protection of an Albanian Turk called Petrit Bassam Kastrati, who runs a restaurant directly below where I'm standing, and now they've broken cover. In the last four days, they've received two faxes, and I'd like to know the point of origin.'

'So would I, but so would Five. Why aren't you asking them?'

'We had a line to one of the Albanians. He was killed last night in Glasgow, in sight of my people, as they were about to follow him back here. We had an MI5 operative under cover in the restaurant; he was found dead a couple of hours ago. His handler is currently being held in custody in my building.'

Arrow whistled. 'You don't need to say any more; give me the number.'

'You'll check it and get back to me?'

His friend chuckled. 'What's up, Bob? Not sure you can trust me?'

'Did I call you? You're the only man outside my own team I'm sure I can trust. Adam, if that's a Five number...'

'Then the fall-out will be in my area of operations, so don't you get into it. From the sound of things you were right to take the handler out of play. Can you tell me who it is?'

'Amanda Dennis.'

'Hell, I know Amanda. Are you sure she's a risk?'

'No, but I'm taking no chances.'

'I don't suppose I would either. You say the Albanians have gone. Do you have any idea where?'

'That's the really heavy bit. The only lead I have points to St Andrews, and you know who's there.'

'God almighty!'

'Not quite, but the future Defender of His Faith.' Skinner paused. 'Whatever these guys are here for, it's not a drug run. As of now, it looks like they're a hit team.'

Arrow hesitated for a few seconds. 'There's another strong

possibility,' he ventured. 'In fact I'd say it was almost likelier than an assassination. I did some research after you called me and I've come up with a possible answer. As well as all those criminal activities for which they've become world famous, they have another speciality. They stage kidnappings for ransom. Can you think of a victim with a higher price tag?'

The DCC pondered the suggestion. 'Whatever they're up to,' he said, 'they're equipped for it. We believe that they acquired a load of armaments in Holland; from the sound of things they gave us a sample of their fire-power in Glasgow last night. The guy I told you about, Samir Bajram, was with two locals. He was completing a drug deal, but I reckon he was doing a bit of business on the side, and when Naim Latifi found out, he took him out of play. The car he was in was hit by an anti-tank missile.'

'Jesus.' Arrow whistled again. 'Why make a small bang when you can make a really big one?'

'Adam,' Skinner went on, 'if Five's been penetrated, I've got to keep my distance from them. Can you send me fast back-up, from anywhere?'

The little soldier's sigh sounded full of despair; it gave Skinner no comfort. 'I don't have any specialists, mate. I was with the Secretary of State at Hereford yesterday, and it was virtually empty. The whole world's on fire, and the SAS is fully deployed putting it out. If you want boys in uniform, I'll get them to you, but they won't be trained for that stuff.'

'Can you alert the protection squad?'

'I'll alert the Palace. But, Bob, from what you say, this thing, whatever it is, could go down any time. An instant military operation isn't practical; the police will have to deal with it themselves.'

At his words, a great wave of dread swept over Skinner, and he felt the tension burn within him. 'Adam, if we're right about this, the stakes are higher than anything I've ever faced. I don't know if we can handle it.'

'Mate,' the old Arrow's voice came down the line, 'I've seen you in action. I don't think there's anything you can't fookin' handle.'

'Thanks for your confidence,' the DCC said, ironically.

'I'd rather you were on this than anyone else. I'll run down that number for you. Is there anything else I can do?'

'First get me an exact location; I need to know precisely where he is. Also, could you get me a chopper? We need to get to St Andrews as fast as we can. I'll alert the Fife force, but it'll take them time to get an armed team out there.'

'I can do that: there's one on standby at Redford Barracks. I'll put a detachment of soldiers in it too. Give me a location.'

'My headquarters building. It can land on the football field. It'll take me fifteen minutes to get back there.'

'How many passengers?'

'There'll be three of us.'

'No problem. Do you want firearms?'

'We'll take our own: we're familiar with them.'

'Let's hope you don't have to use them. I'll be in touch.'

'I hate helicopters,' said a voice from behind him. He turned to see McIlhenney and Mackenzie, the latter wearing a mournful expression.

'Who likes them? But there are worse places you could be. For example, you could be locked up in Glasgow. Strathclyde Police are after you two for blowing up Bajram and his cousins.' He headed for the door. 'Come on, there's no time to lose: we've got to get airborne as soon as we can. The future of more things than you can imagine could be in our hands.'

Seventy-eight

Normally, Andy Martin was a patient man, but as five o'clock approached, he found himself beginning to fret. The contact he had made in the General Register Office in Southport had promised him that he would have the information he sought before the day was out, but time was wearing thin.

He was on the point of making a wake-up call when his direct line rang. He snatched it up.

'Bet you thought I was never going to get back to you, Mr Martin,' said an amiable voice.

'That's not a bet I'm going to take, Mr Donald.' He chuckled. The two men had never met, but when Martin had identified himself to the GRO switchboard, he had been put through to the office of the Deputy Registrar General, who had introduced himself as Rex Donald.

He had expected that he might have some difficulty in persuading him to do a search of the English birth, death and marriage registers, but he had found him more than willing to help. Donald had explained that it was policy to co-operate with official requests from the police and other departments, and that he was not hindered by the Data Protection Act.

When Martin had given him the name of the person whose birth he wanted traced, he had listened for a reaction, but had picked up none. He had smiled to himself, wondering how Tommy Murtagh would have taken the knowledge that a high-ranking English civil servant had never heard, apparently, of Scotland's top politician.

'Has your search been successful?' he asked.

'The birth one has, in triplicate,' Donald told him. 'I've found three male children born thirty-six years ago and named Thomas Murtagh. However, only one of them has a mother called Rachel.'

'And the father?' asked Martin, trying to sound matter-of-fact.

'That information is not on the register. Rachel Murtagh was the mother's maiden name.'

'I see. Where was the birth registered?'

'In the city of York, where the mother lived. Obviously, since the mother was single, your second request, for details of her marriage, fell by the wayside. However, I had some additional checking done, just to make sure, and I can tell you that she did not enter into any subsequent union, not in England at any rate. Finally, there is no record of anyone named George Murtagh dying in the year you mention. Is all that helpful?'

'Very. Thank you, Mr Donald.'

'May I ask, Mr Martin, out of sheer, naked curiosity, what's behind your enquiries? Is it a fraud?'

The police officer grinned. 'You could put it that way,' he replied. 'Some people might see it as a very big fraud indeed.'

He hung up, musing over what he had been told. So the story of the motor mechanic's tragic death, the one that Diana Meikle had believed, was a fabrication, and the First Minister's official biography was a lie.

He found himself thinking about the man's sad family background and of his long-gone sister, whose birth certificate, as a Scottish check had revealed, had also been lacking in information on her paternity. How much light could she shed on her brother's world? Suddenly, he found himself thinking about the Herbert Groves Charitable Trust.

He picked up the phone again and called an old friend of his, someone who went all the way back to his Special Branch days. 'Excellent,' he murmured, as the phone was answered.

'Veronica Hacking.'

'Hi, Ronnie. It's Andy Martin. How's the Inland Revenue these days?'

Seventy-nine

Although the sports field was at the back of the building, and out of sight from his room, Skinner knew from the roar that penetrated the thick windows that the helicopter had arrived.

As he stood behind his desk, phone in hand, waiting to be put through to the Chief Constable of Fife, he adjusted the hip holster containing the Glock pistol that he had signed out from the store. A voice sounded in his ear. 'I have Mr Tallent for you now, sir.'

'Thanks.'

'Bob, what's the panic?' The Fife chief sounded slightly annoyed. 'We've got a medal presentation on here, and I've just been hauled out of it. This had better be good, or else.'

Skinner never reacted well to threats, not even from one of the few senior officers he had within the Scottish force. 'Shut up and listen, Clarence,' he barked. 'I'm calling to advise you that two of my officers and I are heading into your territory in hot pursuit of four suspects whom we have reason to believe may be planning something very big in St Andrews.'

'Terrorists?'

'More like mercenaries: Albanian gangsters, heavily armed. We believe they're heading for St Salvator's, which leads us to suspect the worst. Do you have an armed response unit in the area?'

'In St Andrews? Of course not.'

'How long will it take you to put a team together and get them there?'

'I reckon I can do it in an hour,' said the now compliant chief constable.

'We'll be there before them. I have a chopper on the ground

outside, with a small military detachment. When we get there, and your people arrive, I want them operating under my command. We know what the opposition looks like; they don't.'

'That's agreed. I'll be with them.'

'Thanks. What strength do you have there at the moment?' asked Skinner.

'I've got a uniformed station, with a chief inspector in charge.'

'Okay, I'd like you to have someone go to the college, alert the protection officers and let them know I'm on the way.'

'I'll do that. What's your plan?'

'I'm going to fly there, secure the subject and send him in the same chopper to a place of safety, then wait for the arrival of the Albanians. They've left this area, so I believe that to be imminent.'

'I'll get my team on the ground as fast as I can. God be with you.'

Eighty

'The man's done well for himself,' Ray Wilding commented, as he looked at the house. Night had fallen but the stone-clad villa still stood out, illuminated by carefully placed lights in the landscaped garden. 'The oil business must pay as well as they say.'

'All the people in this area have done well for themselves,' Steele reminded him. 'This is pretty up-market territory.'

Wilding checked his watch. 'It's spot on five. Do we wait for him to come back from the office, or do we go in now?'

'If you look at the driveway, you'll see that there are two cars there. Could be he's home already. Let's go in.'

They climbed out of Steele's car and crunched their way through the frozen snow up the path to the front door. Wilding's ring was answered by an attractive woman with jet-black hair, a brown complexion and eyes to match. 'Yes?' she asked, looking at them suspiciously.

'Mrs Aikenhead,' the inspector began, 'we're police officers.' He and the sergeant displayed their warrant cards. 'Is your husband at home?' She nodded. 'In that case, we'd like a word with him. It has to do with the death of his first wife, and the circumstances that led up to it.'

'If you've come to apologise, you're ten years too late.' The voice came from within the hall; they looked past the woman and saw a big, heavily muscled figure leaning against the door frame. 'But come in and tell me your story.' He turned and disappeared into the room behind him.

By the time his wife had shown them through, he was seated in a chair beside the fire. 'Jessie, you don't need to hear this,' he said. She nodded and left the room.

The two officers stood, waiting for an invitation to sit, but none came. 'What have you got to say for yourself?' Chris Aikenhead asked, truculently.

'We've got a few questions, actually,' Steele told him, quietly.

'I hope they make some sense this time, more than that man Pringle did. Is that bastard still on the force?'

'Detective Chief Superintendent Pringle is currently our head of CID, sir.'

'And what about those other two, the pair who fucked up and caused Patsy to kill herself? What were their names again?'

'I think you know their names, Mr Aikenhead.'

The man scowled up at them. 'How could I forget them?' he muttered. 'McIlhenney and Regan.'

'They're both still on the force too. You must know George is, unless you don't read newspapers or watch television. It was his son who was killed in the castle grounds the Sunday before last.'

'Into every life a little rain must fall.' The words were soft, and had a hint of laughter about them. Steele felt Wilding tense beside him.

'That's quite a downpour,' he replied, 'losing your kid. But it didn't just rain on George and Jen Regan: the cloud hovered over Dan and Elma Pringle as well. Their daughter was gassed last week by a heater in her room on Riccarton Campus. She died a couple of days later.'

Aikenhead's eyes held his. 'That's bad luck,' he said, coldly.

'Yes, it was. Fortunately Neil and Louise McIlhenney were luckier: their son was supposed to have a fatal accident up at Hillend on Saturday, but he managed to escape from the man who took him.'

'A real chapter of accidents, from the sound of it.'

'That's what we were meant to think, but thanks to some excellent work in our lab, we can prove they weren't. We're looking at two counts of murder, and one of attempted abduction. Can I take you back through your movements over the last ten days, sir? For example, where were you on Saturday afternoon, when we had that blizzard?'

Chris Aikenhead stared at the two detectives in absolute astonishment: and then, without warning, he exploded into laughter. When finally, it subsided, he shook his head. 'Make it easy for yourselves,' he said, still chuckling. 'Just get the fuck out of my house.'

'You've got it the wrong way round,' Steele snapped back, his patience eroded. 'We have a warrant to search these premises; if you don't start treating our questions with respect I will have a team up here within half an hour and we will take this place apart.'

'You want answers?' Aikenhead shot back. 'I'll give you one answer, and that's all you'll need.' He seized the arms of his chair and pushed himself to his feet. Standing erect and staring down at both of his interrogators, he unbuckled his belt, unfastened his jeans and let them fall to the ground.

His right leg had been amputated just above the knee, and replaced by a prosthesis. He let them stare at it for several seconds, then dropped back into his seat and pulled himself back, awkwardly, into his trousers.

'That's the reason I came off the rigs,' he told them, calmly. 'I lost it ten months ago. I'm getting good on the new one, but only on level ground. Any more questions?'

'Just one,' Steele replied. 'Why didn't you tell us that at the start?'

'Haven't you worked that one out yet? I don't like you guys. It doesn't matter whether it's you two or the other three, you're all the same to me, unsympathetic bastards in suits whose only interest is in getting a result. That man Pringle bullied my Patsy into confessing to something she didn't do; because of that and because of two clowns who couldn't be bothered to see for themselves, she died a miserable death in a prison cell.'

Aikenhead paused; his anger had been replaced by pain. 'You know,' he murmured, 'since I met Jessie, I've actually been trying to forget about it all. I even thought that when my leg got ripped off, some of that old hurt got torn out as well. I was wrong: you guys have brought all of the injustice back, and more. You came in here prepared to accuse me of being a child-killer.'

He shook his head, sadly. Steele looked down at him, feeling awkward and, for once in his life, at a loss for words. 'I'm sorry,' was all he could say, as he and Wilding turned and headed for the door.

They were almost in the hall when Aikenhead called after them: 'What I don't understand is why you picked me. If I had decided to take revenge ten years on, why would I have killed their kids? An eye for an eye in my case would have been their wives.'

Eighty-one

The helicopter flew low and fast through the night skies. It was a big ugly brute of an aircraft, built for functionality and not for comfort. McIlhenney and Mackenzie were strapped into seats at the back with four uniformed soldiers, Skinner in front with the pilot.

It was gloomy: the only illumination came from the instrumentation and from a small night-light in the cabin, but outside and to their left, they could see the lights of the Fife coastal towns, as they swept across the Forth estuary. They were flying over land once more when the radio crackled into life in Skinner's headset.

'Bob, are you receiving me?' a tinny voice asked. 'It's Adam.' The pilot handed the DCC a microphone, showing him a button and pointing to indicate that he had to press to transmit. He took it from him.

'Receiving,' he shouted.

'I've advised the Palace of the possibility of a threat and told them that a detachment is on the way to St Andrews to secure the area. What action have you taken?'

'I've contacted the local chief constable: he's mobilising what resources he can. What will the Palace do?'

'They'll make direct contact with the protection officers on the ground, advise them of the situation and tell them that you're coming. He is in the college, Bob; repeat, in St Salvator's College building, in his private suite. Do you understand?'

'Received and understood. What about the number?'

'I've had no joy with that yet.'

'Keep trying. What do you want me to do with Amanda?'

'Keep holding her. She may be part of it, she may not; we don't

324

know how far it goes yet. But forget that: what you have to do in the next hour will need your full attention.'

'Acknowledged. I'll call you when he's secured.' He put the microphone back in its slot below the instrument panel and stared out into the night. 'How close are we?' he asked the pilot.

'See those lights up ahead, sir? That's it. We're less than five minutes away.'

'Good. When we get there I need you to put us down as close to St Salvator's College as possible. Do you know the town?'

'Yes, but it's dark, sir,' the young lieutenant shouted back. 'Without proper lighting the safest place for me to land would be on the golf course.'

'I'm bothered about someone else's safety, not ours. If it's clear of students I want you to set us down right in the middle of St Salvator's quadrangle.'

'I'll try, sir, but no promises.'

The lights of St Andrews shone ever clearer, made brighter by the blanket of snow that still lay on the ground. As the aircraft swung over the town, Skinner could make out the shape of South Street, then Market Street and, furthest away, North Street, their objective.

'I can't get into the grounds, sir,' the pilot shouted. 'There are a lot of people down there.'

'In that case, set us down in the middle of North Street, but don't cut your engine. I want you to wait, ready to lift off immediately when your next passenger gets here.' He twisted round in his seat to face McIlhenney, Mackenzie and the four infantrymen. 'It's begun on the ground,' he shouted at them. 'We won't know what the situation is until we see it, but remember this, all of you: our only objective is to make the Prince safe and get him out of there. You've all studied photographs of Naim Latifi, the Ramadani brothers and Peter Bassam: if you see any one of them, put him down unless he's clearly unarmed and offering no resistance.'

'You mean shoot them, sir?' All of Mackenzie's customary flippancy had evaporated; even in the surreal light within the cabin, it was clear that his face was ghostly white.

Skinner stared at him. 'Bandit,' he asked, 'are you up for this? You can stay in the chopper if you want, and it will never be held against you. The same goes for you, Neil. You guys have got kids, after all.'

'So have you,' said McIlhenney, tersely. 'And the young man in the college, he's someone's kid as well.'

The DCC looked out of the window to the side. The pilot had taken him at his word: he had switched on his searchlight and was setting the aircraft down in the middle of North Street, next to the university chapel with its tall illuminated tower. The wheels were barely on the ground before Skinner jumped out, the Glock big in his hand and shining silver in the night.

As the pilot had said, they were not alone. A stream of young people were pouring out of Butts Wynd into the thoroughfare. They were running for their lives, and one or two were screaming. Some were bleeding, but the DCC reasoned that if they were mobile they could be cared for later.

'With me,' he ordered, then led his small force in the direction from which the crowd had come, round the corner of the chapel and into St Salvator's quadrangle.

The scene that greeted them was one of total chaos. More students rushed past them, barely noticing their presence. A few were not running; they lay on the ground, ominously still. He looked across the snow-covered grass to the college itself. He had been there once before, when he and Sarah, as guests at a Fife police summer event in the nearby Younger Hall, had been given overnight accommodation.

The doorway that they had used on that occasion no longer existed. It had been blown apart, and only a great gaping hole remained. Another blast had hit the façade of the old building further along. 'Missiles,' Skinner shouted at McIlhenney. 'The protection-squad guys would have secured the building when they got the alert. They just blasted their way in.'

A tall young student rushed towards them, intent on escape. The DCC grabbed him, halting his flight. 'Where is the Prince's suite?' he yelled. The terrified boy gazed at him, shock in his eyes, but the policeman had no time for sympathy. 'Where?' he roared again.

'One floor up, to the left.' Skinner set him free to run into the night. He turned to his six companions. 'You four,' he said to the soldiers.

'You've got carbines, so you're best in the open, I want two of you here to take down any of the targets if they get past us and try to escape this way, and the other two in The Scores, the street behind, covering the back. Neil, Bandit, we're going in.' As two of the infantrymen raced off across the lawn, and the others took position, the three police officers ran towards the newly carved entrance.

The building was ablaze with light: it had not occurred to the attackers to try to cut the power, or they had been completely confident of the effect of their ferocious assault. The trio sprinted inside, each covering the others' backs. The flood of fleeing students had subsided, and the entrance hall was empty . . . of the living, at any rate. A few must have been in the hall when the missile hit, three, Skinner reckoned, although he could not be certain. The bodies of two uniformed police officers, a chief inspector and a female constable lay at the foot of the stairs. They had each been shot at least a dozen times.

'Automatic weapons,' said the DCC, 'keep yourselves close to the ground, boys, and for Christ's sake, shoot first if you have to.' He led the way up the stairs, moving fast and silently.

At his heels, McIlhenney prayed silently, and thought of Lou and the children. He was aware that Mackenzie, by his side, was trembling; but he was pressing on nonetheless, defying his fear.

They reached the top of the stairs, which opened out on to a corridor; they had turned back upon themselves, and so if the student's direction was correct, the Prince's suite would be on their right. A doorway opposite offered some shelter: Skinner tensed himself and dived towards it, trusting that he still had the speed to beat an Albanian's trigger finger and a hail of bullets.

But none came: the corridor was eerily quiet. Taking his life in his hands once more, he stepped out of the doorway, braced and ready to fire.

Outside a door at the end, two figures, another constable and a man in a suit, lay still on the floor. The DCC ran towards them, beckoning his colleagues to follow. The man in plain clothes wore a small gold badge in his lapel, the sign of a protection officer; his right hand still clutched a pistol, loosely. He had been shot several times in the chest and head, and he was beyond help. Skinner felt the gun in his hand; it was warm, as if it had been fired.

The police officer was still alive: he had wounds in his right arm, shoulder and his upper chest, but he was not bleeding profusely, and he was conscious. 'You'll make it,' said Skinner, quietly. 'What's your name?'

'PC Alan McManus.'

'I'm Bob Skinner, from Edinburgh. How many years on the job, Alan?'

'Fourteen, sir.'

'All of them quiet till tonight, I'll bet. Tell me what I need to know.'

'They took him, sir,' the wounded officer replied, weakly and painfully. 'The other protection officer's in the suite; I think he's dead.'

'He is,' McIlhenney murmured. 'Just inside the door.'

'Where did they go?'

'Down the fire escape: there's a door over there that leads to it.'

'How many?'

'Three, but one was wounded.' PC McManus groaned. 'This man here got off a shot before they opened fire.'

'Okay. You just lie quiet now.' Skinner looked at Mackenzie and took pity on him. 'Bandit, you stay here: make him comfortable and make sure that the emergency services get to him as fast as possible.' He turned to McIlhenney. 'Neil, let's get after them. From Sean's map we have to assume that they're heading for the Sea Life Centre. We've heard no shots from outside, so they must have gone before our two soldiers got into position. But if one's wounded that might slow them down.'

They found the door that led to the fire escape, as the constable had described it. The emergency exit swung on its hinges. The DCC saw, with a burst of savage satisfaction, that it was smeared with blood. They trotted down the metal staircase at double time, no longer caring about noise, then found the gate that led out into The Scores.

The roadway was deserted; skeletal trees rose around them, shifting, ghostly figures in the weak glow of the sodium lamps.

'Bob,' McIlhenney whispered, hoarsely, breaking into a run once more. 'Look.' Skinner followed him across the road; on the other side, huddled against a low stone wall, the two infantrymen lay dead, their carbines by their sides. Each had been shot in the back, at close range, and again in the neck, a *coup de grâce*.

'How the hell did the Albanians do that?' the big chief inspector asked himself, aloud. 'Poor bastards; it looks as if they never had a chance.'

'They must have had an outside man too: there were four of them in all, remember, including Bassam. I'd been guessing that the fourth man would be on the boat, but I must have been wrong: it looks as if he was guarding the escape route. Christ, they could almost be gone by now.'

'There are bloodstains on the snow,' McIlhenney exclaimed.

'We follow them.' Taking the dead soldiers' rifles, and their night glasses, they started to run, as fast as they were able on the treacherous, slippery pavements. As they moved down The Scores the blood patches became noticeably larger, showing them the way ever more clearly. They turned off the roadway and on to a path that led across the grass, passing the Martyrs Monument on the left.

They had almost reached the Sea Life Centre, when they came upon the body, lying face down and hunched before them. Mindful of a trap, Skinner kept the rifle on the man, as McIlhenney turned him over, but there was no need: the dead eyes of Amet, the younger of the Ramadani brothers, stared up at the night sky, just as the moon appeared from behind a cloud to bathe his face in silver.

'I can see them,' McIlhenney shouted, looking through the night glasses. 'They're on the jetty, by the Centre.'

Skinner snatched up his own binoculars and focused them. He found the boat, a big fast vessel, built for sheer speed; a stocky, bald-headed man was at the wheel. 'Bassam,' he murmured, moving the glasses until he found the others, a group of three.

The figure in the middle was slimmer and much taller than the other two, well over six feet, but they held him firmly on either side, shoving him towards the boat. 'If they get him on board...' the DCC murmured. He dropped the glasses and raised the rifle, feeling a wave of exultation when he found that it, too, had night vision.

He pressed the butt to his shoulder and found the trio again; they seemed larger through the telescopic sight than in the binoculars. He drew a deep breath and held it, fixed the man on the Prince's right with the red laser dot, and squeezed the trigger, gently so that he would not jerk it. There was no recoil from the weapon, and so he saw the Albanian as he rose up on his toes and pitched forward, tumbling into the boat.

He swung the sight to the other kidnapper. Even as he did so, he saw the young Prince swing a powerful punch at him with his newly freed fist, knocking him sideways and out of the weapon's field of vision.

'Run!' he bellowed, but the command was unnecessary, for the tall young man was already sprinting up towards them. Frantically he swung the rifle, searching through the sight for the second Albanian, before he could start shooting. He heard McIlhenney, beside him, firing into the night, and then he saw the man leaping into the boat, even as its engine roared into life and it began to move away from the jetty. He gave a huge sigh of relief and let the weapon relax in his grasp.

The young man was racing up the path, and more than halfway towards them, when Skinner saw a figure step from the shadow of the Sea Life Centre building and into the moonlight. The man raised his arm, and he saw the silenced pistol, as he trained it on the fleeing Prince. In a blur of movement, he swept the carbine back up to his shoulder, sighted and fired. The figure seemed to stiffen; the gun slipped from his grasp, and he toppled backwards.

And then the young man around whom so much revolved was standing before them, tall, blond, and blessed with his mother's looks. 'I really do hope that you're the good guys,' he exclaimed, breathlessly.

'Seventh Cavalry, Edinburgh branch, at your service, sir,' Skinner replied, then turned to McIlhenney. 'Neil, take the Prince to the chopper, and have the pilot fly you back to our headquarters; not the barracks as previously discussed. Make him secure and comfortable there, then contact the assistant commissioner in the Met who's in charge of royal protection and tell him where he is. I repeat, go to Fettes, not Redford. Understood?'

'I'm with you. Who was that down there, that fourth man you just shot?'

'That's what I'm afraid to find out, but I'm going to have to. Now get out of here, fast, and up to North Street.'

As the two moved off into the night, he heard a confident young voice say, 'Neil, this way, along Murray Park. It's quicker.'

Holding his rifle in both hands, the DCC moved down the path to where the fallen man lay, with his head in the centre of a great dark circle of spreading blood. His limbs jerked uncontrollably, and he had a massive head wound, just above his right ear. And yet he was still conscious.

'Wh-when you fired, did you know it was me?' asked Adam Arrow. The words were a shivering whisper; Skinner had to kneel down to hear them. He did so steadily and with care for he was shaking himself and a great cold fist seemed to be grasping the pit of his stomach, threatening to shatter his self-control.

'I reckoned that it had to be,' he answered, 'when I saw the dead soldiers. I tried to tell myself that it was impossible, but only you knew they were coming. You killed your own men, Adam,' he said, with disgust in his voice as he stared down at him. 'You were here all along, weren't you? When I called you today, and you said you were in the field, you were here.'

'Yesss.'

'What the hell have you done?'

'F-fucked up in the end.'

'You were behind the whole thing? You and Amanda?'

'No.' The whisper seemed to grow stronger. 'Not Amanda: she knew nothing. Rudy Sewell. She reported back to him; never knew he was one of us.'

'One of us? You mean there are more?'

'A few of us; intelligence officers . . . patriots.'

Skinner sighed. 'How often has that been said by traitors?'

'Not traitors! I've served Queen and country all my life. Queen and country, listen. Rudy and I and the others, we believe that young man mustn't become king or he'll destroy the monarchy, like his mother tried to do.'

'You're crazy. He's his father's son as well, you know.'

'He's an idol. He'll take the throne too close to the people.' Arrow shuddered violently, and for a moment Skinner thought that he was going, but instead he seemed to recover some strength. 'The monarchy can't be u-user-friendly, Bob. It represents authority. It's the symbol that guys like me fight and die for. Make it populist and it will die; this country will be rudderless, and everything it has been will be lost. My friends and I decided that we couldn't let that happen.'

'So you set out to kidnap him?'

'No, to make it look like a kidnap. There's a vessel offshore: that's where the speedboat's headed. He'd have been killed as soon as they got him on board, and his body disposed of effectively. But it would have been blamed on the Albanians.'

'So why did you help me? Why did you give me the helicopter?'

'To make it look good,' Arrow wheezed, his voice beginning to fade once more. 'I didn't plan on getting found out . . . ever. None of us did. I knew you wouldn't be here on time; my backup plan if you did corner them was for him to be killed in the battle. I almost made sure of it.' He let out a macabre, choking laugh. 'I wish I'd never taught you to handle a bloody carbine,' he whispered.

'I'd have got you with the Glock,' Skinner murmured. 'Why did you choose to try it here?' he asked. 'Why St Andrews, with all these people around?'

'Logical. It was easier to attack than anywhere else, plus we could get him out by sea.'

'And the leak from NATO intelligence? That couldn't have been part of your plan.'

'That was unfortunate. Nobody would have been any the wiser but for that, until it was all over. The good thing was that the tip came to me, so we were able to manage it. We couldn't ignore it, but Rudy tried to put a lid on it, keep the search in-house. He let Amanda think they were drug-dealers and sent her chasing wild geese around the clubs in Edinburgh, but your people tripped over it.' Arrow gave another violent shudder, and his face twisted with pain. 'Told him he should have kept off your patch,' he gasped. 'We still held all the cards, though, with Amanda, in all innocence, keeping us informed.'

'Why should I believe that she's not a part of it? She might be one of you; Rudy Sewell might be the innocent one.'

Arrow laughed again, another bizarre, croaking chuckle. 'No chance: she'd never have sacrificed her toy boy.'

'Sean? Him and Amanda?'

'Worst kept secret in MI5.'

The DCC felt his knees growing stiff in the cold: he pushed himself to his feet. 'So what happens now?' the gravely injured soldier whispered.

'You might live,' said Skinner. 'People have survived worse head wounds than that.'

'I know. That's why I asked.'

'I don't want to know. I can't see you standing trial, though. That would be a huge scandal; like you say, very bad for the Queen and country you thought you were protecting.' The policeman scowled, gazing into the night. 'Maybe they'll send you to Cuba, like those other poor bastards.'

'Or somewhere worse, getting names out of us, even when there are no other names to give. I don't want that: I've done it myself, so I know how it'll be.' Arrow looked up at him, into his eyes. 'But that's not what I meant. Bob, there's nobody around. If I could move I'd find my gun, and finish it. You wouldn't do me a favour, would you?'

He gazed back down at the man who had been his friend, the man he had once trusted with his own life, without a moment's doubt or hesitation. 'And why should I do that?' he asked, then turned and headed back towards the college.

'Goodbye, Bob,' the weak voice called after him.

'Oh, shit.' Skinner turned, raised the rifle and shot him dead.

He stood there for a while, not noticing the ground around him darken as the moon retreated behind the cloud cover. He was grief-stricken, not for the traitor but for times past, for unswerving loyalty turned to betrayal. Finally he shook himself into action, and walked through the crisp, icy night towards the Martyrs Monument. He heard sirens in the town, as the Fife police contingent, headed, he supposed, by Chief Constable Clarence Tallent, arrived to take control, and as the emergency services began to remove the wounded. Then, rising over all the din, came the roar of a helicopter taking off; he sighed with relief.

He stopped at the great obelisk, numb not just with cold but with everything that had happened that night, took out his cell-phone and switched it on. He found his stored numbers; selected the first on the alphabetical list, and called it. 'Aileen,' he said, when she answered. 'Where are you?'

'I'm at the flat. I've just got in from the office.'

He had lost track of time; he checked his watch and saw to his surprise that it was only seven twenty. The night seemed to have been endless. 'Is your nice new Fiat there?' he asked, making an effort to sound calm and collected.

'Yes.'

'Then, if you would, I'd like you to do something for me. I'm in St Andrews, I've got no transport, I'm freezing and I'm in a slight state of shock. I wonder if you'd come and get me, for right now there's nobody in the world I need to see as badly as I need to see you.'

'Bob, of course I'll come, but you're scaring me.'

'Don't be afraid: the panic's over. When you get here, I'll be with the chief constable, in St Salvator's College. We'll probably have TV crews here by then so comb your hair before you get out of the car. It'll look good, you being here, I promise you.'

'What's been happening?'

'A small war, but we won. It's safe; I wouldn't have you here otherwise. However, before you leave, there's something you have to do, and it's very important. You're the Justice Minister, so I guess you're able to call the Home Secretary in person, about something really urgent.'

'Yes, I suppose so, although I never have.'

'Well, I want you to do so, although by now you might find he's not surprised to hear from you. When you contact him, tell him to contact the Commissioner of the Met and have him arrest a man called Rudolph Sewell. He's an assistant director of MI5. Tell him that it's very important and that he has to do this tonight.'

'And if he asks me why?'

'You could tell him he's upset your boyfriend. If he doesn't buy that, tell him it involves a plot against the state; that should get his attention.'

Eighty-two

Danielle Martin was cutting teeth; she had given her mother a difficult day, and so when Andy had arrived home, he had found himself concentrating on her and her vocally expressed needs.

Finally, the infant had settled down to sleep, and her parents had settled down to supper. Karen could see that he was distracted; as an ex-police officer, she knew the signs. 'CID, is it?' she asked, eventually. 'Have you got a stalled investigation?'

He blinked, fork in hand and looked at her. 'Uh?'

'You were back in Dundee, Andy.'

'I'm sorry, love,' he said. 'I don't like bringing it home with me. But this is a thing I've been working on for Bob, and I'm keen to talk to him about it.'

'I see. That's what these hush-hush meetings have been about, is it? Your forces have a cross-territory job on and you two are sticking your noses in. Honest to God, the one of you's as bad as the other. You're both deputy chief constables, you have perfectly competent criminal investigation departments, but can you leave them to get on with their work? Can you hell.'

Andy smiled at her lecture. 'No, Kar, you're wrong, honestly. This has nothing to do with either of our forces . . . not directly at any rate. We have a political problem, one that needs careful handling or it could affect all of us.'

She shrugged as she poured him more wine. 'If it's that important, what are you waiting for? Call him.'

'I tried earlier on, but I couldn't get hold of him anywhere. He even had his mobile switched off and that's a rarity.'

'Maybe Sarah's come home and they're having a passionate reunion. That'd be nice.'

'You may wish, but don't hold your breath. Anyway, what makes you think he'd turn his phone off for that?'

She laughed, then reached across to the sideboard from her seat at the table, picked the cordless telephone from its socket, and handed it to him. 'Go on,' she urged him. 'Try again, and then maybe you can appreciate the dinner that I went to some trouble to cook for you.'

He took it from her and dialled Skinner's cell-phone; this time it rang out.

'Yes?'

There was a weariness about his closest friend's voice that set him on edge at once; he had known him in many moods, but he had never heard him sound like that. 'Bob, it's Andy. Are you okay?'

'Yeah, sorry, mate. I'm on the move, that's all.'

Martin could hear background noise: people calling out, their voices filled with urgency. 'What's up?' he asked.

'The proverbial balloon,' Skinner sighed, 'but I can't talk about it. Switch on the telly, and I reckon you'll find out soon. What do you want?'

'It's this Murtagh thing: I'm almost certain that Brindsley Groves is his father. The official version's a load of crap: his mother never married, so she was never widowed by any tragic works accident. Groves did his MBA at York, where she lived; Tommy was born around the time he went back to Dundee and joined the family firm.'

'That's very interesting, but really, Andy, I cannot deal with this just now.'

'Will I speak to Neil?' Martin asked.

'No, please don't. He has his hands full as well.'

'Okay, I'll leave it till tomorrow, if you insist, but there's one other thing I wanted to ask you. I checked out the current beneficiaries of the Groves family trust. There are four: Herbert Groves, Brindsley's son, Rowena, his daughter, Tommy Murtagh, and someone called Chris Aikenhead. Do you have any idea who he is?'

It was as if Skinner had been given an instant shot of a powerful stimulant. 'What?' he exclaimed, his voice back to full strength. 'Andy,' he continued, 'if you're desperate to talk to someone tonight, get hold of Stevie Steele, wherever he is. Your investigation and his have just bumped into each other.'

Eighty-three

Aileen de Marco had never driven as fast after dark. She had done as Bob had asked and had heard the Home Secretary's manner change from one of annoyance, to bewilderment and finally to panic, all within thirty seconds. Then, rather than leave Lena McElhone at home to field incoming London calls about which she knew nothing, she had taken her with her in the Fiat. Her presence was a bonus, for Lena was a St Andrews graduate and guided her along the fastest, straightest road to the town.

They kept the radio switched on all the way. The eight o'clock news headlines told them that reports were coming in of an incident in the university town, they gave no details, but reminded listeners that the Prince was a student there.

When they arrived, the whole of North Street was blocked off by armed police, and a contingent of the RAF regiment flown down from Leuchars, but when Aileen identified herself a detective sergeant took them into his charge and led them towards the college.

A small group of journalists, photographers and television crews had been allowed inside the perimeter, under tight control. They recognised the minister and called out to her. She stopped and walked across. 'Wait, please,' she said, stilling their cries. 'I don't know what's happened yet; I'm just going in to be briefed. When I can I'll talk to you.'

As the sergeant led them into the quadrangle, they stopped in their tracks, shocked by the devastation, and the mangled side of the building. Lena gave a stifled scream; she had known it well.

They passed through the bloody hall, where five large white sheets had been laid over the dead, and found Skinner in a room at the back

338

of the building. Aileen had seen him straight from a transatlantic flight, but then he had looked nowhere near as exhausted. He was slumped in a chair, pale-faced and wearing a military flak jacket. A glass of whisky lay on a table near his right hand, which seemed to her to be trembling very slightly.

He stood when he saw her enter. Their eyes met, then they came together in a great shivering hug. 'Thank God you're here to warm me, baby,' he whispered in her ear. 'I thought I was going to freeze to death.'

'Hush, now,' she murmured, stroking his hair. 'It's all right.' The chief constable, Lena McElhone, Bandit Mackenzie, and the detective sergeant all looked away, trying to be as invisible as possible.

When Skinner had stopped shaking, she released him from her embrace and made him sit once more. She turned to Chief Constable Tallent. 'Is the Prince safe?' she asked.

'Yes. There was an attempt to kidnap him, but thanks to DCC Skinner and his men it was foiled.'

'Those . . .' she hesitated '. . . in the hall?'

He understood her question. 'There have been seven fatalities in the building,' he told her. 'Two students killed by the blast and another by gunfire, two of my officers and two members of the royal protection squad.'

'And three outside,' said Skinner, hoarsely, from his chair. 'Two soldiers and one of the kidnappers; his body's down by the Sea Life Centre, being guarded by the military.'

'Can I go there?'

'You don't want to. Anyway, it's off limits to everybody for now.' His eyes were still slightly glazed as he took a sip of his whisky.

She turned back to the chief. 'How many kidnappers were there?'

'Four in all. Three escaped by boat, although Mr Skinner says that one is wounded, possibly fatally.'

'Probably,' the DCC snapped. 'I shot him in the middle of the back, right between the shoulder-blades. He fell into the boat.'

Chief Constable Tallent nodded. 'The RAF have scrambled aircraft and are searching for them. We believe that they'll be meeting up with a larger vessel offshore.'

'Do we know anything about the attackers?'

The chief hesitated.

'It's all right, Clarence,' said Skinner. 'Aileen's entitled to know; anyway, we might as well go public now. They were a gang of Albanians, four of them, and their aim was to collect the biggest ransom pay-off in history. They got paid off all right, and any minute now the RAF will be blowing what's left of them out of the water.' He smiled, weakly. 'That last bit isn't for the press, by the way.'

'Killed trying to escape?'

'They are certainly still armed. They may even have another missile. No chances will be taken.'

'I understand; anyway, that's military business. Chief Constable,' she continued, 'there's a hungry media pack outside. Shall we give them a joint statement for the ten o'clock news programmes?'

'It's very early in the investigation,' Tallent answered, doubtfully.

'What bloody investigation, Clarence?' Skinner snarled; he pushed himself to his feet once more, stripping off the flak jacket and throwing it into a corner. 'We know what's happened, and we know who did it. It's a national issue, there's Christ knows what speculation already, and the people need to be told: most of all they need to be told that the prince is safe and sound.'

He looked at Aileen. 'Get out there and tell them, Minister. Just don't mention the body count, for there are next of kin to be told, and don't mention my name.'

'If she doesn't I will,' said the chief constable gruffly. 'Let's do it, then.'

Aileen was in the doorway, when she turned. 'Bob, I understand that you don't have transport back to Edinburgh. When this is over, can I give you a lift?'

Skinner's tired smile crinkled the lines around his eyes. 'That's very kind of you. Do you have room for DCI Mackenzie as well? His transport's gone too, and I'd hate for him to have to hitch-hike in this weather.'

Eighty-four

The flashing green light on the telephone receiver told Stevie Steele that he had a message as soon as he and Maggie stepped into the house. He pushed the hands-free button, then play-back and listened.

'Stevie, it's Andy Martin here. There's something I've been working on and a name's come up. I've been told I should speak to you about it, urgently. So if you get in at a reasonable hour, say before eleven, give me a call on this number.' Steele grabbed a pen and scribbled as Martin recited. 'Failing that, I'll call you in the office tomorrow, nine sharp.'

'Wonder what that's about?' said Maggie. 'He sounded pumped up. That's not like him: he's usually pretty cool. Go on, give him a call: it's only just gone ten fifteen.'

He nodded and walked through to the play-room, where he picked up the phone and sprawled on the couch. He dialled; Martin picked up on the first ring. 'You're keen, sir,' he chuckled, 'or were you sat beside the phone?'

'You wake the baby, I get grief.'

Stevie smiled, thinking of days to come. 'Sorry to call you back so late, then; we were at a movie. In that case, whatever you want to discuss must be really urgent.'

'Bob Skinner said it was. I spoke to him earlier tonight and happened to mention a name. He sparked on it and said it might relate to an investigation of yours.'

'Try me.'

'Chris Aikenhead.'

Steele smiled. 'Indeed it does, sir,' he said softly. 'Do you want to go first, or will I?'

'Fire away.'

'We've had three incidents here, two fatal, one might have been, all involving the children of police officers who worked on a specific case together. It ended in the suicide of the accused, following which the guilty verdict was turned over by the appeal court. Chris Aikenhead was her husband.'

'Of course: Patsy Aikenhead, the child-minder who killed the baby.'

'That's not what the appeal court decided.'

'Maybe not, but it's what Dan Pringle believes to this day. Are you telling me this Chris Aikenhead killed Ross, and George's kid?'

'No,' Steele replied, vehemently. 'He couldn't have. He's missing half of one leg. The guy I'm looking for ran up a mountain in the snow with Neil McIlhenney's boy, and put Mario McGuire in hospital into the bargain.'

'Ouch! I'd have thought you'd need three legs to do that. So where does that leave you, with him out of the frame?'

'It leaves me looking at the parents of Mariel Dickens, the dead child. That's on my agenda for tomorrow.'

'I reckon you'll be wasting your time. I was the head of CID's gofer in those days: we had a look at the investigation after it went pear-shaped and, from what I remember, the mother was the main bread-winner in the family because the father had severe multiple sclerosis.'

Steele groaned, and made a face at Maggie, who had come to sit beside him. 'If you're right, unless Mrs Dickens is a hell of a woman, that just leaves Patsy's family.'

'And that's where I might be able to help. Have you ever heard of the Groves Charitable Trust?'

'No, sir. Should I?'

'I don't suppose so,' Martin conceded. 'It's a foundation that provides for the family of the owners of Herbert Groves Construction plc, a big construction firm based on my patch. The current beneficiaries include the children of the present boss of the company. They also include Chris Aikenhead.'

'How come?'

'Have you read the papers in the Aikenhead investigation?'

'Yes.'

'Can you remember the name under which Patsy was charged, her full, formal name, that is, as it went on the charge sheet?'

'No, but I didn't pay any attention to that, because I didn't think it was relevant.'

'Sod it. We might as well have waited until tomorrow.'

'Not at all: I've got the file at home with me. It's in my briefcase.'

Maggie jumped up. 'I'll get it,' she called out, as she headed for the door.

'Thanks, love. It's in the bedroom.'

'Was that who I think it is?' asked Martin.

Stevie chuckled. 'You're well out of the Edinburgh loop, aren't you?'

'I didn't realise how much until now. Are you together?'

'Permanently.'

'That's great. I'm happy for you both.'

Maggie returned with the case and handed it to him. Quickly, he spun the combination locks, opened it and took out the file. 'Hold on till I flip through this,' he said, the phone jammed between his shoulder and his ear. 'Let's see,' he mumbled. 'No, not that. Wait a minute, yes. Here it is, a copy of the indictment. She was charged as Cleopatra Aikenhead . . . Patsy for short . . . and her maiden name is given as Murtagh.' He paused. 'Murtagh? That sounds very familiar.'

'Too right it is, Stevie,' Martin exclaimed, not trying to disguise his triumph. 'She is . . . or, rather, was . . . Tommy Murtagh's sister.'

Steele gasped. 'Stone me! That puts the First Minister at the top of the list of people I need to interview. That is one I am definitely not going to do without referring back to the boss. I'd better call him now. I hope I don't wake his kid.'

'Somehow I don't think you'll find him at home. I've just seen the BBC ten o'clock news; check out Ceefax or Sky, if you've got it, and you'll see that he's had a busy night.'

Eighty-five

The drive back was much more gentle and sedate than the women's headlong rush to St Andrews had been. It was also virtually silent, once the radio news round-up was over and they had heard Clarence Tallent's trembling solemnity as he read his statement.

'The attempt was foiled,' he concluded, 'by a team from Edinburgh, headed by Deputy Chief Constable Bob Skinner. That's all we can tell you for now, but we hope to have more information later. Let me repeat: the Prince is safe and has been taken to another location.'

He was followed by Aileen de Marco, her voice steady and grave, as she paid tribute to the rescuers and offered her sympathies, and any effective help and support that her department could give, to the casualties.

When it was over, and he had switched off the radio, Skinner sat in the front passenger seat, staring ahead into the night, thinking about the part of the story he had not told Aileen, or the chief constable, the part they would never know.

He had sent the two surviving soldiers to guard Arrow's body, with orders to allow no one to come near it, not even the police; then he had called the commanding officer of RAF Leuchars and had arranged for it to be removed by helicopter, taken to the air station and kept under guard. He had told him a simplified version of the truth, that the dead man was a member of the intelligence services, and that his presence at the scene could never be acknowledged.

There would be a cover-up: he knew that. Rudy Sewell and the other conspirators would be disposed of in some way. A bullet in the head, explained to relatives as death in the line of duty; military detention, explained as missing in action; or perhaps, in the bizarre world in which they lived, they might simply be dismissed from the service and kept under supervision for the rest of their lives.

Whatever option was chosen, it would not involve a trial. He should have cared about that, but at that moment he did not. Adam Arrow was dead and that was what filled his mind: Arrow, the solid, reliable, resourceful, lethal friend to whom he had always turned in times of greatest danger, knowing that whatever help he needed would be given. He was dead, and he, Bob Skinner, had fired the fatal shot.

And yet he did not feel that he alone had killed him. He had been the instrument, yes, the executioner, in the end, but he truly believed, and knew that he always would, that his instinctive reaction had been one of compassion. The head wound would probably have crippled the man; it would certainly have left him helpless in the hands of his interrogators. Although Arrow had never told him his real name, which had been kept under wraps to protect those close to him, he had shared one of his darkest secrets with Skinner. He had been tortured once, in Ireland, with electricity. He had withstood it for three days, until miraculously he had been saved by SAS colleagues. This time, there would have been no rescue. He would have cracked and, to him, that would have been worse than death.

Arrow had died because of his loyalty, twisted and misguided though his patriotism had been. Skinner tried to live his own life by that principle, but when he thought of his friend, he knew that his variety was a pale imitation of Arrow's. He was loyal to his force, to his colleagues and to his job. On that basis, he could make instant decisions, as he had that night, knowing that afterwards he would be able to justify them to himself and therefore to others.

He was loyal to his children and would die for them. Yet there was someone else who should have been able to command his loyalty, and in that car on the way through that dark night, he realised that she no longer could.

He remembered once looking up the definition of the word: it had been extensive. *'True, faithful to duty, love or obligation towards a person,'* it had begun, then *'faithful in allegiance to sovereign, govern-ment or mother country'*.

As he thought it through, he recognised that, in his own loyalty,

Adam Arrow had been absolute. He had believed in and had suffered in the defence of the institutions that had shaped his country and made it the place for which, ultimately, he had laid down his life. When he had come to believe, truly and completely, that they were facing destruction, he had been prepared to go to any lengths to protect them. People would say that he had been wrong, but he had trusted utterly in his own instincts and in the necessity of what he and his allies were doing.

Ultimately, Skinner recognised, he himself had been loyal to Adam. He had borne no duty or obligation to him: it was love that had given him the merciful bullet. In that moment of blinding clarity, he realised a simple truth that had escaped him for all of his blinkered life: however pure and admirable loyalty was, it could also be destructive.

And, finally, he accepted a second inescapable fact: in his own loyalty to his wife, he had been at best simplistic, and at worst a hypocrite. Throughout their marriage he had professed it, but he had not always been faithful to her, any more than she had to him. Truthfully, he no longer loved her; indeed, he doubted whether he ever had. They had been sustained as a couple only by the sworn duty of marriage, parenthood and the obligations that came with them.

He glanced sideways at Aileen, and as he did, something beautiful happened, something strange and all the more unexpected since it had come in the midst of that awful night. A moonbeam hit the car from the side, and in its light he saw her profile ... only it was not hers alone. He saw Myra's also, his first wife, Alex's mother, his soul-mate, as if the two had blended together.

'I love you,' he whispered in the darkness.

She turned to him and smiled, briefly, before focusing once more on the M90. 'I love you too,' she murmured, 'but let's not tell the two in the back.'

Bob Skinner grinned, and glanced over his shoulder: Mackenzie and McElhone were either asleep, or pretending to be. In Mackenzie's case, at least, he assumed the former; there was little or no diplomacy in his colleague's make-up.

He turned back, facing the road, to see the lights of the Forth Bridge looming up ahead. Twenty minutes later, Aileen swung the Fiat into the rear car park of the Fettes headquarters. As the four climbed out, Skinner took Mackenzie aside. 'Bandit,' he said, 'as soon as you've checked in your firearm, go straight home. I know you called your wife to let her know you're okay, but she'll want to see you, to make sure there are no holes in you that you didn't tell her about.'

'Thanks, boss,' the chief inspector replied, as they stepped inside the building. Then he stopped, looking awkwardly at the floor, anywhere but at the DCC. 'About tonight: I'm sorry.'

'For what, man?'

'I bottled it in there. It wasn't like that night in the club: I was scared.'

'No more than the rest of us were, son. I like healthily scared guys around me in a crisis: they're sharp. The important thing was that, whatever you felt, you kept moving forward. I gave you the chance to back off, and you as good as told me to get stuffed.' He put a hand on his colleague's shoulder. 'You never know, somebody might want to hand out medals for this. If they do, you're getting one, and you'll have earned it. Now go on, lose that Glock and get the hell out of here.'

As Mackenzie left, the DCC led Aileen and her private secretary upstairs and past the reception desk. When they arrived at the command floor, Sir James Proud was waiting in the corridor to greet them. He stepped up to Skinner and shook his hand. 'Well,' he murmured, 'even by your standards, you've had a hell of a night.'

'*More than you'll ever know, Jimmy,*' he thought. Suddenly he found himself close to tears, but he held them back.

The chief constable turned to the minister. 'Ms de Marco, welcome, and thanks for bringing him back. All of you, come into my room.'

They followed him in through the small antechamber. In the office several people were waiting. As the group entered, they burst into applause. Surprised and embarrassed, Skinner took in the faces of Willie Haggerty, Jack McGurk, Ruth Pye, Alan Royston, several other fellow officers and, among them, two people, a woman and a man, whom he did not know. He looked around for Neil McIlhenney and felt a strange pang of relief and reassurance when he stepped out from behind the skyscraper form of McGurk.

The chief thrust a slim glass into his hand, then waved McIlhenney over to join them. 'Gentlemen,' he announced, 'I want you to know that this gathering is entirely spontaneous. When your colleagues heard that something big was afoot, they stayed here, and when they heard the outcome, they all insisted on waiting for your return. I've only got one thing to say, but it's on behalf of a lot more people than are here. Thanks, boys, you've done us proud.'

Skinner looked at McIlhenney; his mouth went tight, and he read the same thing in his friend's heart that he felt in his own. 'Thank you, sir,' he replied, formally. 'We, and Bandit, who's gone home to his wife . . .'

'No, I haven't,' came a tired voice from behind him. 'I got hauled up here.'

'In that case, all three of us thank you for your concern and for your welcome.' He laid his glass down on the chief's table. 'Thanks for that too, Jimmy,' he said, 'but honestly, I can't drink it. Give me a beer and then several more and I'll slaughter them all, but not that stuff. Champagne's for celebrations, and this isn't. The three of us saw people dead on the ground tonight, brother officers, comrades, and kids who just got in the way. Their families will be grieving, and so am I. Thank you for staying, and thank you for caring so much about us. Now, we would like you all to go home.'

He took McIlhenney by the elbow and led him into a corner. 'Where is he?' he whispered.

'Safe. An SAS detachment arrived half an hour ago; they took him out the back way. There was a plane waiting at Turnhouse. He'll be on his way to London by now.'

'*An SAS detachment that was supposed to be deployed elsewhere,*' thought Skinner. 'Thank Christ for that,' he said.

'Back in St Andrews,' the chief inspector asked, 'who was that other man?'

'Nobody. He wasn't there, he never existed. If you have any theories, keep them to yourself, pal, please, for my sake.'

'What man?' McIlhenney murmured.

'Excuse me, Bob.'

Skinner turned to see the force press officer standing before him. 'Alan, what can I do for you?'

'I've got an army of media outside, all wanting to talk to you. Do you want me to set something up? I could use the gym.'

'No way,' the DCC replied, firmly. 'We're not talking to any journalists, not even old John Hunter. Get rid of them. I don't care whether you're polite about it or not. And tell them also that if anyone is thinking about camping outside my house, or Neil's or Bandit's, they should reject it as a very bad idea indeed.'

'Maybe I shouldn't say this, but do you have any idea how much the media would pay for your stories?' asked Royston. 'You could live on it.'

'We couldn't live with ourselves, though,' said McIlhenney. 'So please, Alan, do as you're told.'

As the press officer left, Skinner pointed to the two strangers. 'Who are they?'

'She's Martina Easterland; she's the Scottish representative of the Royal Household. He's from MI6; he says he wants to debrief us. He says that you and Bandit and I have got to stay here when everyone else leaves.'

'Indeed?' The DCC looked at the man until he caught his eye, then summoned him like a schoolboy, with a crooked finger. 'Are you the director general of MI5?' he asked him.

'No,' he replied, startled.

'In that case, you can go away. He's the only person I'm talking to.'

'You'll get the chance,' the man said, almost pouting with displeasure. 'He's on his way up.'

'Tonight?'

'As we speak.'

Skinner smiled, wryly. 'That doesn't surprise me. You will not be involved in our meeting, so you can take the advice I've just given you.'

'Five is compromised; I insist that you speak to me first.'

'Listen,' the DCC barked. 'I'm a tired, angry man with a warrant card in his pocket and a gun on his hip. Who are you to argue with me? Now fuck off!'

His voice had risen as he spoke. Sir James Proud and Aileen de Marco, the only other people left in the room, looked round anxiously. The intelligence officer looked to the chief constable for support, but he simply jerked his thumb in the general direction of the door.

'Hold on a minute,' exclaimed Skinner, suddenly. 'On second thoughts, you stay here.' He turned to McIlhenney. 'Are Bandit and Jack McGurk still around? If they are, bring them here.'

The chief inspector left, and returned, seconds later, with his two colleagues. 'Gentlemen,' the DCC ordered, grabbing the MI6 operative by the shoulder. 'Take this man away, examine his credentials, then detain him until I'm ready to question him.'

'You can't do that,' the stranger protested.

'Sure I can. Hold your arms out wide. Guys, frisk him.'

With Sir James Proud and the Justice Minister looking on, the two detectives patted the man down. McGurk reached his trouser pocket and stopped, reached in and removed a tiny automatic pistol. 'Let me guess,' Skinner laughed, 'you're just looking after that for your wife.'

'I'm an officer of the intelligence service,' the man protested.

'You're also under arrest for illegal possession of a firearm.' He took out his Glock and waved it under his nose. 'Mine's legal, you see; properly signed out from our store. Bandit, Jack, cuff this guy and lock him up.'

'You can't do this!'

'If you have a problem with reality, try closing your eyes and pretending nothing's happening.'

He watched, smiling, as McGurk stripped the man's belt from its loops and used it to tie his wrists together, then, with Mackenzie on his other side, marched him out of the door.

'It's always exciting around you, isn't it?' said McIlhenney, drily, when they were alone once more.

Skinner sighed, mournfully. 'I really wish it wasn't, mate,' he murmured.

'Would you like to know what's happening back in the real world?' the DCI asked. 'You've had a few phone calls this evening, but only three of significance. One was from Alex; I've called her and assured her that you're okay. Another was from Sarah: she's home. That one, I left for you to handle on your own. The third was from Stevie Steele. You'll want to talk to him.'

'Okay. You and Bandit make yourselves scarce while you can. I'll wake the boy and Maggie from their slumbers.' He headed for the door. 'Aileen, once you and the chief are finished, I'll be in my office. Where's Lena?'

'Gone on ahead. She's being given a lift home in a police car.'

He stepped across the hall and into his own room; before switching on the light he drew the curtains, to avoid being filmed or photographed by the cameras outside. As soon as he was settled he took off his holster and opened his safe, put the gun inside, took out a brown foolscap envelope, and locked it once more. He took a beer from his fridge. As he was opening it, Aileen came into the room. He handed it to her and took another.

'What was all that about just now?' she asked, as she pulled one of the visitor chairs round to sit beside him.

'It's what can happen when you piss me off.'

She laughed, then looked at him. 'Did you mean what you said, back on the road, or were you talking to someone else?'

'I was talking to you, and I meant it. Want me to say it again?'

'Yes, please.'

'I love you. Now you.'

She leaned over and kissed him. 'I love you too . . . and I never had anyone else to talk to.'

'Are you happy about it?' he asked her.

'Happy about loving you? How could I be anything else?'

'I'm an obsessive, driven guy, you know, plus I'm married. Most people would say you were asking for trouble.'

'I'm driven too, remember, and when it comes to social justice, yes, I'm obsessive. Why do you ask the question? Didn't you want to fall in love with me?'

He smiled. 'It doesn't make my life less complicated but, yes, I reckon I'm ready for it. I'm still numb from the things I've seen and done tonight, so it's difficult for me to talk about happiness right now, but I've worked out what I feel for you, and it's good.'

'Will you leave your wife? Don't get me wrong,' she added quickly, 'I'm not asking you to. I'll love you from afar if it comes to it.'

He reached out and squeezed her hand. 'Let me deal with that, then tell you how it's going to be. Meanwhile, Minister, you've got a big day tomorrow. You've got to present Mr Murtagh's bloody Police Bill to the Parliament, a task I know you're anticipating with relish.'

She showed him her best sour expression. 'I'm not so sure about that any more. I went along with it to protect you as much as anything else. After tonight, you'll be beyond Tommy's reach; maybe the whole police service will be for a while. A very public resignation tomorrow morning is back on my list of options.'

He tossed her the envelope. 'There's some briefing for your speech. Read it, while I make a call.'

He picked up the phone and dialled. He knew Steele well enough not to be surprised that he was still awake and that the call was answered quickly.

'Stevie? DCC, what have you got for me?'

'A new suspect, sir.'

'So go and pick him up; interview him.'

'It's not that simple, boss. He's Patsy Aikenhead's brother.'

'I don't care if he's Charlie's bloody Aunt, lift him.'

'Patsy Aikenhead's birth name was Cleopatra Murtagh.'

'What? Say that again, just in case I imagined it.'

'My suspect is Tommy Murtagh, sir. He's the right age, he's fit and he's formidably strong. He doesn't quite fit Miss Bee's height profile, but it was a split-second sighting. I've spoken to her again and she acknowledges that she could have been wrong.'

Skinner inhaled, deeply. Aileen, who had barely begun to read, stopped and looked at him. He motioned her to continue, then turned back to Steele. 'You're right, Stevie: you don't just go along and arrest him. We both go, and we tip the press off in advance. But before that, there's something we have to establish. We've got the motive, but have we got the opportunity?'

As he spoke, he remembered something, and his elation began to disappear. 'Just a moment, Stevie,' he said. 'Aileen…'

He might as well have spoken to the pictures on the wall; suddenly the documents from the envelope had grabbed her attention, one hundred per cent.

'Aileen,' he repeated.

She looked up, wide-eyed. 'What? Sorry, Bob.'

'Something I need you to confirm for me: when did Murtagh call you in to tell you about the terrorists?'

'Sunday, last week.'

'What time?'

'I got there at quarter past eight in the evening, and I didn't leave till after nine.'

'Normally, how familiar are you with his diary?'

'Very: his office circulates his engagements weekly.'

'Can you remember where he was on Saturday afternoon?'

'Yes, I can, because I was there too. We had a Labour National Executive Committee meeting in Glasgow.'

Skinner grinned. Some things were just too bizarre to be true. 'I'm sorry, Inspector, but it wasn't him. His alibi is sat right beside me.'

'Oh, damn,' Steele exclaimed, 'back to the beginning again, then. Sorry to bother you, boss.'

'Don't be too sorry yet. Tell you what, Stevie, I think you should take what you've got and see Andy Martin in his office in Dundee, first thing tomorrow morning.'

He hung up and watched Aileen as she read, his smile widening with her eyes. When she was finished she laid the papers back on his desk. 'Bob, this is amazing. How did you get it all?'

'How can I put that?' he replied. 'Let's just say it was good detective work by some people I can trust when the chips are down. Does it add to that list of options you mentioned earlier?'

'Oh, it does,' she said eagerly. 'Very definitely it does.'

'Honey,' he said, 'that's just the tip of the iceberg. Let me give you a little more background on the man who leads our nation.'

Eighty-six

She was awake when he returned home just before eight, in the kitchen making breakfast for herself and the children, while Trish readied them for school. As he came through the door, she thought he looked more tired and dishevelled than she had ever seen him and her heart went out to him. 'Was it bad?' she asked him.

He nodded. 'It was worse than bad, worse than terrible. I'm sorry to be coming in like the cat, but I've been up all night being debriefed.'

'In the circumstances, I won't make the obvious wisecrack. But don't let the kids see you looking like that. Go shave and shower; sleep if you have to.'

'That's a luxury I can't afford today. I don't look that bad, do I?'

'Yes, but that's not what I'm protecting them from. That looks to me like blood on your pants.'

He looked down and saw that she was right. There were dark stains on each of his knees: the blood of Adam Arrow, his dead, anonymous friend, unmourned except by him, and he hoped by a family somewhere, who would be told a discreet lie. He rushed out of the kitchen and upstairs, into his bedroom, where he stripped naked, tearing his clothes off and shoving them into a bag, to be burned in the garden incinerator at the first opportunity.

It was only when he came out of the bathroom in his robe, still towelling his hair dry, that he realised that all of Sarah's familiar things had gone from the dressing-table: her perfumes, her lotions, her potions, and her most personal family photographs, which she had kept there. The bed had not been slept in either: the book that he had tossed on to the duvet after spreading it the morning before was still there, undisturbed. The scene began to answer the questions that had dogged his journey home.

He dressed, casually, and went downstairs: the house was its usual blaze of pre-school activity, with a special excitement because, finally, Mum was home. Yet as soon as he stepped back into the kitchen he realised that there was an edge to it. At the sight of him, Seonaid's eyes lit up, she screamed, 'Daddy!' and rushed over to him as fast as her toddler's legs would carry her.

If Sarah saw the slight, she gave no sign of it, but Bob knew her well enough to realise that the hurt would be there. He snatched up his daughter, and asked her, teasing, 'Have you hugged your mother this morning?' She giggled and tried to bury her face in his shoulder, but he turned her chin gently upwards. 'It's time you did, then. Let's both do it.'

He drew Sarah to him in a clumsy, three-sided embrace, from which he quietly withdrew, leaving her holding her daughter, who threw her arms round her neck and squeezed as hard as she could.

'Have you been teaching her a choke hold?' she asked, but her eyes were grateful nonetheless.

As the boys ate breakfast and Sarah fed Seonaid, Bob made his own, an unhealthy and untypical sausage, black pudding, bacon and eggs. James Andrew watched him jealously: his personal larder was being raided.

Sarah drove them to school. There was still snow on the ground, but it had started to melt, and she was all too aware of the slush-ball havoc that her younger son could cause had the boys been allowed to walk. When she returned, Bob was watching the BBC all-day news channel, seeing, for the first time, how the attack was being reported.

He saw the shots from the night before, and more live from the scene, as the reporter delivered a monologue to camera. He saw Clarence Tallent in the harsh media spotlights, and then Aileen, her name misspelled by the caption writer. He saw the prince, library footage of him in his red student robes. And then he saw himself, the smiling official photograph from the force's annual report, and heard himself described as the hero of the hour.

'Thirty seconds later and it would have been zero, not hero, pal.'

'But it wasn't,' said Sarah, from behind him. 'You came through for him.'

'Took a hell of a risk with his life,' he told her. 'I took a shot in the dark, literally, at one of the guys who was holding him. I got him, but I could just as easily have hit the prince.'

'And if you hadn't taken the risk?'

'They'd have got away, but I suppose the boat might have been intercepted.'

'The boat was destroyed.'

'Was it?' This was news to him, although no surprise.

'They said so earlier; it and the bigger boat that it was meeting. The RAF blew them up; no survivors.'

'Of course not,' he whispered.

'You were well known before,' she said, 'but now you're famous, nationally, internationally.'

'Will it make it more difficult to leave me?' he asked.

'Who said it was ever going to be easy?'

'You will, though; that's what you came back to tell me.'

'Yes, Bob.' She smiled at him, gently. 'Let me guess, you had a hunch?'

'Something like that.'

'I admire you,' she said, 'more than anyone I've ever known, and it would be great to go on being your wife and bask in whatever glory is coming your way. But I can't: because I don't love you, and I don't belong with you. That's the bottom line . . . and it's mutual, isn't it? Go on, admit it. I'm offering you the easy way out; all you have to do is sit there, silent, and let me be seen as deserting you. But don't, please. Tell me what you feel.'

'Don't worry: I won't let it be that way. I don't love you either, Sarah, not any more.'

'Don't cop out now,' she exclaimed, still smiling. 'You never did. Admit it, officer.'

'Not the way I should have, no. When I met you, I was a flawed, lonely guy.'

She looked at him, sadly. 'Bob, you still are.'

'Maybe, but you took it away for a while.'

'And, in the process, became flawed and lonely myself.'

'How's leaving me going to help that?'

'It'll give me a chance to find someone who does love me, the way it's supposed to be.'

'Mr Right, you mean? Watch out for that bastard: usually Mrs Right's expecting him home by midnight.'

She laughed and sat on the sofa beside him. He switched off the television and turned to look at her. 'What happened last night?' she asked him, quietly.

'You saw on the news. Some Albanians tried to hijack the prince and hold him for ransom; Neil, Mackenzie and I, and four soldiers, stopped them.'

'Yes,' she whispered, 'but what else happened?'

'Isn't that enough?'

'There's more. You're wearing it like a cloak.'

'Two of my soldiers were killed. I sent them to a place where someone was waiting.'

'But you didn't know that.'

'I should have guessed, though. I'll never make a general.'

'You are a general,' Sarah retorted. 'But there's still something you're not telling me.'

'Maybe I don't want to; maybe I can't, for your sake.'

'You've told me things in the past. I'm your doctor as well as your wife, remember: you're suffering from post-traumatic shock, I want to know the cause, and I'm bound to keep it confidential.'

'Okay,' he said abruptly. 'I'll tell you one more dark secret, never to be repeated. That attempted kidnapping last night was actually a plot by some right-wing intelligence officers who shared a paranoid fear of what might happen to this country if that boy becomes king. So they used an MI6 asset called Peter Bassam, who'd worked for them in the Balkans till they had to pull him out. He recruited the Albanians, sheltered them in Edinburgh, and kept them fed and quiet until the time was right to attack. We got on their track and put a man in under cover to find them. He was betrayed, and on Saturday night he was murdered. My two soldiers weren't ambushed by the Albanians, but by one of the plotters, who was in St Andrews to make sure that everything went according to plan. When it didn't, he tried to kill the prince, but I spotted him and I dropped him first. Before he died, he told me most of it. The rest of it we got out of an MI6 operative called Miles Hassett, one of the plotters, who was sent up, right into my very office, to find out how much I knew.' He stopped. 'How's that, Doctor?'

'It sounds like the thriller of the year; come on, you made all that up.'

He looked at her and saw that she was frightened. 'No, I didn't; my imagination isn't that good. Oh, yes, the man I killed? It was Adam.'

The colour fled from her face; she had known Arrow. 'It's not true,' she murmured. 'Tell me it's not.'

'I'd love to. I'd love to wake up and find that it never happened. But it did.'

She sank back into the couch, her hands pressed to her cheeks. 'And the morning after I come home to tell you that I'm leaving you. God, Bob, what lousy timing. I'm so sorry. I can't go now, not when you're trying to deal with this.'

He gave a huge weary sigh. 'Who would your staying help, Sarah? Not me. What are you going to do? Take me to bed and hug me till all the monsters go away? You can try, but they won't. I've been dodging the truth about you and me for long enough. I've been hiding behind you for years, tying you to me, watching you become sadder and less of a person as you took second, probably even third place in my life. If you'd come back and said, "Let's try to make it work," I'd have said, "No." So let's do what we know to be right, and let's do it now. I'll move out. I'll find somewhere in Edinburgh.'

'With your politician friend?'

'Maybe, but not straight away, and maybe never. I'm going to need a lot of breathing space for a while. Besides, Aileen's just like me: she's married to her job as well.'

'You sound just right for each other; I hope it works.' She pursed her lips. 'But listen, I don't want you to move out. I've been doing a lot of thinking of my own, and I've found my truths as well. Somewhere along the line, Bob . . . I don't know when exactly; maybe it was when my parents died, but maybe even before then . . . I handed control of my life to you.'

'I've never tried to control you,' he protested.

'I'm not saying you did, honey, but I let you nonetheless. Well, that's over: as of now I'm in charge of my own destiny again. Sarah Grace is coming out of hiding and back into the world, but with a whole new agenda, not like she was before.'

She looked at him, and he could see in her eyes a determination which, he admitted to himself, had been absent for a while. 'For a start, I've had enough of pathology,' she declared. 'Actually, I decided that a while back. Any people I cut up in future will be alive at the time, and hopefully afterwards. Where will that be? Bob, I'm an American, and I'm a doctor, so I'm going home, and back to work. All my property in Buffalo, and the up-state cabin, is on the market and it'll all sell fast. I've spent a lot of time in New York City and I still have friends there. So I'm going to buy an apartment in Manhattan, and I'm going to practise real medicine again. But I won't look after people who can afford me: I'll be a doctor for those who can't.'

He reached out and touched her cheek. 'Well, good for you, Doc.'

'You don't think I'm just being idealistic?'

'The world could use a few more of us idealists. Your parents have left you wealthy. What you're proposing will let a lot of people benefit from it. I only have one problem with your plan. I don't think I want my children brought up in Manhattan.'

She paused, unsmiling, letting his final sentence hang in the air, gathering its own tension around it.

And then she grinned, dispelling it in an instant. 'I knew you'd say that,' she told him, 'and I admit that, for a while, it was a hurdle I couldn't clear. I love my kids, Bob, just as much as you do, and I don't want to be parted from them. But neither do I want them to be caught in the middle of a great adversarial battle between you and me . . . one which I might not win . . . so I'm prepared to negotiate. I recognise that fathers have rights too and, damn it, obligations as well. I made you a promise in Florida: I said that, whatever happened between us, the children would be educated as we've planned. Sure, that was before I'd had a chance to think things through, but now that I have, I'm prepared to stick to it. You did a pretty good job with Alex; I reckon you can handle this lot too, for half the year at least.

'That doesn't mean I'll give up all legal rights,' she said quickly, 'but I could live with joint custody, on the basis that they stay with you during the school term, and that they spend the bulk of their holidays with me. I'll fly them and the nanny over to New York, or to whatever resort we go to. Plus, I'll pay Trish's salary all year round, because I've got a lot more money than you, and I'll contribute half of their school fees. Agreed?'

He closed his eyes; it felt like closing a book. 'Agreed.'

'Good, but there are a raft of conditions.'

'Okay.'

'One, I have visiting rights here, whenever I choose.'

'Okay.'

'Two, until we're divorced, you don't move anyone else in here, at least not while the kids are around.'

'Agreed.'

'Three, when they finish school, they get to decide where they want to go to college, the US or Britain, without pressure from either of us.'

'Agreed.'

'Four, if we did a conventional property split, it would be a hell of a lot better for you than for me, so I propose that we each take away what we brought in: you keep this place and its mortgage, plus your Spanish property, and I keep my parents' entire estate, from which ultimately the kids will benefit.'

'Agreed.'

'Five, we'll always be friends.'

Bob opened his eyes again, and grinned. 'Yes, that too.'

'And six, that you will never ever put your job above the interests of our children.'

'That's a solemn promise.'

She touched his arm. 'I could argue that you broke it last night. Did you have to risk your life?'

'You mean that I should have risked someone else's instead? Do you want me to raise the boys to think like that? Of course you don't. Anyway, I could argue that the maintenance of national security is in their interests.'

'I suppose you're right. What I'm really saying, Bob, is that you're at an age and stage when you don't have to lead every charge.'

'Hopefully, there won't be any more.'

She laughed. 'Are you kidding?'

'Probably, but let me tell you this. I will do everything in my power to discourage our three from following in my footsteps. I want Mark to be an actuary or a maths professor, I want the Jazzer to be a professional golfer, and I want Seonaid to be a doctor like her mum. I will never countersign an application by any one of them to become a police officer.'

'Thanks for that,' said Sarah. 'The trouble is that I've always encouraged them to try to grow up just like their dad, and I don't plan ever to change that.'

'Poor confused wee sods!'

'Maybe.' She dug him in the ribs. 'Hey, pal, know what?'

'Tell me, why don't you?'

'All of a sudden I feel less lonely than I have in years.'

Eighty-seven

Rod Greatorix had called in sick. A wicked cold had been brewing over the weekend, and when he had wakened to find every major joint in his body aching, he had realised that it had turned to flu.

His wife had put up a show of reluctance to give him the phone when Martin had called him, but eventually they had spoken and he had agreed that the DCC and another officer could visit.

He was sitting in a high-backed chair when they were shown into his study, with a sweater over his pyjamas, and wrapped in a heavy dressing-gown. His eyes were rheumy and his nose shone like a red traffic-light. 'Don't get too close,' he warned, but the two callers needed no telling.

'Will it be family flowers only?' Martin asked.

'Very funny,' the invalid grunted. 'Have you just come here to take the piss?'

'No, honest we haven't. Rod, this is DI Stevie Steele, from Edinburgh; he's been working on an investigation that's under wraps for now but likely to go public soon. Before that happens, we've got some questions that need answering, and you might just be the man who can.'

'That's a first,' said Greatorix. 'I've never been interviewed before. What's it about?'

'What do you know about Cleopatra Murtagh, sir?' asked Steele.

'Tommy's sister? Could Andy not tell you that?'

'I could have given him gossip, Rod. I'd rather he heard it from you.'

'If you must.' The older man sighed. 'The girl is believed to be the daughter of my brother-in-law, Brindsley Groves; her mother was his mistress for years, until she died, in fact.'

362

'Believed to be?'

'All right, then, she is his daughter. I had it out with Brindsley at the time and he admitted it to me. He promised that he'd never acknowledge her publicly, but he said that he'd always look after her.'

'Did he make the same promise about Tommy?' Martin's question took his colleague by surprise.

'Why should he?'

'Because Tommy's his son; the official version, the father's death, that's all balls. His mother was single, not a widow, and she lived in York while Brindsley was a student there.'

'Hell's teeth!' Greatorix hissed. 'So it wasn't just a case of looking after him because he was shagging his mother.'

'To come back to the girl, sir,' Steele intervened. 'What happened to her?'

'I don't know. Brindsley sent her to college somewhere, and that was the last I heard of her. Why?'

'Because she's dead: she committed suicide in jail ten years ago, after being convicted of killing a child in her care. The verdict was later overturned.'

'Would Brindsley know that?'

'It's reasonable to suppose that her mother might have told him, she was still alive at the time . . . or that Tommy might, for that matter. He was on the Groves payroll then. But it doesn't matter who told him; he does know, that's for sure. The Groves Foundation's been paying an income to her husband ever since . . . and to Tommy Murtagh, incidentally.'

'The bastard,' Greatorix swore. 'What if those payments can be traced? If my sister ever finds out . . .'

'Are you sure she doesn't know already?'

'Brindsley promised she never would. He told me he supported the girl through the mother's wage packet.'

'What about your nephew and niece?'

'Herbie heard some gossip when he came home from school one summer and started knocking around with the local lads; he'd have been sixteen at the time. He came to me and, again, I made him promise to keep it from his mother. He did, although he told his dad he wanted fuck all to do with him or his business. I don't think Rowena ever knew. She's a snooty wee cow and she never mixed with Dundee kids.'

'Your brother-in-law is late fifties, sir, yes?'

'Fifty-eight.'

'What sort of shape's he in for his age? Good, bad, any major health problems?'

Greatorix laughed. 'You must be kidding. He's a bloody monster. He was an international cyclist when he was young and he still rides his bike; he belongs to the local wheelers. They go up to Montrose and back once a month, and sometimes do longer trips than that. He rides horses too, and he leads a company team in the London Marathon every year. They're his big hobbies, them and his clocks: he collects them and rebuilds them; he's always tinkering with the bloody things.'

He paused, blew his nose and then looked at Steele, sharply. 'You know, you've got me wondering what all this is leading up to, son. But before you get round to telling me, let me stop you. I don't want to know. I'd do nothing for Brindsley, but I'd do everything in my power to protect my sister so, please, don't put me in an awkward position.'

'Fair enough, Rod,' said Martin. 'That's us done anyway.' He and Steele stood. 'I think you should speak to your sister, but for now just you sit there and fester, we'll see ourselves out.'

The inspector nodded. 'Yes, thank you, sir. I hope the flu clears up soon. By the way,' he continued, 'that's a really nice path you've got up to the house; very unusual stone. I've been thinking of renewing my place. Did you do that or was it there when you bought this house?'

'No,' the chief superintendent replied. 'That's one of the few advantages in having Brindsley for a brother-in-law. He has a stoneyard, and those were cut there. You'll never be able to find anything like them down in Edinburgh: they're grey granite and they'll never wear out.'

Eighty-eight

The Scottish Parliament building and its ever-spiralling cost had become an albatross hung round the neck of the restored legislature, but Aileen de Marco had refused to join the ranks of those who railed against it. She was fond of pointing out to the critics that many of the hotel casinos on the Strip in Las Vegas had cost much more, and that in England there were football stadia under construction which were in the same price bracket, or even more expensive.

As she reached the doorway to the chamber, her papers in her hand and Lena McElhone by her side, she felt serene. In the previous twenty-four hours her life had been stood on its head and her future changed. Against that background, she faced her biggest challenge, but she was ready for it.

As she looked into the impressive chamber in which the Parliament sat, Aileen became aware of a figure by her side. 'Ready to go?' Tommy Murtagh whispered.

She smiled down at him, his moustache and his chemically assisted hair, all the happier that she had chosen a pair of her highest heels. 'Never more so, First Minister,' she replied. 'I'm going to do you proud.' She saw him start, and knew that she had taken him aback.

She took her seat, looking around, noting once more all of the features of the fine modern hall, as Sir Stuart MacKinnon, the Presiding Officer, led the members through the business of the day, waiting patiently for her turn to be called. At last it came.

She made her way to the lectern from which ministers addressed the house, laid her folder down and took her notes and briefing from it. 'Mr Presiding Officer,' she began, in a strong clear voice, 'I come here today, as Justice Minister, to present a bill which will make certain changes to the way in which the police service is run in this country.' As she spoke, she saw a tall figure slide unnoticed into a seat in the public gallery. He was dressed in slacks, a black roll-neck sweater and a sheepskin-lined bomber jacket; his steel-grey hair was ruffled and he looked in need of a night's sleep.

'Members will know,' she continued, 'that I was fairly recently appointed to my present post. They will also be aware that parliamentary bills are not drafted overnight. Therefore while I am privileged to be laying this enactment before you, it would be ungracious of me to allow you to believe that I am its author.'

She picked up the speech, which the First Minister's office had prepared for her, and began to read from it. 'The legislation which is set before you will confer upon the First Minister certain rights. He will confirm every appointment at assistant, deputy and chief constable rank, and he will approve all short-lists for interview. In addition, he will have the power to intervene directly in the management of the police, and to impose sanctions. It should be made clear that these powers are sought as a means of safeguarding society against incompetence and excessive zeal, and against their consequences. Of course,' she focused on the paper in her hand, 'these powers are to be seen as benevolent. They will give the police a new degree of openness and a new degree of accountability, and they will be exercised responsibly and in the public interest.'

She laid the speech down, then lifted the printed bill and waved it. 'There you have it, all clear and succinct, a piece of legislation which has the support of our coalition partners, and I believe of the Scottish Socialist Party.' She looked towards the Presiding Officer. 'Incidentally, sir, may I take this opportunity to congratulate our partners on the appointment of one of their number to the new Cabinet post which was announced yesterday morning.'

As Aileen paused, a slight murmur swept through the chamber. 'Any new piece of legislation requires scrutiny,' she continued, 'and the administration which presents it is entitled to be questioned about it.'

She glanced at the Conservative benches. 'I am sure, for example, that the members opposite will express concern that the traditional apolitical position of the police could be compromised if they have to glance in the direction of Bute House before taking important strategic, or even operational decisions. For their part, the instigators of the bill will assure them that there is nothing to fear, that no First Minister would ever allow political or even personal considerations to influence his decisions. Others will suggest that these powers could be interpreted as allowing politicians to look into the heart of forces and to examine covertly the actions of individual officers. Such scaremongering is to be expected, and I will not take the time to refute it here. All I will do is to point out that what is proposed will not put chief constables and their senior colleagues under the scrutiny of politicians in general. No, these powers will be vested in the hands of one person; they cannot be delegated to another minister, not even to the holder of my own office.'

Aileen put both hands on the lectern, looked around the chamber, at Bob Skinner in the public gallery, then at the Presiding Officer. 'So, sir, there is really only one question to be considered, an almost rhetorical question, most people in this chamber would say. Is it conceivable that any First Minister would not exercise these powers impartially, impersonally, and without bias of any sort?'

She picked up a sheaf of paper from the desk in front of her. 'That is the question which I now propose to answer.'

The chamber, she noticed with satisfaction, had gone deadly quiet.

Eighty-nine

As he looked at him across his massive desk it occurred to Andy Martin that there must be many better ways to spend one's life than working for Brindsley Groves. He was happy that he was doing one of them as he felt the wave of impatience and hostility emanating from the man.

'I have to tell you, Mr Martin,' he boomed, 'that I do not take kindly to unannounced visits from anyone, either to my office, my golf club or my home. I thought that your intrusion into my evening last Friday was a piece of cheek; it was quite obvious to me that you coerced my brother-in-law into introducing you. It was improper and unnecessary, as a simple phone call to my secretary would have got you a meeting. I have it in mind to complain to Graham Morton at Rotary tonight.'

The deputy chief constable smiled at the rebuke. 'I'm sorry if I upset you, sir, but I'm pleased that you're not blaming Rod for it.'

'Apology accepted,' Groves growled. 'But don't get above your station in future. Now, what can I do for you, and who's this?'

'This is a colleague of mine, Detective Inspector Steele.'

'Steele? Don't know you.'

'I'm from Edinburgh, sir.'

'What the hell are you doing here, then?'

'Actually,' Martin told him, 'he's here to interview you. He wanted me to have you brought to our headquarters, but don't worry, I poured cold water down his trousers and made him come to you.'

'I should bloody think so,' Groves muttered. 'What's it about, then?'

The DCC looked at him. 'Before we get into that, there's something I have to say. I have a daughter, and if anyone harmed her, I know what I would want to do to them. For all that I wear this uniform, I can't say honestly that I'd be able to restrain myself. I can say honestly that I wouldn't let my rage lie boiling for ten years before I let it out, in whatever way it found to express itself.'

'What are you talking about?' Brindsley Groves's eyes were slits, his shoulders bunched as he leaned on his desk, his big hands clenched together.

'He's talking about you, sir,' Steele retorted. 'I'm not from around here: I don't have to impress you. I'm here to question you about an attack on a boy just outside Edinburgh last Saturday afternoon. Can you tell me where you were on that day?'

'Shopping with my wife,' the man barked. 'I'm sure she'll confirm that.'

'I'm not,' said Martin quietly. 'Not after Rod's told her about Tommy and Cleo, your secret children by the late Rachel Murtagh.'

'Where were you last Wednesday?' Steele asked, before Groves could react.

'I don't know, ask my secretary.'

'And the Sunday before that?'

'Same answer!'

'We believe that you were in Edinburgh, sir. We believe that on that Sunday you abducted and killed George Regan, junior, having followed him from his home, which you had probably been observing over a period of time. We believe that three days later you returned to the city, broke into Ross Pringle's room on the Riccarton campus, and booby-trapped her gas heater, as a result of which she died of carbon-monoxide poisoning.'

'Rubbish!'

'Our scene-of-crime officers are very good, sir. In the lock on her door, they found traces of a strange lubricant. This was subsequently identified as a type of very fine oil used by clock-makers. I believe that's your hobby, sir.'

'Enough!' Groves shouted. 'Get out of my office!'

'We're not going to do that, sir.'

'In that case I'm saying no more without my lawyer present.'

'That's prudent of you, sir. When he gets here, we'll ask you both to accompany us to your home, where officers from the local force will undertake a search. We'll be looking for a match for the lubricant we found.' He leaned sideways in his chair so that he could take two plastic-wrapped objects from his coat pocket. He held up a grubby white sock. 'We'll also be looking for a match for this.' He showed Groves the granite. 'Later we'll go to your company's stone-cutting yard where we'll compare this with the stock that you have there.'

'Do all that,' the man growled, 'but you'll never prove that Patsy was my daughter. Without that, where's the motive?'

'We'll prove it all right, sir,' Steele replied. 'There's the payments from the Groves Foundation to your son-in-law for a start, but just to make sure, we'll do a DNA comparison.'

'Using what?'

'Using the lock of hair that her husband cut from her head before she was cremated.'

Groves sank back into his chair.

'You should have kept your mouth shut, Brindsley,' Andy Martin said, coldly. 'You know, I can't help dwelling on that ten-year gap. Why wait that long? You know what I think? I reckon that you waited for Chris Aikenhead to get back onshore from the oil rigs so that he could take the blame. I mean to say, where else was Stevie meant to look? It's just a pity you didn't keep in closer contact with him, for in the end your planning fell a foot short of perfection.'

Ninety

'With your indulgence, Presiding Officer, I assure you that what I'm about to say is relevant to the issue.'

The chair nodded.

She held up a document. 'This is the official biography of the First Minister, as circulated by both the Labour Party and the Scottish Executive press office.' She heard a splutter from a seat nearby, and a few gasps around the chamber; her eye flashed to the public gallery and caught Bob Skinner's smile. She read the resumé, loudly and slowly. When she reached the reference to his parents, she stopped. 'Members of this House, however indelicate this may sound, I have to tell you that there is one significant inaccuracy there. Mr Murtagh's mother never married; there was no ill-fated motor mechanic. He was born not in Derbyshire, but in York.' She paused as fresh murmuring arose, letting it subside. 'However,' she continued, 'this deception wasn't perpetrated just for mere propriety.'

She held up a piece of paper. 'This is a public document, but it's the kind that hardly ever comes to light unless someone has reason to go looking for it. It's a list of beneficiaries of a fund set up years ago for members of the Groves family of Dundee. Mr Murtagh's name appears on this list, as does that of the husband of his sister, who died in sad circumstances ten years ago. Members will note that his biography describes him as an only child.'

'Aw, Jesus! Enough of this hatchet job.' Tommy Murtagh's face was almost as puce as his hair.

'First Minister!' The rebuke from the chair was sharp and clear.

'Mr Murtagh misunderstands me,' said Aileen. 'I will demonstrate a conclusion shortly.'

She picked up a third document. 'A few weeks ago, the First Minister made a new appointment that was not announced to this Parliament or to the press. Sir John Govan, the eminent and universally respected former Chief Constable of Strathclyde, was replaced as his security adviser by Mr Greg Jay, who was at that time a serving detective superintendent here in Edinburgh. Mr Jay's appointment was not disclosed to his colleagues, neither at that time nor on his retirement from the police service. Members will be interested to know that his job remit was a little different from that of Sir John.'

She waved the paper in the air. 'I had no advance knowledge of his appointment,' she said. 'However, last night, his letter of resignation from the post, addressed to me, was delivered into my hands. I also received his sworn statement, affirming that on the direct instructions of the First Minister, he conducted covert surveillance directed against me and against Deputy Chief Constable Robert Skinner. During this operation, Mr Jay intimidated my civil service secretary, and compelled her to give him information from my private diary. There was a clear purpose to this: the First Minister knew that Mr Skinner, a close personal friend, was likely to be outraged by the surrender of five untried remand prisoners to the US military, although that country had no legal claim upon them. Mr Murtagh used the information gathered. Although our relationship is entirely innocent, he threatened to leak it in such a way that it would have been sensationalised by the tabloid press, to my embarrassment and to that of Mr Skinner's family. Mr Murtagh sought to silence Mr Skinner; he also sought to coerce me into lending public support to this bill and, indeed, into adopting it as my own. He knows now that he has failed.'

A wave of noise swept across the chamber and the gallery, silenced only by Sir Stuart MacKinnon's roar of 'Order!'

'Ms de Marco,' he advised her, sternly, 'I think it would be as well if you drew this unusual speech to a swift conclusion.'

'Certainly, sir. I know that your own office certified this bill as fit for presentation, and I have no problem with that, for you didn't have grounds for refusal. The measures it contains are not inflammatory of themselves ... given the certainty of good will and responsibility in the exercise of the powers it would confer. However, its opponents will argue that there can be no such certainty. In all honesty, I have to admit that my experience over the last ten days or so leaves me unable to disagree with them. In particular I have to ask myself whether I as an elector would want to entrust effective command and control of the police to a man who plots behind his colleagues' backs, and who, in addition, carries the burden of the knowledge that his sister died a suicide in prison, the victim of an apparent miscarriage of justice.'

She picked up the slim volume that was the Police Appointments Bill, Scotland. 'At this point,' she exclaimed, measuring her words, 'it would normally fall to me to commend this measure to Parliament. However, I find that I can only commend it to the dustbin.'

She let it fall to the floor, gathered up the rest of her documents, bowed briefly to the Chair and walked out of the chamber.

Ninety-one

Tommy Murtagh's downfall was swift and sour. Less than an hour after his public denunciation by Aileen de Marco, and after a round of meetings and telephone conversations with those who had been his backers, he called on Sir Stuart MacKinnon in his suite and tendered his resignation as First Minister, to be succeeded temporarily by his deputy, the leader of the coalition partners.

As the news was breaking around the Parliament building, the Justice Minister was driven away in an official car, through a throng of frantically snapping cameras. She had declined, politely, interview requests by the political editors of the BBC, Scottish Television, and Sky, explaining to each of them that she had said in the chamber all she intended to say that day.

The car took her along Abbeyhill and up Regent Road, but it did not stop at St Andrews House. Instead it carried on along Princes Street, past the Christmas lights, turning at the end past the Caledonian Hotel and into Rutland Square.

Bob Skinner was waiting in the entrance hall of the Scottish Arts Club; as usual, it was quiet, and so nobody saw him take her in his arms as soon as the door closed on the street outside. 'You were wonderful,' he whispered. 'None of those people in there, MSPs, journalists and the rest, have ever seen anything like that before.'

'And hopefully never will again,' she told him sincerely. 'Did I look nervous?'

'Nervous? You looked like the Iron Lady herself.'

'God forbid! I was shaking like a leaf in there, all the way through. After it was over, I locked myself in my room. It was almost an hour before I'd got hold of myself again.'

'He's gone, you know; quit.'

'I know. I heard before I left. His private secretary told Lena that he's going to resign his seat as well.'

'Just as well,' Bob muttered. 'You don't want the wee bastard on the back benches throwing daggers into your back every time you're on your feet. When do they choose his successor?'

'The party will choose its new leader; that's how it'll be done. It'll take a few weeks, I guess.'

'Will there even be a contest? Who'll oppose you after that?'

She looked at him, seriously. 'Who says I'm standing? Let's go and grab a coffee.'

They found their way into the deserted lounge, where Aileen poured two cups and brought them to two chairs by the fire. 'Why wouldn't you stand?' he asked at once. 'It's the natural progression of your career.'

'Not everybody might see it that way. I know my party: I scared a lot of people in there today. Sure, the west of Scotland lot might back me, but Tommy's cronies will be out to get even. Plus there's another factor: you and me, and how the press handle it. I laid a lot of personal stuff on the line in my speech, because I had to. I tried to lean as heavily as I could on the word "friend", but the red-tops won't take that at face value.'

'They'll have to,' said Bob, grimly.

'Oh, yes, and when they start probing into your marriage, what happens?'

'They get told to piss off. I'm not discussing that with any hack. Eventually, word will get out, but not yet.' He told her of Sarah's decision to settle in New York, and of the agreement they had reached.

'When will she go?' asked Aileen.

'She stays till Christmas, as we promised the kids. In January, she leaves for Manhattan.'

'And until then how do you co-exist?'

He laughed. 'Do you mean will we sleep together? Are you getting jealous already?'

'You haven't slept with me yet,' she pointed out, 'so I suppose I don't really have grounds for jealousy.'

'If you did, you wouldn't, if you get my drift. Sarah's chosen the spare room, and none of the kids is old enough to notice the difference. Anyway, I'm going to be away for a couple of weeks.'

'Where are you going?'

'London. I've been asked to head an independent investigation into some stuff that's been going on down there. I'm taking Neil McIlhenney with me as co-pilot.'

'Can I come and visit you while you're there?'

'That would be nice, but it's not a good idea. You have to stay visible up here. If you went down to London, the press might follow, and that would be bad news, for a whole lot of reasons.'

'Spooky.'

'Very. Anyway, you'll be too busy being elected First Minister.'

'If I run.'

'Which you will.'

'You know me that well already?'

'Well? Don't I?'

She laughed. 'Yes, I think you do. Too bad about London, though.'

'That's a hell of a place to go anyway. On the other hand . . . what do you have on your plate for the rest of the day?'

'Nothing. Why do you ask?'

'Because my car's outside, and I could make Glasgow in an hour.'